PRIZE STORIES 1966:
THE O. HENRY AWARDS

Prize Stories 1966:
THE O. HENRY AWARDS

Edited by Richard Poirier and William Abrahams

WITH AN INTRODUCTION BY
WILLIAM ABRAHAMS

Doubleday & Company, Inc., Garden City, New York, 1966

Library of Congress Catalog Card Number 21–9372
Copyright © 1966 by Doubleday & Company, Inc.
All Rights Reserved. Printed in the United States of America
First Edition

CONTENTS

PUBLISHER'S NOTE

THE present volume is the forty-sixth in the O. Henry Memorial Award series. No collections appeared in 1952 and 1953, when the continuity of the series was interrupted by the death of Herschel Brickell, who had been the editor for ten years.

In 1918 the Society of Arts and Sciences met to vote upon a monument to the American master of the short story, O. Henry. They decided that this memorial should be in the form of two prizes for the best short stories published by American authors in American magazines during the year 1919. From this beginning, the memorial developed into an annual anthology of the best American short stories, published, with the exception of the years mentioned above, by Doubleday & Company, Inc. Blanche Colton Williams, one of the founders of the awards, was editor from 1919 to 1932; Harry Hansen from 1933 to 1940; Herschel Brickell from 1941 to 1951; Paul Engle from 1954 to 1959 with Hanson Martin co-editor in the years 1954–1956; Mary Stegner in 1960, and Richard Poirier from 1961 until the present volume, with assistance from and co-editorship with William Abrahams since the 1964 volume.

Doubleday has also published First-Prize Stories from the O. Henry Memorial Awards 1919–1963.

The stories chosen for this volume were published in the period from the winter of 1963 to the summer of 1964. A list of the magazines consulted appears at the back of the book. The choice of stories and the selection of prize winners are exclusively the responsibility of the editors.

INTRODUCTION: PRIZE STORIES 1966

CHANGE in the American short story is so gradual and so imperceptible that one can't, in the manner of a fashion reporter or trend-spotter, announce a dramatic "new direction" with each appearance of this annual collection. On the whole, what was true in 1965 is true this year also, and almost certainly will prove true in 1967—that the American short story is still of legitimate interest to serious readers, and as notable for its variety and vitality as it has ever been. What is most heartening of all is the continuing emergence of new, talented young writers—like Georgia McKinley, Tom Cole, and Maureen Howard—and the welcome they receive not only in the "little magazines," but in magazines of national circulation, in *Carolina Quarterly* and *The New Yorker*, in the *Atlantic* and *Kenyon Review*, and so forth. Indeed, more than half of the stories in the present collection are the work of new writers.

Change is gradual and imperceptible, but it occurs. Writing some twenty years after the end of World War II, one knows that "the postwar American short story" exists, a recognizable phenomenon in the same way as, for example, "the 1965 story" is not, and that it is recognizably different from the American short story of the 1920s and 1930s. In general, the postwar writers have consolidated and made secure the explorations and advances of their famous predecessors. The need for stylistic innovation is no longer deeply felt; hence the apparent conventionality of surface in the postwar short story. In fact, a story by Flannery O'Connor is as revolutionary as a story by Hemingway, the former in the spirit and vision that animates it, the latter in its "technical" invention.

That the writers of the 1920s, novelists and poets as well as short story writers, were engaged in a literary revolution is a fact of literary history. By 1939, however, the problem of an experimental style had been resolved, or taken as far as it could go for the moment, or reached a dead end. In this sense, *Finnegans Wake*, which was published at the end of the thirties, is a monument and an epitaph. But the revolution had resulted in more than enough masterpieces to justify it—in the prewar short story alone, there were a succession of enduring achievements, from Sherwood Anderson's "I am a Fool" to Faulkner's "The Bear."

Admittedly, living through an age of revolution is more exciting and glamorous than to grow old in an age of consolidation, and this may well explain the complaint one sometimes hears that stories have "fallen off," that they are not what they were in the Great Days, and a list of "classics" is introduced as evidence. An impressive list, to be sure. But it would be possible to draw up a list of postwar stories of comparable excellence. (We have no wish, however, to set up a competition in the matter: the famous stories of the prewar period are by now so encrusted with fame that it is exceedingly difficult to read them freshly, as they were read when they were first published. And surely one of the pleasures of reading contemporary stories is that one does so before they have been glazed and varnished by Reputation.) Consider, as a convenient example of the variety and vitality of the postwar short story, a list of first-prize winners in this O. Henry series since Richard Poirier became its editor. In 1961 there was "Tell Me A Riddle" by Tillie Olson; in 1962, "Holiday" by Katherine Anne Porter; in 1963, "Everything That Rises Must Converge" by Flannery O'Connor; in 1964, "The Embarkment for Cythera" by John Cheever (which was later broken into fragments and scattered through the pages of Mr. Cheever's novel, *The Wapshot Scandal*); in 1965, "Revelation," another extraordinary story by Miss O'Connor; and this year, "The Bulgarian Poetess" by John Updike. Miss Porter, of course, is one of the major figures in the history of the prewar short story, but as "Holiday" made abundantly clear, she has continued to write with undiminished power. The others, with one tragic exception, are very much among the makers and shapers of the postwar short story. The exception is Flannery O'Connor, whose death at thirty-nine was an incalculable loss to American literature. It is a source of pride that three of her stories were awarded first prize in this series, the last, "Revelation," only a few weeks before her death.

We have been speaking of "the postwar short story." If, as we believe, it is written more often than not in a style that chooses not to call attention to itself, whether in the language and rhythm of everyday discourse or in an elaborate vocabulary and syntax that so accords with its subject as to appear "natural," in what way then can it be said to be characteristic? Chiefly, in the troublesomeness and complexity of its subjects, which reflect in an exact, albeit highly personal way the troublesomeness and complexity of contemporary life, so that even the social comedy of Nancy Hale's "Sunday Lunch" has concealed at its center the bomb-shelter in the garden.

It is not our intention to explain or justify each of the stories we have chosen: their merits should be apparent not only to apprentice writers in search of "solutions" and to connoisseurs versed in the subtleties of the form, but also to readers who couldn't care less about such matters and want only a "good read." Two of the stories, however, John Updike's "The Bulgarian Poetess" and Tom Cole's "On the Edge of Arcadia" deal with a similar theme in so strikingly different a fashion that they may be usefully singled out for comment. In each, the theme is one that has fascinated a long line of our writers, from Hawthorne to the present—the relation of Americans and Europeans. But if the theme is by now traditional, how contemporary in their attitudes towards it these stories are, light years distant not only from Henry James but from Hemingway and Scott Fitzgerald.

The theme becomes the explicit subject of Tom Cole's story, but its presentation, from the title itself—not *in,* but *on the edge* of Arcadia—to its final sentence is deliberately equivocal, irresolute, ambiguous. Nothing in the world is as simple as it once was (that lost dream of Arcadia!), least of all the relations between Americans and Europeans, or to put it another way (the way we think now) the relation of America to those countries abroad that depend upon it for assistance, the "charity" of Mr. Cole's story. The subject, in life as in fiction, is a good deal more complex than we would wish it to be, no longer to be defined in sweeping contrasts, the good Americans against the wicked, worldly Europeans. Mr. Cole's poet and sculptor are abroad not, as once would have been the case, for "civilization"—they have quite enough of that already!—but for something simpler and different, perhaps the primitive virtues of the aged peasant whom they encounter by chance in the Greek countryside. The question quickly offers itself: shall he be allowed his poverty, the hardness of his life, as the romantic sculptor insists, or shall he be helped by money, as the sentimental poet would like? There is a complication: the aged peasant, embodiment of the primitive virtues though he is, has in fact lived and worked in America. America, in fact, has defeated him and sent him back to this primitive landscape from whence he came. Now, impassively—with dignity, or cunning?—he cries Poor, to the delight of the sculptor who sees in his poverty a beautiful dignity and simplicity denied to Americans. But the poet sees it otherwise: would not the old man prefer to be Rich, as the poet's grandfather, himself an emigrant, has become in America? Thereafter each of the Americans behaves with a consistency that is pleasing to himself and displeasing to the other. And the old man? Mr. Cole's artfully told fable reminds us once again of the difficulties of right action, and even more of the difficulties of knowing what right action is. His story ends, as it must, with a question: as close to the truth as one is likely to come nowadays.

For Mr. Updike, the traditional theme, which has provided Cole with his story, is no more than a point of departure. His hero, very much a postwar creation, is an American author, sent abroad by the State Department as a cultural emissary to countries beyond the Iron Curtain (or as Mr. Updike, with the sympathy of an artist not a cold warrior chooses to call it, "the mirror"). The story is told in political terms, and politics, properly, is what the story appears to be about: what cultural mission is not a *political* act, even the meeting under official auspices of an American novelist and a Bulgarian poetess, in a time when politics count as love most certainly does not. But love, as Mr. Updike's American author observes, "remains . . . one of the few things that deserve meditation." And that, in the guise of a rueful comedy of international politics, is what he has written: a subtle, disquieting, and touching meditation on love and loss.

Mr. Updike is endowed with formidable talents, but it is not often that he turns them as in this case to the conventional short story. His triumph here is that he has been able to report its surface and to imagine its heart with equal conviction. Even without knowing that he himself had been sent abroad on a cultural mission, one feels that this is how it must be: those fatuous embassy receptions, those extraordinary conversations and interrogations—"Your own works? Are they influenced by the *nouvelle vague?* Do you consider yourself to write *anti-romans?*" As for Bech and Vera Glavanakova, those lovers whose love is so transitory as hardly to exist, who can give each other no more than an autographed book of poems, an autographed novel, how readily we assent to their love, and immerse ourselves in the pathos of their situation, which is, in its own fashion, a part of the troublesomeness and complexity of modern life.

It is characteristic of stories of this kind and period that the author

is not anxious to underline or to take credit for the pathos he cre-
ates: he believes in the power of the story to create a reality of its
own. The anti-novel, as Mr. Updike's story ruefully reminds us, has
become a cliché of international literary conversation, but no one
has yet had cause to speak of the anti-story, perhaps because to tell a
story continues to be a natural and necessary human activity. Or at
least, we would have it so.

WILLIAM ABRAHAMS

PRIZE STORIES 1966:
THE O. HENRY AWARDS

JOHN UPDIKE was born in Pennsylvania in 1932 and has published nine books—two collections of short stories, two volumes of verse, four novels, and a book of parodies and essays. He lives in Ipswich, Massachusetts, with his wife and four children. Two stories by him have appeared in previous O. Henry Prize Story collections—"Wife-Wooing" in 1961 and "The Doctor's Wife" in 1962.

The Bulgarian Poetess

Your poems. Are they difficult?"

She smiled and, unaccustomed to speaking English, answered carefully, drawing a line in the air with two delicately pinched fingers holding an imaginary pen. "They are difficult—to write."

He laughed, startled and charmed. "But not to read?"

She seemed puzzled by his laugh, but did not withdraw her smile, though its corners deepened in a defensive, feminine way. "I think," she said, "not so very."

"Good." Brainlessly he repeated "Good," disarmed by her unexpected quality of truth. He was, himself, a writer, this fortyish young man, Henry Bech, with his thinning curly hair and melancholy Jewish nose, the author of one good book and three others, the good one having come first. By a kind of oversight, he had never married. His reputation had grown while his powers declined. As he felt himself sink, in his fiction, deeper and deeper into eclectic sexuality and bravura narcissism, as his search for plain truth carried him further and further into treacherous realms of fantasy and, lately, of silence, he was more and more thickly hounded by homage, by flat-footed exegetes, by arrogantly worshipful undergraduates who had hitchhiked a thousand miles to touch his hand, by querulous translators, by election to honorary societies, by invitations to lecture, to "speak," to "read," to participate in symposia trumped up by ambitious girlie magazines in shameless conjunction with venerable universities. His very government, in airily unstamped enve-

2

lopes from Washington, invited him to travel, as an ambassador of the arts, to the other half of the world, the hostile, mysterious half. Rather automatically, but with some faint hope of shaking himself loose from the burden of himself, he consented, and found himself floating, with a passport so stapled with visas it fluttered when pulled from his pocket, down into the dim airports of Communist cities.

He arrived in Sofia the day after a mixture of Bulgarian and African students had smashed the windows of the American Legation and ignited an overturned Chevrolet. The cultural officer, pale from a sleepless night of guard duty, tamping his pipe with trembling fingers, advised Bech to stay out of crowds and escorted him to his hotel. The lobby was swarming with Negroes in black wool fezzes and pointed European shoes. Insecurely disguised, he felt, by an astrakhan hat purchased in Moscow, Bech passed through to the elevator, whose operator addressed him in German. "*Ja, vier,*" Bech answered, "*danke,*" and telephoned, in his bad French, for dinner to be brought up to his room. He remained there all night, behind a locked door, reading Hawthorne. He had lifted a paperback collection of short stories from a Legation window sill littered with broken glass. A few curved bright crumbs fell from between the pages onto his blanket. The image of Roger Malvin lying alone, dying, in the forest—"Death would come like the slow approach of a corpse, stealing gradually towards him through the forest, and showing its ghastly and motionless features from behind a nearer and yet a nearer tree"—frightened him. Bech fell asleep early and suffered from swollen, homesick dreams. It had been Thanksgiving Day.

In the morning, venturing downstairs for breakfast, he was surprised to find the restaurant open, the waiters affable, the eggs actual, the coffee hot, though syrupy. Outside, Sofia was sunny and (except for a few dark glances at his big American shoes) amenable to his passage along the streets. Lozenge-patterns of pansies, looking flat and brittle as pressed flowers, had been set in the public beds. Women with a touch of Western chic walked hatless in the park behind the mausoleum of Georgi Dimitrov. There was a mosque, and an assortment of trolley cars salvaged from the remotest corner of Bech's childhood in the nineteen-twenties, and a tree that talked— that is, it was so full of birds that it swayed under their weight and emitted volumes of chirping sound like a great leafy loudspeaker. It was the inverse of his hotel, whose silent walls presumably contained listening microphones. Electricity was somewhat enchanted in the Socialist world. Lights flickered off untouched and radios turned themselves on. Telephones rang in the dead of the night and breathed wordlessly in his ear. Six weeks ago, flying from New York, Bech had expected Moscow to be a blazing counterpart and instead saw, through the plane window, a skein of hoarded lights no brighter, on that vast black plain, than a girl's body in a dark room.

Past the talking tree was the American Legation. The sidewalk, heaped with broken glass, was roped off, so pedestrians had to detour into the gutter. Bech detached himself from the stream, crossed the little barren of pavement, smiled at the Bulgarian militiamen who were sullenly guarding the greenish heaps of shards, and pulled open the bronze door. The cultural officer was crisper after a normal night's sleep. He clenched his pipe in his teeth and handed Bech a small list. "You're to meet with the Writer's Union at eleven. These are writers you might ask to see. As far as we can tell, they're among the more progressive."

Words like "progressive" and "liberal" had a somewhat reversed sense in this world. At times, indeed, Bech felt he had passed through a mirror, a dingy flecked mirror that reflected feebly the capitalist world; in its dim depths everything was similar but left-handed. One of the names ended in "-ova." Bech said, "A woman."

"A poetess," the cultural officer said, sucking and tamping in a fury of bogus efficiency. "Very popular, apparently. Her books are impossible to buy."

"Have you read anything by these people?"

"I'll be frank with you. I can just about make my way through a newspaper."

"But you always know what a newspaper will say anyway."

"I'm sorry. I don't get your meaning."

"There isn't any." Bech didn't quite know why the Americans he met irritated him, whether because they garishly refused to blend into this shadow-world or because they were always solemnly sending him on ridiculous errands.

At the Writer's Union, he handed the secretary the list as it had been handed to him, on U.S. Legation stationery. The secretary, a large stooped man with the hands of a stonemason, grimaced and shook his head but obligingly reached for the telephone. Bech's meeting was already waiting in another room. It was the usual one, the one that, with small differences, he had already attended in Moscow and Kiev, Yerevan and Alma-Ata, Bucharest and Prague: the polished oval table, the bowl of fruit, the morning light, the gleaming glasses of brandy and mineral water, the lurking portrait of Lenin, the six or eight patiently sitting men who would leap to their feet with quick blank smiles. These men would include a few literary officials, termed "critics," high in the Party, loquacious and witty and destined to propose a toast to international understanding; a few selected novelists and poets, mustachioed, smoking, sulking at this invasion of their time; a university professor, the head of the Anglo-American Literature department, speaking in a beautiful withered English of Mark Twain and Sinclair Lewis; a young inter- preter with a moist handshake; a shaggy old journalist obsequiously scribbling notes; and, on the rim of the group, in chairs placed to suggest that they had invited themselves, one or two gentlemen of ill-defined status, fidgety and tieless, maverick translators who would turn out to be the only ones present who had ever read a word by Henry Bech.

Here this type was represented by a stout man in a tweed coat leather-patched at the elbows in the British style. The whites of his eyes were distinctly red. He shook Bech's hand eagerly, made of it almost an embrace of reunion, bending his face so close Bech could distinguish the smells of tobacco, garlic, cheese, and alcohol. Even as they were seating themselves around the table, and the Writer's Union chairman, a man elegantly bald, with very pale eyelashes, was touching his brandy glass as if to lift it, this anxious red-eyed inter- loper blurted at Bech, "Your 'Travel Light' was so marvellous a book. The motels, the highways, the young girls with their lovers who were motorcyclists, so marvellous, so American, the youth, the adoration for space and speed, the barbarity of the advertisements in neon lighting, the very poetry. It takes us truly into another dimen- sion."

"Travel Light" was the first novel, the famous one. Bech disliked discussing it. "At home," he said, "it was criticized as despairing."

The man's hands, stained orange with tobacco, lifted in amaze- ment and plopped noisily to his knees. "No, no a thousand times. Truth, wonder, terror even, vulgarity, yes. But despair, no, not at all, not one iota. Your critics are dead wrong."

"Thank you."

The chairman softly cleared his throat and lifted his glass an inch from the table, so that it formed with its reflection a kind of playing card.

Bech's admirer excitedly persisted. "You are not a *wet* writer, no. You are a dry writer, yes? You have the expressions, am I wrong in English, dry, hard?"

"More or less."

"I want to translate you!"

It was the agonized cry of a condemned man, for the chairman coldly lifted his glass to the height of his eyes, and like a firing squad the others followed suit. Blinking his white lashes, the chairman gazed mistily in the direction of the sudden silence, and spoke in Bulgarian.

The young interpreter murmured in Bech's ear. "I wish to propose now, ah, a very brief toast. I know it will seem doubly brief to our honored American guest, who has so recently enjoyed the, ah, hospitality of our Soviet comrades." There must have been a joke here, for the rest of the table laughed. "But in seriousness permit me to say that in our country we have seen in years past too few Americans, ah, of Mr. Bech's progressive and sympathetic stripe. We hope in the next hour to learn from him much that is interesting and, ah, socially useful about the literature of his large country, and perhaps we may in turn inform him of our own proud literature, of which perhaps he knows regrettably little. Ah, so let me finally, then, since there is a saying that too long a courtship spoils the marriage, offer to drink, in our native plum brandy *slivovica*, ah, firstly to the success of his visit and, in the second place, to the mutual increase of international understanding."

"Thank you," Bech said and, as a courtesy, drained his glass. It was wrong; the others, having merely sipped, stared. The purple burning revolved in Bech's stomach and a severe distaste for himself, for his role, for this entire artificial and futile process, focussed into a small brown spot on a pear in the bowl so shiningly posed before his eyes.

The red-eyed fool smelling of cheese was ornamenting the toast. "It is a personal honor for me to meet the man who, in 'Travel Light,' truly added a new dimension to American prose."

"The book was written," Bech said, "twelve years ago."

"And since?" A slumping, mustached man sat up and sprang into English. "Since, you have written what?"

Bech had been asked that question often in these weeks and his answer had grown curt. "A second novel called 'Brother Pig,' which is St. Bernard's expression for the body."

"Good. Yes, and?"

"A collection of essays and sketches called 'When the Saints.'"

"I like the title less well."

"It's the beginning of a famous Negro song."

"We know the song," another man said, a smaller man, with the tense, dented mouth of a hare. He lightly sang, "Lordy, I just want to be in that number."

"And the last book," Bech said, "was a long novel called 'The Chosen' that it took six years to write and that nobody liked."

"I have read reviews," the red-eyed man said. "I have not read the book. Copies are difficult here."

"I'll give you one," Bech said.

The promise seemed, somehow, to make the recipient unfortunately conspicuous; wringing his stained hands, he appeared to swell in size, to intrude grotesquely upon the inner ring, so that the interpreter took it upon himself to whisper, with the haste of an apology, into Bech's ear, "This gentleman is well known as the translator into our language of 'Erewhon.'"

"A marvellous book," the translator said, deflating in relief, pulling at his pockets for a cigarette. "It truly takes us into another dimension. Something that must be done. We live in a new cosmos."

The chairman spoke in Bulgarian, musically, at length. There was polite laughter. Nobody translated for Bech. The professorial type, his hair like a flaxen toupee, jerked forward. "Tell me, is it true, as I have read"—his phrases whistled slightly, like rusty machinery—"that the stock of Sinclair Lewis has plummeted under the Salinger wave?"

And so it went, here as in Kiev, Prague, and Alma-Ata, the same questions, more or less predictable, and his own answers, terribly familiar to him by now, mechanical, stale, irrelevant, untrue, claustrophobic. The door opened. In came, with the rosy air of a woman fresh from a bath, a little breathless, having hurried, hatless, a woman in a blond coat, her hair also blond. The secretary, entering behind her, seemed to make a cherishing space around her with his large curved hands. He introduced her to Bech as Vera Somethingova, the poetess he had asked to meet. None of the others on the list, he explained, answered their telephones.

"Aren't you kind to come?" As Bech asked it, it was a genuine question, to which he expected some sort of an answer.

She spoke to the interpreter in Bulgarian. "She says," the interpreter told Bech, "she is sorry she is so late."

"But she was just called!" In the warmth of his confusion and pleasure Bech turned to speak directly to her, forgetting he would not be understood. "I'm terribly sorry to have interrupted your morning."

"I am pleased," she said, "to meet you. I heard of you spoken in France."

"You speak English!"

"No. Very little amount."

"But you *do*."

A chair was brought for her from a corner of the room. She yielded her coat, revealing herself in a suit also blond, as if her clothes were an aspect of a total consistency. She sat down opposite Bech, crossing her legs. Her legs were very good; her face was perceptibly broad. Lowering her lids, she tugged her skirt to the curve of her knee. It was his sense of her having hurried, hurried to him, and of being, still, graciously flustered, that most touched him.

He spoke to her very clearly, across the fruit, fearful of abusing and breaking the fragile bridge of her English. "You are a poetess. When I was young, I also wrote poems."

She was silent so long he thought she would never answer; but then she smiled and pronounced, "You are not old now."

"Your poems. Are they difficult?"

"They are difficult—to write."

"But not to read?"

"I think—not so very."

"Good. Good."

Despite the decay of his career, Bech had retained an absolute faith in his instincts; he never doubted that somewhere an ideal course was open to him and that his intuitions were pre-dealt clues to his destiny. He had loved, briefly or long, with or without consummation, perhaps a dozen women; yet all of them, he now saw, shared the trait of approximation, of narrowly missing an undisclosed prototype. The surprise he felt did not have to do with the appearance, at last, of this central woman; he had always expected her to appear. What he had not expected was her appearance here, in this remote and abused nation, in this room of morning light, where he discovered a small knife in his fingers and on the table before him, golden and moist, a precisely divided pear.

Men travelling alone develop a romantic vertigo. Bech had already fallen in love with a freckled Embassy wife in Prague, a buck-toothed chanteuse in Rumania, a stolid Mongolian sculptress in Kazakstan. In the Tretyakov Gallery he had fallen in love with a recumbent statue, and at the Moscow Ballet School with an entire roomful of girls. Entering the room, he had been struck by the aroma, tenderly acrid, of young female sweat. Sixteen and seventeen, wearing patchy practice suits, the girls were twirling so strenuously their slippers were unravelling. Demure student faces crowned the unconscious insolence of their bodies. The room was doubled in depth by a floor-to-ceiling mirror. Bech was seated on a bench at its base. Staring above his head, each girl watched herself with frowning eyes frozen, for an instant in the turn, by the imperious delay and snap of her head. Bech tried to remember the lines of Rilke that expressed it, this snap and delay: *did not the drawing remain/that the dark stroke of your eyebrow/swiftly wrote on the wall of its own turning?* At one point the teacher, a shapeless old Ukrainian lady with gold canines, a *prima* of the thirties, had arisen; cried something translated to Bech as "No, no, the arms free, *free;*" and in demonstration executed a rapid series of pirouettes with such proud effortlessness that all the girls, standing this way and that like deer along the wall, had applauded. Bech had loved them for that. In all his loves, there was an urge to rescue—to rescue the girls from the slavery of their exertions, the statue from the cold grip of its own marble, the Embassy wife from her boring and unctuous husband, the chanteuse from her nightly humiliation (she could not sing), the Mongolian from her stolid race. But the Bulgarian poetess presented herself to him as needing nothing, as being complete, poised, satisfied, achieved. He was aroused and curious and, the next day, inquired about her of the man with the vaguely contemptuous mouth of a hare—a novelist turned playwright and scenarist, who accompanied him to the Rila Monastery. "She lives to write," the playwright said. "I do not think it is healthy."

Bech said, "But she seems so healthy." They stood beside a small church with whitewashed walls. From the outside it looked like a hovel, a shelter for pigs or chickens. For five centuries the Turks had ruled Bulgaria, and the Christian churches, however richly adorned within, had humble exteriors. A peasant woman with wildly snarled hair unlocked the door for them. Though the church could hardly ever have held more than thirty worshippers, it was divided into three parts, and every inch of wall was covered with eighteenth-century frescoes. Those in the narthex depicted a Hell where the devils wielded scimitars. Passing through the tiny nave, Bech peeked through the iconostas into the screened area that, in the symbolism of Orthodox architecture, represented the next, the hidden world—Paradise—and glimpsed a row of books, an easy chair, a pair of ancient oval spectacles. Outdoors again, he felt released from the unpleasantly tight atmosphere of a children's book. They were on the side of a hill. Above them was a stand of pines whose trunks glistened with ice. Below them sprawled the monastery, a citadel of Bulgarian national feeling during the years of the Turkish Yoke. The last monks had been moved out in 1961. An aimless soft rain was falling in these mountains, and there were not many German tourists today. Across the valley, whose little silver river still turned a water wheel, a motionless white horse stood silhouetted against a green meadow, pinned there like a brooch.

"I am an old friend of hers," the playwright said. "I worry about her."

"Are the poems good?"

"It is difficult for me to judge. They are very feminine. Perhaps shallow."

"Shallowness can be a kind of honesty."

"Yes. She is very honest in her work."

"And in her life?"

"As well."

"What does her husband do?"

The other man looked at him with parted lips and touched his arm, a strange Slavic gesture, communicating an underlying racial urgency, that Bech no longer shied from. "But she has no husband. As I say, she is too much for poetry to have married."

"But her name ends in '-ova.'"

"I see. You are mistaken. It is not a matter of marriage; I am Petrov, my unmarried sister is Petrova. All females."

"How stupid of me. But I think it's such a pity, she's so charming."

"In America, only the uncharming fail to marry?"

"Yes, you must be very uncharming not to marry."

"It is not so here. The government indeed is alarmed; our birth rate is one of the lowest in Europe. It is a problem for economists."

Bech gestured at the monastery. "Too many monks?"

"Not enough, perhaps. With too few of monks, something of the monk enters everybody."

The peasant woman, who seemed older to Bech than he was but who was probably under thirty, saw them to the edge of her domain. She huskily chattered in what Petrov said was very amusing rural slang. Behind her, now hiding in her skirts and now darting away, was her child, a boy not more than three. He was faithfully chased, back and forth, by a small white pig, who moved, as pigs do, on tiptoe, with remarkably abrupt changes of direction. Something in the scene, in the open glee of the woman's parting smile and the unself-conscious way her hair thrust out from her head, something in the mountain mist and spongy rutted turf into which frost had begun to break at night, evoked for Bech a nameless absence to which was attached, like a horse to a meadow, the image of the poetess, with her broad face, her good legs, her Parisian clothes, and her sleekly brushed hair. Petrov, in whom he was beginning to sense, through the wraps of foreignness, a clever and kindred mind, seemed to have overheard his thoughts, for he said, "If you would like, we could have dinner. It would be easy for me to arrange."

"With her?"

"Yes, she is my friend, she would be glad."

"But I have nothing to say to her. I'm just curious about such an intense conjunction of good looks and brains. I mean, what does a soul do with it all?"

"You may ask her. Tomorrow night?"

"I'm sorry, I can't. I'm scheduled to go to the ballet, and the next night the Legation is giving a cocktail party for me, and then I fly home."

"Home? So soon?"

"It does not feel soon to me. I must try to work again."

"A drink, then. Tomorrow evening before the ballet? It is possible? It is not possible."

Petrov looked puzzled, and Bech realized that it was his fault, for he was nodding to say Yes, but in Bulgaria nodding meant No, and a shake of the head meant Yes. "Yes," he said. "Gladly."

The ballet was entitled "Silver Slippers." As Bech watched it, the word "ethnic" kept coming to his mind. He had grown accustomed, during his trip, to this sort of artistic evasion, the retreat from the difficult and disappointing present into folk dance, folk tale, folk song, with always the implication that, beneath the embroidered peasant costume, the folk was really one's heart's own darling, the proletariat.

"Do you like fairy tales?" It was the moist-palmed interpreter who accompanied him to the theatre.

"I *love* them," Bech said, with a fervor and gaiety lingering from the previous hour. The interpreter looked at him anxiously, as when Bech had swallowed the brandy in one swig, and throughout the ballet kept murmuring explanations of self-evident events on the stage. Each night, a princess would put on silver slippers and dance through her mirror to tryst with a wizard, who possessed a magic stick that she coveted, for with it the world could be ruled. The wizard, as a dancer, was inept, and once almost dropped her, so that anger flashed from her eyes. She was, the princess, a little redhead with a high round bottom and a frozen pout and beautiful free arm motions, and Bech found it oddly ecstatic when, preparatory to her leap, she would dance toward the mirror, an empty oval, and another girl, identically dressed in pink, would emerge from the wings and perform as her reflection. And when the princess, haughtily adjusting her cape of invisibility, leaped through the oval of gold wire, Bech's heart leaped backward into the enchanted hour he had spent with the poetess.

Though the appointment had been established, she came into the restaurant as if, again, she had been suddenly summoned and had hurried. She sat down between Bech and Petrov slightly breathless and fussed, but exuding, again, that impalpable warmth of intelligence and virtue.

"Vera, Vera," Petrov said.

"You hurry too much," Bech told her.

"Not so very much," she said.

Petrov ordered her a cognac and continued with Bech their discussion of the newer French novelists. "It is tricks," Petrov said. "Good tricks, but tricks. It does not have enough to do with life, it is too much verbal nervousness. Is that sense?"

"It's an epigram," Bech said.

"There are just two of their number with whom I do not feel this: Claude Simon and Samuel Beckett. You have no relation, Bech, Beckett?"

"None."

Vera said, "Nathalie Sarraute is a very modest woman. She felt motherly to me."

"You have met her?"

"In Paris I heard her speak. Afterward there was the coffee. I liked her theories, of the, oh, *what*? Of the *little* movements within the heart." She delicately measured a pinch of space and smiled, through Bech, back at herself.

"Tricks," Petrov said. "I do not feel this with Beckett; there, in a low form, believe it or not, one has human content."

Bech felt duty-bound to pursue this, to ask about the theatre of the absurd in Bulgaria, about abstract painting (these were the touchstones of "progressiveness;" Russia had none, Rumania some, Czechoslovakia plenty), to subvert Petrov. Instead, he asked the poetess, "Motherly?"

Vera explained, her hands delicately modelling the air, rounding into nuance, as it were, the square corners of her words. "After her talk, we—talked."

"In French?"

"And in Russian."

"She knows Russian?"

"She was born Russian."

"How is her Russian?"

"Very pure but—old-fashioned. Like a book. As she talked, I felt in a book, safe."

"You do not always feel safe?"

"Not always."

"Do you find it difficult to be a woman poet?"

"We have a tradition of woman poets. We have Elisaveta Bagriana, who is very great."

Petrov leaned toward Bech as if to nibble him. "Your own works? Are they influenced by the *nouvelle vague*? Do you consider yourself to write anti-*romans*?"

Bech kept himself turned toward the woman. "Do you want to hear about how I write? You don't, do you?"

"Very much yes," she said.

He told them, told them shamelessly, in a voice that surprised him with its steadiness, its limpid urgency, how once he had written, how in "Travel Light" he had sought to show people skimming the surface of things with their lives, taking tints from things the way that objects in a still-life color one another, and how later he had attempted to place beneath the melody of plot a counter-melody of imagery, interlocking images which had risen to the top and drowned his story, and how in "The Chosen" he had sought to make of this confusion the theme itself, an epic theme, by showing a population of characters whose actions were all determined, at the deepest level, by nostalgia, by a desire to get back, to dive, each, into the springs of their private imagery. The book probably failed; at least, it was badly received. Bech apologized for telling all this. His voice tasted flat in his mouth; he felt a secret intoxication and a secret guilt, for he had contrived to give a grand air, as of an impossibly noble and quixotically complex experiment, to his failure when at bottom, he suspected, a certain simple laziness was the cause.

Petrov said, "Fiction so formally sentimental could not be composed in Bulgaria. We do not have a happy history."

It was the first time Petrov had sounded like a Communist. If there was one thing that irked Bech about these people behind the mirror, it was their assumption that, however second-rate elsewhere, in suffering they were supreme. He said, "Believe it or not, neither do we."

Vera calmly intruded. "Your personae are not moved by love?"

"Yes, very much. But as a form of nostalgia. We fall in love, I tried to say in the book, with women who remind us of our first landscape. A silly idea. I used to be interested in love. I once wrote an essay on the orgasm—you know the word?—"

She shook her head. He remembered that it meant Yes.

"—on the orgasm as perfect memory. The one mystery is, what are we remembering?"

She shook her head again, and he noticed that her eyes were gray, and that in their depths his image (which he could not see) was searching for the thing remembered. She composed her fingertips around the brandy glass and said, "There is a French poet, a young one, who has written of this. He says that never else do we, do we so gather up, collect into ourselves, oh—" Vexed, she spoke to Petrov in rapid Bulgarian.

He shrugged and said, "Concentrate our attention."

"—concentrate our attention," she repeated to Bech, as if the words, to be believed, had to come from her. "I say it foolish—foolishly—but in French it is very well put and—*correct.*"

Petrov smiled neatly and said, "This is an enjoyable subject for discussion, love."

"It remains," Bech said, picking his words as if the language were not native even to him, "one of the few things that still deserve meditation."

"I think it is good," she said.

"Love?" he asked, startled.

She shook her head and tapped the stem of her glass with a fingernail, so that Bech had an inaudible sense of ringing, and she bent as if to study the liquor, so that her entire body borrowed a rosiness from the brandy and burned itself into Bech's memory—the silver gloss of her nail, the sheen of her hair, the symmetry of her arms relaxed on the white tablecloth, everything except the expression on her face.

Petrov asked aloud Bech's opinion of Dürrenmatt.

Actuality is a running impoverishment of possibility. Though he had looked forward to seeing her again at the cocktail party and had made sure that she was invited, when it occurred, though she came, he could not get to her. He saw her enter, with Petrov, but he was fenced in by an attaché of the Yugoslav Embassy and his burnished Tunisian wife; and, later, when he was worming his way toward her diagonally, a steely hand closed on his arm and a rasping American female told him that her fifteen-year-old nephew had decided to be a writer and desperately needed advice. Not the standard crap, but real brass-knuckles advice. Bech found himself balked. He was surrounded by America: the voices, the narrow suits, the watery drinks, the clatter, the glitter. The mirror had gone opaque and gave him back only himself. He managed, in the end, as the officials were thinning out, to break through and confront her in a corner. Her coat, blond, with a rabbit collar, was already on; from its side pocket she pulled a pale volume of poems in the Cyrillic alphabet. "Please," she said. On the flyleaf she had written, "to H. Beck, sincerelly, with bad spellings but much"—the last word looked like "leave" but must have been "love."

"Wait," he begged, and went back to where his ravaged pile of presentation books had been and, unable to find the one he wanted, stole the Legation library's jacketless copy of "The Chosen." Placing it in her expectant hands, he told her, "Don't look," for inside he had written, with a drunk's stylistic confidence,

Dear Vera Glavanakova—
  It is a matter of earnest regret for me that you and I must live on opposite sides of the world.

MAUREEN HOWARD was born in Bridgeport, Connecticut, and graduated from Smith College in 1952. She now lives in New Brunswick, New Jersey, with her husband who teaches literature at Rutgers University, and a small daughter. She has published two novels: *Not a Word About Nightingales* (1962) and *Bridgeport Bus* (1965). An earlier story (also "Bridgeport Bus") appeared in the 1962 O. Henry Prize Story collection.

Sherry

DURING the war, when I wasn't quite twenty, I began to come to New York two or three times a year to visit my cousin Sherry. New York as I knew it with Sherry has nothing to do with my life now; returning years later, I am still a novice in the city. Her world was constructed of distorted pieces of time: workaday nights, supper at dawn, dreams in the afternoon—toast, coffee, and a quick shower in the evening.

The only way my cousin and her friends ever let on that they knew the moon still drew the tides, that the stars still moved in the heavens—not on Forty-fifth Street—was in their devotion to the big aluminum sun lamp under which they "took five." When the girls came back to Sherry's after the last show in whatever club or chorus line they were working, they all—except Sally, the Negro singer—had a go at the big bulb. As I watched, hunched and happy in my corner, there was always a lovely body smeared with oil turning under the ultraviolet rays. Aside from the uniform orange pallor which the show girls imagined was natural, nothing in their routine acknowledged the day, or allowed that there were other places in the city besides all-night automats, late subways, blue-lit bars and bright swinging rooms at four o'clock in the morning.

I used to arrive in New York in the late afternoon on Saturday and find my way to the newest address I had for Sherry, for in those days she was never with the same friends or in the same apartment. Back home it took hours of cajoling my mother and the aunts before I could get away to the bus station and make the train in Bridgeport. I was told I had no business with Mary Elizabeth in New York when they didn't know where she lived, or with what kind—and Mary Elizabeth (last seen in one of those dirty little news sheets with her bum bare to the world) had no business with me. I promised myself to get to the city early to see the Metropolitan Museum or a play, or to walk in the busy streets, but they got the best of me: I was always late. I would come from the everlasting darkness of the platform in Grand Central into a radiant palace, the main waiting-room. There in an antechamber I would clean up and apply the "Raven Red" lipstick I dared not wear at home. With my mouth the color of dried blood, I sauntered down to the Oyster Bar for a bowl of chowder, a black coffee and a puff on whatever cigarette came in the fanciest package. Outside, New York was not the movie-land of flashing neon, blinding marquees and bright windows I now expect; it seemed all office buildings—thick, high, menacing—blacked out for the duration. The time was right; Sherry would be getting up.

To greet me she wore a silk dressing gown of a confused oriental design—mandarin neck, kimono sleeves—and her eyes, slits puffed with sleep, were fittingly exotic. As soon as I arrived, the rush to the chorus line began. There was only one uncluttered moment, time enough for one of the changing cast of characters to say, "You must be Sherry's cousin!"—not that I resembled Mary Elizabeth in any way; I looked such a hick, bumbling through the hall with my suitcase.

"Something to eat, Ag? A cup of coffee?" Sherry displayed her hostess smile, and I'm sure she thought there was a tasty sugar plum somewhere. She *wanted* one for me, but I knew there was only the stale metallic coffee, the bleak icebox with a quart of skimmed milk and a few forgotten apples.

"No, I've eaten."

"I tell you what—" Sherry said, inspired in the old way—"I tell you what, Mary Agnes, we'll go over to Aunt Lil's and ask for ice cream and she'll come through with enough money for the movies. . . ." "I tell you what, Mary Agnes; after we do the dishes we'll go down to the drugstore and buy a *Silver Screen*; we'll work on my Ginger Rogers routine, we'll play pinochle. . . ." "I tell you what, Mary Agnes, we'll send out for sandwiches at the theater and you can have a big milk shake." So it was at all times for Sherry: life might seem a little makeshift right now—no parents, crabby aunts, hand-me-down clothes; but it was only a matter of making it through a single gray moment into the bright future. And I must say she escaped the dingy days of our childhood. If in the end things didn't turn out right it wasn't her fault. She tried; she made it; it was just that the big world was not what she imagined.

In those days when I visited Mary Elizabeth I found myself waiting on the edge of a bed while her friends threw stockings and slips from their jumbled bureaus and spidery drying racks. I remember trying to tuck my big feet out of the way, scrunching myself to the wall, but if I suggested waiting outside Sherry turned to me in surprise: "You just came, honey. When can I see you?" And the girls agreed I was no trouble at all. It was years before I sensed that they created the confusion of mismatched hose, tipped-over cologne bottles and make-up stains on the dresser—the scene lit by an infuriating fifteen-watt bulb over the mirror. To have me sitting around the house at breakfast time would have disrupted an ordinary household, but none of Sherry's friends wanted to be mistaken for ordinary Betty Boops who ate cereal in the morning. They all practiced wackiness as a religion: they worked hard and long on outlandish pompadours and upsweeps, silver eyelids and glistening talons. Then, coated with ideal artificiality, they went forth into the unsuspecting street, onto a shocked bus, into the glare of the dressing room, where they started all over again to defeat the bit of nature that *would* show through on their pretty faces. They were all simple girls—like Mary Elizabeth—with simple names. Once she shared an apartment with singing sisters from Milwaukee—Jean, Jane and Joan—I never sorted them out.

No matter how ardently Sherry tried for the bizarre effect with pitch mascara and false fingernails, she had a natural beauty which the most extreme maculations could not destroy. Her hair was red, not at all that Irish-red that brings the obvious stare, but the color of black roses, a mysterious shade that women try to imitate without success. With Sherry all was real: her hair, her height, the bones of her cheeks, the cleft in her chin—and her smile was as fresh the last time I saw her as it was the night years and years ago when her mother, old, finished at thirty, carried her up the back steps into our kitchen. My mother and Francis and I stood weighted with sleep while this child we had never laid eyes on, Mary Elizabeth Hurley in an outgrown coat, smiled at us as though we had invited her to a grand birthday party, right then, that minute.

"We'll give her some warm milk," Mary Elizabeth's mother said, "and put her to bed." But the child—almost a year older than me, almost seven—had to show us her pretty, impractical shoes with T straps. Her baby girl legs, without leggings, were red from the cold night air; her dress was taffeta with a sash, the sort I wore only for Sunday. Soon we were all having ginger-ale and cookies—at three o'clock in the morning.

"Where's Jack, then?" my mother asked.

"Off. He's gone off." Mary Elizabeth's mother took off her close felt hat, and then we could see her hair, the same depth of red she had given her child, hanging in dead broken strands over her ears.

"Gone for good this time," she said. "We'll not see him again."

"You've no such luck," my mother said gently. And she was right; he did come back soon—to watch his young wife die.

He was Black Irish, handsome Jack Hurley; he sat in our front room during that awful week, sobered-up in a cloud of cigar smoke, waiting for God to be merciful—until the very last hour, after the priest had gone; then, cursing himself, he knelt by the bed, where the woman who grew beautiful again as she died put out her frail hand with great effort—to comfort him.

Mary Elizabeth told us her father could sing and play the banjo and the mandolin and slide a quarter into his cuff and make the fifty-cent piece in his hand disappear.

"Nobody will contradict that," my mother told her crossly if she was within hearing, and soon our pretty cousin understood it was best to tell me—Francis didn't believe—her marvelous stories about Jack Hurley and other imaginary princes, in secret, behind the couch or up on the attic stairs. Sometimes at Christmas Jack Hurley sent cheap jewelry which Mary Elizabeth raised from the cotton wadding with reverence—like St. Thérèse pictured on a holy card accepting the rosary from the Virgin's hand—and she would wear the little necklace or bracelet until her neck or wrist was ringed with green and the green turned black. Then my mother scrubbed her skin raw, and tears hung on her dark lashes. One ring her father sent with a yellow stone set in golden prongs tore her face in the night, and Aunt Mae, helping my mother bathe the sores with lysol solution, said he must have got that one out of a Cracker Jack box.

Jack Hurley never remembered his daughter's birthday—none of the grownups did, for I suppose though they had to take her in as a child of seven they didn't want to celebrate her clouded birth. I don't know actually when or where she came to be, but Sherry told me once in New York that her parents had run off together to Providence—much in love, so happy that all those fat hens couldn't hold them. From bits I overheard I presume she was born in a charity ward to a frightened girl with another fake ring on her finger while Jack Hurley disported himself (that was the word they used) in a barroom.

It didn't take long for the sweet sadness of her mother's death to wear off and the edginess to come back in the aunts' voices. Mary Elizabeth was another mouth to feed, another body to dress, and we heard that often enough. It didn't take long for her to learn that she was lovelier than other girls, even in faded dresses and cut-down coats, so she smiled and helped with the dishes to get ten cents for her dancing lessons or for the piano lesson with the music Sister after school. No, it never occurred to me, towering on spindle legs above the children my own age, gaping down at the top of their heads through steel-rimmed glasses (which finally uncrossed my eyes), to be affronted by her beauty.

"She has Catherine's hair," they said fondly. "She has his eyes." That was all she did have, after all: the remarkable smile, the glorious red hair, the chin dented with the shadow of her father. Later, after Sherry had used her looks to get other treats: furs and checkbooks—a free ride beyond anything her aunts could imagine—I often thought that was all she had and nothing more.

My Uncle Peter would take her on his knee, and poor Jim, Mae's silent asthmatic husband, would chase her around the table with a wheezy laugh. My father, who never could manage my long limbs, took Sherry under his arm and swung her easily, almost dropping her to the floor, then catching her; and up she flew again through the stuffy living room with giggles and shrieks of delight. They forgot for a minute where they were and made the close brown room a wild, dangerous ring for their acrobatic feats. The truth was that her uncles loved to play with her; such feminine grace, though only in a child, recalled their own lost charm of manhood which had been nicely put aside by the scrubbing, cooking, endlessly-talking women they had married. And Sherry (Mary Elizabeth to them, of course) knew instinctively how to wink at her admirers, how to toss her head of bouncing ringlets and arch her black eyebrows in surprise at every kiss.

If I make her sound like a detestable coy child, a baby movie star, I give the wrong impression. She had a talent for loving men, for giving herself freely, which she did not defile till years later, long after most women have deceived even themselves. The lonely kid throwing her arms around our Uncle Peter's neck was no different than the nervous woman in the best restaurant smiling at some man over the corpse of an extravagant fish: Sherry meant it every time.

In eighth grade her legs suddenly grew long and sleek, and she could tap the whole length of the auditorium platform in twirls— and did for the class one afternoon—her skirt twirling up too, exposing pink garters, until the frenzied rapping of Sister Edmond called a halt. Mary Elizabeth would not dance for graduation—let Lou Magee recite the funny piece where she took off a lady going to the dentist.

"But I can sing," Mary Elizabeth said, and began "Mexicali Rose" with all her heart. Then we were transported from that damp school basement with the water running in the toilets down the hall to an unfamiliar place of yearning flesh and sad withdrawal. Hers was a thin voice, high, forced into the low lusty throbs of the blues—a poor imitation to be sure, but how did the eighth grade of St. Augustine's know, how did Sister Mary Edmond know? Sherry wailed, a woman before us, of the disasters that would come upon us soon enough; and she sang at graduation finally, bound into a white organdy dress meant for a child. She sang out for everyone else's parents: "Hark, hark the lark at Heav'ns gate sings and Phoebus 'gins arise."

In the Freshman Talent Show at high school there was no holding her back. A whole new audience of boys from all over town whistled and stamped for more after she exhausted her two dance routines. There was her shape, undeniable now, and her hair brushed back into waves blending into the red velvet curtain on the stage. She was admired in Pappadoulous' Sweet Shop all afternoon while I did the Latin homework for us both on the dining-room table. If I envied her, it was only for a moment, when one of the perfect boys in saddle shoes and a pork-pie hat came, breaking the terrible dullness of our house with lively shuffling and patronizing good will until the queen made her entrance. And she was, without seeking the title, the queen of Central High, gracious in the corridors, stately in class, a presence in the girls' lunchroom—never with unseemly pride, but with the inherent simplicity of royalty in her plain clothes.

"Come along, Ag," she would say on a sunny afternoon when a carload of boys waited in front of our house, and she would lure some poor sap who wanted to gaze at her into asking me. I was vulnerable on different grounds then, and couldn't stand the contempt in their eyes, the gagging politeness in their mouths, so I preferred to stay at home with my library books. Later on, when Sherry wanted me to come to New York, it didn't matter: I had accepted myself, an ugly cousin, my sharp nose pressed against the sweet-shop window.

There are many girls who come to flower at the silly age of fifteen or sixteen and hold their loveliness like perishable blooms. I am shocked to meet them in the stores downtown and discover them wilted at twenty, bodies already turning to hard pods, closed to possibility and change. It might have happened to my cousin if she had fallen in love with one of her high-school beaux; but she never really had a chance even for that deadening solution; she was too spectacular for our factory town.

I can't come up with the answer to Mary Elizabeth, any more than *she* could, though a Park Avenue psychiatrist furnished her with long plausible stories to tell. There was the rootlessness of Jack Hurley in her that wanted nothing to do with two-family houses and supper at six o'clock; and like her father she was always performing just a little—her walk, her smile, the inventions that brightened the evenings when we sat together at algebra and French. Being no one at home but an orphan with a name that was bad cess and a burden to my mother who was looking for crosses to bear, Mary Elizabeth hoped in her adolescent fantasy to be someone even grander than Aunt Lil, who had married a lawyer, to dwell in a land more magical than the one green hill across the river where rich people lived. For years, while I learned to accept a hall-bedroom and the lonely oblong of my face, I told that incredible person in the mirror, substance of myself, that it was her beauty that set her free. Such nonsense: that perfection of form trapped her; she became a rare animal, a spirit caged within her own body.

Mr. Garafano, the used-car dealer, gave us a ride home after Glee Club one day in a Packard convertible the color of heavy cream with caramel leather seats. It was spring and anyone could see us, including my mother on her way to the second-day bread store. We thought it odd that Mr. Garafano complimented Mary Elizabeth (he called her "Red") on her height when I was three inches taller, and though she never took a ride again he was not discouraged: when we came around his corner on the way to school Mr. Garafano lingered at the front of his lot. He was fat and forty and smelled of cigars—a big laugh—quite a different matter from the young druggist, Mr. Shea, who began to pay for our sodas and give Mary Elizabeth perfume samples. He was handsome in a lanky way and kidded around with us about boys, but when summer came he spent an indecent amount of time watching out the window to see Mary Elizabeth come down the street, and he ran out and wound the awnings up and down, talking to her about serious matters: movies, dancing, love, her family, his family. When he came to the boiling point Tom Shea would ask her to come into the cool dark store where fans blew the air and the smooth marble counter took the heat out of your hands. He would fix her a cherry Coke. Such innocence is touching, but she was still a little girl and he was a man, I suppose, so one Saturday night in August we all woke up to the noise of glass breaking and found that young Shea had dropped his bottle on our front walk. My father helped him out of the barberry, and with lovesick eyes going all over Mary Elizabeth's pajamas, Tom said, "I must have lost my way."

That fall when she would have been a cheerleader and the Princess of Transylvania in *Sweethearts*, Aunt Lil came up with the money to send Mary Elizabeth away to the Sisters of Mercy. There she played field hockey and girl's basketball and went through a religious period (with the same fervor she called forth for her analysis). It was novel for Sherry to be holy and calm, to conjure emotions from the depths of an inexperienced heart—to exist on guilt, self-abnegation, humility. The demands of the role were great; I'm glad I missed the performance. She came home at Christmas ten pounds lighter from the spiritual indulgence, more shapely than ever; she paraded all the way up the center aisle to communion in her blue serge uniform, a small black mantilla draped over her head—more enchanting than any bride in white. All our bells rang—the phone and the front door—but Mary Elizabeth turned her suitors away with a saintly sigh and the secret smile of one who has the higher calling. Then, invited to the golf club across the river she went out on New Year's Eve and danced till morning. I was waiting in the hall for her, listening for the sound of a car, but she came walking up our hill alone, and when I let her in she ran down the hall to the bathroom.

"Come in, Ag," she whispered. Under the borrowed evening wrap her dress was torn; a gardenia, crushed and brown, hung from the tattered ruffle. We spent an hour washing the mud spots out of the skirt, but the dress was ruined.

"Silly old fool!" Mary Elizabeth wailed, despairing over the limp net, "Silly old fool!"

I didn't know what to ask. "How was the party?"

"Dreamy. A big band—I got to sing two numbers in front of a real mike, and the leader said any time he needed a girl. . . . Oh, that silly old fool," she cried again, finding another rip where her heel had caught the underskirt.

"Who?"

"Dr. Morrisey." (She had gone to the golf club with young Jim Morrisey: I had watched from a dark corner in the hall when he came to the door with a corsage.)

"Well, Jimmy put rye in his ginger-ale to prove he's a man. He passed out, and his father gave me a ride home."

"How awful!" I said, not having the slightest idea what could have happened. "Are you all right?"

"Oh, sure." Mary Elizabeth laughed. "He didn't mean anything." Then she sat down on the side of the bathtub. "Oh, Ag," her voice was young and bewildered, "why does it always have to be me?" The question seemed easy enough to answer.

Back at school, she taught the can-can to the Senior Sodality, smoked in the cellar, and got herself dismissed before Easter. Aunt Lil, whose colored girl had left to have a baby, took her in for the housework and didn't allow Mary Elizabeth out of the yard. In May my father went to bed one night and never woke up. My mind was so full of him laid out in Conley's funeral parlor that I never noticed how my brother Francis was making himself useful in Aunt Lil's garden.

Francis used to wait for me after school and we'd go visit Mary Elizabeth in her respectable prison. I sat on the slatestone porch, which was one of the features of Lil's house and which she had learned to call a terrace. The only time Lil gave us a thought, when she was home at all and not out playing bridge, was when she stuck her head out the sun-parlor door and said, "Don't sit on the cold stone, Agnes, you'll catch cold in your bowels."

No doubt there were buds on the rambler roses—held within delicate tendrils until their time came—and surely the apple tree snowed down on us, promising so much more than the stunted wormy fruit it bore each fall, but I saw only the throbbing heart of red carnations (chosen because they hold up so well) trailing the golden motto "Beloved Husband" into the magnificent box in which Mr. Conley set my father stiffly to rest. In the murky funeral home, which seemed to me a vestibule of fitting horror for the grave, clots of flowers blocked my vision: gladiolas and snapdragons wired and puttied into wreaths, sweetheart roses in a baby cross—"Our Dear Father"—and bouquets big enough to open a bank. Tributes to the florist's art appeared on every page of my Gallic Wars. I wore a black skirt, and the sight of this might bring to mind, between the successive *gaucheries* of M. and Mme. Perichon on their imbecilic voyage, other arrangements for death: the hasty purchase of our mourning, the warehouse of caskets down in New Haven, a dazzling display of varnished boxes lined with velvets and silks in pale colors to compliment the morbid tones of the embalmer's palette. Then I saw again the dresses, rose and pale green like the slabs I sat on, dresses banked by the rentable palms, dresses of lace and crepe, unwearable garments of no size, slit all the way down the back to "fit" a woman wasted or bloated in death.

In my aunt's yard the sun was bright and warm. Along each side was a strip of garden neglected since the old Yankee schoolteacher had sold the house to my Uncle Peter, though the tulip and daffodil bulbs still yielded up a few weak blossoms, and forgotten plants pushed up out of habit through years of dry stalks and a blanket of leaves. No one in our family had any use for gardening: they had heard enough of poor potato crops and pitiful Mayo squashes to ever want to kneel to the earth again. Indeed I heard Lil tell a neighbor that her family had been "in agriculture," as though my grandfather was a gentleman farmer, breeding fancy apples or prize cows. Childless, bustling woman that she was, Aunt Lil had developed a sharp eye for clutter of any kind, and I suppose that looking out beyond the sterile tidiness of her kitchen one day she saw her back yard and thought Francis might clean it up.

Neither my brother nor Mary Elizabeth had the slightest notion of what they were about when they went out together in that spring sunshine. One of them would rake as the other hacked at the rubble, and then they would sit together on the grass and talk till supper time. It was a slow business, clearing away the brittle stems and matted leaves, and Francis carried off the debris in a peach basket and dumped it to rot behind the garage. They scratched at the ground with metal claws, uprooting what they thought were weeds, until they drew an ugly rim of black soil around the grass and only the obvious flowers were left—naked and humiliated. Aunt Lil was pleased, for now the yard looked like one of her pantry shelves, stark and irreproachable before the world—and she believed that the world saw and cared about the state of shelves and closets and fingernails.

What's worth telling?

When they asked me, "What were you up to, Miss, that you couldn't see?" I didn't have an answer—then. There was nothing to see: on my lap a geometry book, black perimeters defining truths within range of a sophomore—each day a new proposition, another proof. The yard, inscribed around us in a black line of earth, holds the three of us, Francis and Mary Elizabeth and me, forever, the last of our childhood dumped behind the garage. We are circumscribed by one another and by the knowledge of what would become of us as sure as my father is by his damp-proof box.

"What kind of fool were you then?" The same kind I am now. They dug in the ground; they sat on the grass. Sometimes, not often, they came to be with me on the stone porch.

Francis wore his mourning tie still and looked a likely candidate for the seminary. My mother had always wanted it for him and claimed on occasion that she had heard his call (an unnatural voice whispering from the rectory). My brother was handsome and about to graduate from high school with his clubs and teams set down next to his picture in the yearbook: History, Junior Service, French, Thespians, Glee Club, Swimming, Basketball, Cross Country—and Class Secretary. It's a wonder Francis turned into such a dull man —but maybe the tribute under his name summed him up too well: he was voted "Most Affable." Active and happy—taking showers, training his hair, studying, serving Mass—too important to mope with me and Mary Elizabeth in our projections of black lucite and smoked mirrors, marabou and Leslie Howard. It kept him busy the whole time to be the most affable Francis X. Keely.

What *did* I think then when he didn't go to graduation practice and missed the Senior Prom? Why, that his life, like mine, had stopped on the edge of our father's grave. And "that one," as my

mother called Mary Elizabeth forever after, as if her name would
bring the Devil back to live among us, "that one" shuffled off to
Buffalo on the porch, her breasts bouncing, her red hair beating her
back in a rhythm of life. She costumed herself in an old cotton dress
of Aunt Lil's which she drew tight at the waist with a belt—pathetic,
a ravaged heroine of post-war *realismo* breathing desperation and
desire. Well the hell with that: this was still the Depression for us
and I was fifteen years old. The hell with that and other after-
thoughts.

I drooped my head down between my high shoulders and sucked
sadness from the air. We were studying *Hamlet* in English. It's hard
to imagine a more personal reading of the play than mine.

" 'Tis not alone this inky cloak, good mother. . . ." I stalked the
misty cemetery where the sod was not yet settled over my father, and
appeared in a nurse's cape behind Conley's blessed candles (which
were not lit until we arrived at the funeral "home"). I swept away
the sickening floral arrangements—"What?" I said with a cynical
laugh, "these for a man to whom you gave not the tribute of one
flower while he lived." Or, switching roles, I tripped, maddened,
down the altar steps in a dance modeled on Mary Elizabeth's Fred
Astaire number and confronted my mother and aunts in their black
hats with fennel and rue tied in packets like the sachets they gave
each other on birthdays. "Hey non, nonny," I sang, for I could see
this much: that they were bitter women with empty complaints who
at last had gained a terrible dignity in their widow's weeds and their
ceremonious weeping; their fragile minds shattered, they moaned
lunatic sentiments: "He went peaceful," "A beautiful death," "Never
a word," "It's those behind who suffer"—and by the time it was over
they came to believe that my father was a sneaky fellow who slipped
off without warning.

One Friday night the mad world became real, and like other tragic
figures I was left alone: my father, my brother, my cousin Sherry, all
the people I loved, had been taken from me—in the normal course
of affairs, I might say, because death, shame, a boy going off to college seem like childhood diseases compared to the larger plague. It
was coming to the summer of 1939. There was nothing left but report cards and the pomp of Francis' graduation ceremony—nothing
but the joyless procession of hot days and wasted hours. Summer
idleness had settled upon us already, and with the garden work finished we three sat on the porch every afternoon, our only project to

get ten cents out of Aunt Lil for the Good Humor man. We might have been inmates of a hospital set out to get some warmth in our bones, so it was difficult to tell them why God gave me eyes.

"There's a lot went on under your nose, young lady. You just better come down to earth, Ag."

It had been a Friday; perhaps I know that only because Lil still tells the story: "It was a Friday night," she says. "I remember Mary Elizabeth wouldn't eat the haddock. Nice filets I got to poach in milk, but she never would eat half the perfectly good food we put in front of her. . . . I did everything for that girl."

It seems Mary Elizabeth got up in the middle of the meal to make it to the movies; I know it was one of the first times she was let out of the house. I went down to church with my mother that night to pay for the Month's Mind Mass for my father—so Francis went to Poli's with Mary Elizabeth, and on Saturday morning "the whole thing was clear." I've always wondered at that phrase, because to me there's never been anything about it that wasn't muddy. Aunt Lil got up to take a seltzer because the coconut pie was a little heavy, and hearing a noise like breathing below, she went downstairs to find them "at it" on her couch. "The blouse open," she says. "I thought it was an animal, and I told her, you are no better than a *low* creature. . . ." And the story goes on—Francis seduced while carrying incense up the center aisle, Sherry doing a belly dance on her mother's deathbed while Jack Hurley strums the ukulele at the foot of the Cross.

On Sunday Sherry was gone, with the mayonnaise jar full of pennies off the pantry shelf and all the money she could filch from Lil's purse. She was sixteen and they never tried to find her, never saw her again except in the newspapers, smiling over her shoulder with her rump bared. We stood in the bus station together, knocking our shins into the suitcase Lil had bought for her to go to the nuns.

"Oh Boy," she said, "I'm finally getting out of this rotten town."

"It wasn't your fault."

"Sure it was," Mary Elizabeth said looking down at her flesh as though it were separate from her, the embodiment of an impossible child. "For weeks I told old Francis to chase his tail; but it's always my fault."

I handed over her winter coat, wet from the heat of my arm, and at least five men rushed up to help with her suitcase. When she turned on the step of the bus to wave goodbye her gesture was big;

her smile dramatized the moment: she was already on stage and she hadn't even left home. In her high-heeled shoes, bright with Shinola, and with a brave Carmen mouth, she was gone from us. The crowd of strange men who looked up at her seemed a chorus of male dancers, ready to follow her with whatever grace they could muster into the stinking hot recesses of the Bridgeport Bus.

The summer heat settled into the rooms of our downstairs flat, never to leave; even during thunderstorms when the air blew the curtains, it never got inside to us. Days moved slowly—Francis went off to mow lawns in Lil's neighborhood and I read stacks of library books with sticky red and green covers: mysteries and novels and everything of Eugene O'Neill that was in print—and behind each uneventful day was the figure of my mother, a mound of lard melting on the kitchen stool, fingering the bankbooks until their pages were transparent with grease, tucking them in and out of their snug envelopes with a trembling that tensed us all. Where was the money to come from? It was certainly unfortunate (by this she meant unfair) of my father—Lord have mercy on him—to die when Francis was ready to go to college.

"May he rest in peace," she said with an unforgiving edge to her voice that echoed across town towards St. Michael's cemetery. May he rest in peace while she goes begging to her sisters.

Nights I lay on my bed and wondered where Mary Elizabeth was now that she wasn't sharing my room, now that I no longer listened for her admirers coming up the hill on hot nights: the shy smitten druggist, the butcher, the baker, the candlestick maker ensnared with passion in the barberry.

"Rich man, poor man, beggar man, thief. . . . Count your buttons, Aggie." I could hear the promise in her voice, as if she was sitting on the other bed brushing out her hair, sparks crackling in the dark—my nightdress *tied* at the neck; I didn't have a button to my name.

Where is she now? Where is all that spring sadness I felt in Aunt Lil's garden? Faded at the end of summer, burnt out, like my father, like the patch of grass in our yard. By now Lil's penny jar was empty; where would the money come from? There was never any real doubt that Francis would go off to Fordham in the fall, and it seems now that other events didn't surprise us. We stopped only for a moment (as the aunts did when that girl ran off) to cluck at the war—not at the enemy—and went on with the bedlam of our lives: years that

went by like the pages of a calendar flipping by on Poli's screen to
the swelling strains of "Tipperary."

But the days were long. "Another day, another dollar," my mother
said jauntily—she thought it was a happy phrase—and hustled me
off each morning—not to school, for I was sixteen and could be put
on as extra help in the zipper factory, where I sat sorting government orders stamped RUSH. I had to finish paying for our happy
home. I had to pay for Francis to study 16th century logic and
rhetoric with the Jesuits. I thought of Mary Elizabeth, and stole a
fifty-cent piece out of my pay envelope each week and put it in a
candy box, which was hers. Francis walked among the righteous. He
found himself in the NROTC and at a desk and on a ship and with
a war. He was thrown against a gangway. Mamma pin a rose on me.

Something was going to happen. I felt that for a couple of years,
saw the expectancy somewhere between my bird-beak nose and the
slope-off of my chin—in my mouth to be exact. I thought there
might be words that mattered, like the song of a Chinese maiden
perhaps, stark and elliptic, or the street cry of a French whore, *sym-
bolique* and endearing in its shrillness, but my tongue went dry, my
lips cracked, and when the words came they were cheap sarcastic
replies to my mother, invective without wit, without meter, without
imagery. Nothing was going to happen. I had nothing to say.

At home the months went by. We were two fish in a bowl, my
mother and I, drowsing in mid-water, suspended in liquid slime,
chasing specks, darting at each other in pecking motions, sustaining
ourselves automatically in the staleness with some low-grade will to
go on for no reason. Francis wrote in navy lingo from the Good Ship
Lollipop about a matey life on board a secret ocean. My mother
prayed for him—a jumbledy gurgling:

"Lite uv adjuz prayfruz, lilisuv fiel prayfruz, Virgin mose pure prayfruz—prayfruz who have recoursa Thee." She started, never to end, a
series of novenas, fretted about ration books and got slipped an occasional bag of sugar by a Democratic committeeman who had always been sure of the Keelys' vote. In the zipper factory I sorted,
stapled, filed, then was put to typing routine letters for the president
—Dear Major Spoolfiddle: Your contract (USQMC/100257z/42m)
for 150,000 total-slide khaki tapes, as acknowledged in our letter of
March 14th, etc. . . . I pasted defense stamps in books with the
Minute Man on the cover, wore a snood and flappy slacks, carried
spam sandwiches in a black tin box, grew nearly six feet tall, and

earned a First Aid certificate by wheezing the air out of my co-work-
ers (drowning victims), bandaging their head wounds, and cutting
off their flow of blood. I ran around our block in an air-raid helmet
carrying a blank piece of paper from Mr. Dunn to Mike Ford in three
minutes. History made up the meaningless games I would have
learned to play in any case.

It took a while to figure out: a postcard with a fat lady in bloomers running out of a Chick Sales. A printed caption, *Let's get to the
bottom of this, cutie!*, and written on the other side: "Will be in
New London with USO Sunday, Love, Sherry." Among other things
I learned that day was the story of Mary Elizabeth's new name. A
flamenco dancer claimed that in a spotlight her hair was the color of
aged sherry—blood of his native land—and so he had named her
that, Sherry, during a two-week run at a Newark nightclub. She
never used her real name again. In a few years when she blithely ordered Tio Pepe at the best bars in New York, Sherry said, "He was a
Frenchman—you know, *haute monde* with a title—and he insisted
upon 'Chérie.'" Then she repeated something which had been said
to her: "Well, it became Sherry—corrupted like everything else, I
guess." But in the full sun of an April afternoon with the Thames
River dazzling and the air full of music and the roaring whistling
sailors, the name Sherry Henderson seemed as natural to her as Mary
Agnes Keely was to me.

"How did you manage it, Ag?" she asked. "I never thought you'd
be able to get away from them."

"I told them I was doing a Sunday shift at the plant."

"That's the ticket!" She sounded as if we were still in league and
had escaped from the house for an afternoon show. As nearly as I
can remember she never mentioned any of the family again, and
when I spoke of my mother, of Francis, of Aunt Mae or Uncle Peter
—as I had to since there was no one else to make up my scenes—
she listened with little comment. From that day on I might have
been any friend she had shared a room with in one of those many
apartments. I might as well have brought her up to date on the ail-
ments of a family she had never seen.

We sat on the grass under the criss-cross of two-by-fours supporting
the temporary stage at the submarine base in New London. There
was bunting with stars and stripes tacked up around us, and the
sun shone through the gaps. Near us three little dogs, two poodles
and a mutt, strutted and yapped through a rehearsal of their act—

sitting up, praying, playing dead and jumping through imaginary hoops—and for a minute it looked like the Hawaiian girls in hula skirts with long tangles of hair and paper hibiscus blossoms were going to outnumber the rhumba dancers in wedgies and fruited turbans; but then another cluster of banana heads and ruffled breasts scurried out of the barracks across the way and there were more rhumbas than hulas. We talked about the places she had been: Pensacola, Fort Benning, Camp Kilmer. You were always singing and dancing—you never knew whether there'd be a stage and a mike or whether you'd have to sing off the back of a truck.

"Gee!" I said, fascinated by the dots of flaming rouge at the inner corner of her eyes, the streaks of white grease on her eyelids, her cherry lips coated with oil, and the pink shading on the lobes of her ears. White birds fluttered in a cage, white rabbits nibbled the air, impatient for false bottoms and secret pockets—all of this, though magic to Sherry too, was yet natural. And so I felt that Sunday, with the band booming, the M.C. warming up the boys with jokes about their officers, the gray warships lolling like harmless zoo mammals, that she danced through strangeness as most of us stumble through houses we know, accepting an irrational arrangement of doors and hallways, getting on with the business of the day. The notion persisted in my head for years that she was at home in the marvels of her world; but of course there are mornings when you can't find your way down the hall to the bathroom, when passages are sealed: then midgets and amplifiers, klieg lights and diamonds in the navel are freakish distortions in a macabre scene—gothic, unmanageable, disordered.

A heavy-set man with talcum powder on his beard and a rose in the buttonhole of his uniform came over to Sherry when he had nothing else on his mind.

"How's it going, kid?"

"Pretty good, Stu."

He wandered off in the direction of his comic cigar, and came upon us again through a slit in the bunting.

"How's it going, kid?"

"Just fine, Stu," Sherry said with a smile. "This heat is murder on the make-up."

"Powder it down again, kid, before you go on." Stu took her head in his manicured hands, examined her mouth and eyes with professional interest. He flicked a swarm of gnats away with a green silk handkerchief.

"A coming talent," he said. "Remarkable girl."

At last Sherry explained, rather defensively I thought, "This is my cousin."

"Is that so?" He bit the tip of a new cigar, moistened it with a sucking of his lips and tongue and went off to see about the line of hulas filing up the steps to the whooping of sailors and the twanging undulation of guitars. The dog trainer threw bits of biscuit in the air and the poodles leapt high—one, then another, in perfect time with the little mutt in a paper ruff and clown hat popping up on the fifth beat and tumbling down in a sorry heap.

"Stu's the manager of our outfit," Sherry said. In a moment he came back.

"You've got five minutes, baby." We stood up and shook our skirts, and I looked at my shoe while Stu fastened the hooks at the back of Sherry's dress. Then—unbelievable to me—he ran his fingers up her legs, straightening the seams of her stockings—soft fingers with clear nail polish and a chunky onyx ring.

"Don't give them any more than two numbers," he said, "I want to be in the buses by seven o'clock."

"Shiny face—I know, honey." Sherry twisted her mouth in a grimace that recalled her answers to the nuns.

Stu—foppish, middle-aged, blatantly handling the beautiful girl —was the first of many agents, managers, patrons: Mert, Sol, Jerry, Tonkey, the Colonel. I came to take them pretty much for granted, and towards the end I always expected some stocky gent to show up when I visited Sherry in New York. The man would enter her apartment, or be in his place already, a scotch and soda in hand, wearing a blue cashmere suit, white-on-white shirt, initialled silk tie, cuff links, ring, cologne—all the appurtenances of control. Like all the rest of them, Stu took particular notice of her clothes, her hair, her figure. Like no other breed of men they were concerned with fabrics and style, and I even got used to chatting with Sol about the length of her skirts and agreeing with the Colonel that she should avoid anything but dramatic hats.

"A simple cotton is all Sherry needs," said Stu, "nothing fancy, a little sweetheart neck like the girl back home. That's what the boys want, see—" He spit cigar juice.

I took a seat out front, on the end of a bench next to a sailor with a long face the color of oatmeal and tried to imagine his girl back home. Sherry, smiling big enough for all the boys in the world, sang "Don't sit under the apple tree with anyone else but me . . . ," and it didn't matter that the lyrics were supposedly sung by a man—on the battlefield, say, or in the bowels of a submarine—all that existed was the sea of male voices cheering, rising in waves to her. Sherry spread her arms wide to welcome them all—oatmeal face, baby lieutenant and weathered old commander. It didn't matter to the USO that her voice was thin, untrained and rasped on the high notes as she sang the third number.

"Stu will give me hell," she said, afterwards, blotting her tears, "but I can't help it . . . they were all so darling to me. See, Ag, here's the picture I send them for a pin-up." Mary Elizabeth in another simple cotton blown up over the knees, on a swing all twined with blossoms—apple blossoms, back yards, girl's hair massed on shoulders, fuzzed sunlight—the pay-off.

"Well, Sherry," I said, "Sherry!"

I left her at the door of a gray barracks. A man's voice called, and she hurried up the steps into her wonderland of yapping dogs, sweat, cold cream, rabbit pellets, and Stu with a bottle of Kentucky Moon come to the door to find her.

Mert said, "I see her as the exotic type, black jersey and an upsweep."

"How's that . . . ?" I hadn't been listening. We were standing outside the theater waiting for Sherry and some of her friends to come out after a performance of *Oklahoma!* The crowd was more interesting than Mert, her agent, whom I'd been telling yes, oh fine, all evening.

"Sherry should come to the theater in a cab."

"Yes."

"Get a press agent."

"Oh fine."

"Shouldn't waste her time on some two-bit band player."

"Yes." Sherry could do worse than show up at the clubs around town with a certain star, all to be arranged by him, Mert.

"Oh fine."

"I see it this way," Mert said. "Columbia Pictures may take an interest in the girl, but I happen to know they're loaded with All-American kids . . . besides, she could get typed, bad idea at this stage in her career. As I see it, *Oklahoma!* is a springboard, but she's no comic, see—a natural yes, but what she needs is to show a versatility—an exotic quality for the switch: black jersey halter, furs, upsweep."

"Fine," I said. "Fine."

"This Columbia Pictures deal could be very big." Sherry came out in a raincoat and saddle shoes, her cheeks scrubbed, her hair held back by an elastic band. This started Mert again: "If you want to stay in the chorus the rest of your life that's all right with me too, you know. I could very easily arrange for you to make the columns next week, but I mean if you go around looking like Miss Nobody. . . ."

"Jesus, I'm only going back to my place with the kids."

Mert pointed out the whole disaster with one finger brutally jabbed into my shoulder.

"That's just it, that's just the angle with this baby. She thinks she's working in Kresge's—going to have a few beers with the girls." He turned, hacked in the gutter, and one sweet act suggested another:

"Thumb your nose at Columbia Pictures, sweetheart—it's no skin off my back."

"This is my cousin," Sherry said with exaggerated patience, "we are going to have a little fun."

"A lousy sax player," he growled.

"Some two-bit sax player," Mert heckled, and scurried off towards war-dim Times Square: clickety click click clickety—that one wore taps on his shoes.

Some two-bit sax player was Tony De Angelo, the big handsome product of an Italian father and an Irish mother out on Staten Island—though I'm not sure how Sherry ever found this out, because more than any of her show-biz friends Tony created the impression of having always lived in midtown Manhattan. For him there was no harking back, no hatred for a crowded house with oilcloth on the table and cooking smells in your clothes. He existed now, only now, at the moment he stood before you: tall, jazzy, self-absorbed, product of the whole yearning American psyche with its Jack Armstrong heart cut out.

During the run of *Oklahoma!* Sherry lived at some good addresses, old places on the West Side with doormen and mahogany elevators; and Tony always had his key. As I talked to her at three in the morning her eyes seldom left the door. Tony would be coming in half an hour—in ten minutes, in five seconds.

"Well, you know how it is with late subways if you miss one, kid. . . . don't crump on me now, Ag"; Sherry would brighten with her stage smile. "Tony's going to be here in a minute."

So I nursed another can of beer until it was warm from my hands and flat. The girls in the show came in and gossiped for a while, timing themselves under the sun lamp. They assumed that Sherry was waiting for Tony, like a housewife with dinner on the stove. They thought it was kind of cute, and I remember one storybook blonde who was inspired to write long letters to her guy in the Marines on pages and pages of blue stationery while we waited for Tony.

"So tell me," Sherry said, and I talked. Her face was full of anxious devotion, the injured beauty of her mother, and she blinked at the closed door through which he would come.

"So tell me," she said.

I told her all the goddamn nonsense on my mind, talking to the four walls in a drowsy monologue. I wondered if I could absent myself from the nausea of daily life, from the factory with its everrunning day—put a net on my mind so it wouldn't get caught in the gears. Then I wouldn't have to address myself to the cafeteria slop or the Red Cross collection or the damn figures on the time sheet. They could be made natural functions of the body, and I would have control over all that was stupid and necessary.

"Why, Ag, I thought you liked your job."

"I am giving myself to eight hours a day at a zipper factory, and if you count the overtime there's nothing left but supper and a bath."

"Look, honey, this show's been running for nearly a year, and all I know is I get on that stage every night and put out."

"But then," I said, "safety guards presume you have two arms and all your fingers to begin with. . . ."

"Ag, do you think Tony'll want coffee when he comes in?"

Those nights waiting for Tony became my favorite times. I recall them as triumphant, and if Sherry didn't understand, Jean and Jane and Dolly and Peg never got it at all: they had learned to sit and smile at oddities, and I was just another mad thing, like the bum who picked theater programs out of the gutter every night on Forty-fifth Street, the fat lady in the delicatessen who had been Miss

Binghamton of 1932, and the men who spoke the gibberish of army maneuvers or Wall Street while they waited to be taken off and fondled in a taxi. I was Sherry's skinny high-toothed "little cousin" (tall as a man). Three or four times a year I made it to New York at dusk, ate my chowder at Grand Central, stood through the whole of *Oklahoma!* with its bright days and blue love-song nights: good snared by evil with "adult" touches.

"Suppose a man," (I didn't mention Francis) "were to follow the expected road without any hitches, become nothing more nothing less than his training and his character dictated . . . it'd be like the life of a larva moth."

Sherry was on the floor, going through her dance exercises, stretching towards the door.

"He could be a very nice guy."

"But of course," I said, "I only talk like this while we're waiting for Tony."

"He's working a small club downtown." She arched her back, her arms working overhead in a graceful plucking—"and that's why Tony's late." She was Mary Elizabeth justifying some shamefully cheap trinket Jack Hurley sent to our house with the postage half paid.

Tony De Angelo was worth waiting for, I suppose—and then again he wasn't worth the tip of her little finger. He let himself into the apartment whenever he pleased, and usually stopped to light a cigarette or run a comb through his hair before he gave her so much as an insolent smile. He stood before us for a moment to be admired, which wasn't hard for me after months of doughfaces at the factory. He was grand and big and stuck in your eye. Sherry feasted: his thick black hair grew in waves close to his head, except for a forelock which flopped boyishly. His face was heavy, square at the temples, square at the chin, with a frankly Italian nose, almost Roman but ever so slightly askew—busted once, a miracle considering how often Tony enraged people. His eyes—I don't think they were brown or black, but a dark color of his own—private, skimming over the objects before him (people were objects to Tony) as though nothing commanded his attention. At last he settled on Sherry, and his gaze was a benediction. There was damn little that Tony could appreciate without a sneer, but Sherry was on the list with the world's greatest trumpet player, Harry James, the big radio networks, and custom-made suits.

"Tony has bedroom eyes," a model said one night—but that was wishful thinking. He looked through your clothes all right, but it wasn't your body that interested him, it was whatever crippled thing hid inside: the nasal Brooklyn accent of an actress trying to sound like Katherine Cornell, the parrot mind of a script writer, the fear in a tough Master Sergeant. I was not a member of their beautiful-bodies club and when Tony De Angelo looked at me I like to think I puzzled him. There was no deception in my hungry adolescent form: I was the cynical clown, the sensitive spinster, the hell-of-a-good kid.

"Mary Agnes, how's the girl?" His words sounded like a joke, and I can imagine him thinking:

"You have no secrets, do you, sweetheart? You plan to make that a way of life."

If Sherry made coffee Tony would say, "Not right now. I'll have that Canadian Club." And when she poured him the best liquor she could buy, he flicked it away.

"What have you got in the house? Fruit? Maybe I'll have some scrambled eggs to start."

Then she watched him eat, and asked (as if the management had sent her), "Is everything O.K.?"

"Great," Tony said, but in some small way—his finger tapping on the burnt edge of toast, his fork held to let the egg dribble through the tines—he let her know how hopeless she was as the Little Woman.

I never set eyes on Tony De Angelo before three o'clock in the morning, and he was always perfectly dressed, often in a tuxedo with wide glossy lapels, so if he hadn't come in with his bulbous sax case he might have been arriving from one of those prewar parties I had seen in the movies, with frozen-faced extras fox-trotting around the pillars. I was to understand, and so were the kids who lived with Sherry—she told us with misty eyes—that Tony "could not fight for his country." They wouldn't even have him in the U.S. Marine Corps band. There was something damaged (a vague internal organ which she described on different occasions as the kidney, the liver, the pancreas)—just something that made him unfit.

It was true: there were many sad stories during the war, but when I think of it now I can't imagine that Tony De Angelo would have been any less bitter if he had sweated out his days in glory on a Pacific island. Sherry and her friends had big enough hearts to accept

his tragedy, and so that covered the situation nicely. Injustice for
Tony was so much bigger than a lousy medical fact—it was the whole
deal that brought him into the world in a four-family house on Staten
Island, that gave him a musical facility but no original talent, that
made him expect because he was one gorgeous kid he could have
something besides hard luck—and by the time Sherry met him he
was not even angry, just using one setup after another for whatever
it was worth: a drink, a few dollars, a woman.

Maybe his style was unfamiliar then: we were involved in a spiritual renaissance, and we hoped, we cared, while Tony, convinced of
personal destruction, played his own game. He was a prophet: youth
turned silent, moody and selfish—sick because it knows that nobody
wins. What mattered to Tony was lonely nervous grace—his night-
time body beating to the rhythm of the band, shut off from the
dancers, finding its momentary salvation in a note that came off—as
good as sex. Once at the Palladium I saw him in his ecstasy—but only
once, because Sherry did not like to watch him play. If Tony were
around now, exactly as he was twenty years ago, he would be a
cliché—but then, ah then, he was a remarkable bastard.

"A terrible bastard," Little Dot said in her lady-like drawl,
". . . and Sherry could have a lead in the road show, but she's sitting
around for him . . . it's one handout after another." Little Dot was
wiry and resilient, the only one of Sherry's friends who ever made a
name for herself. She had worked hard training a sweet lyric soprano
voice for years, and when her first big chance came on the Major
Bowes Amateur Hour she lost to a quadruple amputee who played
(with a spoon held in his teeth) "God Bless America" on nails stuck
into a cigarette carton.

"You wouldn't catch me jumpin' through a hoop for that bastard."

Little Dot went right on with her scales. I took up going to night
school to learn whatever useless pleasantries existed in poems and
stories—to learn something apart from the zippers which evolved
each year like a Darwinian species: grew longer, smarter, more dura-
ble, only to be killed off by superior models with better teeth, more
adaptable bindings. My mother, praying for Francis, who was in
Washington and later got that piece of gangway in the thigh, was
inspired to return to the arts. She created a cake made without butter
or sugar and only one egg. It stuck like paste on the teeth. She made
a display of weeny figures for her Civil Defense class with peanut
shells for bodies and pipe cleaners for limbs, and set them in cigar

boxes: peanuts straddled peanuts, performing (one hoped) artificial respiration; healthy peanuts carried sick peanuts on a snip of old blanket; there were peanuts in tourniquets and arm slings, peanuts with concussions and complex fractures, and one old peanut (modeled after the bedridden ancient of our block) being evacuated in an Indian handclasp seat by two sturdy peanut wardens to the cellar of the Congregational Church. Sherry continued her chorus-girl role in *Oklahoma!*

Sherry Henderson's career was a child's dream—that was the maimed thing Tony De Angelo saw. There were at least three screen tests maneuvered for her by a bull-neck named Jerry, and she was content to come back from the Coast and pretend she was interested in her future; but she would have chucked the whole business in one minute if Tony had agreed to teach dance and music with her —which was, of course, Sherry's idea. We were hiding the liquor in the bottom of a closet, because of his kidney or liver or pancreas, and I was delivering a facetious sermon to myself on the advantage of developing my given peculiarities—no chest, long nose, sunken eyes —into full-fledged eccentricities.

"Do something with what God gives you," I said, "for His mercy is unbounded. We have only to look around us to discover there is a Great Intelligence behind the intricate patterns of the Universe, and it is our duty to discover further the purpose for which the Good Lord put us here . . . , for He moves in strange and mysterious ways."

"Put that pint in the shoe box, Ag."

"It is our duty to discover ourselves as part of the Divine System, for surely with this body I am meant to carry a burden on my back, and these eyes must see deep into the machinery of souls—yes, even into my own faltering soul; and the nose . . . the nose must smell out corruption and decay."

"Oh, stop it," Sherry cried. Her hair was all crazy from stooping in the closet. "You're always laughing lately, never serious for a moment. We do what we must. We do what we can. I could give tap lessons, you know, and teach ballroom dancing. Tony could teach the sax and probably the accordion if he would only settle down."

"You must be kidding," I said.

"Yes." Big tears washed the mascara down her cheeks. This was wilder than any of the mad schemes for fame and fortune she ever had back home. She actually conceived of rented rooms up over a drugstore in some sizeable outpost, "The De Angelo's" painted on the window and rows of kiddy legs wriggling around on highly polished floors—"with my foot I tap, tap, tap, with my hands I clap, clap, clap"—while Tony listened to farts exploded out of a cheap instrument by an unwilling boy. I saw the curtain of faded chintz that separated the "studio" from the little room with the sink and hot plate. I saw Tony and Sherry (thought to be a little on the flashy side) grown to forty, still holding tight to a New York concept of themselves, eating out in bad restaurants, playing the accordion and singing at weddings in the BPOE Hall.

Tony came in and said, "How about a drink."

"I don't have a thing in the house."

"Look around, Baby . . . ," and she went directly to the closet and brought out the bottle.

So the next time I came to New York Tony was unable to work, though he still came in at four o'clock in his tux. Sherry had set him to songwriting, where the real money was. On top of a Steinway she had rented for him there were three songs pencilled out—notes, lyrics, titles and all—"Why so Bitter, My Sweet?", "When Bonnie Comes Marching Home" (about a WAC who left her love behind), and "Love Letters in the Sky" (a pilot who is afraid to declare his feelings except when he is gunning Japs in a B-47). Tony's socks and underwear were all over the bedroom, his razor on the sink, and he slept in the bed where I had last seen Little Dot propped up with pillows memorizing the score of Cosí fan tutte. I can't say that I was shocked, for I don't suppose that even I thought they had been playing post office all this time. That night Tony was snarly, got drunk, passed out on the living-room floor, and we had to drag him to bed. Sherry loosened his shirt collar, took off his shoes, and smoothed that wild forelock back out of his eyes.

"Poor Tony . . . ," she said looking at me, and we both knew that things weren't going to improve.

When he left her she went on the road with a second company of the show, singing those bright songs all over the country, dancing and whooping, shouting out about the beautiful morning. She made a movie which I saw eight times. When Dane Clark entered a small night club she said "Good Evening," and tried to check his hat.

"Where the boss?" Dane asked.

"Over at the bar," Sherry answered. Later she screamed when the shots went off, an unconvincing shriek, and she wouldn't answer the hard old detective.

"I only work here, Mister."—Sherry was never good at répartee. Her features, blown up on the screen, were not the common doll-face the role called for: her high cheek bones and cleft chin were too powerful facing the perceptive camera: she looked as if she had wandered into this contrived piece out of a drama on the Irish Rev-olution—moving close-ups of faces with "character," damp, darkness and meaningful death.

My mother and the aunts weren't much for movies, and I never let on that Mary Elizabeth could be seen down at Poli's because I knew that all they'd go for was the net stockings, the cleavage, the "low types" wished into existence by their literal minds. I cut my class in Great Thinkers of the Western World to study what I saw in Sherry's eyes—the crease of doubt forming on her brow, the air of acceptance in the droop of her bare shoulders. Though she was only twenty-three she had gone through one life already; I could see that, and I walked out of the theater while Dane Clark was still dying, while the lights were still on in the night classes at the high-school, illuminating the sophistries of Mr. Ruggiero and Miss Flynn as they argued free-will and determinism. The two-bit sax player was gone forever, and I hated him for the years he had taken from Sherry. Later, during her "mature" phase, she told me he had married a neighborhood girl out on Staten Island and had two kids and worked in a shoe store.

Sol was a loud-mouth puffed eunuch who had great success in shaping the careers of female comics, and he was sure that what Sherry had was a flair for dancing, a kind of rag-doll in a Baby Snooks routine he had devised, the surprise being that when she pulled off the Harpo Marx wig and the Harold Lloyd glasses there was a real pretty girl who sang a couple of sweet ballads. It was blistering hot the night Sol and Sherry and I went down to the Village to show the act to a very big man who was opening a new club. Sol advised Sherry on her costume in a lilting falsetto.

"The simple backless number, Dear . . . no jewels . . . ruins your neck," and he pursed his lips in disgust at me, done up in my best Bemberg sheer:

"Why don't you go to a newsreel?"

But I went along, paid the cab driver, and watched from a leopard-skin booth while Sol and Sherry dealt with the very big man. The club was to be a jungle with a lot of African masks, bamboo tables that caught the stockings, and a ceiling weighted with oppressive greenery. A pair of caged monkeys chattered over the bar.

"Zow, *some* people!" Sherry cried out in an effeminate voice, an imitation of *Maitre* Sol. She slid onto the dance floor as if kicked in the seat of the pants and attempted to get up on rubber legs; she pulled a great big Times Square funny comb from no-place and further mucked up her blonde wig.

"I'm gonna sing a little song," she said with a croak in her throat. "Why don't you Voo-Do-Do what you did did did before. . . ."

I walked out to the street where a gang of little children in filthy underpants were working to unscrew a fire hydrant. I thought I could watch anything as long as it wasn't Sherry clowning in the veldt, but the sight of the screaming kids—sweaty, no doubt tired, for it was past ten—nauseated me and brought to mind the six gray mollusks (the color of their dirty hands) I had swallowed whole at the Oyster Bar. Sad they seemed, those oysters, exposed on their icy bed and wanting nothing more than to contract into the known darkness. Slowly I went to the hydrant and we pulled together: the straining little fingers and my own scrawny hands; we pulled in a hush of effort until the geyser shot into the sleepless night-city. Squealing with relief the children performed a frantic dance; shiny bare limbs, freshened, made clean.

The audition—that's what they called it—was over when I went back. Sol and the very big man sat on rattan stools at the bar celebrating their mutual distrust. They toasted Sherry with cuba libres. I watched from behind the glistening leaves of a paper tree.

"I'm glad you like the act," Sherry said—that good face full of hope once more.

"We'll talk about the act, honey," the big man reassured her with several pats on the fleshy part of her back.

"Oooo, you naughty boys," Sol chided the monkeys who were very busy in their cage; and then they saw me in the mirror, my dress shrunk up over my knees, my hair soaked into kinks, an untamed freak of nature after a tropical storm.

After the war there were two musicals; one closed in Boston, the other petered out in the City before I got to see her. Then Sherry sang, restrained, intimate, in supper clubs—which was less embar-

rassing than most of her ventures—and it was in this role of sophis-
ticated *chanteuse* that the Colonel discovered her. Beneath the
show-biz patina and the undercoat of spoiled innocence he detected
the expansive, natural girl. The Colonel had wives; oh yes, but no
woman challenged him like Mary Elizabeth. That was his trade: he
had rebuilt a European city from the ruins of war and occupation,
restored its dignity with a fine respect for history, set it to live and
grow once again. Now he was revitalizing a great newspaper that
was sick unto death. He was rich and bright and powerful.

The marriage came as a surprise, a telegram I found opened on the
hall table when I returned from work one day. My mother's voice
called out to me with a tremble of excitement:

"Ag—Ag, is that you?" She was on the phone, and it must have
been a difficult moment for her, not knowing whether to continue
her damnation of Mary Elizabeth—satisfying in the mouth like
chocolate creams—or to come hustling through the dining room to
exact testimony from me of Sherry's depravity. The verdict she had
already reached.

"Don't you tell me you never saw the man on one of your sneaky
'visits,' Ag Keely."

"I never even has heard of him," I said in my grandmother's jibing
brogue.

"Throw insults on the grave—that's good, Miss."

"I don't know who he is."

My mother plumped herself out like a proud fat pigeon. "That
name," she said with malicious pleasure, "he's a Jew!"

The Colonel was a Jew, but all that was left was a story now and
again with a Yiddish expression and a dreamy painting by Chagall
hanging in the dining room over a fine carved cabinet (which I was
expected to admire).

Was Sherry Catholic any more? The question was irrelevant. Her
new mode was ultimately enlightened, free of the limitations of any
simple identity. The first time I saw Sherry and Colonel Leavit together I tried to understand the cosmopolitan perfection he aimed
at, but in minutes my head was fuzzed by martinis and I felt the
three of us floating in a soft white room to a melody plucked from
a fragile box.

He was fifty, Colonel Harry, Daddy of All the Ages; he wanted
the best for his little orphan girl (even *that* was in a literary tradi-

tion), and he never failed to have something in his pocket for me
too—the rag-picker cousin.

"We can't use our tickets to the Philharmonic, Mary Agnes," he'd
tell me. "I want you to come down here and enjoy yourself. Bring a
friend."

"Oh, Harry, she can't just hop a train," Sherry said.

She was right. Still the offer was like a crisp five dollar bill.

He was fifty. That didn't seem old: it seemed right. His head was a
phrenologist's dream, bare and gleaming, with bumps that I read
—without even knowing the science—as intelligence, creativity,
success. And since he had no hair, one looked hard at his face: lean,
composed, a model of a commander whose kindly eyes made the
people around him want to perform in style. His whole body was
lean, and I never knew until Sherry told me—oh much later—that
he worked out at a gym every day.

I don't know why I found that disappointing; he worked damn
hard at the "image" of himself, as hard as he now worked on the
ailing newspaper or had worked over the demolished city. Those
quiet evenings I was invited to share—they were carefully conceived.
His scheme for Sherry was delicate, but its process was superhuman,
and of all his plans the only one she took to was the study of music:
she learned to play the harpsichord.

"Tasteful beginners' pieces," he said, "nicely done all the same."
He knew her voice was good only for a few songs after dinner, so
we listened to her in a white drawing room sing sad short *lieder*
in memorized German. To me it was all strange and perfect, and like
the thick herbaceous liqueur I rolled on my tongue I believed in it;
but surely the Colonel knew that their life came out of bad historical
novels.

"Tomorrow let us ride over to the Manor House in the pony cart."

"Oh yes, that will be gay," Miss Agnes said, letting drop her
needlework that she might dream a while of her new bonnet, looking very pretty indeed in the orangery.

Gold flowers blooming in gold pots, Sherry in a green velvet gown,
covering her arms to the wrists, open at the throat. Her look says,
"Ain't it the berries, Ag!" And the Colonel, in a smoking jacket,
talks of pleasure: *his*—in having me with them—"one of the people
Sherry loves."

Other treasures: a frieze of saints given by a grateful city—part
of itself—to take away with him; the edition of *Parnasse contem-*

porain bound in pearly leather—"of particular interest to you. . . ."
The wine I couldn't possibly know . . . everything real in the way
heaven must be: softly lit, with one all-caring God.

Their bed (I see it when led off to wash the Château Lafite-
Rothschild out of my sweater) is big enough for a host of lovers,
high up on a dais—a throne yes, but to me more like the altar in my
parish church, its canopy hung with starched lace, thick embroidered
initials on the spread: His and Hers intertwined, scrambled. I saw
IHS: Harry, Sherry, Leavit, the bottom nodule of the "L" strangely
shortened for the sake of the design. "To God who giveth joy to my
life." Maybe it was that: ascending those green (for hope) carpeted
steps onto the consecrated kingsize mattress—was that what became
impossible?

At the table Sherry, now learned in sauces and salads, had to be
followed closely as to which fork—and that peculiar small knife for
a russet pear with the leaves left on, or a platinum-blond apple; and
grapes (Lord, they must be fake), frosty, purply. But no!—she cuts
them apart with a scissors! The salt sits in open silver shells with
midget spoons, and the coffee cups are doll-size.

Sherry *tried* with all that food and wine business, but she never
could make herself eat the special smelly cheeses—or brains or kid-
neys or sweetbreads. I could tell just the way she ate—not seeing the
elaborate entrees the Colonel ordered—veal and chicken and
tongue: larded, farced, and truffled in glossy gelatine—that she
might as well be eating Mae's overcooked meat loaf swimming in
canned tomatoes. She hid peanut butter in a jar labeled Queen Bee
Hormone Jelly, and Ritz crackers under her lingerie.

"It's a terrible sign of a regression, Ag. . . ." The Colonel had sent
her to a Park Avenue psychiatrist so she'd know all about herself—as
well as George III tea pots and pre-Colombian sculpture. She wasn't
always happy—Colonel Harry knew that, admired it even—and no
doubt he expected the analysis to tap a vein of hidden meanings and
obscure desires in his beautiful girl. But Sherry was still a "C" student: she took to the idea in her own way, began to read inspira-
tional literature, do-it-yourself salvation kits. Harry was infuriated;
he had given her Kierkegaard and Nietzsche.

He staged a quiet evening of Camus—I was included—and she
bubbled over about "inner resources" and "building towards personal maturity."

"I'm going to send you this book, Mary Agnes, by this woman . . ."

"Now my Darling," the Colonel said; "Mary Agnes knows she can charge any book she wants on my account at Brentano's."

"Yes, Harry . . . by this woman, Ag, this wonderful woman whose child died of leukemia."

Her recommended readings arrived at our house, and I found the books opened on the hall table—the Overstreets and Norman Vincent Peale—and I heard my mother behind her evening paper.

"Protestant . . . ," and, making what was to her a logical connection, "Jew." I put the books, which seemed sticky with childish optimism, under my bed; my mother never dusted there because her heart started racing. "Jesus, Mary, and Joseph . . . no one to help an old woman."

At night after I had escaped into my homework from the endless days of my life at the zipper factory, I fell asleep under my student lamp and I heard Sherry call from her stack of goodness-readings under the bed (where as a girl she used to hide her contraband movie magazines):

"Say, Mr. and Mrs. North are over at the Rialto, Ag—Let's go; I'll get twenty cents easy if I sing down at the firehouse."

". . . just because a person has been disturbed by a difficult family situation doesn't mean that they have to react to a relationship without commitment. . . ." Sherry was on her favorite theme, and I could see the Colonel's disappointment as he suffered the obvious phrases she had picked up on the couch. He was bewildered by defeat.

"Well, what did you expect," I thought; "there's nothing in my cousin for a doctor to heal. Sherry is all surface. That's what's great about her: if she's sad, there are tears, a black mood that clears at the first dose of peanut butter. And she is happy every time she puts on that big mink coat you gave her. You know the smile."

We were both wrong: the Colonel for wanting her complex, and I was a fool to think that she was simple.

For five years I journeyed to the City when I could get loose, partook of their hospitable dream, became one of the mottled images reflected in that ancient mirror which Colonel Leavit hung at the end of his palatial salon. Thirty, I was thirty years old (which would have made her thirty-one), and by then the Colonel had built up several anemic industries. Projecting into the future, he saw the growth-potential in fiberglass, in prefab houses, in tranquilizers, in television; and he began to take a lady painter—Bryn Mawr and bor-

SHERRY

ing to Sherry—out to fashionable restaurants while his wife went to bed with headaches. He escorted Little Dot to the opening night of the Metropolitan Opera. And then, when he flew out to the Coast to buy old Academy Award pictures, Sherry produced the grand finale.

"What will I say to Harry?" she asked, and turned the question into a tipsy song, "What'll I tell Harry, Harry. . . ." She stumbled through forgotten dance routines.

"Nothing, I guess."

She wouldn't have to say a thing: all the kids were there, even little Dot, who didn't stay long because she was much too fine for them now, but all the lamp-tanned chorus girls and all the dainty men who had not aged a minute, and Sol and Jerry and some of the way-back USO girls who were married now and brought their husbands in from the suburbs for free eats, and lots of people no one had ever seen before. Sandwiches ground into the Aubusson carpets, club soda spilled into the harpsichord, and all those wines were pulled out of the carved cabinet from their tilted mellowing sleep and drunk like gallons of *paesano*. On one side of the bed there was a blind man who played the electric organ in nightclubs. He sat up stiffly, laughing and drinking, his white cane stuck through the lace. Someone had tied a brassière on his head, and behind him on a pile of coats a girl was cruelly used. I didn't want to see more, so I left my good coat and walked out in the rain.

How did Sherry look: desiccated, hard, a hearty bitch? Not at all. She looked frail from the trying years of a fraudulent marriage, stretched in the neck and arms, bones and veins without much flesh, but with hair the color of red maples, and her song, "Tell Harry, Harry . . . ," was gay.

She had walked out, way beyond his control, away from the elaborate parlor game he had made into the good life. The act was over for me too, and I regretted that mutation of reality which had made our evenings together a séance—on my part a dabbling in the mysterious and occult. For a while there had been no factory, no zippers, no dinners at Sticky-Bun Inn where you presented Therese Sielinski with an orchid corsage and a Mirro-Matic Pressure Cooker and wishes for many sunny days of married life. With no mother, no Lil, no Mae with a breast removed; without them you are sinking into the white softness, your body suspended in a million goose feathers sewn in sacks of sky blue silk. Think now of what you learn

and what you read: Blake in night school, Villon in translation. You
will speak through them to us, misty-footed angel: in your mouth
are the phonemes of a strange mellifluous language. You will trans-
form the ugliness of our landscape; you will tell us what it means.
. . . Speak, monkey, speak—and I moaned from my horrifying
past.

"Love is like the lion's tooth." It ended so. No more artichokes,
no more golden apples; only the reality of Florence Flynn and Mr.
Ruggiero—my intellectual milieu—squabbling in the high-school,
this time about D. H. Lawrence in Modern British "Lit."

"One individual has a responsibility not to destroy the core of
another individual," Sherry explained after the divorce. "Harry
wanted me to look his way, act his way, but he didn't care anything
about me inside."

"No," I said. We were having lunch at Stouffer's on Fifth Avenue
after my morning with Shakespeare at Columbia. I had the distinct
impression that all around us the ladies were talking about their
lives in the same way, or about their clothes—as important as their
lives.

"He never understood that he must respect me as a person." She
wore a floppy brown hat that covered up her hair, and the mink coat
was thrown over the back of her chair. I had not seen her out in the
daylight in many years, and on the avenue the winter sun had
caught every line. The girl that Colonel Leavit had preserved in
candlelight was gone. Sherry could have been any faded beauty; the
spectacle was over.

"Yes," I said.

"I feel I can breathe again, Ag, and dance. Listen, I have this
wonderful voice coach, a sweetheart who says he can get me right
back to work; not that I have to, but it's my old compulsion—
Harry never touched it—of having to give myself. . . ."

"Yes," I said. We must have looked a sight, me hunched over a
parfait, skinny and dry, probably in one of those sexy knit suits I
wore to fool the public, and Sherry wiping the floor with mink,
wearing the biggest diamond in the world—third finger right hand.

"The Colonel never had friends. They were always business con-
nections pretending to be buddies. It wasn't all Boccherini and Bel-
gian endive, I'll tell you, Ag."

"Gosh!"

Her new apartment was in a shining glass building on Sutton Place, as friendly as a hospital, with the instruments for living laid out about the white walls: plastic wood tables at the end of the couch, a deep Naugahide chair with a stand big enough for an ashtray and a drink. Here the portly men sat with scotch-and-soda, bourbon-on-the-rocks, gin-and-bitters. They were all "sweethearts," "real cuties" who wanted to help a girl out. She went to Acapulco for rest and sunshine with an advertising man who put her in a detergent commercial.

I left my books to watch my mother as she watched Sherry (she never recognized her) as a worried housewife in a laundromat, a pleasant woman aging fast with the problems of sink stain and bathroom odor. Soil and deep-down grime drove her nearly to tears.

"I just can't seem to get things *clean* any more." Then up came a snappy dish with a pile of whiter-than-white towels and laughed right in Sherry's face.

"Why don't you use the new miracle tablet, a combination of gentle bleach and power-plus detergents that makes laundry day the happiest day in the week."

"A tablet? Not on *these* filthy collars!" Sherry held up a shirt ringed with greasy body dirt.

My mother heaved herself out of her chair and hurried to the kitchen. Now that she had grown so *very* big her walk was labored and she put out her hand for support, first on the back of a dining-room chair and then on the buffet.

"Want anything, Ag?"

How delighted Mary Elizabeth looked, and she chuckled with Mrs. Goody Two-Shoes, right there in our front room with the *filet* curtains and the furniture, the same as when she left.

"I guess my troubles are over," Sherry said, but she was a bad actress and the line didn't ring true. I felt when she left the laundromat she was doomed to droopy tresses or nasal congestion; and what's more she knew it.

Mother was having a run on jelly doughnuts in the months Sherry's commercial was shown and she would come back with two soft clumps oozing scarlet tapioca jelly.

"Have one, Ag."

"I couldn't."

"Aren't you going to hear the weather?" she asked as I went back to my studies. "Well, I'm sure I'm privileged to have got a look at you at all."

I wasn't a girl any more and night-time visits to New York had lost their charm. After a few expense-account dinners with Sherry and one of her "sweethearts" I gave it up. Should I say I gave her up? Anything I had to say to her would sound preachy, the envious moralizing of an old maid, and why should I accuse her when she could still riffle through the bottom drawer of used emotions and come up with that best of smiles meaning jolly days, tomorrow, just around the corner? Her personal psychology was as out of date as the Depression song she used to sing about a pocket full of dreams. The world had changed on her. There was an insatiable lust for things: great-assed cars, freezing chests like coffins, magic boxes; love-play in the supermarket, sexual poking at sealed meats and cake mixes, the thrill of climax as the register rings—the check-out counter. She didn't know what was happening, and I closed my door, unable and unwilling to cope with her life or mine. I had something of a problem at this time: Jim Neary, son of one of my mother's cronies, went so far as to declare an interest in stumping into the future with me. He had a limp and taught the fifth grade. He gave me a bottle of Blue Grass cologne and a little collie dog, but that is another story of misplaced trust and self-destruction, a melodrama starring my brother Francis (now an FBI agent) and my mother who breaks her hip in a cemetery outside of Buffalo.

To be honest, I had not talked to Sherry in years. Waiting for Tony I had talked *at* her; I had talked *around* her with the Colonel, but all I had said directly to my cousin was "Gee Whiz!"—a line straight out of the funny papers delivered with a look of bug-eyed amazement long after she ceased to amaze. I discovered more of the City in daylight after my Saturday-morning class at Columbia than I had in all the years of her night life, which now seemed trite for both of us. I'm sure it was as hard for Sherry to go on with the show—pulling out new wonders for the relative from out-of-town— as it was for me to come on all incredulous at out-sized menus and happy-pills. What she had in mind now that she was free was a comeback, this time off-Broadway, the real theater—Art. The last time I saw her she was sitting on the floor surrounded by piles of new paperbacks: Brecht, Ionesco, Genet, and the plays of Yeats. The man in the Naugahide chair (Scotch Manhattans and ladies' sportswear) smirked indulgently, said his daughter was interested in all that up at Sarah Lawrence. I said I had to get my train, but Sherry with her brand new smile asked, "What do you think, Ag? Now that I won't have to play the *ingenue?*"

Almost a year later the Christmas card came with a drawing of a parrot in a golden cage. "Season's Greetings from Sherry Leavit and Jamie."

Since I never envisioned her cleaning a cage and setting out parrot food, I presumed there was a new "sweetheart" in her life—until she telephoned late one January night.

"Glory be to God!" My mother held her hand where she imagined her heart was. "I thought it was something wrong with Francis or one of the children."

". . . Wonderful," I said.

"This is the break I've been waiting for." Sherry used the same old words the same old way. "You'll see it in the papers, but the show isn't announced yet. It's got everyone: Merman, Leonard Bernstein."

"Gee!"

"It's tremendous, exciting. Listen to Jamie. Listen to beautiful baby; he was so happy for me I cried; honest, he *knows* that something great has happened. Listen to Jamie." I listened to Jamie's guttural squawks, which grew louder and soared to a piercing crescendo.

"Are you going to sing?" I asked, turning my back on my bird of prey, who was pretending to watch the Late Show. There was a flapping and scratching at the other end.

"It's not quite set, Ag. *The Gershwin Years* is a whole ninety minutes, a spectacular, and of course they need lots of kids."

"Wonderful!"

"He's right here on my shoulder, my baby Jamie."

She had given her heart for the last time.

"Lord forgive me," mother said, "I thought it was Francis."

Sherry was right. I couldn't have missed *The Gershwin Years*, one of those cultural gestures on behalf of the network and a paternalistic oil company. I didn't say a word at home and—small wonder—my mother went over to Mae's, lured by fudgy brownies. Alone in the darkness I waited for Sherry; girls swayed and sang, girls with giant Ziegfeld plumes wafted down the glittering stairs of our M-G-M dreams; girls drifted through arty mobiles in leotards. They were all young—Sherry fifteen years ago—with painted inexpressive faces and elastic bodies—a lifetime removed from the beautiful woman with a past, weighted with mink and diamonds in Stouffer's, picking her way through the days with a man or a parrot or another hope.

"George Gershwin came up from the Lower East Side, from a confining study of the classics to the restless jazzy world of discordant newness. . . ."

It went on like that, a man's voice giving me all this about the American dream, the search, fulfillment; but the first half hour was over and I had not seen Sherry. Then the scenes from *Porgy and Bess*—nothing doing there unless they put her in black face. I looked at the screen so damn hard—more young girls swooping about the Eiffel Tower. I thought I had missed her, perhaps unrecognizable behind a feathery fan, disguised by a boa—and then I thought, my God, she never made it—all these kids jumping around and Sherry out of the business for so many years.

Ten minutes left, and my solemn commentator grew more lugubrious as he spoke again of Paris in the twenties: Gershwin had wanted much more than success . . . , O.K., O.K., yes, Fitzgerald, Picasso, Hemingway, Joyce, and as our own greatest spokesman for the expatriates, Gertrude Stein, said: "Everybody was twenty-six. Hemingway was twenty-six. I was twenty-six. The world was twenty-six." It was Mary Elizabeth reading the words out in a high faltering voice, toneless, uncomprehending. It was so bad, but I counted on Sherry not knowing.

Come to think of it, I counted on a lot: on an unbroken line that I followed, like a child's puzzle in which you draw your pencil from 1 to 2 to 3, through a maze of numbers and come out with the not so very hidden picture of our pig-eyed house snuggled in nightmare juxtaposition up to the zipper factory—Mother supporting the whole teetering works, old Atlas of the daily continuum. I counted on some freshly shaven gent with a Sulka tie to tell Sherry how talented she was, though maybe her style was more in the Arlene Francis line: wit and chiffon. I counted on getting up and going to work and coming home to Henry James. I counted on Sherry slipping into her mink coat and eating a peanut butter sandwich. I counted on the only death being inside me, an increasing numbness of some mysterious vital organ, like Tony De Angelo's kidney or liver or pancreas. But Sherry didn't even bother to switch off the set.

She went straight to the medicine cabinet of her luxury bathroom, and when the woman who ran the vacuum over the wall-to-wall carpet came in she found the daytime *Price Is Right* blaring and thought that strange because usually if Mrs. Leavit was up she liked the old movies.

They notified the Colonel, who was in Washington about a contract for nose cones, and by the time her show-biz friends remembered my name she was buried in a non-sectarian cemetery on Long Island. A man I'd never heard of called me at the office and I took the next bus to Bridgeport and changed to a midmorning train to New York—as if something could be done. When the superintendent let me into Sherry's apartment he drew back the curtains, and there was the bright spring East River, sunlight on the water, green branches along the embankment. A toy tug fitted out with little men hauled a flat black freighter out to the sea—gay flags, a pretty world from this height, like the magic blackness embroidered with stars and strings of electric lights which had been Sherry's.

In a while the Colonel came with Little Dot. She was anxious about a rehearsal of *Traviata* at City Center.

"Harry dear," she said, "perhaps Miss Keely would like something of Sherry's." They offered a brooch I had never seen her wear, but then there were demanding screams from the bedroom, and we ran in to find Jamie—yellow and red and green with glassy eyes. He was in a flap and repeated again and again words we had not been trained to understand. Little Dot, always the prima donna, glanced at her watch.

"We called the ASPCA and I thought somehow that we should be here. Harry or someone. . . ." Then she looked at me with a wan smile, perfect for the last act, the final brave aria.

"Would you like him? Would you like the bird?"

I said I found him disgusting. Colonel Leavit, full of understanding, brought me out to the living room again. He picked up his topcoat of some rich wonderful material, and said by way of consolation, "She was beautiful, beautiful."

"Yes."

We looked around at her plain room before we left, for Little Dot had decided that, after all, the doorman could deal with the parrot.

"Terrible place," the Colonel said, "no character."

I telephoned Francis from Grand Central, and as soon as I heard his voice I knew I would not have to tell him about Mary Elizabeth. He had read it in the paper.

"Don't say anything to them at home—please Francis, that's just what they'd like."

He said yes, and then asked, "Tell me Ag, was there time—did she have a priest?"

TOM COLE was born in Paterson, New Jersey, and was educated at Harvard. His first published story, "Familiar Usage in Leningrad," won an Atlantic First award and was a prize winner in the 1962 O. Henry collection. Atlantic-Little, Brown published his first book *An End to Chivalry* in the fall of 1965. He has taught English, Russian, and other subjects at the Commonwealth School in Boston and at M.I.T. where he is now Lecturer in Humanities. He is married and lives in Boston.

On the Edge of Arcadia

IT WAS April, and they were driving across Greece in a Fiat, two young Americans, a sculptor and a poet, both fellowship winners. They had come from Rome, and they were on their way to Athens. Rounding a curve through the silver of Peloponnesian spring, they abruptly came upon an array of fabrics in strips along the roadside, all the colors of autumn and of fire waving in the wind. They saw shawls, blankets, saddlebags, crude tapestries—red, burnt orange, mustard bordered with scarlet—all, beyond suspicion, the work of hands native to this valley, as the sculptor immediately knew, bellowed, in fact—*Holy Christ!*—and sitting by that clothesline of raging splendors, an old man. His face, as they flashed by in the sun, seemed carved, Sophoclean. Behind him, there was a hint of whitewashed walls, a suggestion of chickens; then it was gone.

On they drove, but not far. The poet's forehead almost went through the windshield as the sculptor slammed on the brakes.

"That's it!" announced the sculptor. "That is the work of the human hand! See how it comes out of nowhere? Like a storm. A vision!" He banged the heel of his hand against his head, and in general made hectic and meaningful tableaux.

They were stopped near two mountains and three goats. With the ignition off, they could hear, beneath the wind, downhill water

—springs, brooks, streams that had still been snow when these travelers had left Rome. Above them to left and right, then falling continuously below, the world curved and coiled in fields of young wheat, olives, pale grasses: a shifting play of green and silver down into the sun, dotted here and there with a bent black crone.

"That's what we've come for, Rick," said the sculptor.

"That's what *you've* come for, Slugger."

The sculptor gave back an ominous look. His face was, curiously, his family's face, of southern California money, sunburnt and belli-cose beneath sandy thatch. With a slight twist of his soul, Slugger could have been at this moment sounding off in a locker room in-stead of seeking the work of the human hand in the Peloponnesus. The thought of that possible twist in his soul could drive him mad.

He launched into an effusion, and Rick disconnected his ear-drums, letting his mind sail out upon that landscape for which his nostalgia was lately getting out of control. He wanted to dive face-first into that young wheat, to let his body soak into the curve of a hill, to hear passing bells, wind, the plodding of beasts, never again to write a prize-winning ode On Reading a Letter From Alice James to Her Brother Henry in Mount Auburn Cemetery During Warbler Migration, never again to be bright, cocky, irreligious, ambitious, indifferent, shallow, all the things he felt himself, somewhat un-fairly, to be.

"—good look at his *face?*" Slugger was asking, with dangerously accelerating veneration.

"The old man's face?" said Rick.

"Well, yeah. What did you think?"

Rick said, cautiously, that the old man's face, what he had glimpsed of it, seemed good, patient, handsome.

"Ricky, it was a work of art! Carved out of stone. Nothing extra. No fat, no cowardice, no greed. Just that pride, that dignity these people have."

It was an obsession of Slugger's.

The only people left in the world with natural dignity were the Greeks and the Spaniards. And that, only in the deep countryside. He had recently discovered the Spanish Civil War, and spent half a year constructing a towering bronze "To the Spanish Dead." Now he was sketching faces, bent bodies, coiled landscapes toward an-other mountain of bronze, "To the Greek Living."

"Why do you think he had all that stuff hanging out there?"

"Maybe for the world to see. Leaves, bright feathers. I doubt they're for sale."

Rick was not in the mood to bargain with another penniless octogenarian.

"What do you say?" asked Slugger, already shifting into reverse.

Rick laughed bleakly as the Fiat lurched backward. It was a chance in a lifetime; they just *had* to talk to that old prince (that is, Rick had to talk to him: his Greek was primitive; Slugger's, non-existent); they *had* to see what the hands around here could still make (which was, of course, Slugger's major obsession: soon there was going to be nothing in the world made by human hands). What they had found in Greece so far were cynical imitations, which could almost fool Rick but not Slugger. He had fumed and raged through Delphi, Arakhova, Olympia, Sparta; only in one or two villages hanging under the bleak eaves of Arcadia did he begin to see what he needed: through dark doorways to shops where the mountain folk came to haggle, crude magnificence hanging from wooden pegs. But he was a hard bargainer, although Rick, whose preference was always to overpay with a winning smile, had to do the talking. Not to bargain hard, according to Slugger, was to let real Mediterranean people down. To pay too much, to tip too easily, was to sap their dignity—that priceless treasure—in return for a handful of filthy pennies. He was sick of Europe pimping and grimacing and scraping and lying for money—worse than America; in Rome, where he had been sculpting that year, worst of all—and he had worked himself into a frenzy of premeditated reverence for the Greeks as the last Men in Europe, natural princes every one, at least in the mountains, who could not be bought off, who had pride, whom Hemingway would still have admired, with the result that he squeezed every last drachma, in the name of Greek dignity, until it howled.

This was a strange turn, for Slugger by nature was almost imbecilely generous, the despair of his wife and his gallery, giving away work, sketches, Mexican treasures to anyone he cared for (a numberless horde), while Rick himself, that gusher of alms along the road ("Take. Eat. This is my body, this is my blood, this is a 30 percent tip") was a skinflint among his own, never committing a semicolon to paper without payment on the spot, inscribing his name large in books he lent to his mother. By now, they were both a mess about money. Slugger had refused to be driven above two dollars in one Arcadian haggling, when the equivalent of three

would have brought him a peasant masterpiece unobtainable anywhere else in the world, and could only nod his head, grim and
huge, while Rick tore the marginal thirty drachmas into shreds and
threw them out the car window, to float a thousand feet down upon
flocks and poppies: a curious rain. Rick was then put in charge and
emerged, yesterday, from the shop of a blatant old tourist-trapper in
Nauplion bearing a rug and a smile. Slugger took one look, charac-
terized the rug as "machine-made" and the smile as "shit-eating."
The rug had cost twenty-five dollars, which was as nothing compared with the cost of the smile, payment exacted by sculptor from
poet; but today was another day, at least for Slugger.

Upon seeing the same car approach twice on the same afternoon,
this time backward, the old man bestirred himself.

Slugger was bulky, Rick lean, the old man taller than either of
them and his posture straight as an archaic charioteer's as he held
his arms forward. "Young men," he said. "Welcome, young men."

Slugger nudged Rick, who said "Good-day to you, sir" in Greek,
clumsily, smiling in self-deprecation.

"Sir," chuckled the old man and gestured them toward his place.

Then he chuckled again—"Sir!"—delighted with his private re-
flections. His jacket and trousers, both black, were frayed into
shininess; his shirt was open at the throat, letting escape tufts of
white hair which also sprouted from his ears; and his neck, cheekbones, forehead, chin were spare—thongs and bones and print of
wind—nothing excessive, as Slugger had said, except perhaps the
venerable vagueness of his eyes, which Rick might have called a trifle
overdone. On his pure white shock of hair, the country cap sat so
high that the sun from behind blazed into an aureole for it to float
upon.

Slugger was beside himself.

"Sir," Rick began again, and then joined in the chuckle for reasons that escaped him.

Both young men pointed to the brilliance of the weavings as their
explanation. Seen at close hand, the colors and patterns were less
startling, not so pyrotechnical, but deep, domestic, strong.

"Beautiful," the poet said. "We saw. On the road. Beautiful
work."

"Yes, indeed it is. Family work. We have fine hands in the
family." The old man held his hands up into the sunlight with

grave emaciated fingers spread as if they were the loom, to which Slugger responded with such nods and convulsions of empathy that one of the hands came down to pat him on the shoulder. Men of hands. Toilers, carvers, builders. They understood each other.

There was a pause.

Domestic beasts cackled and groaned. The birds of spring held forth. Beyond, the earth fell away in grains, groves, and ravines. The sculptor nudged the poet.

"You sell?" Rick said, his face abysmal with tact.

"I sell?" repeated the old man.

They nodded.

"Because, we buy," said Rick.

"You buy?"

Nods.

"I sell, you buy?"

Nods.

The old man burst into laughter. He still had his teeth, not all of them rotted. The cords of his throat quaked, until his wheezes subsided into an apology. Now he patted both of them on the shoulders, saying, no, no, he did not sell, but asking, courteously, whether the young men were not, perhaps, Americans?

"Yes."

He pointed to himself. "Woo-stir."

"Woo-stir?"

"Woostir, Mass." His English clipped them like a sniper's shot. "I been there twelve years, boys."

They laughed uneasily while the old man wheezed again into the face of the sun. "Oh, yeah, boys. I left in 'thirteen. Right before the big war, over here. Whaddya think of that?"

"Fifty years ago," the poet said.

"Oh, yeah. Fifty-one years I been sittin' here."

Through gaps in the gorgeous fabrics, they peeked at the family's hamlet. There was a medlar pear tree and a thick, dark table against the limed wall, yards scratched and meager, beyond a mountain slope scrolled partway up with green, flecked at the top with ice.

"Nice stuff, huh?" The old man extended a Sophoclean arm toward the fabrics. "Shirts, clotes, bags . . ."

"Clotes?" Rick repeated.

Slugger, quiet and serious, said that it was more than nice stuff.

It was the best, strongest, most alive work of this kind they had seen anywhere in Greece.

The old man took down one of the smaller shawls and a bag, and settling into his straight chair that faced the road, spread them across his lap. The sun beat fully into his eyes and upon that splash of colors in his lap.

Rick said that he knew some girls at Bennington who would sell their souls, if any, for that one bag.

Smiling, the old man accepted the compliment.

Slugger was bent over the weaves, tracing out the patterns across the rough wool with his fingertips. There were subdued diamonds of blue and brown that he hadn't noticed from a distance. And staggered borders of black, crosses of dark green running through and around the scarlet stridencies, transforming mere stridency into brilliance—as he explained to Rick, who listened with half an ear.

But the old man nodded gravely as Slugger held forth; then asked whether he, in America, was a weaver.

Slugger laughed when he said no, patted their host on the crown of his country cap, called him "old-timer," all of which pleased the old man immensely. Again he pointed to his chest.

"I weave," he said.

"You wove these?"

"No, no. In Woo-stir, boys. Mill hand. Then I started doin' fine. Then I got poor."

There was a silence.

"Oh, yeah, boys. Bad luck. I'll tell ya . . ." He shook his head. "Bad luck," he said again, this time in Greek.

Silence again. All three shook their heads.

The sun beat down on the empty road; the weavings fluttered.

Rick finally produced the oration he had been rehearsing for the past five minutes: Sir did not sell these things. Now they understood. But a thing they did not understand. Why were the things out under the sun? For the world? To see?

The old man crinkled his eyes, staring slyly up at Rick. Then he beckoned him closer, poured a flood of Greek and an ancient mustiness into his face. Rick grinned foolishly, shook his head, until the monologue began to end with fragments about his not trying any longer to pretend (the old man joyfully wagging a finger at him): he should admit it: he was a Greek boy, or at least of Greek parents.

Rick, whose hair was pitch black, whose face was lean and olive, protested, shook his head again with a smile, started to say something in broken Greek, which set the old man off into yet happier circles, embellishing his totally incomprehensible arguments. It began to be clear that there were eavesdroppers somewhere behind the arras, for whose benefit, partly, the old man was building his delicious scene.

"What's he saying?" asked Slugger.

"I haven't the foggiest," said Rick, playing the Englishman abroad.

The old man turned to Slugger. "Come on," he said, with another finger-wag. "Your friend. He's a Greek fella. Right?"

"Everybody seems to think so," said Slugger. "Same thing in Italy."

"Also in China," Rick said.

Now the old man was in splendid spirits, but Slugger was growing ominous, with his arms hanging at his sides. ("Banter," he had been known to say, "is not my line.") He raised his right arm, in which the muscles played, but noticing the attentiveness with which the old man eyed it, grew embarrassed and nodded his head instead toward the weavings. "I was wondering why you have all this fantastic stuff out here."

"Funny you should ask that," said Rick.

And the old man told them. There was a girl in the family, his young niece. It was long time for her to marry. But where can boys be found around here? In the village they all went away, at least all the good ones, just as he himself had once left. Now they had a boy coming to see, from the north. This boy ("A suitor?" Rick interposed. "That's it," said the old man), this boy would come to see what the family had to offer. First he would look at all the family's things (the old man leaned forward, lowered his voice: now they were three Americans in mockery of the Old World). He would count the sheep. He would look at the teeth of the horse. He would feel the chairs. He would ask what the . . . thing was that they could give him ("Dowry," Rick interposed again, and Slugger nudged him to shut up). But, this family was poor. Their only treasure was the weavings the women had done. Beautiful work, as the boys said. Fine family work. So, that is what they could give, and it was out in the air today to make it fresh. Then if the boy liked the sheep, the horse, and the shawls, he would say, "OK. Where's the girl?"

The old man called out, peremptorily, and from a few steps away a woman appeared. "That's her," he said to Slugger and Rick.

She was in the compulsory black, with apron and kerchief and heavy socks. Her face, pleasant but perhaps too strong, almost masculine, was already lined. The Americans bowed, and she smiled shyly, with powerful teeth.

The old man ordered her to withdraw, then called another order to her back.

"So that's it, boys. She's twenty-four, see?" He peered for a reaction, which they did not give. "My wife's brother's son's daughter," he said, looking questioningly at Rick.

"Grandniece."

"That's it. If she gets married this time, that's nice. Up north, it's nice. If no, then you see those ladies out in the fields? Thirty, forty years workin' on the ground, then under it."

There were the makings of another silence. But a Mercedes passed, and they could have talked about war or German tourists if the grandniece had not reappeared, carrying a tray with a bottle of white wine and tumblers instead of the expected Turkish coffee.

"Like retsina?" the old man asked, and nodded toward his kaleidoscopic lap, where the woman carefully placed her tray. She began to remonstrate with him, pointing to the wine and the weavings, but he waved her away.

She paused to look at them. "*Amerikaniki?*"

Rick answered that they were.

"Good," she said, very slowly, as if for children, "Good!" gesturing toward them and to her great-uncle and back again, giggling. The old man again raised his hand, and in a flurry of affirmation, she was gone.

Three brimming glasses were ready. The old man held his high to admire the sun pouring through in an amber shaft, illuminating the mists of sediment that swirled faintly before his eyes. He asked, half apologetically, whether they knew Greek wine, which was very strong and had the taste of the resin.

"We know. We like it."

They toasted each other's health, and drank. The young men had thirsts from the road, eliciting a wheeze from the elder. "Hey! We're not in Woostir, boys. Here we don't do like that. Insult, if the glass gets empty. Here."

Again they studied the wine motes in their tumblers. The Americans were free to move about in the light, whereas the old man was imprisoned in his chair, beneath shawls and tray, with the sun blazing into his face, probing every crevice in its hide, and surely, said Slugger (beginning to move his chair about), hurting his eyes. The old man waved him off. It seemed that he preferred trying to outstare the sun, and he wanted them in front of him so that they could talk.

Slugger had now begun to study the old man's face with bald intensity. The victim was half amused, half puzzled. He adjusted his cap, held his refilled glass up into the sun again, and peeked around to see whether the fixed stare was still upon him. It was.

Rick laughed. "My friend wants to make a portrait of your head."

"Picture? Sure. Got a camera, boys?"

"No, no. He's a sculptor."

"Sculptor?" The old man smiled, in docile incomprehension. He and Rick had made a game of the gaps in his English.

The young man molded the air with his hands. "You know, you know. Sculptor—*glyptos!*"

"Oh. *Glyptos, glyptos.* Sure. But what you wanna make *my* face for, boys?"

Slugger was already at work with charcoal pencil and sketch pad. "You're a very beautiful old man."

"Thank you."

"Hold still, now."

"OK," said the subject, very happy.

Afraid to move, he pointed to the wine tumblers, which Rick made to brim again.

Now there was not a silence among them, but a moment of justified quiet. Slugger's pencil scratched back and forth while he murmured occasionally those soothing words that good portraitists and doctors know: "good . . . that's fine . . . just hold that . . . just a bit more . . . there." Rick was free to prowl about, savoring the spell of spring and retsina, studying rocks and fabrics, medlar pears and mountains. He chased a few chickens, stared at rapacious silhouettes (eagles? vultures?) that wheeled against the sun, exchanged cynical glances with the goat, and waved to the grandniece, who smiled blindingly and disappeared, seeming to leave her teeth behind. He wandered back to the road, admiring his friend's crouched concentration and wondering again that nature made provision for such present rage and potential cruelty to be expended through the point of a pencil or into the hammer's head that beat on bronze. They had taken this trip on the urging of Slugger's wife, who said he was growing "completely impossible" cooped up in Rome. All the bronzes that he cast out of his private agony had recently fetched "handsome prices" at a New York show. The danger that he might wax rich and famous was apparently rousing his demon. So he and Rick ("you're his only sane friend") had jumped from rock to rock, from an archaic smile to a golden lion, watched the sun rise from the walls of Mycenae and watched it set through the doors of a Byzantine chapel secluded amid its collection of cypresses, frescoes, hawks, sea, and clouds; and they had haggled over crafts, and now the great forearm instead of threatening a wife was sketching a relic. Rick himself studied the time-ravaged face as it tipped up toward the sun that had burned it into leather and bleached its eyes. He looked at it carefully, for the first time, and then at its version on the sketch pad; and he grew troubled.

"You've made him look like one of my grandfathers," Rick said to the sculptor. "It's uncanny."

Slugger grunted.

"He does look a little like my grandfather. The thin one." And turning to the old man, "You look like my grandfather."

"Where?" the old man said, smiling pleasantly. "Your grandfather?"

"Look *like*. You resemble him. Same face, except for the sunburn."

"Same face? No kidding."

"You know," Rick said, "he came from a village. Probably like yours."

"No kidding. Greek fella?"

"No, no, no. Don't start that again. From . . . Slavic country. But he told me there were hills, and chickens."

"Yeah? Well, that's it. That's what we got."

". . . last couple of lines here. Don't move around too much, now . . ."

Rick was excited. "You know, he came as a mill hand, too. My grandfather. A weaver. It's strange, the same story, but . . ."

"Bad luck?" The old man, eager, turned to Rick. "He got bad luck, too?"

"No. No. As a matter of fact, he had good luck."

Silence, except for the pencil's rasp.

"He had very good luck. He made money, had a big family, got through depressions, wars."

"*I* made money, boys!"

Slugger threw down his pencil, in disgust at talk, as the old man tried to pitch himself up from the chair but managed only to spill the wine bottle.

Only a few drops were left. All three watched the blots swell on blazing crimson.

"*I made money!*" the old man repeated.

He sat back, first closing, then covering his veined eyes. Slugger seemed abruptly anxious to go, Rick not.

"Business. I was a kid. Your age. Her age. Doin' fine."

Silence. Slugger, pacing.

The old man uncovered his eyes—vague, errant eyes. "What's he do now?"

"He?" Rick said. "Oh. He's dead. Dead for six years."

The old man said he was sorry.

"No. He had good luck. Things worked out well for him."

"Mill hand."

"Started as a mill hand. Like yourself. He bought some looms. Eventually he did very well, in ladies' blouses. House in town, house in Maine. 'Just like the czar,' he used to say. 'Summer Palace, Winter Palace.'"

The old man had ceased listening. He turned toward Slugger. "Luck. We had the store. I—work in factory, work in store. I'm the one, speak English for the family. Money. I want to come back here. Fight the Turks, see my mother. On a ship."

"What happened?" said Slugger.

"Lost it."

"What do you mean, lost it?"

"Lost it," said the old man, and lapsed into vagueness.

Slugger lay his sketch—his blueprint of the old man's physical dignity—on the tray, with a phrase meant to cover offerings, sympathies, and farewell. But Rick said, quietly, "What was it like, in Worcester?"

And the old man astounded them with a prose poem. With fragments, solecisms, and waning breath he composed a 1900 town of great singularity, where the snow was always filthy as it lay and the gray winter wind never ceased to howl, where a thousand city horses reeked in disease and confinement and people, pinched by work, grew mean while the racket of the factories hung everywhere on their heads. He told them how he wrote back, and later people wrote back to him, of the golden land where everything was fine, and it was a lie.

Suddenly his eyes were unveiled, and his face, amid its creases, was intelligent.

Then he kicked at a clump of poppies at his feet, and the hairs seemed to resprout from his ears. "Boys," he said, "I'm poor."

They still said nothing.

"Poor. Nothing. I got nothing. See?"

He did not pull out his pockets to wave emptily in the breeze as other men might, but held his palms forward for the Americans to see, one for the sculptor and one for the poet. He held them gracelessly before him, angling his fingers sharply downward to make the cords in his papery old wrists extrude and strain, and the Americans had time to observe that his palms, those blighted contour maps, were indeed empty, while his eyes, as occluded now as any Worcester winter, watched them.

So they were held for another long moment.

The poet cleared his throat, made tragic murmurs. The sculptor shuffled his feet. Eyes watched from a window. Goats rang their neck bells. Then the old man let his hands drop. "Yeah, that's it, boys. That's the way it is."

"I'm sorry," the poet said. "It's a terrible thing."

"Fifty years. Fifty years I been poor."

"Terrible," said the sculptor.

"Nothing here," the old man announced, waving at the medlar pear tree. "Hills and chickens. That's right. That's what we got. But he got the luck. Better man."

"*Luckier* man," said Rick. "That's not the same thing."

"Luck," the old man said, staring down the valley. "He could give to his family. That's what I wanted. That's what's good."

"Now look, old-timer." Slugger took a solid grip of the old man's shoulder, that compilation of matchsticks. "His grandfather got into all kinds of tax brackets selling underwear. Huzzah for him. But did he ever take a boat back to fight the Turks? He never lived out here where the gods used to live. Spent his life in a place like Worcester; you haven't missed a thing. He never saw these mountains, these eagles. He probably never found out what a good day's work feels like in the sun. And you've worked." Slugger turned over one of the hands and tapped its ancient calluses. "You can't kid me, about 'sitting here.' You've worked. You've seen the lambs, the new wheat, every year. Every year. Just look at this stuff around you." He pointed again at the waving fabrics. "You're alive. He's dead. You're drinking wine in your own place in the sun. He's dead six years. So I'm not so sure who's luckier."

(Lies, thought Rick. You're damn well sure this old fossil is luckier, because he slipped out of the clutches of the Industrial Monster. That's your only and absolute standard.)

The old man was quiet for a moment, while spring with wheat fragrance, birds, drifting silver clouds, outdid itself. The road was still except for a horse cart three bends below, and there was not a sound that Homer might not have heard.

"He's dead for six years," said the old man, and then with great dignity: "I'm poor for fifty."

Slugger smote himself on the brow.

Hearty thanks were offered, in two languages, for the wine, and praise, in one, for the excellence of this family's skills. The old man stepped fragilely along toward the Fiat, disregarding thanks and praise. A knot of women, varied in sizes but all in black, materialized to watch from a distance, behind the abandoned chair and against the weavings.

For a chance to speak English to fine boys, for the "real fine picture," the old man was grateful. He asked where they were going (Athens), and where after that (back to Rome), and where they had been (Paris, Istanbul, San Francisco, and so forth), and he pointed to himself, then to the hamlet with its beasts and fruit trees, saying there was the place *he* was going to, today, and tomorrow, and also where he had come from, and where he was highly likely to go the day after tomorrow.

"Poor," he said.

He had the young men pinned now against the side of the car. To let the door open outward they would have had to push him aside.

It was as if he were enamored of the word itself. He tapped both their arms and again intoned it.

"Poor."

Slugger and Rick eyed each other. Their friendship was not deep,

but its silent vocabulary could easily meet the challenge of a verb:
Give? and a noun: money?

Give money?

Slugger's southern California face clouded over.

"Wait," the old man said.

He hobbled off impulsively to his chair, picked up the woven bag,
then put it down and picked up the shawl instead, and returned
with it to the Americans, who watched him and each other.

The old man stepped up to them, holding forth the shawl, which
glowed, and looked straight into their eyes. His own eyes made their
bleared demand in silence, while the sun again seemed to carve his
face, casting shadows in the depths below his cheekbones, blazing
on the white hair that escaped beneath his cap and on the ravages
of his brow and the harsh stubble about his chin and neck.

Now they could give, thought Rick. They could give easily, and
they knew it. And they knew they wanted to give, each in his own
style: that was the right and generous and American thing to do
(CARE packages and United Fund thermometers danced in his
head). But poor Slugger's notions of manliness, dignity, pride still
existing in a few rocky corners of the earth—in proximity, at least,
to certain museums and archaeological sites; that there were still
men who wanted simply to be accepted as men and who would
not be bought. And what would their five or ten dollars do for this
man (surely they were not going to give him more)? Would they
change the conditions of his life? Were they going to give equal
amounts, in all fairness, to all the old men in the Peloponnesus?
Wasn't it merely to relieve themselves of a bad moment that they
would plunk their bribe into his ruined old palm? To let themselves
off the hook so that they could enjoy their taverna in Athens tonight? But it was so easy to give, if that's what he wanted. There
he was, waiting in the sun: Still Life with Shawl. So easy, if it would
give him a sweeter week or two. How many did he have left?
And probably he was corrupted, by Worcester. For half a century he
had been a Sophoclean decoration for this roadside while through
his head America was still spinning (time-is-money-what's-in-it-for-
me-got-to-look-out-for-yourself, boys). A wedding gift for the grandniece. Tactful. A fat price for the shawl. Was that what he was
angling for, after all? A bargaining, slightly elaborate with pathos?
Right on the Athens road, how many tourist cars per week, all looking for handmade genuine, and sensitive to deprivation at 50 percent

above the market price. But if Slugger were right: that all he wanted was a human ear once or twice in his dwindling life, a chance at the mysterious consolation of singing one's sorrow in broken English to someone who listens and is gone, an exchange of hospitable wine for nothing but the blessing of talk—?

The sculptor had already accepted the shawl, clasped the proffered old hand, exchanged a forthright *vale,* and was in the car by the time Rick had drawn out his wallet and selected nine bills fresh from American Express—450 drachmas, about fifteen dollars. These he placed in the old man's left hand while he shook the right one (strong, but twig-dry), saying, "Good-bye. Here's a bit of luck from my grandpa." It came out badly. The old man said nothing, merely letting the bills lie in his upturned old claw, staring vaguely at Rick's shoulder. The poet's face burned as he slammed the door.

The Fiat roared off.

Slugger was too choked with rage to speak. Rick saw with astonishment that tears had welled up in his friend's eyes.

Then his own forehead was almost grazing the windshield again. They screeched, stalled.

Slugger had hold of the back of his head—sweat-hot grip—and forced him to look through the rear window.

"Look. Damnit, look!"

Rick saw the old man with his back turned to them, reduced by distance, framed against the upland groves, his white hair catching the sun as he walked, stiffly. The sun was slanted enough to give each step its illuminated puff of dust, until he had passed through the crimson weavings, leaving his chair behind.

They stared at each other wordlessly, then Slugger released his grip of Rick's neck and looked instead at his own palm, as if examining it for loathsome contagion.

The poet settled down to difficult thoughts as Slugger reached for the starter. The engine picked up its spark, gas was fed, and they were in motion again, backward.

"Slugger," Rick said.

But he was talking to his friend's neck and shoulders, which strained for rearward vision, while the voice, mingling with the engine's whine, muttered out the window something about "nobility . . . apologize. . . ."

"Pay attention now, Slugger. How about calling an end to this farce?"

But they had reached the scene of the crime, against the undulant curtainings. Engine, off.

Slugger leapt out. He slammed the door so hard that the Fiat quivered on its springs. Then he was standing, triumphant, in the middle of the road, looking down at a handful of crumpled bills.

"That noble old bastard," he said, shaking his head. "That's what he thinks of your money. That noble old bastard!"

Rick waited.

"All right, friend," called the sculptor, too stridently for this mild valley. "Pick it up!"

"What do you mean, pick it up?"

"You heard me," Slugger said. "The money. Get out, right now, and *pick it up.*"

"I believe you're trying to sound like Marlon Brando," Rick said. Slugger bolted back to the car. His face had blotched with anger.

"You going to do it on your own?"

Rick searched his friend's eyes for some sign of a human being. "No."

And Slugger grappled him from the car, pulling Rick's right arm with both hands. Rick was not so heavy as his friend, but neither was he afraid to fight him. He was simply unable to suspend disbelief. Slugger had his arm twisted up behind now, and half dragged, half pushed him to the middle of the road, where lay the lethal clump of bills.

"Pick 'em up, Rick, and the farce is over."

"No."

Now the arm was twisted up almost to his head. It began to interest Rick to know whether or not the sculptor was actually willing to break a friend's arm in the name of an idea, but then the pain grew amazing and he was being pushed down also by a heavy wet hand on the scruff of his neck. Slugger was forcing his face down into the little pile of paper as an enraged master pushes a dog's nose into its own filth, to teach it. That is, to break it. The comparison interested Rick as he smelled the oil and dust of the road, but then the choice was simply to let his arm crack or to swing a wild left back into his friend's crotch or to pick up the money.

He picked up the money.

After they had driven downward for a while through the valley, where spring was silver-green and the branches threw laceworks of racing shadows, Slugger said, "I'm sorry, Rick."

The poet concentrated on light and shade, olive trees and rock.

"What I mean to say is, I'm sorry up to a point. I apologize for my bad behavior. You do the same."

Rick looked back steadily. "I don't recall any bad behavior on my part."

The sculptor bristled: "God*damn* me for trying to smooth things out! You haven't learned a damn thing from this, have you? About human dignity, about—"

"Yes," Rick said, "as a matter of fact, I have."

Something in his tone finally quieted the sculptor. He looked through the windshield and down the road toward the next stage of his pilgrimage.

The poet opened his fist, where lay the fifty-drachma bills, much crushed and wadded—three of them, to be exact: which were all, apparently, that had dropped from the old man's hand, or that he had chosen to throw down.

Then Rick closed his fist again.

LEONARD MICHAELS was born in New York, attended New York University, the University of Michigan, and the University of California at Berkeley. He is currently teaching at the University of Michigan while working on his doctorate. He has published stories in *Audit, Playboy,* and *The Massachusetts Review.*

Sticks and Stones

I<small>T</small> was a blind date. She met me at the door and smiled nicely, but I could tell she was disappointed. Fortunately, I had brought a bottle of bourbon, an expensive brand, though not a penny too much for a positive *Weltanschauung.* I felt disappointed, too. We finished the bourbon and were sitting on the couch in her livingroom. She stuttered the tale of her life and named her favorite authors. I had never before met a girl who stuttered. Our hands became interlocked and hot, our knees touched and both of us were crying. I cried for her. She, moved by my tears cried for me, and through me for herself. Beyond the room, our sobs, and her breaking, retrogressive voice, I heard church bells and the scream of a bird. I squeezed her hands, shook my head and staggered from the couch to a window. The glass broke. I fainted and fell down the night. Minutes later I awoke on a porch just below the window and she was kneeling beside my head, smoking a cigarette. I heard her voice repeating consonants, going on with the story of her life—a bad man, accident and disease. Broken glass lay about me like stars. Church bells rang the hour, then the half hour. I lay still, thinking nothing, full of mood. Cloth moved smoothly across her thighs when she breathed and rocked to the measures of her story. Despicable as it may seem, that made me sexual. I lifted on an elbow. The sight of my face with the moon shining in it, surprised her. She stopped telling her story and said, "No, I d-don't want t-to. . . ." Our eyelids were thick with water. We shook like unhealthy, feverish things.

There was a reason for not having called her again. Shame, disgust, what have you? I know that when I saw her in the street I would run. I saw her there often, and I ran hundreds of miles. My legs became strong, my chest and lungs immense. Soon I could run like a nimble dog. I could wheel abruptly, scramble left or right and go for half the day. I could leap fences and automobiles, and run from roof to roof, springing deadly air shafts, snapping in middle flight to gain the yard that saved my life. Once I caught a sparrow smack in my teeth and bit off his head. Spitting feathers and blood, I felt like an eagle. But I was not, and good things, however vigorous, come to an end. At least for me. I was neither Nietzsche, Don Juan, nor Chateaubriand. My name was Phillip. As I resolved to stand and started practising postures, a friend who knew the girl came and said she wasn't reproachful. I ought to call her on the phone. It didn't sound true, but he insisted. She wanted to see me again, at least as an acquaintance. The reasons were good and clear. She would be spared the implications of my flight. I could rest in body and mind. Next time I saw her in the street I ran faster than before, my hair flying, my eyes big. I ran half the day and all that night.

My friend came again. Running alongside, he shouted that he had had her too. We stopped.

"Do you mind?" he asked. It had bothered him so much he couldn't sleep.

"Mind?" I kissed him on the cheek and slapped his back. Was I happy? The answer is yes. I laughed till my sight was bleary. My ribs, spreading with pleasure, made a noise like wheezy old wood. My friend began laughing, too, and it was a conflation of waters, lapping and overlapping.

A crooked nose and small, blue eyes—Henry. A nose, eyes, a curious mouth, a face, my own felt face behind my eyes, an aspect of my mind, a habit of my thought—my friend, Henry.

The sight of him was mysterious news, like myself surprised in a mirror, at once strange and familiar. He was tall and went loose and swinging in his stride. Degas dreamed the motion of that dance, a whirl of long bones through streets and rooms. I was shorter, narrower, and conservative in motion. A sharp compliment striding at his side. As Henry was open, I was close, slipping into my parts for endless consultation, like a poker player checking possibilities at the belt. He and I. Me and him.

Such opposite adaptations contradict the logic of life, abolish Darwin, testify to miracle and God. I never voiced this idea, but I would think: "Henry, you ought to be dead and utterly vanished, decomposed but for the splinter of tibula or jaw bone locked in bog, or part of a boulder, baked, buried, and one with rock." I meant nothing malicious; just the wonder of it.

Now, in company, Henry might grin, expose his dearly familiar chipped front tooth, and whisper, "Tell them how you fell out the window."

"Out the window," people would shout. "You fell out the window? What window?"

I told the story, but declined the honor of being hero. "No, no, not I—this fellow I know—happened to him. Young man out of a job, about my age, generally sick, depressed about life and himself. You must know the type—can't find meaningful work, spends a lot of time in the movies, wasting. . . .

"It was suggested he call a certain girl named Marjorie, herself out of work, not seeing anyone in particular. He asked why out of work. They told him she had had an accident and lived on the insurance payments. Pretty girl? 'Not what you would call pretty. Interesting looking, bright.' So he called and she said glad to see him, come by, bring something to drink. She had a stutter. It annoyed him, but not so much as her enthusiasm. Anyhow, he was committed. He went with a bottle, and though she was interesting looking, he was disappointed and began straight in to drink and drink. Perhaps disappointed, too, she drank as fast and as much. The liquor qualified their sense of one another and themselves. Soon they sat on the couch and were full of expectations, drinking, drinking, chatting. He told her about his life, the jobs he had lost, how discontented he felt, and about his one good friend. She followed in a gentle, pleasing way, ooing and clucking. He said there were no frontiers left, nothing for a man to do but explore his own mind and go to the movies. She agreed and said she spent a lot of time just looking in a mirror. Then she came closer and told him about her life. He came closer, too, and fondled her fingertips. She had been raised in an orphanage. He pressed her palms. She had gone to work in a factory. He held her wrists. In an accident at the factory, her leg was bashed and permanently damaged. His hands slid up and down her arms. She limped slightly but the company paid. She didn't mind the limp. He shook his head no. The scars on her face, though, made

her look a bit tough; that bothered her. He moaned. She pulled up
her dress, showed him the damage, and he began to cry as he
snapped it down again. She cried, too, and pulled it back up. He
stumbled from the couch, crying, punching his fists together as he
went to the window. Trying to open it he fell through and was
nearly killed."

People loved the story and Henry cackled for more.

"You're such a jerk," he said. My heart lunged fiercely with
pleasure.

How I carried on. My friend urged me. I carried on and on. Everyone laughed when I fell out the window. No one asked what happened next. Anyhow, the tale of abused and abandoned femininity
is pathetic and tediously familiar. Only low, contemptible men who
take more pleasure in telling it than doing it, would tell it. I stopped
for a while after I had a dream in which Henry wanted to kill me.

"Me?" I asked.

"That's right, scum. You!"

Only a dream, but so is life. I took it seriously. Did it warn me of a
disaster on the way? Did it indicate a fearful present fact? I studied
Henry. Indeed, his face had changed. Never a handsome face, but
now, like his face in the dream, it was strangely uncertain, darker,
nasty about the edges of the eyes and mouth. Dirty little pimples
dotted his neck, and the front chipped tooth gave a new quality to
his smile, something asymmetrical, imbecilic and obscene. He looked
dissolute and suicidal.

He rarely came to visit me anymore, but we met in the street. Our
talk would be more an exchange of looks than words. He looked at
me as if I were bleeding. I looked at him quizzically. I looked at him
with irony; he returned it with innocence. He burst out laughing, so
I smiled and looked ready to share the joke. He then looked blank,
as if I were about to tell him what it was. I grinned, he sneered. He
smiled, I frowned. I frowned, he was pained. He looked pained, I
looked at my shoes. He looked at my shoes, I looked at his. We
looked at one another and he mentioned having seen a mutual
friend.

"An idiot," I said.

"A pig," he added.

"Intolerable neurotic."

"Nauseating . . . psychotic."

Then silence. Then he might start, "You know, his face, those weirdly colored eyes. . . ."

"Yes," I would say. The eyes were the color of mine. I yawned and scratched at my cheek, though I wasn't sleepy and felt no itch. Our eyes slipped to the corners of the squalid world and life seemed merely miserable.

Afterwards, alone in my apartment, I would have accidents. A glass slipped out of my hand one night, smashed on the floor and cut my shin. When I lifted my pant leg to see the cut, my other leg kicked it. I collapsed on the floor. They fought with kicks and scrapes, back and forth till both legs lay bleeding, jerky, broken and jointless.

Lose a job, you will find another; break an arm, it soon will heal; ditched by a woman, well

I don't care if my baby leaves me flat,
I got forty 'leven others if it come to that.

But a friend! My own felt face. An aspect of my mind. He and I. Me and him. There were no others. I smoked cigarettes and stayed up late staring at a wall. Trying to think, I ran the streets at night. My legs were remarkably strong. My lungs were thrilled by darkness. Occasionally, I saw Henry and he, too, was running. With so much on our minds, we never stopped to chat, but merely waved a bit and ran on. Now and then we might run side by side for a couple of hundred miles, both of us silent except for the gasping and hissing of our mouths and the cluttered thumping of our feet down the night. He ran as fast as I. Neither of us thought to race, though we might break silence after some wonderful show of the other's speed and call: "Hey, all right." Or, after one of us had executed a brilliant swerve and leap, the other might exclaim, "Bitching good."

Alone, going at high moderate speed one night, I caught a glimpse of Henry walking with a girl. She seemed to limp. Curious, I slowed and followed them, keeping well back and low to the ground. They went to a movie theatre. I slipped in after they did and took a seat right behind theirs. When the girl spoke, I leaned close. She stuttered. It was Marjorie. They kissed and throughout the film, she coiled slow ringlets in the back of his head. I left my seat and paced about in the glassy lobby. My heart knocked to get free of my chest and glide up amid the chandeliers. I pressed a hand to it. They seemed much in love, childish and animal. He chittered little monkey things to her. There was a coy note in her stutter. They passed without noticing me and when they stopped under the marquee, I was able to stand nearby. Henry lighted a cigarette. She watched as if it were a spectacle for kings. As the fire took life in his eyes, and smoke sifted backward to membranes of his throat, she asked, "What did you think of the m-m-movie, Hen Hen?" His glance became fine, blue as the filament of smoke sliding upward and swaying to breezes no more visible, and vastly less subtle, than the myriad, shifting discriminations that gave sense and value to his answer. "A movie is a complex thing. Images. Actors. I can't quite say." He stared at her without a word, then sighed. She clucked helplessly. All was light between them. It rose out of warmth. They kissed.

Now I understood and felt much relieved. Henry had always cared a great deal about movies and he had, at last, found someone to whom he could talk about them. Though he hadn't asked me to, I told my story again one evening in company. My voice was soft, but enthusiastic:

"This fellow I know, ordinary chap with the usual worries about life, had a date to go to the movies one night with a girl who was quite sweet and pretty and a wonderful conversationalist. He found her dressed and ready to leave when he arrived. She wore a faded gingham blouse, a flowery print skirt and sandals. She limped a bit and had a vague stutter. Her nails were bitten to the neural sheath in finger and toe. She had a faint, but regular tic in her left cheek, and throughout the movie, she scratched her knees.

"It was a foreign movie about wealthy Italians, concerned mainly with a statuesque blonde and a dark, speedy little man who circled about her for two hours like a house fly. At last, weary of his constant buzz, she reclined on a bed in his mother's apartment, and he did something to her. Afterwards she laughed a great deal, and, near the end of the movie, she discovered an interlocking wire fence. Taking hold of it with both hands, she clung there while the camera moved away and looked about the city. The movie ended with a study of a street lamp. It had a powerful effect on this fellow and his date. They fell in love with each other before it was half over, and left the theatre drunk on the images they carried away of the blonde and the speedy little man. He felt the special pertinence of the movie to their human essences, and as she limped and he shuffled beside her, he was speechless. She honored his silence and was speechless, too. Both of them being consciously modern types, they did the thing quickly as soon as they got to her apartment. An act of recognition. A testimony, he thought, to their respect for one another. Perhaps an agreement to believe their love was more than physical. Any belief needs ritual; so this one. Ergo, the beastly act. Unless it's done, you know, 'a great Prince in prison lies.' Now they could know one another. No longer drunk, however, they sat dishevelled and gloomy on her livingroom floor. Neither looked at the other's face, and she, for the sake of motion, scratched her knees. At last, she rose and went off to take a shower. When the door shut behind her, he imagined he heard a sob. He got up, put out his cigarette, went to the window and flung himself out to the mercy of the night. He has these awful headaches now and constant back pains, and wishes the fall had killed him."

People thought it was a grand story. Henry looked at me till his eyes went click and his mouth resolved into a sneer.

"Ever get a headache in this spot?" he asked, tapping the back of his head.

"Sometimes," I answered, leaning toward him and smiling.

"Then look out. It's a bad sign. It means you've got a slipped disc and probably need an operation. They might have to cut your head off."

Everyone laughed, though no one more than I. Then I got a headache and trembled for an hour. Henry wanted me to have a slipped disc.

Such a man was a threat to the world and public denunciation was in order. I considered beginning work on a small tract about evil, personified by Henry. But I really had nothing to say. He had done me no injury. As for my dream, however, that was obviously the truth: he wanted to kill me. Perhaps, inadvertently, I had said or done something to insult him. A gentleman, says Lord Chesterfield, never unintentionally insults anyone. But I didn't fancy myself a gentleman. Perhaps there was some aspect of my character he thought ghastly. After all, you may know a person for centuries before discovering a hideous peculiarity in him. I considered changing my character, but I didn't know how or what to change. It was perplexing. Henry's character was vile, so I would change mine. I hadn't ever thought his character was vile before. Now, all I had to do was think: "Henry." Vile, oh vile, vile. It would require a revolution in me. Better that than lose a friend. Was it indeed? No; better to be yourself and proud. Tell Henry to go to hell. But a real friend goes to hell himself. One afternoon, on my way to hell, I turned a corner and was face to face with Marjorie. She stopped directly in my path and smiled. Behind her I could see flames, and fluttering dimly down the wind came the sound of prayer.

There was no reason to run. I stood absolutely rigid. She blushed, looked down and said hello. My right hand whispered the same, then twitched and spun around. It slipped from the end of my arm like a leaf from a bough. She asked how I had been. My feet clattered off in opposite directions. I smiled and asked her how she had been. Before she might answer anything social and ordinary, a groan flew up my throat. My teeth couldn't resist its force and it was suddenly in the air. Both of us marvelled, though I more than she. She was too polite to make anything of it and she suggested that we stroll. The groan hovered behind us, growing smaller and more contorted. While she talked of the last few months, I nodded at things I approved of. I approved of everything and nodded without cease until my head fell off. She looked away as I groped for it on the ground and put it back on, shouting hello, hello.

How could I have been so blind, so careless, cruel and stupid? This was a lovely girl. I, beast and fool, adjusting my head, felt now what I should have felt then. And, at the same moment, I felt that Henry was marvelous. "Seen any movies lately?" I asked.

She stuttered something about a movie and Henry's impressions of it. The stutter was worse than I remembered, and now that I looked, her face seemed thin, the flesh gray. In her effort not to stutter, strain showed in her neck. As if it were my habitual right, I reached and took her hand. She continued to stutter something Henry had said about the movie, and didn't snap her hand back. I was touched. Tears formed in my nose. "Thank you," I whispered. "F-for what?" she asked. We were near an empty lot. I turned abruptly against her, my lips quivering now. She said, "Really, Phillip, I d-don't w-want. . . ." With a rapid hand I discovered that she wore no underpants. We fell together. I caught sight of her some time later as she sprinted into the darkness while groans issued from my mouth. They flew after her like a flock of horrid bats.

It was a week before Henry came to see me, though I was certain I had heard the bell a hundred times. Each time, I put out my cigarette and dragged to the door, ready for a punch in the face, a knife or a bullet. In the middle of the night, I found myself sitting up in bed, my eyes large and compendious with dark as I shouted, "No,

Henry, no." Though I shouted, I had resolved to say nothing or little when he finally came. Not a word would shape my mouth if I could help it. A word would be an excuse. Even self-denunciation was beyond decent possibility. If he flung acid in my face, I would fall and say, "Thanks." If he were out in the hall with a gun and fired point blank into my stomach, I might, as I toppled, blood sloshing through my lips, beg forgiveness. Though I merited no such opportunity, I hoped there would be time for it. If I could, while begging, keep my eyes fixed on him, it would be nice.

After three days passed and he still hadn't come, I thought of hanging myself. I tied a rope to the lightbulb, made a noose and set a chair under it. But I couldn't, when I experimented, manage to open the door and then dash to the chair and hang myself without looking clumsy, as if I were really asking to be stopped. On the other hand, I didn't want to practice, become graceful and look effete. I considered poison: open the door, hello, down it goes, goodbye. Or fire: set myself on fire, shrivel in flames while spitting curses on my head.

Despite all this I slept well most of the week, and on several nights I dreamed of Marjorie. We did it everytime. "Is this the nature of sin?" I asked. "This is nature," she said. "Don't talk." I discovered a truth in these dreams: each of my feelings was much like another, pity like lust, hate like love, sorrow like joy. I wondered if there were people who could keep them neat. I supposed not. They were feelings and not to be managed. If I felt bad I felt good. That was that.

The idea made me smile. When I noticed myself smiling, I chuckled a bit, and soon I was cackling. Tears streamed out of my eyes. I had to lie down on the floor to keep from sinking there. I lay for a long time digging my nails into my cheeks. When I came to myself, I stared up at the ceiling and thought about the nature of ideas. Pascal, Plato, Freud. I felt kin to men like that. Having ideas, seized as it were. I had had an idea.

When I heard the doorbell I knew immediately that I had heard it. The ring was different from the phony ringing during the week. It was substantial, moral, piercing. It set me running to answer, dashing between tables and chairs, leaping a sofa, lunging down the hall to come flying to the ringing door where I swerved, careened and came back to where I had been. A voice more primitive than any noise the body makes, said:

"Let the son of a bitch ring."

My lips slid up my teeth and my ears flattened to the skull. I found myself crouching. Muscles bunched in my shoulders. I felt a shuddering stiffness in my thighs. Tight as bow strings, tendons curled the bones of my hands to claws. The bell continued to ring, and a hot, ragged tongue slapped left and right across my muzzle. I smelled the sweet horror of my breath. It bristled my neck and sent me gliding low to the ringing door, a noiseless animal, blacker and more secret than night.

Henry out there, stood dying in his shoes, ringing in his gruesome demise. My paws lifted and lopped down softly. Blood poured me, slow as steaming tar, inevitably toward the door. My paw lay on the door knob. It turned. I tugged. Nothing happened. He rang again and I shouted, "Can't open it. Give a shove." While I tugged, Henry shoved. I twisted the knob and he flung himself against the other side. A panel was dislodged and I had a glimpse of his face, feverish and shining. A blaze of white teeth cut the lower half. The door stayed shut. We yelled to one another.

"All right. Give it everything."

"Here we go."

The door opened.

Henry stood in the hall, looking straight into my eyes. The crooked nose, the blue eyes. The physical man. Nothing I had felt, absolutely nothing, could accommodate the fact of him. I wondered for an instant if it were actually Henry, and I looked rapidly about his face, casting this and that aside as I searched, like a man fumbling through his wallet for his driver's license and identification cards while the trooper grimly waits. Nothing turned up to name him Henry. I pushed the left eye away and the right eye into his ear, the nose I kicked any old place, and the lips I wound up like rubber bands and flicked off down the hall. Even the familiar tooth left me unimpressed, though I plucked it out of his gum and dropped on the floor to test the ring for truth. It was futile. Henry's features made no more sense than a word repeated fifty times. The physical man, Henry, Henry, Henry, Henry. Nothing. I wanted to cry and beg him to be Henry again, but instead I snickered and stepped back. He came inside. I took a package of cigarettes from my pocket and offered it to him. He stared, then shook his head. The movement was trivial, but it was no. No! It startled me into sense. I put the cigarettes back into my pocket and sighed. The breath ran out slowly and steadily, like sand through an hour glass. This was it. He followed with a sigh of his own, and then said, "I guess this is it."

"I guess," I murmured, "it is."

"Yes," he said, "it is," and took a long deep breath, as if drawing up the air I had let out.

I began to strangle. Neither of us spoke. His blue eyes were like flecks of glass or bright, flickering birds. I coughed. He cleared his throat in a sympathetic reflex. I coughed again. He cleared his throat once more. I coughed a third time, and he waited for me to stop, but I continued to cough, more convulsive each time. I was barely able to see, though my eyes bulged. He asked if I wanted a glass of water. I nodded and remained doubled forward wiping my bulging eyes. When he returned with the water I seized it and drank. He asked if I wanted another glass. I said, "No thanks," and coughed again, a rasping, rotten-chested hack. He rushed away for another glass. I saw it trembling in his hand when he returned. His sleeve was wet to the elbow. "Thanks," I said and seized it again.

"Go on, go on, drink."

I drank half the water.

"Finish it," he urged.

I finished it slowly.

"You ought to sit down."

I went to a chair and sat down. My head rolled in a dull, feeble way, and a moment passed in silence. Then he said:

"There has been enough of this."

I stood up instantly.

He looked at me hard. I tried to look back equally hard, as if his look were an order that I do the same. His height and sharp little eyes gave him the advantage. "Yes," I said, shaking my head yes.

"Months of it. Enough!"

"I'm responsible," I muttered, and that let me put force into my look. "All my fault," I said, the force accumulating.

"Don't be ridiculous," he answered, frowning. The light in his eyes split like drops of mercury, flew off, struck my forehead and ran down in beady rivulets as though I had been crying from the hairline. "I don't blame you for anything," he said, his voice low and strong. "You want to kill me and I don't blame you for that. I'm no friend. I betrayed you."

"Kill you?"

"I came here expecting death. I am determined to settle for nothing less."

"Don't be absurd."

"Absurd? Is it so absurd to want justice? Is it so absurd to ask the friend one has betrayed to do for one the only possible thing that will purge one?"

He had moved an inch closer to me and seemed to be restraining himself, with terrific difficulty, from moving closer.

"Shut up, Henry," I said. "I have no intention of killing you and I never wanted to do such a thing."

"Ha! I see now."

"You don't see a thing, Henry."

"I see," he shouted and slapped his head. "I see why you refuse to do it, why you pretend you don't even want to do it."

He slapped his head again very hard.

"I see, Phillip, that you're a moral genius. That by not killing me you administer cruel, perfect justice."

"Henry, get a hold of yourself. Be fair to both of us, will you."

"Don't hand me that liberal crap, Phillip. Don't talk to me about fair. You be fair. Do the right thing, the really merciful thing. Kill me, Phillip."

I started backing toward the door, my hands stuffed deep between my lowest ribs. Henry shuffled after me, his little eyes wild with fury and appreciation. "No use. I will follow you until you show mercy. I will bring you guns and knives and ropes, vats of poison, acids, gasoline and matches. I will leap in front of your car. I will. . . ."

Whirling suddenly, I was out the door. Henry gasped and followed, tearing for a grip on the back of my head. We went down the night, Henry ripping out fists of my flying hair and jamming them into his mouth so he might choke. The night became day, and day night. These a week, the week a month. My hair was soon gone from the back of my head. When it grew in again he ripped it out again. The wind lacerated our faces and tore the clothes off our bodies. Occasionally, I would hear him scream, "I have a gun. Shoot me." Or, "A rope, Phillip. Strangle me." I had a step on him always and I ran on powerful legs. Over the running years, they grew more powerful. They stretched and swelled to the size of trees while my body shrank to the size of my belt and my head descended. At last my arms disappeared and I was a head on legs. Running.

ELIZABETH SPENCER has published five novels, three set in Mississippi where she was born and lived until going to Italy in 1953, and two set in Florence, Venice, and Rome. She and her husband now live in Montreal. Miss Spencer has also published some twenty stories in *The New Yorker* and other magazines, one of which, "First Dark," was included in the O. Henry Prize Stories of 1960.

Ship Island

THE French book was lying open on a corner of the dining-room table, between the floor lamp and the window. The floor lamp, which had come with the house, had a cover made of green glass, with a fringe. The French book must have lain just that way for two months. Nancy, coming in from the beach, tried not to look at it. It reminded her of how much she had meant to accomplish during the summer, of the strong sense of intent, something like refinement, with which she had chosen just that spot for studying. It was out of hearing of the conversations with the neighbors that went on every evening out on the side porch, it had window light in the daytime and lamplight at night, it had a small, slanting view of the beach, and it drew a breeze. The pencils were still there, still sharp, and the exercise, broken off. She sometimes stopped to read it over. "The soldiers of the emperor were crossing the bridge: *Les soldats de l'empereur traversaient le pont*. The officer has already knocked at the gate: *L'officier a déjà frappé—*" She could not have finished that sentence now if she had sat right down and tried.

Nancy could no longer find herself in relation to the girl who had sought out such a good place to study, had sharpened the pencils and opened the book and sat down to bend over it. What she did know was how—just now, when she had been down at the beach, across the boulevard—the sand scuffed beneath her step and shells lay strewn about, chipped and disorderly, near the water's edge. Some

shells were empty; some, with damp drying down their backs, went
for short walks. Far out, a long white shelf of cloud indicated a distance no gull could dream of gaining, though the gulls spun tirelessly
up, dazzling in the white light that comes just as morning vanishes.
A troop of pelicans sat like curiously carved knobs on the tops of a
long series of wooden piles, which were spaced out at intervals in the
water. The piles were what was left of a private pier blown away by
a hurricane some years ago.

Nancy had been alone on the beach. Behind her, the boulevard
glittered in the morning sun and the season's traffic rocked by the
long curve of the shore in clumps of breasting speed. She stood looking outward at the high straight distant shelf of cloud. The islands
were out there, plainly visible. The walls of the old Civil War fort
on the nearest one of them, the one with the lighthouse—Ship Island—were plain today as well. She had been out there once this summer with Rob Acklen, out there on the island, where the reeds grew
in the wild white sand, and the water teemed so thick with seaweed
that only crazy people would have tried to swim in it. The gulf had
rushed white and strong through all the seaweed, frothing up the
beach. On the beach, the froth turned brown, the color of softly
moving crawfish claws. In the boat coming home through the sunset
that day, a boy standing up in the pilothouse played "Over the
Waves" on his harmonica. Rob Acklen had put his jacket around
Nancy's shoulders—she had never thought to bring a sweater. The
jacket swallowed her; it smelled more like Rob than he did. The
boat moved, the breeze blew, the sea swelled, all to the lilt of the
music. All twenty-five members of the Laurel, Mississippi, First Bap-
tist Church Adult Bible Class, who had come out with them on the
excursion boat, and to whom Rob and Nancy had yet to introduce
themselves, had stopped giggling and making their silly jokes. They
were tired, and stood in a huddle like sheep; they were shaped like
sheep as well, with little shoulders and wide bottoms—it was somehow sad. Nancy and Rob, young and trim, stood side by side near
the bow, like figureheads of the boat, hearing the music and watching the thick prow butt the swell, which the sunset had stained a
deep red. Nancy felt for certain that this was the happiest she had
ever been.

Alone on the sand this morning, she had spread out her beach
towel and stood for a moment looking up the beach, way up, past a
grove of live oaks to where Rob Acklen's house was visible. He would

be standing in the kitchen, in loafers and a dirty white shirt and an old pair of shorts, drinking cold beer from the refrigerator right out of the can. He would eat lunch with his mother and sister, read the paper and write a letter, then dress and drive into town to help his father in the office, going right past Nancy's house along the boulevard. Around three, he would call her up. He did this every day. His name was Fitzrobert Conroy Acklen—one of those full-blown Confederate names. Everybody liked him, and more than a few—a general mixture of every color, size, age, sex, and religion—would say, when he passed by, "I declare, I just love that boy." So he was bound to have a lot of nicknames: "Fitz" or "Bobbie" or "Cousin" or "Son" —he answered to almost anything. He was the kind of boy people have high, undefined hopes for. He had first seen Nancy Lewis one morning when he came by her house to make an insurance call for his father.

Breaking off her French—could it have been the sentence about "l'officier"?—she had gone out to see who it was. She was expecting Mrs. Nattier, their neighbor, who had skinny white freckled legs she never shaved and whose husband, "off" somewhere, was thought not to be doing well; or Mrs. Nattier's little boy Bernard, who thought it was fun to hide around corners after dark and jump out saying nothing more original than "Boo!" (Once, he had screamed "Raw head and bloody bones!," but Nancy was sure somebody had told him to); or one of the neighbor ladies in the back—old Mrs. Poultney, whom they rented from and who walked with a cane, or Miss Henriette Dupré, who was so devout she didn't even have to go to confession before weekday Communion and whose hands, always tucked up in the sleeves of her sack, were as cold as church candles, and to think of them touching you was like rabbits skipping over your grave on dark rainy nights in winter up in the lonely wet-leaf-covered hills. Or else it was somebody wanting to be paid something. Nancy had opened the door and looked up, and there, instead of a dozen other people, was Rob Acklen.

Not that she knew his name. She had seen boys like him down on the coast, ever since her family had moved there from Little Rock back in the spring. She had seen them playing tennis on the courts back of the hotel, where she sometimes went to jump on the trampoline. She believed that the hotel people thought she was on the staff in some sort of way, as she was about the right age for that—just a year or so beyond high school but hardly old enough to work in town. The weather was already getting hot, and the season was falling off. When she passed the courts, going and coming, she saw the boys out of the corner of her eye. Were they really so much taller than the boys up where they had moved from, up in Arkansas? They were lankier and a lot more casual. They were more assured. To Nancy, whose family was in debt and whose father, in one job after another, was always doing something wrong, the boys playing tennis had that wonderful remoteness of creatures to be admired on the screen, or those seen in whiskey ads, standing near the bar of a country club and sleekly talking about things she could not begin to imagine. But now here was one, in a heavy tan cotton suit and a light blue shirt with a buttoned-down collar and dark knit tie, standing on her own front porch and smiling at her.

Yet when Rob called Nancy for a date, a day or two later, she didn't have to be told that he did it partly because he liked to do nice things for people. He obviously liked to be considerate and kind, because the first time he saw her he said, "I guess you don't know many people yet?"

"No, because Daddy just got transferred," she said—"transferred" being her mother's word for it; fired was what it was. She gave him a Coke and talked to him awhile, standing around in the house, which unaccountably continued to be empty. She said she didn't know a thing about insurance.

Now, still on the beach, Nancy Lewis sat down in the middle of her beach towel and began to rub suntan lotion on her neck and shoulders. Looking down the other way, away from Rob's house and toward the yacht club, she saw a man standing alone on the sand. She had not noticed him before. He was facing out toward the gulf and staring fixedly at the horizon. He was wearing shorts and a shirt made out of red bandanna, with the tail out—a stout young man with black hair.

Just then, without warning, it began to rain. There were no clouds one could see in the overhead dazzle, but it rained anyway; the drops fell in huge discs, marking the sand, and splashing on Nancy's skin. Each drop seemed enough to fill a Dixie cup. At first, Nancy did not know what the stinging sensation was; then she knew the rain was burning her. It was scalding hot! Strange, outlandish, but also painful, was how she found it. She jumped up and began to flinch and twist away, trying to escape, and a moment later she had snatched up her beach towel and flung it around her shoulders. But the large hot drops kept falling, and there was no escape from them. She started rubbing her cheek and forehead and felt that she might blister all over; then, since it kept on and on and was all so inexplicable, she grabbed her lotion and run up the beach and out of the sand and back across the boulevard. Once in her own front yard, under the scraggy trees, she felt the rain no longer, and looked back curiously into the dazzle beyond the boulevard.

"I thought you meant to stay for a while," her mother said. "Was it too hot? Anybody would be crazy to go out there now. There's never anybody out there at this time of day."

"It was all right," said Nancy, "but it started raining. I never felt anything like it. The rain was so hot it burned me. Look. My face—" She ran to look in the mirror. Sure enough, her face and shoulders looked splotched. It might blister. I might be scarred for life, she thought—one of those dramatic phrases left over from high school.

Nancy's mother, Mrs. Lewis, was a discouraged lady whose silky, blondish-gray hair was always slipping loose and tagging out around her face. She would not try to improve herself and talked a lot in company about her family; two of her uncles had been professors simultaneously at the University of North Carolina. One of them had written a book on phonetics. Mrs. Lewis seldom found anyone who had heard of them, or of the book, either. Some people asked what phonetics were, and others did not ask anything at all.

Mrs. Lewis now said to her daughter, "You just got too much sun."

"No, it was the rain. It was really scalding hot."

"I never heard of such a thing," her mother said. "Out of a clear sky."

"I can't help that," Nancy said. "I guess I ought to know."

Mrs. Lewis took on the kind of look she had when she would open the handkerchief drawer of a dresser and see two used, slightly bent carpet nails, some Scotch Tape melted together, an old receipt, an unanswered letter announcing a cousin's wedding, some scratched negatives saved for someone but never developed, some dusty foreign coins, a bank deposit book from a town they lived in during the summer before Nancy was born, and an old telegram whose contents, forgotten, no one would dare now to explore, for it would say something awful but absolutely true.

"I wish you wouldn't speak to me like that," Mrs. Lewis said. "All I know is, it certainly didn't rain here."

Nancy wandered away, into the dining room. She felt bad about everything—about quarrelling with her mother, about not getting a suntan, about wasting her time all summer with Rob Acklen and not learning any French. She went and took a long cool bath in the big old bathroom, where the bathtub had ball-and-claw feet painted mustard yellow and the single light bulb on the long cord dropped down one mile from the stratosphere.

What the Lewises found in a rented house was always outclassed by what they brought into it. Nancy's father, for instance, had a china donkey that bared its teeth in a great big grin. Written on one side was "If you really want to look like me" and on the other "Just keep right on talking." Her father loved the donkey and its message, and always put it on the living-room table of whatever house they were in. When he got a drink before dinner each evening, he would wander back with glass in hand and look the donkey over. "That's pretty good," he would say just before he took the first swallow. Nancy had often longed to break the donkey, by accident— that's what she would say, that it had all been an accident—but she couldn't get over the feeling that if she did, worse things than the Lewises had ever imagined would happen to them. That donkey would let in a flood of trouble, that she knew.

After Nancy got out of the tub and dried, she rubbed Jergens Lotion on all the splotches the rain had made. Then she ate a peanut-butter sandwich and more shrimp salad left over from supper the night before, and drank a cold Coke. Now and then, eating, she would go look in the mirror. By the time Rob Acklen called up, the red marks had all but disappeared.

That night, riding down to Biloxi with Rob, Nancy confided that the catalogue of people she disliked, headed by Bernard Nattier, included every single person—Miss Henriette Dupré, Mrs. Poultney, and Mrs. Nattier, and Mr. Nattier, too, when he was at home—that she had to be with these days. It even included, she was sad to say, her mother and father. If Bernard Nattier had to be mean—and it was clear he did have to—why did he have to be so corny? He put wads of wet, chewed bubble gum in her purses—that was the most original thing he ever did. Otherwise, it was just live crawfish in her bed or crabs in her shoes; anybody could think of that. And when he stole, he took things *she* wanted, nothing simple, like money—she could have forgiven him for that—but cigarettes, lipstick, and ashtrays she had stolen herself here and there. If she locked her door,

he got in through the window; if she locked the window, she suffo-
cated. Not only that, but he would crawl out from under the bed. His
eyes were slightly crossed and he knew how to turn the lids back on
themselves so that it looked like blood, and then he would chase her.
He was browned to the color of dirt all over and he smelled like salt
mud the sun had dried. He wore black tennis shoes laced too tight at
the ankles and from sunup till way past dark he never thought of
anything but what to do to Nancy, and she would have liked to kill
him.

She made Rob Acklen laugh. She amused him. He didn't take anything Nancy Lewis could say at all to heart, but, as if she was something he had found on the beach and was teaching to talk, he, with
his Phi Beta Kappa key and his good level head and his wonderful
prospects, found everything she told about herself cute, funny, absurd. He did remark that he had such feelings himself from time to
time—that he would occasionally get crazy mad at one of his parents
or the other, and that he once planned his sister's murder down to
the last razor slash. But he laughed again, and his chewing gum
popped amiably in his jaws. When she told him about the hot rain,
he said he didn't believe it. He said "Aw," which was what a boy
like Rob Acklen said when he didn't believe something. The top of
his old white Mercury convertible was down and the wind rushed
past like an endless bolt of raw silk being drawn against Nancy's
cheek.

· In the ladies'-room mirror at the Beach View, where they stopped
to eat, she saw the bright quality of her eyes, as though she had been
drinking. Her skirts rustled in the narrow room; a porous white disc
of deodorant hung on a hook, fuming the air. Her eyes, though blue,
looked startlingly dark in her pale skin, for though she tried hard all
the time, she never seemed to tan. All the sun did, as her mother was
always pointing out, was bleach her hair three shades lighter; a little
more and it would be almost white. Out on the island that day, out
on Ship Island, she had drifted in the water like seaweed, with the
tide combing her limbs and hair, tugging her through lengths of
fuzzy water growth. She had lain flat on her face with her arms
stretched out before her, experiencing the curious lift the water's
motion gave to the tentacles of weed, wondering whether she liked
it or not. Did something alive clamber the small of her back? Did
something wishful grope the spiral of her ear? Rob had caught her
wrist hard and waked her—waked was what he did, though to sleep
in water is not possible. He said he thought she had been there too

long. "Nobody can keep their face in the water that long," was
what he said.

"I did," said Nancy.

Rob's brow had been blistered a little, she recalled, for that had
been back early in the summer, soon after they had met—but the
changes the sun made on him went without particular attention.
The seasons here were old ground to him. He said that the island
was new, however—or at least forgotten. He said he had never been
there but once, and that many years ago, on a Boy Scout picnic. Soon
they were exploring the fort, reading the dates off the metal signs
whose letters glowed so smoothly in the sun, and the brief sum-
maries of what those little boys, little military-academy boys turned
into soldiers, had endured. Not old enough to fill up the name of
soldier, or of prisoner, either, which is what they were—not old
enough to shave, Nancy bet—still, they had died there, miserably far
from home, and had been buried in the sand. There was a lot more.
Rob would have been glad to read all about it, but she wasn't interested. What they knew already was plenty, just about those boys.
A bright, worried lizard ran out of a hot rubble of brick. They came
out of the fort and walked alone together eastward toward the dunes,
now skirting near the shore that faced the sound and now wandering south, where they could hear or sometimes glimpse the gulf.
They were overlooked all the way by an old white lighthouse. From
far away behind, the twenty-five members of the Adult Bible Class
could be overheard playing a silly, shrill Sunday-school game. It came
across the ruins of the fort and the sad story of the dead soldiers like
something that had happened long ago that you could not quite remember having joined in. On the beach to their right, toward the
gulf, a flock of sandpipers with blinding-white breasts stepped pecking along the water's edge, and on the inner beach, toward the
sound, a wrecked sailboat with a broken mast lay half buried in the
sand.

Rob kept teasing her along, pulling at the soft wool strings of her
bathing suit, which knotted at the nape and again under her shoulder blades, worrying loose the damp hair that she had carefully
slicked back and pinned. "There isn't anybody in that house," he
assured her, some minutes later, having explored most of that part
of the island and almost as much of Nancy as well, having almost, but
not quite—his arms around her—coaxed and caressed her down to

ground level in a clump of reeds. "There hasn't been in years and years," he said, encouraging her.

"It's only those picnic people," she said, holding off, for the reeds would not have concealed a medium-sized mouse. They had been to look at the sailboat and thought about climbing inside (kissing closely, they had almost fallen right over into it), but it did have a rotten tin can in the bottom and smelled, so here they were back out in the dunes.

"They've got to drink all those Coca-Colas," Rob said, "and give out all those prizes, and anyway—"

She never learned anyway what, but it didn't matter. Maybe she began to make up all that the poor little soldiers had missed out on. The island's very spine, a warm reach of thin ground, came smoothly up into the arch of her back; and it was at least halfway the day itself, with its fair, wide-open eyes, that she went over to. She felt somewhat historical afterward, as though they had themselves added one more mark to all those that place remembered.

Having played all the games and given out the prizes, having eaten all the homemade cookies and drunk the case of soft drinks just getting warm, and gone sightseeing through the fort, the Bible Class was now coming, too, crying "Yoohoo!," to explore the island. They discovered Rob hurling shells and bits of rock into the surf, while Nancy, scavenging a little distance away, tugged up out of the sand a shell so extraordinary it was worth showing around. It was purple, pink, and violet inside—a palace of colors; the king of the oysters had no doubt lived there. When she held it shyly out to them, they cried "Look!" and "Ooo!," so there was no need for talking to them much at all, and in the meantime the evening softened, the water glowed, the glare dissolved. Far out, there were other islands one could see now, and beyond those must be many more. They had been there all along.

Going home, Nancy gave the wonderful shell to the boy who stood in the pilothouse playing "Over the Waves." She glanced back as they walked off up the pier and saw him look at the shell, try it for weight, and then throw it in the water, leaning far back on his arm and putting a good spin on the throw, the way boys like to do—the way Rob Acklen himself had been doing, too, just that afternoon.

"Why did you do that?" Rob had demanded. He was frowning; he looked angry. He had thought they should keep the shell—to remember, she supposed.

"For the music," she explained.

"But it was ours," he said. When she didn't answer, he said again, "Why did you, Nancy?"

But still she didn't answer.

When Nancy returned to their table at the Beach View, having put her lipstick back straight after eating fish, Rob was paying the check. "Why not believe me?" she asked him. "It was true. The rain was hot as fire. I thought I would be scarred for live."

It was still broad daylight, not even twilight. In the bright, air-conditioned restaurant, the light from the water glazed flatly against the broad picture windows, the chandeliers, and the glasses. It was the hour when mirrors reflect nothing and bars look tired. The restaurant was a boozy, cheap sort of place with a black-lined gambling hall in the back, but everyone went there because the food was good.

"You're just like Mama," she said. "You think I made it up."

Rob said, teasing, "I didn't say that. I just said I didn't believe it." He loved getting her caught in some sort of logic she couldn't get out of. When he opened the door for her, she got a good sidelong view of his longish, firm face and saw the way his somewhat fine brows arched up with one or two bright reddish hairs in among the dark ones; his hair was that way, too, when the sun hit it. Maybe, if nobody had told him, he wouldn't have known it; he seemed not to notice so very much about himself. Having the confidence of people who don't worry much, his grin could snare her instantly—a glance alone could make her feel how lucky she was he'd ever noticed her. But it didn't do at all to think about him now. It would be ages before they made it through the evening and back, retracing the way and then turning off to the bayou, and even then, there would be those mosquitoes.

Bayou lovemaking suited Rob just fine; he was one of those people mosquitoes didn't bite. They certainly bit Nancy. They were huge and silent, and the minute the car stopped they would even come and sit upon her eyelids, if she closed her eyes, a dozen to each tender arc of flesh. They would gather on her face, around her nose and mouth. Clothlike, like rags and tatters, like large dry ashes of burnt cloth, they came in lazy droves, in fleets, sailing on the air. They were never in any hurry, being everywhere at once and always ready to bite. Nancy had been known to jump all the way out of the car and go stamping across the grass like a calf. She grew sulky and de-

spairing and stood on one leg at a time in the moonlight, slapping
at her ankles, while Rob leaned his chin on the doorframe and
watched her with his affectionate, total interest.

Nancy, riddled and stinging with beads of actual blood briar-
pointed here and there upon her, longed to be almost anywhere else
—she especially longed for New Orleans. She always talked about it,
although, never having been there, she had to say the things that
other people said—food and jazz in the French Quarter, beer and
crabs out on Lake Pontchartrain. Rob said vaguely they would go
sometime. But she could tell that things were wrong for him at this
point. "The food's just as good around here," he said.

"Oh, Rob!" She knew it wasn't so. She could feel that city, hanging
just over the horizon from them scarcely fifty miles away, like some
swollen bronze moon, at once brilliant and shadowy and drenched
in every sort of amplified smell. Rob was stroking her hair, and in
time his repeated, gentle touch gained her attention. It seemed to
tell what he liked—girls all spanking clean, with scrubbed fingernails,
wearing shoes still damp with white shoe polish. Even a fresh
gardenia stuck in their hair wouldn't be too much for him. There
would be all sorts of differences, to him, between Ship Island and the
French Quarter, but she did not have much idea just what they
were. Nancy took all this in, out of his hand on her head. She decided
she had better not talk anymore about New Orleans. She wriggled
around, looking out over his shoulder, through the moonlight, toward where the pitch-black surface of the bayou water showed in
patches through the trees. The trees were awful, hung with great
spooky gray tatters of Spanish moss. Nancy was reminded of the
house she and her family were living in; it had recently occurred to
her that the peculiar smell it had must come from some Spanish moss
that had got sealed in behind the panelling, between the walls. The
moss was alive in there and growing, and that was where she was
going to seal Bernard Nattier up someday, for him to see how it felt.
She had tried to kill him once, by filling her purse with rocks and
oyster shells—the roughest she could find. She had read somewhere
that this weapon was effective for ladies in case of attack. But he
had ducked when she swung the purse at him, and she had only gone
spinning round and round, falling at last into a camellia tree, which
had scratched her. . . .

"The Skeltons said for us to stop by there for a drink," Rob told
her. They were driving again, and the car was back on the boulevard,

in the still surprising daylight. "What did you say?" he asked her.
"Nothing."

"You just don't want to go?"

"No, I don't much want to go."

"Well, then, we won't stay long."

The Skelton house was right on the water, with a second-story, glassed-in, air-conditioned living room looking out over the sound. The sofas and chairs were covered with gold-and-white striped satin, and the room was full of Rob's friends. Lorna Skelton, who had been Rob's girl the summer before and who dressed so beautifully, was handing drinks round and saying, "So which is your favorite bayou, Rob?" She had a sort of fake "good sport" tone of voice and wanted to appear ready for anything. (Being so determined to be nice around Nancy, she was going to fall right over backward one day.)

"Do I have to have a favorite?" Rob asked. "They all look good to me. Full of slime and alligators."

"I should have asked Nancy."

"They're all full of mosquitoes," Nancy said, hoping that was O.K. for an answer. She thought that virgins were awful people.

"Trapped, boy!" Turner Carmichael said to Rob, and banged him on the shoulder. Turner wanted to be a writer, so he thought it was all right to tell people about themselves. "Women will be your downfall, Acklen. Nancy, honey, you haven't spoken to the General."

Old General Skelton, Lorna's grandfather, sat in the corner of the living room near the mantel, drinking a Scotch highball. You had to shout at him.

"How's the election going, General?" Turner asked.

"Election? Election? What election? Oh, the election! Well—" He lowered his voice, confidentially. As with most deaf people, his tone went to extremes. "There's no question of it. The one we want is the one we know. Know Houghman's father. Knew his grandfather. His stand is the same, identical one that we are all accustomed to. On every subject—this race thing especially. Very dangerous now. Extremely touchy. But Houghman—absolute! Never experiment, never question, never turn back. These are perilous times."

"Yes, sir," said Turner, nodding in an earnestly false way, which was better than the earnestly impressed way a younger boy at the

General's elbow shouted, "General Skelton, that's just what my daddy says!"

"Oh, yes," said the old man, sipping Scotch. "Oh, yes, it's true. And you, Missy?" he thundered suddenly at Nancy, making her jump. "Are you just visiting here?"

"Why, Granddaddy," Lorna explained, joining them, "Nancy lives here now. You know Nancy."

"Then why isn't she tan?" the old man continued. "Why so pale and wan, fair nymph?"

"Were you a nymph?" Turner asked. "All this time?"

"For me I'm dark," Nancy explained, but this awkward way of putting it proved more than General Skelton could hear, even after three shoutings.

Turner Carmichael said, "We used to have this crazy colored girl who went around saying, 'I'se really white, 'cause all my chillun is,'" and of course *that* was what General Skelton picked to hear. "Party's getting rough," he complained.

"Granddaddy," Lorna cried, giggling, "you don't understand!"

"Don't I?" said the old gentleman. "Well, maybe I don't."

"Here, Nancy, come help me," said Lorna, leading her guest toward the kitchen.

On the way, Nancy heard Rob ask Turner, "Just where did you have this colored girl, did you say?"

"Don't be a dope. I said she worked for us."

"Aren't they a scream?" Lorna said, dragging a quart bottle of soda out of the refrigerator. "I thank God every night Granddaddy's deaf. You know, he was in the First World War and killed I don't know how many Germans, and he still can't stand to hear what he calls loose talk before a lady."

"I thought he was in the Civil War," said Nancy, and then of course she knew that that was the wrong thing and that Lorna, who just for an instant gave her a glance less than polite, was not going to forget it. The fact was, Nancy had never thought till that minute which war General Skelton had been in. She hadn't thought because she didn't care.

It had grown dark by now, and through the kitchen windows Nancy could see that the moon had risen—a moon in the clumsy stage, swelling between three-quarters and full, yet pouring out light on the water. Its rays were bursting against a long breakwater of concrete slabs, the remains of what the hurricane had shattered.

After saying such a fool thing, Nancy felt she could not stay in that kitchen another minute with Lorna, so she asked where she could go and comb her hair. Lorna showed her down a hallway, kindly switching the lights on.

The Skeltons' bathroom was all pale blue and white, with handsome jars of rose bath salts and big fat scented bars of rosy soap. The lights came on impressively and the fixtures were heavy, yet somehow it all looked dead. It came to Nancy that she had really been wondering about just what would be in this sort of bathroom ever since she had seen those boys, with maybe Rob among them, playing tennis while she jumped on the trampoline. Surely the place had the air of an inner shrine, but what was there to see? The tops of all the bottles fitted firmly tight, and the soap in the tub was dry. Somebody had picked it all out—that was the point—judging soap and bath salts just the way they judged outsiders, business, real estate, politics. Nancy's father made judgments, too. Once, he argued all evening that Hitler was a well-meaning man; another time, he said the world was ready for the Communists. You could tell he was judging wrong, because he didn't have a bathroom like this one. Nancy's face in the mirror resembled a flower in a room that was too warm.

When she went out again, they had started dancing a little—a sort of friendly shifting around before the big glass windows overlooking the sound. General Skelton's chair was empty; he was gone. Down below, Lorna's parents could be heard coming in; her mother called upstairs. Her father appeared and shook hands all around. Mrs. Skelton soon followed him. He was wearing a white jacket, and she had on a silver cocktail dress with silver shoes. They looked like people in magazines. Mrs. Skelton held a crystal platter of things to eat in one hand, with a lace handkerchief pressed between the flesh and the glass in an inevitable sort of way.

In a moment, when the faces, talking and eating, the music, the talk, and the dancing swam to a still point before Nancy's eyes, she said, "You must all come to my house next week. We'll have a party."

A silence fell. Everyone knew where Nancy lived, in that little cluster of old run-down houses the boulevard swept by. They knew that her house, especially, needed paint outside and furniture inside. Her daddy drank too much, and through her dress they could perhaps clearly discern the pin that held her slip together. Maybe, since

they knew everything, they could look right through the walls of
the house and see her daddy's donkey.

"Sure we will," said Rob Acklen at once. "I think that would be
grand."

"Sure we will, Nancy," said Lorna Skelton, who was such a good
sport and who was not seeing Rob this summer.

"A party?" said Turner Carmichael, and swallowed a whole an-
chovy. "Can I come, too?"

Oh, dear Lord, Nancy was wondering, what made me say it? Then
she was on the stairs with her knees shaking, leaving the party, leaving with Rob to go down to Biloxi, where the two of them always
went, and hearing the right things said to her and Rob, and smiling
back at the right things but longing to jump off into the dark as if
it were water. The dark, with the moon mixed in with it, seemed to
her like good deep water to go off in.

She might have known that in the Marine Room of the Buena
Vista, down in Biloxi, they would run into more friends of Rob's.
They always ran into somebody, and she might have known. These
particular ones had already arrived and were even waiting for Rob,
being somewhat bored in the process. It wasn't that Rob was so
bright and witty, but he listened and liked everybody; he saw them
the way they liked to be seen. So then they would go on to new
heights, outdoing themselves, coming to believe how marvellous
they really were. Two fraternity brothers of his were there tonight.
They were sitting at a table with their dates—two tiny girls with
tiny voices, like mosquitoes. They at once asked Nancy where she
went to college, but before she could reply and give it away that her
school so far had been only a cow college up in Arkansas and that
she had gone there because her daddy couldn't afford anywhere else,
Rob broke in and answered for her. "She's been in a finishing school
in Little Rock," he said, "but I'm trying to talk her into going to the
university."

Then the girls and their dates all four spoke together. They said,
"Great!"

"Now watch," said one of the little girls, whose name was Teenie.
"Cootie's getting out that little ole rush book."

Sure enough, the tiniest little notebook came out of the little
cream silk bag of the other girl, who was called Cootie, and in it
Nancy's name and address were written down with a sliver of a gold

pencil. The whole routine was a fake, but a kind fake, as long as Rob
was there. The minute those two got her into the ladies' room it
would turn into another thing altogether; that she knew. Nancy
knew all about mosquitoes. They'll sting me till I crumple up and
die, she thought, and what will they ever care? So, when the three of
them did leave the table, she stopped to straighten the strap of her
shoe at the door to the ladies' room and let them go on through,
talking on and on to one another about Rush Week. Then she went
down a corridor and around a corner and down a short flight of
steps. She ran down a long basement hallway where the service
quarters were, past linen closets and cases of soft drinks, and, turning another corner and trying a door above a stairway, she came out,
as she thought she would, in a night-club place called the Fishnet,
far away in the wing. It was a good place to hide; she and Rob had
been there often. I can make up some sort of story later, she thought,
and crept up on the last barstool. Up above the bar, New Orleans-
style (or so they said), a man was pumping tunes out of an electric
organ. He wore rings on his chubby fingers and kept a handkerchief
near him to mop his brow and to swab his triple chins with between
songs. He waved his hand at Nancy. "Where's Rob, honey?" he
asked.

She smiled but didn't answer. She kept her head back in the shadows. She wished only to be like another glass in the sparkling row
of glasses lined up before the big gleam of mirrors and under the
play of lights. What made me say that about a party, she kept wondering. To some people it would be nothing, nothing. But not to
her. She fumbled in her bag for a cigarette. Inadvertently, she drank
from a glass near her hand. The man sitting next to her smiled at
her. "I didn't want it anyway," he said.

"Oh, I didn't mean—" she began. "I'll order one." Did you pay
now? She rummaged in her bag.

But the man said "What'll it be?" and ordered for her. "Come on
now, take it easy," he said. "What's your name?"

"Nothing," she said, by accident.

She had meant to say Nancy, but the man seemed to think it was
funny. "Nothing what?" he asked. "Or is it by any chance Miss Nothing? I used to know a large family of Nothings, over in Mobile."

"Oh, I meant to say Nancy."

"Nancy Nothing. Is that it?"

Another teaser, she thought. She looked away from his eyes, which glittered like metal, and what she saw across the room made her uncertainties vanish. She felt her whole self settle and calm itself. The man she had seen that morning on the beach wearing a red bandanna shirt and shorts was standing near the back of the Fishnet, looking on. Now he was wearing a white dinner jacket and a black tie, with a red cummerbund over his large stomach, but he was unmistakably the same man. At that moment, he positively seemed to Nancy to be her own identity. She jumped up and left the teasing man at the bar and crossed the room.

"Remember me?" she said. "I saw you on the beach this morning."

"Sure I do. You ran off when it started to rain. I had to run, too."

"Why did you?" Nancy asked, growing happier every minute.

"Because the rain was so hot it burnt me. If I could roll up my sleeve, I'd show you the blisters on my arm."

"I believe you. I had some, too, but they went away." She smiled, and the man smiled back. The feeling was that they would be friends forever.

"Listen," the man said after a while. "There's a fellow here you've got to meet now. He's out on the veranda, because it's too hot in here. Anyway, he gets tired just with me. Now, you come on."

Nancy Lewis was always conscious of what she had left behind her. She knew that right now her parents and old Mrs. Poultney, with her rent collector's jaw, and Miss Henriette Dupré, with her religious calf eyes, and the Nattiers, mother and son, were all sitting on the back porch in the half-light, passing the bottle of 6-12 around, and probably right now discussing the fact that Nancy was out with Rob again. She knew that when her mother thought of Rob her heart turned beautiful and radiant as a seashell on a spring night. Her father, both at home and at his office, took his daughter's going out with Rob as a means of saying something disagreeable about Rob's father, who was a big insurance man. There was always some talk about how Mr. Acklen had trickily got out of the bulk of his hurricane-damage payments, the same as all the other insurance men had done. Nancy's mother was probably responding to such a charge at this moment. "Now, you don't know that's true," she would say. But old Mrs. Poultney would say she knew it was true with *her* insurance company (implying that she knew but wouldn't say about the Acklen company, too). Half the house she was renting to the Lewises had blow right off it—all one wing—and the upstairs bathroom was ripped in two, and you could see the wall-papered walls of all the rooms, and the bathtub, with its pipes still attached, had got blown into the telephone wires. If Mrs. Poultney had got what insurance money had been coming to her, she would have torn down this house and built a new one. And Mrs. Nattier would say that there was something terrible to her about seeing wall-papered rooms exposed that way. And Miss Henriette Dupré would say that the Dupré house had come through it all ab-so-lootly intact, meaning that the Duprés had been foresighted enough to get some sort of special heavenly insurance, and she would be just longing to embark on explaining how they came by it, and she would, too, given a tenth of a chance. And all the time this went on, Nancy could see into the Acklens' house just as clearly—see the Acklens sitting inside their sheltered game room after dinner, bathed in those soft bug-repellent lights. And what were the Acklens saying (along with their kind of talk about their kind of money) but that they certainly hoped Rob wasn't serious about that girl? Nothing had to matter if he wasn't serious. . . . Nancy could circle around all of them in her mind. She could peer into windows, overhearing; it was the only way she could look at people. No human in the whole hu-man world seemed to her exactly made for her to stand in front of and look squarely in the eye, the way she could look Bernard Nattier in the eye (he not being a human, either) before taking careful aim to be sure not to miss him with a purseful of rocks and oyster shells, or the way she could look this big man in the red cummerbund in the eye, being convinced already that he was what her daddy called a "natural." Her daddy liked to come across people he could call that, because it made him feel superior.

As the big man steered her through the crowded room, threading among the tables, going out toward the veranda, he was telling her his life story all along the way. It seemed that his father was a terri-bly rich Yankee who paid him not to stay at home. He had been in love with a policeman's daughter from Pittsburgh, but his father broke it up. He was still in love with her and always would be. It was the way he was; he couldn't help being faithful, could he? His name was Alfred, but everybody called him Bub. The fellow his father paid to drive him around was right down there, he said, as they stepped through the door and out on the veranda.

Nancy looked down the length of the veranda, which ran along the side of the hotel, and there was a man sitting on a bench. He had on a white jacket and was staring straight ahead, smoking. The highway curled around the hotel grounds, following the curve of the shore, and the cars came glimmering past, one by one, sometimes with lights on inside, sometimes spilling radio music that trailed up in long waves and met the electric-organ music coming out of the bar. Nancy and Bub walked toward the man. Bub counselled her gently, "His name is Dennis." Some people in full evening dress were coming up the divided walk before the hotel, past the canna lilies blooming deeply red under the high, powerful lights, where the bugs coned in long footless whirlpools. The people were drunk and laughing.

"Hi, Dennis," Bub said. The way he said it, trying to sound confident, told her that he was scared of Dennis.

Dennis's head snapped up and around. He was an erect, strong, square-cut man, not very tall. He had put water on his light-brown hair when he combed it, so that it streaked light and dark and light again and looked like wood. He had cold eyes, which did not express anything—just the opposite of Rob Acklen's.

"What you got there?" he asked Bub.

"I met her this morning on the beach," Bub said.

"Been holding out on me?"

"Nothing like that," said Bub. "I just now saw her again."

The man called Dennis got up and thumbed his cigarette into the shrubbery. Then he carefully set his heels together and bowed. It was all a sort of joke on how he thought people here behaved. "Would you care to dance?" he inquired.

Dancing there on the veranda, Nancy noticed at once that he had a tense, strong wrist that bent back and forth like something manufactured out of steel. She also noticed that he was making her do whatever it was he called dancing; he was good at that. The music coming out of the Fishnet poured through the windows and around them. Dennis was possibly even thirty years old. He kept talking the whole time. "I guess he's told you everything, even about the policeman's daughter. He tells everybody everything, right in the first two minutes. I don't know if it's true, but how can you tell? If it wasn't true when it happened, it is now." He spun her fast as a top, then slung her out about ten feet—she thought she would certainly sail right on out over the railing and maybe never stop till she landed in the gulf, or perhaps go splat on the highway—but he got her back on the beat and finished up the thought, saying, "Know what I mean?"

"I guess so," Nancy said, and the music stopped.

The three of them sat down together on the bench.

"What do we do now?" Dennis asked.

"Let's ask her," said Bub. He was more and more delighted with Nancy. He had been tremendously encouraged when Dennis took to her.

"You ask her," Dennis said.

"Listen, Nancy," Bub said. "Now, listen. Let me just tell you. There's so much money—that's the first thing to know. You've got no idea how much money there is. Really crazy. It's something, actually, that nobody knows—"

"If anybody knew," said Dennis, "they might have to tell the government."

"Anyway, my stepmother on this yacht in Florida, her own telephone—by radio, you know—she'd be crazy to meet you. My dad is likely off somewhere, but maybe not. And there's this plane down at Palm Beach, pilot and all, with nothing to do but go to the beach every day, just to pass away the time, and if he's not there for any reason, me and Dennis can fly just as good as we can drive. There's Alaska, Beirut—would you like to go to Beirut? I've always wanted to. There's anything you say."

"See that Cad out there?" said Dennis. "The yellow one with the black leather upholstery? That's his. I drive."

"So all you got to do," Bub told her, "is wish. Now, wait—now, think. It's important!" He all but held his hand over her mouth, as if playing a child's game, until finally he said, "Now! What would you like to do most in the world?"

"Go to New Orleans," said Nancy at once, "and eat some wonderful food."

"It's a good idea," said Dennis. "This dump is getting on my nerves. I get bored most of the time anyway, but today I'm bored silly."

"So wait here!" Nancy said. "So wait right here!"

She ran off to get Rob. She had all sorts of plans in her head.

But Rob was all taken up. There were now more of his friends. The Marine Room was full of people just like him, lounging around two big tables shoved together, with about a million 7-Up bottles and soda bottles and glasses before them, and girls spangled among

them, all silver, gold, and white. It was as if while Nancy was gone
they had moved into mirrors to multiply themselves. They were talking to themselves about things she couldn't join in, any more than
you can dance without feet. Somebody was going into politics, somebody was getting married to a girl who trained horses, somebody was
just back from Europe. The two little mosquito girls weren't saying
anything much anymore; they had their little chins glued to their
little palms. When anybody mentioned the university, it sounded
like a small country the people right there were running *in absentia*
to suit themselves. Last year's Maid of Cotton was there, and so, it
turned out, was the girl horse-trainer—tall, with a sheaf of upswept
brown hair fastened with a glittering pin; she sat like the mast of a
ship, smiling and talking about horses. Did she know personally
every horse in the Southern states?

Rob scarcely looked up when he pulled Nancy in. "Where you
been? What you want to drink?" He was having another good evening. He seemed to be sitting up above all the rest, as though
presiding, but this was not actually so; only his fondness for every
face he saw before him made him appear to be raised up a little, as
if on a special chair.

And, later on, it seemed to Nancy that she herself had been,
among them, like a person who wasn't a person—another order of
creature passing among or even through them. Was it just that nothing, nobody, could really distract them when they got wrapped up
in themselves?

"I met some people who want to meet you," she whispered to
Rob. "Come on out with me."

"O.K.," he said. "In a minute. Are they from around here?"

"Come on, come on," she urged. "Come on out."

"In a minute," he said. "I will in a minute," he promised.

Then someone noticed her pulling at his sleeve, and she thought
she heard Lorna Skelton laugh.

She went racing back to Bub and Dennis, who were waiting for
her so docilely they seemed to be the soul of goodness, and she said,
"I'll just ride around for a while, because I've never been in a
Cadillac before." So they rode around and came back and sat for a
while under the huge brilliant overhead lights before the hotel,
where the bugs spiralled down. They did everything she said. She
could make them do anything. They went to three different places,

for instance, to find her some Dentyne, and when they found it they bought her a whole carton of it.

The bugs did a jagged frantic dance, trying to climb high enough to kill themselves, and occasionally a big one crashed with a harsh dry sound against the pavement. Nancy remembered dancing in the open air, and the rough salt feel of the air whipping against her skin as she spun fast against the air's drift. From behind she heard the resonant, constant whisper of the gulf. She looked toward the hotel doors and thought that if Rob came through she would hop out of the car right away, but he didn't come. A man she knew passed by, and she just all of a sudden said, "Tell Rob I'll be back in a minute," and he, without even looking up, said, "O.K., Nancy," just like it really was O.K., so she said what the motor was saying, quiet but right there, and definitely running just under the splendid skin of the car, "Let's go on for a little while."

"Nancy, I think you're the sweetest girl I ever saw," said Bub, and they drove off.

She rode between them, on the front seat of the Cadillac. The top was down and the moon spilled over them as they rode, skimming gently but powerfully along the shore and the sound, like a strong rapid cloud travelling west. Nancy watched the point where the moon actually met the water. It was moving and still at once. She thought that it was glorious, in a messy sort of way. She would have liked to poke her head up out of the water right there. She could feel the water pouring back through her white-blond hair, her face slathering over with moonlight.

"If it hadn't been for that crazy rain," Bub kept saying, "I wouldn't have met her."

"Oh, shut up about that goofy rain," said Dennis.

"It was like being spit on from above," said Nancy.

The needle crept up to eighty or more, and when they had left the sound and were driving through the swamp Nancy shivered. They wrapped her in a lap robe from the back seat and turned the radio up loud.

It was since she got back, since she got back home from New Orleans, that her mother did not put on the thin voile afternoon dress anymore and serve iced tea to the neighbors on the back porch. Just yesterday, having nothing to do in the hot silence but hear the traffic stream by on the boulevard, and not wanting a suntan and

being certain the telephone would not ring, Nancy had taken some
lemonade over to Bernard Nattier, who was sick in bed with the
mumps. He and his mother had one room between them, over at
Mrs. Poultney's house, and they had stacks of magazines—the
Ladies' Home Journal, McCall's, Life, and *Time*—piled along the
walls. Bernard lay on a bunk bed pushed up under the window, in
all the close heat, with no breeze able to come in at all. His face was
puffed out and his eyes feverish. "I brought you some lemonade,"
said Nancy, but he said he couldn't drink it because it hurt his gums.
Then he smiled at her, or tried to—it must have hurt even to do
that, and it certainly made him look silly, like a cartoon of himself,
but it was sweet.

"I love you, Nancy," he said, most irresponsibly.

She thought she would cry. She had honestly tried to kill him
with those rocks and oyster shells. He knew that very well, and he,
from the moment he had seen her, had set out to make her life one
long torment, so where could it come from, a smile like that, and
what he said? She didn't know. From the fever, maybe. She said
she loved him, too.

Then, it was last night, just the night before, that her father had
got drunk and made speeches beginning "To think that a daughter
of mine . . ." Nancy had sat through it all crouched in the shadows
on the stair landing, in the very spot where the moss or old seaweed
back of the panelling smelled the strongest and dankest, and
thought of her mother upstairs, lying, clothed, straight out on the
bed in the dark, with a headache and no cover on and maybe the
roof above her melted away. Nancy looked down to where her father
was marching up to the donkey that said, "If you really want to look
like me—Just keep right on talking," and was picking it up and
throwing it down, right on the floor. She cried out, before she knew
it—"Oh!"—seeing him do the very thing she had so often meant to
do herself. Why had he? Why? Because the whiskey had run out on
him? Or because he had got too much of it again? Or from trying
to get in one good lick at everything there was? Or because the advice he loved so much seemed now being offered to him?

But the donkey did not break. It lay there, far down in the tricky
shadows; Nancy could see it lying there, looking back over its
shoulder with its big red grinning mouth, and teeth like piano keys,
still saying the same thing, naturally. Her father was tilting uncertainly down toward it, unable, without falling flat on his face, to

reach it. This made a problem for him, and he stood thinking it all
over, taking every aspect of it well into account, even though the
donkey gave the impression that not even with a sledgehammer
would it be broken, and lay as if on some deep distant sea floor, toward which all the sediment of life was drifting, drifting, forever
slowly down. . . .

Beirut! It was the first time she had remembered it. They had said
they would take her there, Dennis and Bub, and then she had forgotten to ask, so why think of it right now, on the street uptown,
just when she saw Rob Acklen coming along? She would have to see
him sometimes, she guessed, but what did Beirut have to do with it?

"Nancy Lewis," he said pleasantly, "you ran out on me. Why did
you act like that? I was always nice to you."

"I told them to tell you," she said. "I just went to ride around for
a while."

"Oh, I got the word, all right. About fifty different people saw
you drive off in that Cadillac. Now about a hundred claim to have.
Seems like everybody saw those two characters but me. What did you
do it for?"

"I didn't like those Skeltons, all those people you knew. I didn't like
those sorority girls, that Teenie and Cootie. You knew I didn't, but
you always took me where they were just the same."

"But the point is," said Rob Acklen, "I thought you liked me."

"Well, I did," said Nancy Lewis, as though it all had happened a
hundred years ago. "Well, I did like you just fine."

They were talking on the street still. There had been the tail of a
storm that morning, and the palms were blowing. There was a sense
of them streaming like green flags above the low town.

Rob took Nancy to the drugstore and sat at a booth with her. He
ordered her a fountain Coke and himself a cup of coffee. "What's
happened to you?" he asked her.

She realized then, from what he was looking at, that something
she had only half noticed was certainly there to be seen—her skin,
all around the edges of her white blouse, was badly bruised and
marked, and there was the purplish mark on her cheekbone she had
more or less powdered over, along with the angry streak on her neck.

"You look like you fell through a cotton gin," Rob Acklen continued, in his friendly way. "You're not going to say the rain over in
New Orleans is just scalding hot, are you?"

"I didn't say anything," she returned.

"Maybe the mosquitoes come pretty big over there," he suggested. "They wear boxing gloves, for one thing, and, for another—"

"Oh, stop it, Rob," she said and wished she was anywhere else.

It had all stemmed from the moment down in the French Quarter, over late drinks somewhere, when Dennis had got nasty enough with Bub to get rid of him, so that all of Dennis's attention from that point onward had gone exclusively to Nancy. This particular attention was relentless and direct, for Dennis was about as removed from any sort of affection and kindness as a human could be. Maybe it had all got boiled out of him; maybe he had never had much to get rid of. What he had to say to her was nothing she hadn't heard before, nothing she hadn't already been given more or less to understand from mosquitoes, people, life-in-general, and the rain out of the sky. It was just that he said it in a final sort of way—that was all.

"I was in a wreck," said Nancy.

"Nobody killed, I hope," said Rob.

She looked vaguely across at Rob Acklen with pretty, dark-blue eyes that seemed to be squinting to see through shifting lights down in the deep sea; for in looking at him, in spite of all he could do, she caught a glimmering impression of herself, of what he thought of her, of how soft her voice always was, her face like a warm flower.

"I was doing my best to be nice to you. Why wasn't that enough?"

"I don't know," she said.

"None of those people you didn't like were out to get you. They were all my friends."

When he spoke in this handsome, sincere, and democratic way, she had to agree; she had to say she guessed that was right.

Then he said, "I was having such a good summer. I imagined you were, too," and she thought, He's coming down deeper and deeper, but one thing is certain—if he gets down as far as I am, he'll drown.

"You better go," she told him, because he had said he was on his way up to Shreveport on business for his father. And because Bub and Dennis were back; she'd seen them drift by in the car twice, once on the boulevard and once in town, silenter than cloud, Bub in the back, with his knees propped up, reading a magazine.

"I'll be going in a minute," he said.

"You just didn't realize I'd ever go running off like that," Nancy said, winding a damp Coca-Cola straw around her finger.

"Was it the party, the one you said you wanted to give? You didn't have to feel—"

"I don't remember any party," she said quickly.

Her mother lay with the roof gone, hands folded. Nancy felt that people's mothers, like wallpapered walls after a hurricane, should not be exposed. Her father at last successfully reached the donkey, but he fell in the middle of the rug, while Nancy, on the stair landing, smelling seaweed, asked herself how a murderous child with swollen jaws happened to mention love, if love is not a fever, and the storm-driven sea struck the open reef and went roaring skyward, splashing a tattered gull that clutched at the blast—but if we will all go there immediately it is safe in the Dupré house, because they have this holy candle. There are hidden bone-cold lairs no one knows of, in rock beneath the sea. She shook her bone-white hair.

Rob's whole sensitive face tightened harshly for saying what had to come next, and she thought for a while he wasn't going to make it, but he did. "To hell with it. To absolute hell with it then." He looked stricken, as though he had managed nothing but damaging himself.

"I guess it's just the way I am," Nancy murmured. "I just run off sometimes."

Her voice faded in a deepening glimmer where the human breath is snatched clean away and there are only bubbles, iridescent and pure. When she dove again, they rose in a curving track behind her.

HARRY MARK PETRAKIS has published two novels, *Lion at My Heart* and *The Odyssey of Kostas Volakis*. His most recent book is a collection of short stories, *Pericles on 31st Street*. He has won a number of awards and lectures extensively, reading his stories to college and club audiences across the country. He is at work on a new novel, *A Dream of Kings*, scheduled for publication in 1966.

The Prison

H ARRY KLADIS met Alexandra when he was forty-five and she was forty. For twelve years he had worked with his father in their small candy store. She was a librarian at the neighborhood branch. He admitted to himself that she was not very pretty and a little older than he would have wished but he was drawn to her by the soft abundance of dark hair that she wore to her shoulders and by an air of shyness he suspected concealed loneliness as distressing as his own. One night after she had been coming into the candy store for almost three months, he mustered the courage and asked to take her out. He was so pleased when she accepted that he insisted she take three pounds of her favorite chocolate mints as a gift.

On their first date they walked for hours and talked endlessly. In the beginning they tried shyly to suggest they were accustomed to dating many others. After a while this posturing seemed foolish to both of them. He told her about a girl, handsome and raven-haired, that he had lost to a bolder man years before. She told him of a salesman, tall with sensitive eyes, who held her devotion until transferred to another territory he ceased to answer her letters. These melancholy recitals drew them together. They were delighted to find they both enjoyed concerts and chop suey with black pekoe tea and almond cookies. After a month of seeing each other several evenings a week they accepted with grateful happiness that they were in love.

Two weeks before the day scheduled for their wedding, Harry's

father died. Returning from an evening with Alexandra, Harry found
the old man in the back room of the store where he had suffered a
stroke while mixing a batch of fresh milk chocolate.

They recognized it would have been unseemly to marry so close
upon death and they delayed their wedding for a few months.
Harry wished to sell the store as soon as possible. He had studied
accounting some years before and considered taking additional
courses to qualify himself for that profession. But his mother insisted he keep the thin security of the store that was all her husband
had left to provide for her old age. The first weeks after the funeral
seemed merely to sharpen the blades of her sorrow.

"My father and I were all she ever cared for," Harry said to Alexandra. "He is gone now but she wonders what will happen to me if
I sell the store and cannot make a go of accounting."

"You will be a good accountant," Alexandra said. "I have my job
to help out. It will be better for your mother in the long run."

"I should have made the decision years ago," Harry said and he
was ashamed. "I never really cared for the store but I have let the
years slide by." He turned away to conceal his distress. "Just a while
longer," he said. "I don't want to press mama in her grief now. Just
a little longer."

But he could not make chocolates as well as his father and business fell off. The price he might have received for selling the store
declined as well. He worried and worked for longer hours. At the
end of six months from his father's death they postponed their wed-
ing once more.

His mother's continued despair confused him and made him un-
happy. They tried to include the old lady in the things they did but
she did not care for music and could not stand the sight or smell of
chop suey. In desperation to appease her relentless grief they spent
most of their evenings at home with her. She talked ceaselessly of
the past and of joining her husband in death to remove herself as
a burden on Harry. He spent the evening assuring her of his love
and devotion. The only moments he managed alone with Alexandra
were during the brief period when he walked her home. Then be-
deviled by the evening of his mother's lament, he had little to say.

He insisted that Alexandra attend the concerts alone. He remained
behind to listen to his mother stitch the bleak patches on the hours
before he could flee to bed.

"Sitting in with me instead of being out with her," his mother said and a long sigh came wracked from her flesh, "She must resent me and blame me for so much."

"She does not blame you for anything, Mama," Harry said. "She has never spoken a single word against you."

"I want you to marry," his mother said. "I want you to be happy." She looked in dismay at her son. "You were our only child. You are my life now. I would swear to die tonight if you thought I did not want your happiness."

"Stop it now," Harry said. "When Alexandra and I are married, you will live with us and we will look after you."

The old lady shook her head somberly. "You were two years old when your father's sister Sophoula died," she said. "The last ten years of her life she lived with us. I bathed her and fed her and cleaned up her slop. I would say my prayers at night and ask God to forgive me because I hated her on my back and wished her dead." She paused and with her dark dried fingers made her trembling cross. "There were nights I would hear her calling to me," she said. "I would hold my ears and make off I was asleep. And she would call in a voice like a bird for a long time." She bared her teeth in a harsh and cold smile. "My sins have come home to roost. I am the old woman now."

"What more can I say, Mama?" Harry asked. "As long as I live I will love you and look after you. And Alexandra will love you as I do."

The old lady looked at him silently for a long time. He felt himself reduced to the condition of a child unaware of reality and the grim shades of life. She rose slowly and heavily to her feet.

Harry kissed her goodnight with tenderness. For a moment she clung to him fiercely. He felt her fear of death and loneliness riot through his own flesh.

Winter passed into spring. The hours of daylight grew longer. From blossoming gardens in the park came the aroma of new flowers. Within the foliage of trees sounded the shrill-throated songs of birds. In the twilight the moths writhed their wings about the streetlamps. The young lovers whispered and laughed in the sheltered groves beyond the walk.

With the coming of spring, Harry and Alexandra felt their spirits rising. Sunday afternoons they spent looking for an apartment with an extra bedroom. They talked confidently of the future. The season filled them with new strength.

On the last Sunday in April they found a bright apartment not far from the park and only a few blocks from the library and candy store. Alexandra was enchanted with it but Harry could not subdue his apprehension. He could already feel the dark somber attendance of his mother. And closing their bedroom door at night would not shut out her brooding presence.

Afterwards they walked silently in the park. They passed old men with bony faces who sat on benches like withered roosters soaking up the sun, old men who bore the marks of neglect and impending death.

"We will take the apartment!" Harry spoke in a furious effort to break free. "We will go back and take it."

"You did not want it," Alexandra said quietly. "We have been searching for a place like that for weeks and when we found it you did not want it."

He fumbled helplessly for her hand and felt her slim-boned fingers against his palm. "In every room I could feel my mother," he said. "Like all the curtains were drawn and the shades pulled down."

"She cannot live alone," Alexandra said. "We have to work it out."

"She is sure we will come to hate her," he said. "Maybe she is right. I love her and feel a terrible pity for her. I love you too and I don't know what to do."

They paused before a deserted bench and sat down. He put his arm around her slim shoulders and drew her close.

"When I found you I had given up hope of love," she said quietly. "I had put that dream away like a flower pressed between the pages of a book." She moved her head slightly and he felt her breath against his throat. "Now I brush my hair as I did when I was a girl. Every mirror makes me realize I am no longer young. I want you to love me and find me beautiful. I want you to love me before I grow old."

"We will work things out," Harry said and for a moment tightly closed his eyes. "We won't lose each other. We will work things out."

Summer passed. The hours of daylight grew shorter. Dusk and dark advance as the autumn nights closed in. The earth stirred and waited for the winter.

His mother grew more feeble. She could not bear to be alone and in the afternoon had a neighbor woman help her to the store. She sat in a corner and watched Harry as he worked. In the evening the neighbor returned and took her home so that she could prepare Harry's supper. She sat watching him silently as he ate.

Afterwards he helped put her to bed. She was driven with fear that death would claim her while she slept so she delayed sleeping as long as possible, holding Harry's hand, and talking aimlessly of the past. There were moments when she looked at her son with a strange burning pity. "There is no answer for us on this earth," she said and made her cross. "God save you by taking me soon."

After she slept Harry went to his bed on the couch in the next room and lay awake for a long time. Finally weary and tormented by his thoughts, he fell asleep.

In December of that year Harry and Alexandra parted. They had been seeing each other less frequently as the weeks passed, each meeting marked by a silent grievance and rebuke. They were lonely away from one another and yet miserable when they were together. He made the suggestion, trying to hold back his tears, and she mutely agreed.

That night Harry did not go home. He knew his mother would be in terror at being alone but he remained all night in the store and mixed more chocolate than he would be able to use in months. He kept all the lights burning and tried furiously to keep busy. In the dawn when weariness finally overcame him, he sank down on a chair and lay his head on the table smelling of sweet chocolate. In that moment he envied his father who was dead.

For almost three years Harry did not see Alexandra. From an acquaintance he knew she still worked at the library. He was often tempted to walk by the library in the hope of catching a glimpse of her. He was afraid she might see him and this kept him away.

He saw her often in his dreams. Her thin mournful face and the long hair about her pale cheeks and her slim fingers quiet in her lap. In the morning he woke unrested and faced the day with a burden on his heart.

His mother grew a little stronger. Now that she had him to herself she made fewer demands upon him and let him alone. They never spoke of Alexandra.

He had always been careful about his diet but as time went on he ate as much as he wished and gained weight. When he shaved in the morning he was repelled at how suddenly he seemed to have aged. He was not yet fifty but he felt much older.

More and more did the pattern of his life assume the dimensions that had governed the last years of his father. He rose early and went to the store. He worked through the day and in the evening went home to eat the supper his mother prepared. Afterwards he sat and read the paper while she rocked silently in her old chair. When she was in bed he smoked a cigar as furtively as his father had done because she had always complained about the rank odor. He had trouble sleeping and after a while began using sleeping pills that a doctor prescribed.

In the beginning of the fourth year after he and Alexandra separated, his mother died. A cold had plagued her for several weeks. She ran a high fever and had to be moved to the hospital. The fever blazed up and down in spurts while she struggled fiercely to live. A priest came and dispensed the last rites. She died late one night in her sleep.

After the funeral Harry returned to the flat alone. He walked slowly about her bedroom. Every possession of hers, every article of clothing or spool of thread seemed to belong to someone he could hardly remember. He felt suddenly as if she had been dead for a long time.

He went for a walk. Without awareness of direction he found himself across the street from the library. In a panic that Alexandra might see him for the first time in three years on the day of his mother's funeral, he fled back home.

In the next few days he kept thinking about Alexandra. He yearned to go to her and yet shame kept him away. He studied himself in the mirror and mourned how seedy he had become. He determined desperately to diet again and brushed his hair in a way that concealed the growing patch of baldness.

After closing the store in the evening he detoured on his way home to pass the library. He stood hidden in the darkness of the small park across the street. When she came out and started to walk home he knew that he still loved her and had always loved her.

One night when he stood beneath the shadow of the trees a longing to talk to her overcame his shame and fear. When she emerged from the library he crossed the street and called out her name.

It was a strange moment. She did not seem surprised to find him there. He was stunned at the sight of her and the changes that three years had made. She looked much older than he remembered, the last traces of youth gone. He trembled knowing that he too had changed and that she might see her own ravages reflected in him.

They walked home together as they had done so many times in the past. He was careful not to walk too close beside her. For a block they were silent and then they spoke a little. She had become head librarian. He mentioned a concert he had attended a few months before.

They paused before her building. He was about to say goodnight and try and muster the courage to ask to see her again.

"Would you like some tea?" she asked quietly.

For a moment, choked by gratefulness, he could not speak. They walked slowly up the stairs. He sat in her small parlor while she heated water in the kitchen. Everything appeared the same. The rows of books and records in the corner, the photograph of her dead parents, the small plaster bust of Beethoven on the mantle. The room even retained the delicate scent of her powder and he leaned back slightly and closed his eyes. He felt for an overwhelming moment that he was back where he had always belonged.

She brought in the pot of tea and set the cups upon the small table. She poured carefully and filled a plate with a few almond cookies. He had not eaten them in years.

"Do you still like chop suey?" he asked gently.

She shook her head. "Not anymore," she said. Her hands, pale and slim-fingered, moved restlessly about the cups of fragrant tea.

"I don't care for it anymore either," he said. He was silent a moment, wondering if he had suggested too much.

When he finished his tea he rose slowly to his feet. He wanted to stay longer and yet was afraid to ask.

She brought him his coat. "You have gained weight," she said.

He fumbled hurriedly into the concealment of the coat. "I have started to diet again," he said.

"Your cheeks have no color," she said. "And you are growing bald."

He made a mute and helpless gesture with his hands.

"Do you find me changed?" she asked and a certain tightness had entered her voice.

"Hardly at all," he said quickly. He was sorry the moment he uttered that naked lie.

"Three years have passed," she said and the words came cold from her lips. "I was not young when you first met me. I am much older now."

"Alexandra," he felt a furious need to console her. "Alexandra," he drew a deep breath and then could not control the wild tumble of words. "Can you care a little for me again? Can you let me love you once more?"

She made a stiff and violent motion of her arm to silence him. He was shocked at the fury blazing suddenly in her eyes.

"Three years are two words," she said. "Two words easy to say. But three years are a thousand lonely nights and a thousand bitter cups of tea and a thousand withered flowers."

She raised her hand and struck him hard across the cheek. "For the thousand lonely nights!" she said and the words came in flame. "For the thousand bitter cups of tea! For the thousand withered flowers!" She struck again more fiercely than before.

He turned then and fled. He went quickly out the door, down the stairs to the sidewalk, across the street into the darkened doorway of a closed store. He stood there seeing the dark reflection of his face in the glass and felt his heart as if it were about to bust. He began to cry, the tears running down his stinging cheeks. And he did not know in that terrible moment of despair whether he was crying for Alexandra or for himself.

VERA RANDAL was born in New York City, was educated in New York schools and at Connecticut College. She and her two children live in New York. Her short story "Waiting for Jim" was included in Martha Foley's Best American Short Stories of 1964. Sections from *The Inner Room*, her first novel, have appeared in *The New Yorker* and *The Saturday Evening Post*.

Alice Blaine

SHUT up! Jesus God, can't you shut up awhile?" the voice said. It was a loud voice—solid, rough, heavy. "Shut up, now, Miss Parrington. It's three o'clock in the morning."

For a moment, I thought it had smothered the other voice—the slim reed voice—by its weight. I stared into the deep red that was the light coming through my closed lids, and waited for the red to darken to the black of sleep. The reed voice began again, soft, clear, tireless. "One, two, three, four, five, six, seven," and on and on. I built a little white fence in the redness and watched tiny lambs leaping over it. "Twenty-two, twenty-three, twenty-four . . ." The lambs were soft gray, with their coats tightly curled and with pink ribbons tied around their necks. They were like the toy lamb John bought Jenny eight years ago, like the toy lamb before Jenny hugged and chewed and loved it into a state of near unrecognizability. "Sixty-seven, sixty-eight, sixty-nine . . ." The little white fence was gone, and I saw Jenny on her cot—dark lashes curling against rosy skin, one arm flung back over her head, the other clutching the limp, battered lamb to her chest. "Eighty-four, eighty-five, eighty-six . . ." Surely it wasn't time to get up yet. Jenny and Pete weren't awake. Even the baby was quiet. "Ninety-nine, a hundred, a hundred and one . . ." And I was tired. God, I was so tired.

"Quit it now, Miss Parrington," the heavy voice said. "Keep that up much longer, you'll have me as nuts as you are."

The counting stopped. Through the silence came the sound of running water, and anxiety was layered on anxiety, a child's tower of blocks mounting shakily. Had I left a faucet on in the kitchen or bathroom? Perhaps Jenny or Pete had gone to get a drink. "John," I said, choking on the thick gag of sleep that stuck in my throat. "John, wake up."

"One, two, three, four, five, six," the reed voice began again. "Seven, eight, nine . . ."

"John," I said, more firmly this time. I heard my voice echo strangely—*John, John, John*, ever softer and smaller, until it was gone. A dark nucleus of fear sprang tentacles, and I shut my eyes tighter, until my forehead wrinkled and ached with strain. Still the tentacles grew, thin black threads weaving and winding inside me, crawling damp down my neck and binding my icy clenched hands.

The reed voice, interrupted, started over with cool, even persistence. "One, two, three, four, five . . ."

"John." I reached out my arm, moving it sidewise to touch John, to wake John. My knuckles touched a flat, hard, unyielding surface. There was the sound of running water. I was in the water. "John!" I shouted. This was no nightmare from which I would wake. "John!" I screamed. And I opened my eyes to the nightmare from which I knew, with a knowledge deeper and surer than words, I would not wake. *John! John!* My voice bounded from the high white ceiling and the white-tiled walls, weaving itself into a mad fabric of sound. *John!*

"Now, Mrs. Blaine, don't you go getting started with that John stuff," she said. She was standing over me, towering above the canvas sheet that covered the tub where I lay—a massive jailer of a woman in a blue cotton uniform, her heavy arms mottled red and white. "Miss Parrington's been counting for over an hour. Don't you go getting started, too."

"John," I said tentatively, hopelessly now.

"John's not here," she said. Her cheekbones were wide and jutting under oily skin. Her straw-colored hair was pulled up from her scalp and fastened in a tight little knot on top of her head. "There's nobody here but us—just you and me and them." With a meaty hand, she gestured toward the three other tubs in the room. "Next thing, we'll have Mrs. Haggerty singing 'Rockaby Baby.' You go back to sleep. Hear?"

Some part of me, I observed in a fashion that was almost detached, had been here before in this huge white room with the tiled walls and the running water. Some massive inner sponge had absorbed detail upon detail: the tubs covered with canvas, the cut-out holes through which heads came like strange growths, the feel of the canvas sling under me, the doorless cubicles—toilets—against one wall, the line of washbasins against the other. It was familiar, all of it—blond head to my right, soft wispy brown in front of me, and next to it the fourth head, darker brown, curling. Through a large, open archway in the uppermost part of the wall I could see into the next room, see the line of narrow, high cots on wheels. All familiar, and my terror receded bit by bit until there was only the dark nucleus—also familiar. "John!" I shouted almost cheerfully. *John! John! John!*

She bent down until her flat red face was close to mine, and I read her name, embroidered white on the pocket of her uniform. "Miss Jorgensen." But of course it was Miss Jorgensen. The name, too, was in a tiny cell of my inner sponge, seen before, heard before, correct. "Correct," I said, my voice curiously loud in my ears. *Correct, Correct, Correct.* I could see the coarse, oily pores of her skin, and the blackheads in her wide, flat, almost bridgeless nose. Also correct. "Right, Miss Jorgensen," I said. "Check and double check, right and correct. O.K."

The head sprouting from the canvas-covered tub on my right turned, the head with its gleaming spun-gold hair and its exquisite, cut-glass face. The counting girl. I sought a name in my sponge but couldn't find it. "Hi, friend!" I shouted across the stretch of white-tiled floor that separated us. "How you doing?"

Her eyes stared, fixed, seemingly unseeing. Then she closed them, opened them, blinked several times, and moved her finely shaped mouth soundlessly.

"Can't hear you, chum!" I yelled. My voice bounced from the wall to greet me like an old friend. *Chum! Chum! Chum!* my voice said. And very softly, *Chum.*

"Be quiet, Mrs. Blaine," Miss Jorgensen said, her face still close to mine. "You want to create a ruckus like last night?" Her breath was hot against my cheek and foul-smelling, and her face seemed to be swelling like some monstrous balloon, inflated from a hidden source. "Get yourself wrapped in cold sheets again. You wouldn't like that much, would you?"

"Why don't you just go to hell?" I yelled into the swelling balloon face. "You'd be in proper company there, sister."

"You'd better watch yourself, Mrs. Blaine," Miss Jorgensen said, grinning.

I moved my legs up and down in the water a couple of times, experimentally, and stirred up a fine churn. "Go to hell."

The soft wispy brown head in front of me twisted until I could see about three-quarters of the face—a monochrome, eyes slightly darker than hair, sweet-curving pinkish-tan mouth. "Ah, now we have Mrs. Haggerty with us," Miss Jorgensen said. "Isn't that nice? Isn't that just the nicest thing?"

"Good morning," I said, and, seeking a name, this time I found one. "Good morning, Jan. How's the water in your private pool?"

"Same as usual," she said, sweet-faced, sweet-voiced. "Damp."

"That's a shame," I said. "Maybe Miss Jorgensen will fix it. Or go to hell. Or sit down."

The balloon face hovered above mine a moment longer, then floated upward as Miss Jorgensen straightened, turned, and settled herself in her chair under the wall light. "Don't you two start cutting up, now," she said, her voice thudding, heavy with finality.

"Wouldn't think of it," I said, listening for echoes. I tried it an octave higher, and a little louder. "Wouldn't think of it. Would you, Jan?"

"I'd think of it," Jan said. "Sure, I'd think of it. Why shouldn't I think of it?"

"I don't know," I said in my new, high voice. "Maybe you should think of it."

"I can't," Jan said sadly, and her sweet, upcurving mouth drooped. "My head's all thick inside."

The sadness in her voice floated toward me and settled, a pale-gray cloud. "We could sing!" I shouted through the cloud. "How about if we sang a little something?"

"We could sing," Jan said.

Miss Jorgensen sighed vastly, her whole huge self heaving in the straight-backed wooden chair. "You could be quiet, both of you, like Miss Rogers over there. She never carries on like you do."

I looked over at the fourth tub, next to Jan's, at the damply curling brown head motionless against the canvas sheet, the upside-down face soft and flushed. "God help us." The words wrote themselves across the inside of my skull in heavy black letters. "God help us.

God help us." I read them twice through, and then blinked hard to make them go away. "O.K., then. Let's sing."

" 'Onward, Christian Soldiers,' " Jan announced in a small-girl voice—a child before the weekly school assembly, pleased, shy, a little frightened.

"Great!" I shouted. "Real rousing and great. You start her off, O.K.?" From my right came a soft, mewing sound. The golden girl was watching me, moving her lips, whimpering. "What does she want?" I yelled at Jan. "She's saying something, but I can't make it out."

"Who?" Jan said vaguely.

"Her." I jerked my head sidewise. "I can't seem to remember her name."

Jan knit her tan brows briefly, then nodded above the flat stretch of canvas. "Binnie," she said. "Her name's Binnie."

"Oho!" I said. "Well, what does she want?" I listened again to the whimper, rising in volume. "What's up, Binnie girl?"

Jan had twisted about, her chin resting on the canvas. "Binnie," she said. "Binnie, it's me. It's Janet."

The golden head jerked erect. The whimpering stopped. "Janet," Binnie said in a cool, clear little voice.

"That's right," Jan said encouragingly. "Janet. Don't you like 'Onward, Christian Soldiers'? We could sing something else, couldn't we, Alice?"

"Sure," I said. "Sure, we could sing something else."

"You could be quiet," Miss Jorgensen said from her chair under the light, the words thumping. "You could go to sleep."

"It's not that," Binnie said, her beautiful face expressionless, the pupils black in her light-gray eyes. "I have to go to the bathroom." Pink tinged the white cheeks.

"Oh," Janet said. And, to Miss Jorgensen, relaying a message, "She has to go to the bathroom."

"Let her go, then. Who's stopping her?" Miss Jorgensen's fat pink tongue crawled forward between her teeth and licked at her lower lip.

"How the hell do you expect her to get out of that tub?" I yelled.

"Who expects anything?" Miss Jorgensen's voice was softer, with a remote quality in it.

"She said she'd hit me if I messed in my bed again," Binnie said hoarsely. "I have to get up."

"Get her out of that tub!" I shouted.

Miss Jorgensen was silent, her tongue moving from side to side over her lip, one hand stroking her upper thigh rhythmically.

"You bitch." Jan's voice was too sweet, too gentle.

"Bitch!" I yelled. "Bloody bitch. Get her out of there."

Miss Jorgensen did not appear to hear us. Her face was reddening. Slowly her tongue moved back and forth over her lower lip, slowly her hand stroked her heavy thigh, outlined now under blue cotton. She was watching Binnie, her eyes remote and foggy, staring at that beautiful head held upright on its stalk-straight neck. Binnie's head started to shake in denial, but for another moment her face remained impassive. Then it twisted, contorted, her head fell briefly forward and then back against the canvas. "One, two, three," Binnie said, eyes closed. "Four, five, six, seven, eight . . ."

Fury gathered until I was swollen with it. Jan had turned away, closing her soft brown eyes. "Eighteen, nineteen, twenty," Binnie counted. "Twenty-one, twenty-two, twenty-three . . ." My mouth was dry with rage, and my throat ached with it. "Get me a drink of water," I said. "I want a drink."

Miss Jorgensen's eyes cleared and came back into focus. Her face paled a little. She shook herself all over like some large animal after a bath. "Such a fuss," she said complacently. "The water's changing in those things all the time."

"I'm thirsty," I said. "I want some water."

Miss Jorgensen leaned back in her chair. "Go to sleep."

"I want some water."

"O.K., O.K." Miss Jorgensen rose wearily.

She walked past me, a moving blue mountain, toward the water cooler that I knew without looking stood in the corner, at a sharp angle from the top of my head. "One, two, three," Binnie counted. "Four, five, six . . ." Jan lay quiet, eyes closed, upper teeth biting into lower lip, and in the fourth tub the girl with the curling brown hair remained motionless, a statue carved of flesh. I sucked at the insides of my dry mouth. At first there was nothing, but then the saliva came, collecting in a warm little pool under my tongue, rising to the roof of my mouth. I waited, tense, listening for the sounds of Miss Jorgensen's returning footsteps. "Eighteen, nineteen, twenty," Binnie said. "Twenty-one, twenty-two, twenty-three . . ."

Miss Jorgensen was back, standing above me, bending toward me, a cone-shaped paper cup in her hand. She bent lower and lower until there was only that huge, swelling red obscenity of a face. Only that face, the face of some monstrous ugliness bigger than all of us, stronger than all of us. And I spat.

"Forty-four, forty-five, forty-six," Binnie said. "Forty-seven . . ." My spittle was on Miss Jorgensen's face, just under her left eye, rolling down her round, reddening cheek. Miss Jorgensen's eyes were gleaming, sharp, brilliant with fury. She reached into her pocket for a handkerchief and wiped her cheek. Then, rising a little, she lifted one heavy hand close to my cheek and drew it back, watching, calculating the distance. Inside me, fear crouched, cowering, but I held my head rigid. Binnie was counting off the seconds: "Sixty-one, sixty-two, sixty-three . . ."

Miss Jorgensen's uplifted arm was poised, a punitive club. "Sixty-nine, seventy, seventy-one," Binnie counted.

Miss Jorgensen's arm trembled and dropped to her side. "They might just believe you." She laughed—a thick, unamused sound in the back of her throat. "Lunatic," she said contemptuously, standing over me. "Crazy, raving lunatic."

Gray morning light came through the two windows, one on either side of the washbasins that lined one wall. It was morning, then. But what morning? In front of me, Jan lay in one tub, asleep, and in the other the curly-haired girl remained, frozen. Binnie was gone, though. A newcomer, with dark-red hair and a very white face, was in her tub. Miss Jorgensen was gone, too, replaced by a rosy little student nurse, her blue-and-white striped uniform covered with a starched white apron, a wide-winged bird of a cap perched on her head, and her stubby-fingered child hands folded primly in her lap. What day? Time, dough in a bowl, rose, doubling, trebling in bulk, and I was in the middle of the swelling, yeasty mass—lost. "What day is it?" I asked.

"Thursday," the little student said. "How are you, Mrs. Blaine?"

Thursday. I stretched in the tepid water, wiggling my toes, and a thought, a shiny bright firefly, glowed and was gone. "O.K.," I said. "Waterlogged."

She looked at her watch. "You'll be getting out in a bit."

"Goodo. Great. Also hurrah." My firefly was back, this time with friends. They flickered, danced about in a frenzy, and formed themselves into a question mark, complete with dot at bottom. "What Thursday?"

"Gee, I'm not sure, Mrs. Blaine. The fourteenth. Maybe the fif-teenth."

"Oho. Maybe the fifteenth." I considered the high white ceiling. I stared lengthily at Jan's wispy hair. I glanced at the red-headed girl in the tub next to me. "Where's Binnie?"

"Miss Parrington? She's in bed, sleeping."

"Right," I said. "O.K. What's the redhead's name?"

"Mrs. Barr. You remember, Mrs. Blaine. She's been on the hall quite a while."

"Right," I said. "Mrs. Barr. Kate." Thursday, the fifteenth. Maybe the fourteenth. But time moved forward, not backward. At least, time used to move forward, not backward. The girl was a bit off on her dates. It should be—what? The fifteenth of what? "Which fifteenth?"

"I beg your pardon, Mrs. Blaine," the girl said. "Which fifteenth?"

"Month. Which month?"

"It's July, Mrs. Blaine," she said.

"July?" I laughed, somewhat uneasily. "Look, kiddo, you can't just dispose of a couple of months like that. If this is July, what, pre-cisely, happened to June, and a sizable slice of May?"

"You've been ill, Mrs. Blaine. You're getting better now."

"Ill? Me? It's John who's been ill, youngster." It's John who's been ill. John. John. My head was filling with fog—murky, gray green.

"You've been ill."

I was moving through fog, blind with it. John. Blind with it, deaf with it, dumb with it, hands outstretched, groping.

"But you're better now. You're doing just fine now."

I was falling over the edge, into a great nothingness. I closed my eyes, and I was falling, and my stomach was falling faster than the rest of me, and I was going to be sick. I heard a retching, gagging sound, and that was me, about to be sick.

"You're going to be all right, Mrs. Blaine. You're really much bet-ter than you were."

I opened my mouth and gulped warm, humid air.

"Honest, Mrs. Blaine."

"Honest, kiddo?" I looked at her. She was standing at the side of the tub, incredibly young, with her skin soft and pink as a baby's, and the whites of her eyes very clear, very white. And I had a sud-den vision of myself, seen—when?—in the narrow strip of glass above the line of washbasins, a hollow-cheeked creature, tall, gaunt, with wild black hair strangely streaked with gray, and eyes red-veined, slightly mad but undeniably mine. "You've been here before, haven't you?"

"Yes," she said. "I've been on Four for almost a week."

"Four?"

"It's—" She hesitated, then continued. "It's the disturbed hall."

The disturbed hall? A boulder loomed in my path. I examined it briefly, and skirted around it. "I'm afraid I don't remember your name."

"Johnson," she said. "Susie Johnson."

"I used to be pretty good on names. Now I'm not sure I know my own."

"That's just the shock treatments, Mrs. Blaine. Everyone has that trouble. You don't have to worry about it any."

"Everyone." I looked at her, and it seemed incredible that anyone could be that young, unlined, untouched. "How old are you, youngster? Miss Johnson."

"Eighteen."

"Eighteen. Well, I've got ten years on you. That is, if I haven't lost a year or two in this madhouse." Madhouse—the word had slipped out from behind tightly locked doors. All right, then, I thought wearily. All right, all right.

"You haven't lost a year."

"Good," I said. "O.K." Jan was awake again, turning, smiling—good old friend, old Jan. "Greetings, Janet," I said.

"Thank you," Jan said. "Good morning."

"Jim-dandy morning." It was better with Jan awake. "I was going to tell Miss Johnson something. She's eighteen."

"Is she?" Jan said. "That's nice."

"So I was going to tell her the hell with it. Might take her years to figure it out for herself. To hell with it, Miss Johnson."

"To hell with what, Mrs. Blaine?"

"With it," I said, enthusiastic now. "Don't you think to hell with it, Jan?"

"Yes," Jan said. "I think to hell with it. I think maybe we're in it. Hell, I mean."

"Nope," I said. "We're in another, very similar but not identical, place. What's the name of it, Miss Johnson?"

"Woodlands, Mrs. Blaine. It's the shock that makes you forget."

"Yeah," I said. "Woodlands. Woodlands, Jan lamb. Inmates of. That's where we are."

"Same thing," Jan said, yawning widely.

"No, ducko," I said, and I was about to explain that it was merely similar when Jan's head jerked forward.

They were bringing a girl into the next room, a skinny, short girl in a white hospital gown that flapped open in the back. Her almost skeletal body had gone limp, as if in protest, and two student nurses were half pulling, half carrying her. "Let me go! Let me go! Let me go!" she was screaming in a thin, high, not quite human voice. A tall, lean nurse followed them, moving across the room with swift competence. The nurse moved out of sight. The students pulled the gown off the girl, and she was framed in the archway, under the brilliant ceiling light—naked, emaciated, with her pelvic bones jutting sharp, and her legs sticks with round, swollen knees. "Let me go! Let me go!" she screamed, writhing feebly between the two stocky students.

The nurse was back in view, in her hands a sheet dripping on the white tiled floor. I shivered, remembering with my flesh the inescapable icy wetness. They were surrounding her now, the three of them, binding her, mummylike, lifting her onto one of the high wheeled cots. "Let me go!" she screamed, a bound animal, immobile under the shining light, only her head moving frantically from side to side.

"She's starved," Jan said. "God, she can't weigh more than sixty or seventy pounds."

"She's starving herself," Miss Johnson said. "She's sick."

I lay in the water, watching the white, competent nurse walk briskly away, followed by one of the students, watching the second student settle herself on a high white stool next to that twisting, tortured head. The head was thrashing from one side to the other and back again, over and over. Then the head was centered, still, and the body rose, resting on head and feet, curving upward, fixed in a thin arc of anguish. And I remembered when Jenny was born and I was lying on a high wheeled table, bound down, screaming into a black cone that covered my face. A voice was saying, "Take it easy, now. It's almost over." I was screaming into the blurry blackness. "Take it easy," the voice said. I could feel my body rising from the table, and my insides were being ripped to bloody bits.

I could feel myself curving, arching in the tepid water. "Take it easy, Mrs. Blaine," Miss Johnson said.

Somewhere someone was screaming, "I can't stand it! I can't!"
And then the words blurred and there was only the scream.

The room was tiny, the walls pale powdery blue, the floor black
asphalt tile, the ceiling tan dotted squares, some sort of soundproof
material. I sat up and swung my legs over the side of the cot,
a tightly webbed affair, metal legs cemented down, the mattress thin,
hard, leather-covered. I stood up with the tile cool against my bare
feet and paced the area, length and width. Vaguely, a childhood
game returned to me. "You may take six giant steps, Alice," I told
myself. "May I?" I asked myself cagily, remembering the rules of the
game just in time. "Yes," I told myself. "Yes, you may." Six giant
steps took me to a small square window at the far end of my cell. I
looked out through the double-paned glass into a courtyard, deeply,
lushly green with summer, splashed here and there with clumps of
flowers, red and yellow. It was July. Someone had told me it was July.
I was aware abruptly that I was naked except for a short white
hospital gown open in the back, and, reaching behind, I clutched at
the bottom edges in sudden embarrassment. I turned then and
walked to the other end of the room; this, too, had a small window
of double-paned glass. Through it I could see a section of the black-
floored, white-walled corridor. On a table against the wall, Binnie
sat, golden, cross-legged, clad in the same scanty fashion as myself.
She was swaying up and back, gently and rhythmically. Her long yellow hair was a glory. Her lips were moving as she swayed.
"Binnie!" I yelled. "Hey, Binnie!" I banged at the door with my
palms and then my knuckles, and winced with the pain. I looked at
my hands. They were red front and back, and the knuckles looked
raw. There was a brown scab on my right hand. I must have been
hammering at the door before, hammering at great length, but I
couldn't remember. I turned away—away from the corridor, away
from Binnie—and I walked the short distance to the window, turned,
walked, paced the cell floor.
"It must be hell to be caged," John said to me once. "It must be
hell." We were sitting on a bench in the Central Park Zoo, eating
peanuts we'd bought from a vender, throwing one occasionally to a
bright-eyed squirrel who had joined us. In front of us, the hyena
paced, a mangy, gray, nervous creature, moving endlessly across the
width of its cage, keeping close to the bars, eyes fixed on the concrete floor, dreaming God knows what dreams of freedom lost. "We

ought to get him out," John said. "Christ, someone ought to get him
out."

"Yes," I said. "Someone ought."

John's hair flamed orange in the summer sun. His face was all flat
planes and angles, a prism face, changing with each shift of position,
each passing shadow. "It must be hell to be caged," he said. I could
feel him tense next to me, leaning forward slightly, following with
his eyes the up-and-back movements of the hyena. "It must be hell."

"Mmm," I said. I was tense, too, watching, swaying a little from
side to side. Part of me was pacing with that mangy animal, up and
back, up and back. I stood suddenly, holding out a hand to John,
"Let's run," I said. "Let's climb a tree. Let's go rowing."

"O.K." John stood beside me, skinny and very tall, so tall that I
felt almost small next to him. He smiled down at me, and his eyes
were soft and brown and beautiful. "Let's walk. Let's find a place.
O.K.?"

"O.K.," I said. We wandered through the Park that afternoon as
we had wandered all that sun-drenched, golden summer. And we
found a place, very quiet and hidden and green. Afterward, I lay
there watching the leaves make shadowy patterns on John's shirt.
I was eighteen that summer. Just eighteen.

Six giant steps. You may take six giant steps to the window that
will not open, Alice, six giant steps to the door that will not open,
Alice. God, God, God. I sat on the cot with its legs cemented into
the floor, and I stared at the floor, and then I twisted off the bed
and knelt, bare-kneed, on the floor. God, holy, suffering God. Once,
there was a God to whom I used to pray—a gentle, bleeding God.
I knelt long hours at the side of another bed, our bed. Only let this
war be over and John be all right. Only let John be all right. I had a
thin gold ring then that cut into my finger when I pressed my hands
together. Only let John be all right. I looked again at my hand, my
naked, raw-knuckled, ringless hand, my lost hand that was a piece
of my lost self.

There was the sound of keys jangling, the sound of a door opening,
and I rose, clutching the hospital gown in the back, reddening for
the indecent shortness of it. One of the young doctors stood just
inside my cell, one of the blurring bunch of brown-suited, tweed-
suited, fair-haired, dark-haired young men, nameless, sometimes
faceless young men who had been flickering in and out of view, half

caught by a broken camera, projected on a misshapen screen. "My ring," I said. "Where's my ring?"

This one was in gray flannel, pale, with heavy lemon-colored hair and thick, soft curving lips. "Good morning, Mrs. Blaine," he said, his voice sweet and cold as Italian ice. "Your ring's quite safe. You'll get it back when you're better." A small, compact Oriental-looking nurse stood just in back of him, silent and watchful. "How are you feeling?"

"Jim-crack dandy." I yanked my mouth into a grin. "Just great. Where are my clothes?"

"You won't be needing them this morning."

"I won't?" Curiosity twinned with terror, and I abandoned them both.

"No," he said. "Not this morning."

An obese young girl, her arms and legs dripping with flesh, and her face white and puffy and sullen under greasy black hair, appeared in the doorway, stepped inside, and stood next to the nurse. She was wearing a beltless cotton sack of a dress, not quite clean, and dirty tennis shoes with open, dragging laces. "It all stinks," she said. "Christ, it stinks."

"Now, Miss Rich," the nurse said flatly, indifferently. "You don't want to go on like that."

The blond young man turned to the nurse. "I think Mrs. Blaine might walk around a bit," he said. He had an immaculate white handkerchief in his jacket pocket, and he was blurring, blurring until there was only the handkerchief, and an image arose, superimposing itself on the cool blond young man. My father was there—gray suit, white handkerchief. My father was there telling me to go and get a cup of coffee.

"It stinks as much out there as it does in here," Miss Rich said.

"It's the smell of death," I said. "Like a filthy animal being sick in a corner."

Miss Rich smiled a yellow-toothed smile in the middle of puffy whiteness. "It sure does stink."

"All right, now, ladies," the compact, almond-eyed nurse said. And we were walking into the corridor, the blond young man—or was it my father?—Miss Rich, myself. The nurse came last, stopping to lock the door with one of the keys that hung in a bunch from a rope tied round her waist. The white walls stretched long, broken on one side by windowed cell doors, on the other by arches, openings to the room with the tubs and the cots on wheels. Student nurses, blue-and-white splotches against the black floor and white paint, lounged about, strolled in low-heeled shoes, into focus and then out. I dug my knuckles hard into my eyes, looked again, and there was Binnie, beautiful Binnie, still cross-legged on the wooden table, still rocking. "Hi, Binnie," I said.

She looked up without stopping her backward, forward movement. Her eyes flickered with faint recognition, her lips parted slightly, closed again, and she was gone, buried somewhere in that beautiful rocking body. I wanted to cry. "Sissies cry," John used to say scornfully when we were little kids. I could see him again, my red-headed idol, two years older than I was, smarter than anyone, my brother's best friend. And I could hear his high, strong voice. "Sissies cry."

"It stinks, huh?" Miss Rich said.

"Right," I said. "You bet."

She was standing close to me, almost directly in front, smelling of sweat and old dirt, with a thick growth of black hair on her arms and bare legs, and fuzz on her upper lip, like an adolescent boy. Her eyes were small and dark and sunken, and the flesh of her cheeks swelled almost to her lower lids. "I've been here a year," she said proudly. "Anything you want to know about this stinking dump, you just ask me."

"Right," I said. "I'll do that." It was then that I noticed the two little holes, one on either side of her head, healed-over indentations. My hands rose in panic to my own head. Had they hacked my brain, too? I felt slowly, carefully, moving the tips of my fingers from my cheekbones upward to the hairline.

"Before that, I was in high school. I was one smart girl," Miss Rich said.

"Yes." I dropped my hands to my sides.

"You just ask me. Ask me anything."

"O.K."

"You want to know where your friend is?"

"Friend?"

"Janet. Your friend Janet."

"Yes," I said. "O.K. Where's my friend Janet?"

"There," Miss Rich said triumphantly, jerking her heavy, butchered head to the right. "There she comes."

And there Jan came, walking down the corridor in a hospital gown and canvas slippers, one arm outstretched, hand moving along the wall, as though she was having difficulty keeping her balance. "See?" Miss Rich said. "You just ask me. I'm one smart girl."

"You are that," I said.

"Know why none of you have any clothes this morning?" She shifted her sunken eyes swiftly from Binnie to Janet to me.

"Why?"

"Shock this morning." She grinned her yellow grin, then she turned away, shouting over her shoulder, "You just ask me."

A lounging student nurse moved from her place against the wall. "Going somewhere, Miss Rich?"

"To hell," Miss Rich said, lumbering down the corridor, a clumsy, shapeless animal, with a crisp, tiny-waisted, blue-dressed girl walking firmly and evenly beside her. The long hall filled suddenly with a wild imitation of laughter. "To hell!" Miss Rich shouted.

Shock. We were going to shock. Terror rose, wave upon icy wave, and I was shaking with it, standing there with my back pressed against the locked door of my powder-blue cell. No one to turn to, no place to run to, nowhere to hide. Across the narrow corridor, Binnie sat, cross-legged, rocking. To my left, a dozen or more students roamed about, seemingly unheeding but quick, I remembered bitterly—quick and strong with the strength of numbers. To my right, still more students wandered, bright-blue clusters of them. It seemed that they were multiplying in amoebalike fashion until the hall was thick with them, its entire length pockmarked blue.

Jan was groping her way closer, her hand against the wall, and her wispy hair all in points over her forehead, like a wild woods creature. I could see her pale-brown eyes. I could see the black fear in their depths. "I'm scared, Alice," Jan said in a very small, trembling voice.

I fought my way desperately to the surface of my own terror. "It's O.K., kiddo," I said. "It'll be O.K." But my lungs were full of it, and my mouth was sour with the taste of it, and my voice was an alien voice.

"This time they'll kill me. I know," Jan said. I could feel her hand cold and wet on my forearm. "I don't want to die." The black fear in the depths of her eyes was growing now, turning the pale brown darker, casting strange shadows over the sweet, soft-curving young face.

I had seen this fear before, in another pair of eyes—brown eyes flecked with gold, John's eyes. On the morning of that day, three of us were standing in another corridor, another black-floored, white-walled corridor that smelled of Lysol and soap and alcohol and, faintly, of ether—an ugly clean smell to mask all the ugly dirty smells of sickness and death. My father was there—white pocket handkerchief, sharply creased trousers, my tall, cool, tidy father—and another man, too. The new doctor, the specialist, a short, round, spectacled little man, bald, staring at the floor in silent corroboration of a look on my father's face, a slight pressing together of the lips, a slight pinching of the nostrils. Nothing really, but enough. I leaned back against the corridor wall, the palms of my hands pressed flat against it. "Well?" I said. "What, Dad?" But I knew. I had read the encyclopedia the night before, under "B," "Blood," under "Blood, diseases of the."

My father made a soft, moist, throat-clearing sound. "You know what, Alice."

"Yes." The wall against which I was leaning seemed to be tilting backward. My father's fingers dug sharply into my shoulder, and the wall righted itself. "How long?"

His fingers were hard and strong. A nerve was jerking at the corner of his eye. "Tell her how long, Doctor."

The little round man raised his eyes from the floor, toy eyes behind thick lenses. "Four weeks. Six. Maybe eight."

"No," I said, a single, jagged, bleeding syllable.

"I'm afraid yes." He shrugged plump shoulders. "We'll do what we can. Unfortunately, there's not much to do." Again plump shoulders rose and fell. "I'm sorry."

"No," I said.

"Listen to me, Alice," my father said, and his fingers were pressing into my flesh.

"If you'll excuse me." The little round man turned away, then back again. "I'm sorry." And then he was moving down the corridor, walking almost noiselessly, with his arms sticking out from his round body and his bald head gleaming pink.

"I can't stand it," I said numbly.

"You're in good company," my father said. "Many of us can't stand it." His hand dropped from my shoulder. "Somehow we stand it. Somehow."

"I cannot."

"A man lives only once," my father said. "A man dies only once.

Perhaps," he said hesitantly, "perhaps for this little time we should think of this, of him. And afterward—"

We walked side by side the couple of dozen steps to John's room, I on boneless legs that it seemed must give way. "Do you want me to go in with you?" my father said.

I shook my head. "Does he know?"

"I think he knows."

I pushed open the wood-framed canvas half door. John was lying there, whiter than the sheet. It was as if some monstrous vampire had sucked him dry of life. His left arm was strapped to a board, and dark blood was dripping, drop after drop, down from an inverted bottle, down through long rubber tubing, into a vein in his wrist.

I sat on a wooden chair next to his bed. John opened his eyes slowly, as if with great effort. "Hi, Alice," he said. He tried to smile. I could see how hard he was trying to smile. "Hi, John." And I saw his eyes with the golden flecks gone. I saw the black fear.

"How are the kids?"

"They're O.K.," I said. "Mother is taking real great care of them." I grinned with stiff lips. "They're even learning table manners."

"I'd like to see them."

"You'll see them. You'll come home soon and see them."

"I want to see them here."

"O.K." Somehow, without willing to do so, I had slid off the chair and was on my knees with my head bent and my mouth touching John's upturned palm. And I was screaming my single bloody syllable inside my skull, "No! No! No!" over and over again. After a while, I raised my head. John's eyes were closed. I could see the pale-blue lines of veins on his almost transparent lids. I could see the tears seeping beneath his orange lashes.

Through the timeless afternoon the blood dripped, drop after drop, and it stained his lips and cheeks pale pink. And inside me unshed tears were dripping, drop after drop, in time with that dark, useless blood.

"All right, ladies. Let's go now," the lean nurse said briskly. We had been edged somehow to the end of the corridor, edged or led or dragged, we in the short hospital gowns. We were surrounded on three sides—the first a locked door, the second a short stretch of wall, the third a solid line of students. Before us was the archway into the huge white room with its line of wheeled cots. Jan stood next to me, quivering, cringing against the wall. She slipped her cold wet hand into mine. "Let's go, ladies." The lean nurse stood close to the archway, hands on hips. Her hair was cut in straight bangs. She had a look of weary patience on her thin-cheeked, long-nosed face. "Ladies."

Two of the students led Binnie through the archway. She walked quietly between them, with her head lowered. The calves of her legs were round and solid like a little child's, and her hair streamed golden to her waist.

"Get up now, Mrs. Barr," another student said. She was standing next to the girl with the dark-red hair.

"It's all over." Mrs. Barr's voice moved feebly in the same direction as her unfocussed eyes.

The students split in half, and the halves grown whole stooped, one on either side of Mrs. Barr—Katherine, I remembered—putting their hands under her armpits, lifting her to her feet. She slumped between them, and stumbled forward as they started to walk. "It's all over," she said weakly. "Leave me alone. It's over."

"All right, ladies. Mrs. Haggerty, Mrs. Blaine," the lean nurse said.

Jan's fingernails were cutting into the palm of my hand. Her skin was cold against my cold skin, wet against my wet skin. "I'm scared," she said in a thin whine. Her hand was pulling backward toward the wall, pulling mine along with it.

"God," I said. And it wasn't my gentle, suffering God I was naming. It was a different God, a God John had brought back with him from the war, a vast unself-conscious something, on whose mighty meaningless breath we came into being and perished.

"I'm so scared," Janet whimpered. "I'm so scared."

Miss Johnson separated herself from the roadblock of young girls and walked over to us. She raised herself on the toes of her oxfords to whisper in my ear. "This is the last time, Mrs. Blaine. You'll be back in an hour, having toast and coffee."

Fear pressed into my throat with powerful fingers, and my voice was half strangled. "Thanks, youngster." But each time had been the last time. Christ, even a murderer was electrocuted only once. Miss Johnson was pulling at my free hand, and I was moving forward toward the archway, with Jan walking beside me, tugging backward like a reluctant child, but keeping pace, step for step. She no longer spoke. She just whimpered.

Inside the high-ceilinged white room, Binnie was already lying on one of the cots, wound in a wet sheet, with only her left arm free.

Beyond her, the skeletal girl lay, similarly wrapped and silent, and on the farthest of the six cots Mrs. Barr—Katherine, I remembered again—was moving her free hand up and back in front of her eyes. From the next room, the room with the tubs, three students brought the frozen girl, Miss Rogers. She neither moved nor spoke. Her eyes remained closed; her hair curled damply over her forehead. All the time they were wrapping her lovely, flat-bellied, delicately breasted young body in that sheet, she never moved. It was as if she were dead, except for the up-and-down movements of her chest. I envied her.

Jan was next, stripped, wrapped, and lifted—not struggling, just whimpering. And then I was standing naked, and my short white gown was in Miss Johnson's hands. She tossed it behind her. All I could think for a moment was that I hated my long, skinny feet, with their misshapen large toes and purplish-pink nails. The wet sheet was warm and I was on the end cot, with Miss Johnson standing beside me.

Each of us had our own student now, and the lean, blond nurse with the weary, patient face was wiping Mrs. Barr's upper arm with a piece of cotton, picking up a hypodermic needle from a tray held by an attendant—Miss Jorgensen, or her twin—jabbing the point into loose flesh, plunging the plunger, moving on.

"It's nothing," Miss Johnson said soothingly. "It's just some stuff that sort of dries everything up so things don't get too messy."

Suddenly the skeletal girl yelped like a puppy.

"It's nothing," Miss Johnson said.

Binnie was silent as the needle went into her arm, and so was the frozen girl. Jan's whimper rose slightly in volume and pitch, and then fell and continued.

"It's nothing," Miss Johnson said. "Honest."

"Honest Injun Joe," I said in my strangled voice, and jerked a bit. It was nothing. "Now what?"

"Now we wait a few minutes," Miss Johnson said.

We waited, and the inside of my mouth got dry. Miss Johnson fetched a small piece of ice from a cardboard container the attendant was holding. Then the wheeled cots started moving through the archway, Mrs. Barr's (Katherine's), the skeletal girl's, Binnie's, Miss Rogers', Jan's. Miss Johnson's stubby child hand was close to my head, and we were moving, last in line, through the open archway, down the short stretch of corridor, and through the door at the end, now unlocked and standing open. The door closed behind us. I could hear the jangle of keys.

"I'm scared." My voice? Jan's voice? Mine, I decided.

"I'd be scared, too, I guess," Miss Johnson said. "It's the last time. It'll be all over soon." We were moving through a labyrinthal underground passage, through doors that unlocked before us and locked behind us. "We're almost there now."

"There?"

"Hall Six," Miss Johnson said. "Remember? The old ladies who have the big room move out for a while, and the doctors use it for shock."

"Nice of the old ladies," I said hoarsely. My throat ached, I was so scared. We went through the last door, wheeled cot after wheeled cot. The door closed. The key turned. The corridor was crowded with elderly ladies in house dresses, in sweaters, with felt slippers on their feet. A red-faced, madly cheerful-looking lady with a head of magnificent white hair drifted by, cradling a rag doll tenderly in her arms.

The cots rolled along, close to the wall, down toward the end of the corridor. There they stopped. Miss Johnson stopped. I stopped. A little woman walked up to me, a dry, tight, wrinkled mummy of a woman, the most alive thing about her the sparse yellow-white braids around her head. She poked at me with her forefinger.

"Go along, now," Miss Johnson said gently.

The old woman shook her head. "Do you know that I am Mary, Mother of God?"

"Go along," Miss Johnson said.

"And pray for me," I whispered as she turned away.

The first of the line of cots, Mrs. Barr's cot, was being wheeled into the shock room. We moved up a bit, and stopped in front of a door-shaped cutout in the wall. I looked into a small, square room, shabbily furnished with a worn sofa and a couple of wooden chairs. The walls were a dark, sick green. Four women were in the room, wearing pajamas and robes, two pacing about, two sitting stiffly, side by side on the sofa.

"They're from the front halls. They'll go in after you," Miss Johnson said.

"You mean they walk here by themselves? You mean they wait for this?" They could run, and didn't. I would run. Christ, I was so scared. The skeletal girl was being wheeled in, and we moved up an-

other three or four feet. Soon I was going to die. Soon. When the
little remaining space was covered.

"They're probably feeling miserable," Miss Johnson said. "When
you feel awful enough, you try anything."

"Doctor, don't kill me. I didn't do it. Please don't kill me." The
voice of the skeletal girl was off pitch with sickness and fright. I
could hear the murmur of a man's voice, and then a click. I waited
for the answering click. It was over. She was lying on her narrow cot
under the glaring spotlight. She was unconscious now. God, I wished
I were.

Binnie's turn, and again we moved. Click. I counted to five before
the second click. I could feel my heart banging inside my chest, and
the sweat collecting under my arms. Jan's student was pushing her
into the shock room. Jan was whimpering. Jan was yelling. Click.
"One, two, three, four, five," I counted, moving my lips soundlessly.
Click.

"Here we go now, Mrs. Blaine," Miss Johnson said.

And we were moving, turning, and I was inside that room, in the
center of that room. I was smelling that smell, the smell of fear and
electricity, twisted and knotted by the brightness of the light, the
god-awful sterile whiteness. Strange faces, and that smell. An oxygen
tank in the corner. A sandbag under my back. Someone was leaning
over me, a tall man in a white coat, a thin-faced man with a large
nose and thick spectacles. "Good morning," he said. "How are you?"

"Scared," I said. "Cold, stone stiff."

"It wouldn't help any if I told you not to be, would it?" he said.
"There's really nothing much to it. The being afraid is the worst of
it."

He had very pale-blue eyes, gentle eyes, and a soft mouth. He
looked ugly and kind. And then the face was changing slowly, the
nose growing smaller, the chin and cheekbones sharper, more clearly
defined. The gray-streaked black hair was lighter, reddening. I closed
my eyes, and found somewhere a remaining shred of will. I was going
to die sane. This, at least this. I opened my eyes again. "You're not
John."

"No," he said. "I'm not John. I'm James Engel. I'm one of the
doctors here—yours, in fact. Make a fist now."

"I'm scared of needles," I said.

"Lots of people are. Don't watch. It's not going to hurt much."

I felt the bite of the needle into my vein, and then the curare, like fire.

"That's the bad part," he said. "And it's done."

"My husband."

"Your husband?"

"I want to see him."

"I'm afraid you can't. Can you pick up your head now?"

I lifted my head, and let it drop back on the cot. I could feel myself choking, and I knew it wasn't just fear this time. It was the drug. So I wouldn't get my bones fractured, someone, sometime, somewhere had told me.

"Can you pick up your head?"

I could lift it, just barely.

"You know why you can't see John," he said softly. "Try lifting your head once more."

I tried. I moved my lips but couldn't hear my voice. "I can't do it." And I knew why I couldn't see John.

"Very good. Now open your mouth."

I dragged my jaws apart. I knew I would never see John. Something hard was put between my teeth.

The voice was coming from a great distance now. "It's practically all over. You're going to be fine after a while, you know. And go home."

Home? I could feel something gritty being rubbed on my temples. I could feel the electrodes, one on each side. I had no home.

"This isn't going to hurt. It'll be all over in a minute."

Because John was dead.

"It's all over now."

And it didn't matter if I died, too. It didn't matter. And then I heard the click.

"You wanted to see me?" Dr. Engel said.

"Yes." I sat in one corner of the sofa. He sat in a chair he had pulled around almost directly facing me. The conference room was a very sane-looking little room—sofa, chairs, a couple of small tables, carpet on the floor—a tremendous contrast to the square cell in which I slept, and the octagonal room to which I had graduated from the tubs, a wildly modern affair in which we gathered, we mad ones, to watch carefully chosen children's programs on television and eat pre-cut meat with spoons. "Yes, I did."

He smiled at me, a shy sort of smile that made him seem very young despite the streaks of gray in his hair. He wasn't wearing the long white coat I had seen him in last. His suit was dark, almost black, a bit shiny at the knees and elbows, and his tie was a limp thing, dreary against his rumpled shirt. "I'm glad you did," he said. His pale-blue eyes were moist-looking behind thick-lensed glasses. "I hope I can help. I'd like to." He took a pack of Chesterfields from his pocket, lit one for each of us, and placed the pack and the matches on the corner of the small table in front of me. "It must be rough not being able to smoke as much as you want to."

"It's a minor trouble." I slouched in the corner, stretching my bare legs in front of me. "It's nice to have a whole one, though."

"A whole one?"

"Yes." He was too long, all of him—his hands and his feet, and his long, thin neck. Vaguely, I wondered if he would be able to get all that loosely strung-together boniness back into a standing position. "Jan Haggerty and I have switched to Pall Malls. We break them in half. We get six instead of three that way. But it is nice to have a whole one."

"I'm sorry about that." He was, too. I could tell from the way he said it. "You'll be moving on to the next hall in a week or so. You get half a pack there, I think."

I ground out my cigarette butt, reached for the pack, then stopped, looking at him.

"Go ahead," he said.

I was shaking so hard I had to steady my right hand with my left to get the match to the wavering end of the cigarette. We sat in silence for what seemed a long time after that. We both took fresh cigarettes. He leaned forward, this time, to light mine. "What did you want to tell me?" he said.

"Nothing." The air was banked gray with smoke—soft rolling hills, fog, mist. "Nothing. I've forgotten."

"Have you really?"

"Yes." But the handle of my inner phonograph had moved a short distance and the needle was circling round and round, grinding out the same old words in the same old sequence. "My name is Alice. Alice Blaine. I am twenty-eight years old, and can count to a hundred by sevens forward or backward. I believe I am quite sane."

"You are quite sane," he said.

"I have three children—Jenny, aged eight; Pete, aged four; Tommy, aged two."

"I know that."

"John is dead."

"Yes."

"I am also dead," I said numbly.

"You're not dead. You're very far from dead."

"I feel dead."

"That's different."

"Is it?" I said. "Is it really?"

"It is. Really." He raised his hand and ran his fingers through his gray-black hair. He looked at the ceiling, at the floor, at the scuffed tips of his long shoes, at me. "What did you want to tell me?"

"Nothing. I don't know." I grinned through the heaviness, through the deadness. "I'm sorry I bothered you, and I don't mean to be rude. But—nothing. I'd like it if you'd leave me alone now."

"You know I can't, don't you?" he said.

"I know you can't. It's your job not to."

"It's my job to help. Let me try."

"Help?" I shook my head wearily. "Do you believe in God, Dr. Engel?"

"Sometimes," he said. "I believe in people, which I suppose is a way of believing in God."

"I used to pray, 'Let John come back from the war. Only let John come back from the war.'"

"And he came back."

"Yes. He came back. He wore white gloves for a while, because he had some sort of fungus thing on his hands. Jungle rot. That was all." That was all. That was all that was left to me. A detail. A thousand details. Nothing.

"Your father told me you'd loved John since you were a child."

"Yes." I paused, swallowing hard. "I'd like to see my father."

"I'll tell him. He's been here a number of times."

"Has he?" I said indifferently. "I'd like to see him. I'd like to speak to him about the children."

"I'll tell him."

"We had plans, John and I. For them, I mean."

"You'll be back with them in a while. You'll be able to do what you planned."

"No. I don't think so."

"I think so." He nodded his long head vigorously. "I'm sure so. You haven't said what you wanted to, have you?" He was infinitely patient. "Why don't you? Try it, anyway."

I stood up and walked the length of the small, carpeted room, my tennis shoes sinking down a little with each step. It was different from walking on tile. I turned when I reached the far wall, moved along it, turned again, and tried the door. It was open. The student standing outside it looked at me curiously. I pulled the door closed. Dr. Engel was still sitting, his bony length arranged sloppily in the chair. "I could walk out of here," I said.

He nodded. "You could."

I flung myself in the corner of the sofa. "This is a lousy place."

"It's better than most."

"That's sad," I said.

"It is. Very."

Silence settled, thick and oppressive. I lit another cigarette and squashed it out. I glanced toward the door, half rose, and dropped backward against the cushion.

"Tell me how it happened," he said. "You might feel better if you told me."

"O.K." Because part of me had to tell somebody. I had to tell somebody. "It was the last day. I knew it. It's odd, isn't it? I'd never seen anyone die before, but I knew it was going to be soon."

"Yes." Dr. Engel was separated from me by heavy blue smoke. It was almost as if he weren't there, almost as if I were by myself.

"I had been there all night, sitting on that stiff wooden chair next to John's bed. All night listening to that new, frightening cough, listening to words, half sentences, sometimes hearing my name. There was a lamp on the table next to the bed, very dim. I could see his white, dying face all night, hour after hour."

"Yes."

Hour after hour, holding his hot, dry hand in mine, having him wrench it away as he tossed about, moaning, muttering inarticulately. Toward morning I slept, and when I woke gray light was coming through the window. Someone had turned off the lamp and put a blanket over my knees. I was stiff and aching all over, and there was a smell in the room.

"Alice."

"John." I stood next to the bed, near his white, dying face. His eyes were open, looking at me, really seeing me for the first time in two days. "I'm here, John."

His white lips moved. "Alice." And his eyes closed.

"John," I said. "John." Like a prayer I said it. My fingers pressing the buzzer for the nurse were so numb I could hardly feel them. While I slept, John had pulled off his pajamas, and he lay, fleshless, his clearly marked ribs heaving, the lower half of his body smeared with excrement. Naked and dying.

The nurse came quickly, an elderly, wrinkled, very clean-looking woman. "Would you wash him, please?" I said, gagging on my own voice.

She glanced swiftly at John, at me, and shook her head. "There's no need to bother him." She moved through the room, into the bathroom, and came back with a sheet, which she opened and arranged over him. "Ring again if you want me," she said. "I'm right down the hall."

And I sat on the wooden chair, not thinking, not feeling, frozen all the way through me. Once I thought John said "Water." I stood again, and held the glass with its bent drinking tube to his mouth. He drank, and a moment later the water, tinged red, was foaming at his lips, dribbling down his chin.

Time dragged, a dying man inching his way to the grave. My father came softly and stood beside me. He took his handkerchief from his pocket and blotted John's mouth and chin with it. "I'll stay now. You go out. Get some coffee."

I shook my head.

"Go on," my father said. "Get some coffee. Get something to eat."

"John's dying." Could it be that my father didn't realize this? "He's going to die."

"There's a drugstore right around the corner." My father handed me a couple of bills and some change. "Get some coffee and call your mother. She's waiting to hear from you."

Outside, it was misty. The sky was gray, heavy with clouds, a bundle of dirty wash. I walked down the street, staring at my feet, which were carrying me forward automatically. Step on a crack, break your mother's back. I used to chant that when I was a youngster, and now little Jenny sang it as she skipped home from school. Nothing had changed. Everything had changed. And the Coca-Cola sign in the drugstore window was the same as it had always been. I sat down on the round stool at the counter, and in the mirror I could see my reflection—poor, tired old reflection, looking black under the eyes, as if someone had kicked it.

"You want something, lady?" The young man behind the counter was pimply-faced and popeyed. He didn't have much chin.

"Coffee," I said.

"Anything else? Danish? Corn muffin?"

"Yes. A sandwich. Peanut butter on white."

"For breakfast?" he said admiringly.

"Breakfast? Sure. Why not?"

"No reason, lady," he said. "It's O.K. with me."

I watched as he poured the tan, watery coffee. I watched as he unscrewed the top of the peanut-butter jar, spread the stuff thickly on one slice of bread, topped it with another, divided the square into two triangles.

"Is there a telephone here?"

"Sure, lady," he said. "Right behind you. Against the wall."

I picked up my half a sandwich and walked over to the telephone booth. I pulled the door closed behind me, stuck a coin in the slot, and dialled, listening to the ring of the phone.

"Hello." It was my mother.

"Hello," I said. "Hi, Mom."

"Hello, dear. How are you?"

I lowered the telephone receiver and stared at it, running my fingertips over the smooth blackness. How was I? Was that what she had asked? For an instant I had a vision of my mother, a vision of hallucinatory vividness. She was sitting in her little blue damask chair, cradling her phone against her soft cheek. My mother, an ever-fading after-image of beauty, spreading, softening, smiling very gently, dimpling as she smiled. Sweet mother in her sweet, home-made world. "O.K.," I said heartily. "How are the children?" There was peanut butter stuck behind my teeth.

"The children are fine. Alice, dear?"

"Yes, Mom." I was poking about my mouth with the tip of my tongue.

"Alice. How's John, dear?"

"John?" I bit into my sandwich again and chewed energetically, working my jaws up and down.

"Yes, dear," my mother said. "How is he?"

"Is he?" I swallowed, and stared at the wall of the phone booth. It was gray metal, all covered with little bumps. Someone had scratched a heart on the wall and etched two sets of initials inside it. "He's dying, Mother."

"Alice. Dear. Alice, where are you, dear?"

"I'm in a drugstore, Mom," I said. "I'm eating a sandwich. Peanut butter." Bubbles of laughter were rising through my frozen insides. "John's dying, and I'm here, eating a sandwich." And the laughter burst, bloody, staining my lips, dribbling down my chin, bloody, bloody, bloody.

"Alice. Where are you, dear? Where are you?"

Broken telephone. Where are you, where are you, where are you? I dropped the receiver, and it hung, dangling by its black cord, swaying while I laughed and John lay dying.

Dr. Engel had not moved while I spoke, or perhaps it was just that I had not been aware of any movement. I had not even, after a minute or two, been aware of his presence. Now I saw him again, spread untidily in the chair, with his nose jutting and his blue eyes damp, and the lips of his small, pale mouth pressed tight together. I got up from my corner of the sofa. "I'll go now," I said.

He put his hands on the arms of the chair and pulled the whole, loose-jointed, sloppy length of him erect. He stood next to me, very tall, as John had been tall, and something inside me twisted, and somewhere inside me I felt the slow, constant dripping of tears. "This elation you've been in," he said. "It's the same thing as depression, you know. Two sides of the same coin."

I grinned my stiff-lipped grin. "I'll go now. O.K.?"

"O.K." He lifted his hand and touched my shoulder, barely touched it. "There are many ways of crying."

"Yes." My tears were hidden behind my grinning mask face. "Yes, there are."

"The conventional one has considerable merit. You ought to try it."

"Sissies cry," I said, grinning.

"People cry. People who have been hurt cry."

Inside me the tears were dripping. The tears were seeping under John's closed lids, down his chalky face. I would cry my tears, John's tears, until I died.

"People cry."

Until I died. Until I died. I flung myself face down on the sofa. Dr. Engel was saying something, but I couldn't make out the words. I could only hear a low drone under my own strangled sobs.

PHILIP L. GREENE was born in New York, attended Lowell Technological Institute and New York University. He is an Assistant Professor of English at Adelphi University and was Associate Editor of *Venture* magazine from 1953–1959. "One of You Must Be Wendell Corey" is his first published short story.

One of You Must Be Wendell Corey

L IL WAGNER's marriage was on the rocks when I first met her. She was at a point where her need for spiritual renewal came from Erich Fromm. "*The Art of Loving,*" she said to me with conviction, "if I had known before I met Ben, if I could have talked with my analyst before he went to California. . . ." The Fromm revelation came to me in a surprised voice. Lil's constant seizing of the obvious and investing it with wonder—another secret uncovered to reward her with a new life—kept her in a perpetual cycle of desire, rapt discovery, and flat-eyed disillusionment. Lil was always a cultural idea away. This caused an impasse between her and Ben, who was always on the frontier of an idea. This situation made for a most satisfactory lesion. They knew what was wounding them. Ben was all modernity, in the vanguard of good causes, always in control of the intellectual apparatus rigged for him by the monopolists of the mid-city mind— *Dissent, Commentary,* the *New Leader.* "Can't you see," he said to me once, while Lil was looking vacantly out of the window onto Waverly Place, "that the social mobility of the new class depends on the morality of the cash nexus." Lil said, "Oh, shit," and walked out of the room. Ben stared after her, looked back at me, and went on. "Take Weber's view of the Protestant ethic and update it to give the petite bourgeoisie its function under the new capitalism. What do you have? The little man with just enough illusions to keep him morally bankrupt forever. I mentioned this to my analyst, and do you know what he said? 'Don't you think you're hiding behind all this, Ben.' "

Lil's doctor had called Ben's doctor to discuss a possible separation
—this at the suggestion of Lil, who had thrown herself at the mercy
of a new idea: why shouldn't the transferents involve themselves
directly in the transferers' problems. When Ben found a place on
Hudson Street over a wholesale meat market and refused to put a
phone in, Lil's mother sent him a telegram: "Lil wants to try again.
Please call." Ben called. Possessed with the idea of effecting a moral
sacrifice—he wanted it desperately—he persuaded Lil to a reconciliation. That night, Ben told me later with embarrassing ingenuous-
ness, they got into bed, and he couldn't get an erection. He cried.
Lil laughed at him, and he hit her in the face, once, a short, open-
handed slap. She screamed at him, "You can punch, but you can't
screw, you lousy fat louse."

Shortly after that at a gathering at Marsha Weinstein's house she
told me in a drawn voice that she had given up sex for yogurt and
carrot juice. Marsha, her best friend, was a ballet dancer when she
was not working part-time for Secretaries Anonymous. Marsha's
three abortions had taken the limber out of her legs, which were
running to fat, and she had recommended the Health Shoppe on
Madison Avenue right around the corner from her analyst. Lil had
decided to move in with Marsha, the reconciliation with Ben a wash-
out. Larry Jonas, Marsha's new man, was in Washington doing a
study of pressure groups and would not be back for a while. Larry
had been Lil's boy friend, so she felt a vicarious renewal with Larry
in staying at Marsha's. Larry had been good to her, but after two
years of indecision, she found Ben at a party given by Murray
Abramson, whose book, *Existential Psychodynamics*, had stirred the
psychological community. Murray had studied at the W. A. White
school with Ben before Ben decided to go into his father's medical
supply business. Lil told me that Ben was the warmest, brightest,
tenderest man she had ever met. "I never knew about social consciousness before I met Ben," she said. Ben had admired Larry's work
with the American Civil Liberties Union and knew too that Larry
was sleeping with Lil, so that he found the usurpation of Larry's girl
a moral problem painful enough to engage him full time. "I knew
something was wrong," Lil said, "the night Ben took me home from
Murray's party, but he told me later that he was discussing the problem with his doctor. He had a premature ejaculation; he came all
over my dress before I had time to take it off. He said the Larry problem was a projection of an infantile regression, a kind of Oedipal

return, since he had always thought of Larry as a kind of father figure."

The marriage had gone on like that for four years, deteriorating steadily. Toward the end, I was having dinner at the Cookery with Merle Jonas, Larry's kid brother. We had just come from Max Lerner's third lecture at The New School where Lerner brilliantly illustrated his thesis of the dynamics of American pluralism by showing the bipolar attitude of the nation at large toward abortion, a topic Merle continued with great expertise, over a cookeryburger. "Marsha has had three—one in Jersey, one in Puerto Rico, and one right here on Fifth Avenue. Lerner is right because this problem epitomizes the indigenous moral strength of the American people. In the face of official sanctions against it, there is a remarkable pragmatic will operating."

When Merle told me that Marsha was having some people over and that Lil would be there, I accepted the invitation. I was at loose ends myself and Lil had looked plaintively neurotic the last time I had seen her. I knew that her health-food phase was temporary, and I hoped I might be just the thing to renew her contact with love. She was leaning heavily on her new Frommian world view. Merle had to pick up Tibby Barrett, Lil's old roommate at Oswego State College, who had recently arrived from Goshen and had taken a one and a half on Jane Street just around the corner from the old cat and dog store that was being torn down to make way for a luxury apartment, one of a number around the West Village that were following an artist motif. The Van Gogh and The Rembrandt had already been built. The new one was called The Picasso Arms. Tibby was doing research at *Newsweek*. Merle, who was writing advertising copy, met her for lunch every day in front of the library lions.

When we arrived at Marsha's Lil was sitting on the couch between Murray Abramson and his wife Lisa, who greeted me with a warm voice edged with a Hungarian accent. She was finishing her work at the White school. Murray and Lisa were planning to start a husband-and-wife group therapy experiment. As the husband-and-wife doctor team they would take only husband-and-wife teams as patients. Murray's chapter on existential therapy for marital groups had been published as an article in the *Saturday Evening Post*. When Marsha came in with a tray of stuffed mushrooms she announced that Larry had just called and would be arriving from Washington any minute. Over drinks Lil posed the problem of pre-

non-post-extra-marital relations to Murray. Murray, with Lisa coun-
terpointing in soft Hungarian, suggested that behavioral patterns
weren't subject to moral judgments, only analysis and clarification.
Lil was overwhelmed by the simple logic of Murray's position. Larry
arrived, kissed Marsha and Lil, and added that Murray's view could
be applied to the law; in fact his trip to Washington had shown
that the sociological carry-over into law had in effect reduced the
moral difficulties of law immeasurably. Murray said that he didn't
think of sex as sociological. "Sociology is what happens after the be-
haviorists get finished. Understanding human actions, especially
group action, is the psychologists' business. The sociologist puts
down in his notebook the kind of hors d'oeuvres served in a group.
For the sociologist the great question is: are we or are we not a
stuffed mushroom group?"

Then Murray introduced a game called "Psychology." "Someone
goes out of the room," he explained, "one of the group is 'it,' and
the person excluded is called back and must identify the one chosen
by a series of associational questions. For example, you might ask:
'If this person was a fruit, what kind would he be, or if he was on a
desert island, what five books would he take.' The same question is
asked of all, so there are conflicting answers. Through the pattern of
responses the person who is 'it' can be guessed."

Everything went along all right until Lil went out. She asked: "If
this person was a movie actor who would he be?" Merle was "it."
Merle is a kind of relaxed kid, Crosbyish, who surprises occasionally
with sharp Spencer Tracy-like perceptions. Everybody gave Lil a
tough time, saying things like Mickey Rooney, Donald O'Connor,
Jack Lemmon, when Lil came out with a crazy remark: "One of you
must be Wendell Corey."

That stopped the show. Murray guffawed. "You mean all of us
must be Wendell Corey. How is that for a group label?"

Tibby asked in her bright, flat upstate accent, "Who is Wendell
Corey?"

"I was 'it,'" said Merle, "and I see myself as Gerard Philipe. Wendell Corey never made love to anybody. Always that sour, pinched
face, like he's getting ready to take a crap any minute."

"Maybe that's how Lil sees the world," Murray said, "constipated
non-lovers." Murray thought that was funny, but Lisa gave him a
stony look.

Lil said, "Actually I don't know why it came to me, but I hear he's a big fairy."

"I saw Jimmy Stewart in Washington," Larry said, "with some finky right-wing group. You know, the Hollywood hero acting out the role of patriot. It made me sick."

"But nobody answered the question," Marsha said. "Who is Merle? I vote for James Mason."

"I hear he is Jewish," Lil said. Murray really broke up on that one. "What's so funny?" Lil asked. She was beginning to get sore.

Larry said, "Murray has a big anti-Jewish complex. He is the only analyst in New York who refuses Jewish patients. He even married a shikse."

Lisa smiled. "But I really think Jewish. He must be out of luck."

We finally decided that Merle was Anthony Franciosa, and stopped for coffee and cake. Murray picked it up again at the table. "You are not playing the game right. If you want to show what impression people have of others why not ask some dangerous questions. It's only in discomfort that we find emotional truth. Here's one: If somebody was drowning would this person jump in, call for help, or run away? Or, even better, if this person had a perverse habit, what would it be? That's a good one, because the responder would reveal his own tastes in perversion."

Everybody boldly agreed and I felt then that there really was a difference between intellectual life in the city and the wasteland of suburbia. Murray went out to be the guesser, and we decided on Tibby Barrett as "it," since most of us knew her slightly and it would lessen our personal embarrassment. Murray popped the question about perversion and we went around.

Lisa, sitting in Marsha's Saarinen Womb Chair, was first. She blushed a little, thought for a while, and then said: "If this person had a perverse habit, I would say he likes to smell armpits."

"Not much of a perversion," said Murray. "You know what Freud says about the olfactory sense and primitive man's delight in all smells."

"But this is twentieth-century civilized man," said Lisa. "Who today likes to handle and smell his own excretion?"

Larry, who was next, said loudly, "As a matter of fact, that was going to be my statement about our person, that he likes to smell human feces."

Tibby was next. I figured this was pretty rough stuff for a closed-in upstater, but she came out with a lulu. It almost broke up the game. "If this person was a female and had a perverse habit," she said matter-of-factly, "it would be wearing athletic supporters. Jock straps, you know."

"That's nothing more than locker-room transvestitism," said Murray, "but I'll guess it is you Tibby, because everybody else in the room sees you as anal-oriented. You at least know yourself."

"What does that mean?" asked Merle.

"Probably she thinks she harbors homosexual feelings, and the way to defeat them is to talk about them," answered Murray.

At this point, Lil, who had been crouching in the corner of the couch, said, "I think this whole business is perverse. How everybody enjoys it."

"Verbal sublimation may be a way of riding oneself of a compulsion neurosis toward societally taboo sex feelings," said Lisa.

"But where is love in all this?" asked Lil.

Larry said, "As an old Stalinist friend would say: love is a romantic excrescence of bankrupt bourgeois capitalism."

Everybody laughed, and right in the middle, Tibby farted. "Oops," she said, and before she could blush we doubled up with laughter. Except Lil.

"I think it's a stupid game. Let's talk about something else." But that finished it. We were all ready to go home.

"Now that Larry is back are you going to stay?" I asked Lil. I offered to take her to my place. She agreed and as soon as we got home she showered and went right to sleep. I thought she was faking it, but when I jostled her, she murmured, "Mommy," and began to snore a little.

I told Ben the story some days later. He was back over the meat market on Hudson Street. "You know," he said, "Lil is really all right. I mean that Marsha Weinstein crowd, I hate it." He stared soupily at a glass of warm Scotch. "I read an article in this week's *Reporter* about the fragmented man. This guy said, I think it was Oscar Jones, who wrote that study of the light-skinned Negro as *the* symbol of the alienated man. He's up at Columbia in C. Wright Mills's place. Wasn't that a tragic thing? Anyway, Jones discussed the possibility that we have lost a real work tradition and are seeking substitute gratification through the arts. He calls it cultural tunneling, whereby the true emotions of man, work-directed, have gone underground, so we seek love, not in sex, but in the movies, 'sex's blessed surrogate' he said. Maybe if I make it with Lil again I'll get job satisfaction too. Does that make sense?"

I said that it did, but I wondered why he didn't comment on Lil's sleeping in my bed. I asked him. "Well," he said, "you're no real threat the way Larry Jonas is. I haven't been able to satisfy Lil, so you may be my blessed surrogate."

"But she fell asleep," I said, thinking how nice it would have been to take her in her sleep.

A few days later Ben told me that he and Lil were going to try again and invited me to dinner to celebrate the reconciliation. When I arrived Lil was on the floor in leotards, practicing a leg-raising exercise she learned from Marsha. The "Ode to Joy" was storming out of the record player. Ben was whistling in the bathroom. "I've got a part-time job as a dental assistant," Lil said, as she kept exercising, and then, jumping up, she whispered, "we have decided to try for a baby."

Ben walked in wiping his face with a towel and boomed, "Say, did Lil tell you that we decided to try for a baby." Lil flashed an angry look at him. He went on. "I looked around me, at all the people I know in the Village, and nobody has a family. Maybe they think it's a concession to middle-class attitudes, but it occurred to me that barrenness extirpates life. Listen to the Beethoven. It sings out the triumph of life, but without the child-bearing function man is deracinated, absolutely deracinated. Have a drink."

Lil looked at him, the light going out of her eyes. "Why must you always intellectualize everything. I want a baby because it will be the fruit of me, mine, yours, ours. Don't feelings have a place anywhere?"

"Of course they do. That's what I was trying to say. There must be a return to feeling and away from the highbrow dissection of everything. I can't even read *Dissent* any more. Doesn't Murray say in his book that the existential moment is truly realized in the coital act?"

"Good God, Murray is forty-five years old, Lisa is his third wife, and do you see any kids around the house?"

"What do you know." Ben gulped his drink. "Murray can't have babies, for goodness sake."

"I don't believe it."

"He is sterile. S-T-E-R-I-L-E. Sterile."

I thought of Murray, wavy-haired, graying at the temples, the

image of Jeff Chandler, poor guy, as a psychoanalyst. I didn't believe
Ben either.

"But he is," Ben said. "He told me so at the White school. Why
do you think he was interested in asking those questions about per-
versity? He is capable of intercourse, but he knows the guilt-anxiety
of the act, and he chooses wayward acts as a kind of self-mutilating
penance to his libido. I think those were his exact words to me."

Dinner went along aimlessly and I left shortly after. Ben had put
on a John Cage record, and Lil was in the kitchen washing the floor.
As I closed the door I heard him come into the kitchen. "Come on,
Lil, get off the floor."

The next week I met Merle at Lerner's fourth lecture on American pluralism, this time the dichotomy between our Puritan adher-
ence to monogamy on the one hand, and the new culture's rampant
extra-maritalism on the other, a split which carried directly into the
political arena. Lerner explained that the only way our statesmen
could exorcise private guilt is by being supermoral in our foreign
policy. He called it the Dulles syndrome. I wanted to pursue the
point over a cookery-split, their ice cream special, but Merle broke in.
"I wasn't listening. I broke up with Tibby last week."

"You don't look like you're collapsing over it," I said.

"I'm not. I'm puzzled more by an eerie feeling I have. I might as
well tell you because you'll find out soon enough. A few days after
the break I ran into Lil at the 8th Street Bookstore. She was looking
haggard. The thing with Ben was over, but she said what disturbed
her was the fact that she had been riding on the wings of a new
idea, and her wings had been clipped. She did look like a fallen bird.
She wanted a baby. That was the answer. She knew it. She spoke to
her doctor and all he could say was, 'Do you really want it?' 'I don't
know what I want,' she answered, and he said, 'Tell me what you
think.' She talked a lot. She lies down now, you know, but she
came out depressed. I told her about Tibby and me, and a strange,
desperate look came over her. 'Come up to my place and we'll talk,'
she said, and before I knew it, although I really knew it, we were in
bed. 'I want a baby. I want a baby,' she kept repeating. She was too
hysterical for any honest screwing, and we ended up drinking coffee
in the kitchen. The thing that bothers me is that she was Larry's
girl for quite a while. I mean, he is my older brother."

I asked him if he wanted the affair, and he shrugged. "Who knows
what I want? The thing with Tibby went sour overnight. Really. We

didn't even have a fight. She said, 'I'm moving out,' and I said O.K. I'm not like that. I like to analyze a relationship; that's half the fun. But the lights went out, that's all. So I look at Lil. I mean she probably can be good in bed if she works at it. But she is sick. And there is Larry. And maybe Ben with his crazy moral views will get sore. I like Ben. He was the first guy to give me a sense of social consciousness. I spoke to Marsha this morning and she insisted that I see a doctor. So her analyst arranged for an appointment with a man he recommends. Do you know him? Talcott Weingarten. He's a Sullivanian. I thought of going to Murray, but Marsha laughed. 'You are naive, Merle. You don't go to your friends. He knows too much about you.' I thought that was a funny remark, but I let it go."

I called Ben that night. He was back again at Hudson Street, and he had put a phone in, because, he said, "Who am I kidding? Artificial means of severing communications won't work. I have got to make the break from the inside."

"Why are you breaking?" I asked.

"Actually I'm not. As a matter of fact, for the first time in my life I feel a real spiritual renewal. Why don't you come over and see."

When I got to his place I saw demolition notices on all the stores. A new luxury building was going up. This one, a big placard announced, was to be called The Titian Terrace. When I walked in, Tibby was sitting in a sling chair, holding a copy of *Civilization and Its Discontents*. "It's all in here," she said with a straight face. "He says I'm in trouble because I'm using sex as a sublimation for sex." I laughed and Ben greeted me.

"She really means that Freud is a fraud. Tibby is the answer to all neuroses. She is the incarnation of the love instinct."

"You mean the sex instinct," I offered.

"No, the love instinct. Lil didn't have it. I've been looking for the direct woman all my life. Look at her in the flesh." He went to her and kissed her.

"Ben thinks I am the embodiment of Marilyn Monroe and Jean Harlow. He is cute. I think I'm a quiet Bette Davis. Freud says it's a reaction formation. I refuse to accept my image of myself. I think he's cute too."

Ben said, "You see what I mean. She has insight, a native gift. She is the master of the innocuous apothegm. 'He's cute too.' Could Lil ever say anything like that?"

I said I thought she could. But Ben answered that it didn't matter, and launched into a recital of Tibby's virtues, while Tibby kept looking at him with bemused detachment. After the last breakup with Lil, Ben said he felt like commiting suicide, but despite his despondency he knew that suicide was a failure of moral commitment. He had gone to the Cedar Street Bar for a drink, and Tibby was sitting at a table in the back. She told him about her break with Merle, and suggested that they try something together. She meant it as a joke, but Ben said why not. Tibby moved in that night, and Ben had his first successful love-making in months.

"Do you know what it is to make real love?" he said. "I told my doctor that it was a bourgeois myth kept alive for the sake of promoting wish-fulfilling fantasies and to keep the advertising business going. Did you see that piece in *Commentary* on 'Eros as Money-Making Myth'? It may be true, but nobody has ever seen the archetypal force of the pure, private act. It is positively prelapsarian." Just then Tibby farted.

"Oops," she said, and I noticed that she had learned not to blush as she had done at Marsha's.

Ben turned on her. "What kind of a stupid thing is that to do?"

"I had gas," Tibby said.

About a month later I met Larry and Marsha coming out of the 8th Street Playhouse. *Paths of Glory* was playing. "Film-making of the highest order," Larry said, "absolutely devastating exposure of the military mind. But why cast that right-wing bastard Menjou I can't understand." Marsha thought Larry looked like Kirk Douglas without the cleft. We went to the Limelight for capuccino.

"There's Wilder Benjamin, the movie critic of the *Voice*," Marsha said. "Do you know that he was Lil's first boy friend in the Village?"

"Can you believe it," Larry said, "Ben and Lil are together again. Lil's fling with Merle lasted about a week. Merle came to me and told me that my image haunted the bedroom. He couldn't even get an erection."

"And Ben," Marsha added, "had a terrible fight with Tibby. He accused her of lacking any distinction as a human being. He said he couldn't live with a girl so obtuse about the world around her. So Lil and Ben are back together, and they have decided to attend Murray's husband-and-wife therapy team. They are not going to think about a baby for a while. Murray recommended that Lil go back to dancing classes with me in order to get back to her primal self."

Although it was late when I left them, I wandered over to the

Cedar Street Bar thinking that despite the problems people seem to have, they were alive to the possibilities of existence. It was almost closing time. Two fairies were standing at the bar having a furious argument. The only other person was Tibby.

She was sitting at a table in the corner, looking disconsolate. "I just broke up with Ben," she said, before I could sit down. I ordered two beers, and after a quiet cigarette I asked her if she would like to stay at my place. She agreed.

NANCY HALE, born in Boston in 1908, has published fourteen books, including novels, short stories, and a collection of critical essays on writing, *The Realities of Fiction*. Her most recent publication was an anthology of New England literature. In the thirties she was an O. Henry prize winner and several times represented in that collection. She lives in Charlottesville, Virginia, where her husband is a Professor of English at the University of Virginia. Miss Hale is at present at work on a novel.

Sunday Lunch

THE joyful young clergyman followed his hostess, and his hostess's son and wife, through adjoining sitting rooms and out a door onto an open terrace. The terrace was round in shape and fitted into the angle of a wing to the main house. Its pink bricks were laid in a concentric pattern, and in the middle of it rose the curved-over rim of a brick well, topped by an arch supporting a well sweep. Between terrace and lawn stood willow oaks and mimosas, whose branches made a feathery awning overhead, pinned everywhere with pale-pink mimosa blossoms. Bees were going about their murmurous business in the masses of roses—pink, red, and yellow—that climbed the walls of the remarkable old Maryland house, and a delicious scent drifted through the warm June air.

"Just time for a cozy confab before the others arrive," Mrs. Beneker remarked. She seated herself gracefully on a white iron chair. Pretty and chic, she had the figure of a girl of twenty—a far better figure than her daughter-in-law's—and was dressed in gray linen with white touches. On entering the house after church, she had removed a broad-brimmed gray straw hat before a mirror in the hall and, turning, threw her guest a most complicated smile, compounded of flirtatiousness, recognition of his cloth, and a pretty acceptance of her inability to do other than flirt. "I do think Sunday lunch is a divine institution," she said. "Oh! I've made a sort of joke, haven't I, Mr. Watson?"

He nodded happily. With his dark, shining eyes and graying hair close-cropped to his round head, he looked like a small, friendly animal. Since he had been learning to practice his secret ability, he could hardly wait for people to say things—any things—because he loved them so and they couldn't hurt him anymore and they were so wonderful, with their crazy reserves and their touching braggadocio, their determined frustrations and their self-inflicted suffering. His eyes rested on Mrs. Beneker, and he prayed for her to go on talking. He could hardly come right out and say, "Go on, go on, I can hardly wait to hear the awful things you say." He couldn't come right out and say, "You are my mother and my brethren."

"We've just time to all make quicky friends," she said.

Her beautifully coiffed reddish-tinted hair rose from her pretty neck, around which hung a string of pearls. Mr. Watson's eyes strayed innocently about other visible furnishings of Mrs. Beneker's life—the iron chairs, with their springy wire-mesh seats; the glass-topped bar table set under a willow oak and loaded with bottles, etched glasses, and a silver bucket of ice; the sheer curtains that billowed out through the open French doors; the huge, brilliant-blue pool just beyond the row of trees; the well-tended borders of flowers against the walls of the house; the marble benches. The young clergyman hadn't the faintest conception of what all of this cost; it simply looked nice to him and it was a beautiful day.

The son, a hulking blond fellow, threw himself into one of the iron armchairs and sat blinking up at the sun through baggy lids. He and his wife hadn't been in church; they were coming down the wide front stairs as the others entered the house. Under his jacket he wore a white silk shirt, its neck left open, with a printed silk scarf instead of a tie. He made Mr. Watson feel violence.

Mrs. Beneker's daughter-in-law was big-boned and gawky, with a sulky young face. Her polished chestnut hair swung against her cheek whenever she turned her head. She sat on the opposite side of the well from her husband, staring down, as though with interest, at the concentric brickwork.

"Alec! Make us drinks, please," Mrs. Beneker said crisply. "The wherewithals are on the table."

My! thought Mr. Watson. When people spoke that way to each other, it was like a bump to his consciousness. Often they made his consciousness hurt before they even said anything. Before he had begun to understand that he was a mirror to them, this reflecting had made him so uncomfortable in society that he had been on the verge of becoming a recluse.

Young Beneker got up and lounged heavily across to the bar table. "What'll it be, Reverend?" he asked. He gave Mr. Watson a disarming smile.

Mr. Watson smiled back. "Bourbon-and-water, please," he said in his gentle way.

"Don't *I* get a drink?" the girl said.

"All in good time is soon enough, Audrey," her mother-in-law said without turning her head.

Oh! Mr. Watson thought. He looked placatingly from one woman to the other. "At least they don't let clergymen into the lifeboats first," he said, as a little joke, to the girl. He received from her a reluctant smile.

While Alec was making and bringing the drinks, Mrs. Beneker resumed charge of the conversation.

"We're so glad you're attached to St. James's, Mr. Watson, and we hope to see you often here at Rosemont!" she said, in her perky, challenging way. "Dr. Beecham—such a friend. He married Alec's late father and me. Did he tell you?"

"Not yet," Mr. Watson said.

She smiled. "He surely will! It was Dr. Beecham who went up to marry Alec and Audrey, too, you know. That, of course, was not one of Rosemont's weddings." Mr. Watson listened entranced to Mrs. Beneker's speech. "We are regular communicants at St. James's, except in the winter season, when we go for two months up to be near the Great White Way. There it's dear old St. Thomas's for us!"

It was not just Mrs. Beneker's language, so like a boarding-school girl's, that fascinated Mr. Watson. Underneath, she herself—this shy, stiff, tense little person who was driven to communicate in catchwords—was all the while hiding something. What was she hiding? She was hiding it from everybody. And . . . the secret was not exactly shameful, Mr. Watson felt, groping. Mrs. Beneker's secret was something precious to her, which she sat on like a hen an egg.

Mr. Watson knew it would come to him. All he had to do was let himself go and *be* her. Sometimes he had the most amazing visions of people's inner lives. Until he understood it, he had often made himself ill this way. Once, visiting his cousin Eric, he had felt sicker and sicker, until all at once it was Eric who came down with pneumonia.

"Occasionally when Mother is up near the Great White Way, she goes even farther north and visits Beantown," Alec Beneker said. Instead of being entranced by his mother's girlish speech, he was sneering at it. "Beantown's where I wooed and won Audrey, Mr. Watson," he said, spitting the words, "and brought her back to Rosemont a bride."

"One more in a succession of lovely Rosemont brides," Mrs. Beneker said, not tumbling at all.

"Oh, God," Audrey said.

"Audrey. Dear." Mrs. Beneker inclined her head toward the guest. "Remember where you are."

Mr. Watson smiled blissfully. He didn't care if Audrey did swear. He didn't care what she did, she was so lovely with her glittering hair sweeping her still-childish cheek, so young that even her anger seemed young and almost sweet: fierce, indignant anger—nothing cold about it.

She's cooking up something, the young clergyman thought. She's in the midst of some plot. Is she going to leave him? She feels that way. Go ahead and say anything you like, he thought, at Audrey. Swear all you want. The more you say, the more I know you, and I love to know you.

Audrey Beneker let out a long-suffering sigh and cast her eyes up into the boughs of the willow oaks.

How long, O Lord, how long, Mr. Watson thought along with Audrey.

All this time Alec had not even glanced at his wife but gazed steadily at his mother, smiling faintly and mockingly.

Why is he so venomous? Suddenly, out of the venom, a hint of something new sprang up in Mr. Watson's mind—a feeling full of light and grace. He felt that the two of them were going to be very close, soon.

He asked himself if it were merely the original prenatal relation between them that he sensed, for his faculty always needed this kind of checking. He was pretty sure not. Experience at the hospital psychiatric clinics, when he was in seminary, had taught him to recognize and discount regressiveness. His visions about people always seemed to have to do with the future.

"Mother," Alec Beneker said, eyes never shifting from the graceful little lady in the gray dress, "tell Mr. Watson about this historical old house."

Audrey's eyes jumped to find her husband's. "Hysterical old house," Mr. Watson heard her murmur. It must be some old joke between them. But Alec didn't even glance back at her.

Mrs. Beneker took charge of the conversation again as though it were a refractory horse. Ignoring her son's suggestion, she said, "My old nurse" (Mr. Watson was struck by a wave of hatred from Alec) "—I know that nowadays one isn't supposed to have *had* a nurse, but there it is," she added. "My old Aunt Lucy used to tell me, 'There's a different way fittin' for each and all. What's fittin' for this one ain't fittin' for that one.' That's all I was trying to say to you, Audrey dear, about the presence of Mr. Watson," she said lightly, as to a little girl.

But the young wife wasn't being treated like any little girl. She continued to look away.

"It's fittin' to offer the preacher the first drink, Aunt Lucy would surely agree. But it sho ain't fittin' for the preacher to go first into the lifeboat! Isn't that right, Mr. Watson? The clergy is supposed to be up on deck organizing the singing of 'Nearer My God to Thee.'" She laughed, tinklingly. Mr. Watson nodded. "A crisis is the very time we depend upon our spiritual leaders," Mrs. Beneker went on with wide-eyed earnestness. "I did think it was atrocious a couple of years back—or was it longer?—when some priest—not one of us, praise the Lord—made that pronouncement about fallout shelters. Do you recall it? He said it was a man's duty to own a gun and use it to fight off intruders into his fallout shelter, comes the day of the Big Bang. I suppose he himself would do likewise. That's not very fittin'! Or Christian, either. Is it?"

Alec went on gazing at his parent. The young wife sulked. Mr. Watson smiled and smiled.

"Isn't it nice; you don't hear much about shelters nowadays, do you?" Mrs. Beneker went on, with unshakable social poise and small talk. "I always thought it such a mistake when President Kennedy allowed himself to be quoted—in *Life*, was it?—saying everyone ought to have his own fallout shelter. I can't agree. How about people in cities? How about the poor? That didn't seem very Christian to me, either."

Mr. Watson, accustomed to any number of Sunday irrelevancies from parishioners, smiled some more. Audrey, who had come to the bottom of her drink, held it out mutely toward her husband to be filled. But his eyes never swerved from his mother.

The bees still hummed in the climbing roses. The terrace was deliciously shaded from the midday sun by the awning of tiny leaves. Far beyond the row of sheltering trees, the summer fields could be seen, golden in the sunshine. Audrey held her empty glass, balancing it.

"My own feeling is," Mrs. Beneker said with pretty diffidence, "people should spare time from their busy lives to consult their consciences. Ask themselves what is fittin', when and if the awful day of the Big Bang should arrive. As we pray it will not, of course. The pundits tell us that the danger has become so great that there is no danger anymore." She blinked, and Mr. Watson, like a mirror, blinked with her. "I mean, people need to ask themselves are they worth saving. Then what are they worth saving for? I have come to the conclusion," Mrs. Beneker said, "that the value old people have in a post-Bomb world must be twofold."

She paused, but nobody spoke. The clergyman was struggling with an influx of mystifying impressions. These are what pass for Great Thoughts to her, he thought, groping.

"Twofold," Mrs. Beneker repeated. "After the cataclysm will be a new world. If there is any world left at all! And youth must inherit. The use of the old, in such a world, will be twofold."

"Oh, stop saying 'twofold,'" Audrey murmured.

"Shut up," her husband told her.

"What was all that?" Mrs. Beneker asked.

Audrey got up and walked into the house.

Mrs. Beneker lifted her eyebrows minutely and went on. "A two-fold value," she said. "Both necessarily in relation to the youth. First, to care for them. They will need those with wisdom and tenderness to care for them in their terrible hardships. Second, to teach the youth. It is us oldsters who must pass on the torch of civilization."

Mr. Watson's eyes, moving to Alec's face, drawn by a barrage of dark emotion, winced. She's making him feel . . . murderous.

He hoped he was exaggerating. He often did exaggerate. There was the time when, driving with John Nichols in John Nichols' car, he suddenly had the perfectly clear impression that John was going to push him out of the car, at sixty miles an hour. Instead, in a minute John turned toward him and said, "How can you believe in such rubbish as God?"

"Mother," Alec Beneker said. He peered down into the wavery depths of his drink. "Why don't you tell Mr. Watson about this fabulous old house?"

"What you want me to tell?" his mother said tartly.

"Oh, anything at all. I'm sure he'd be interested in its history. Its quaint ins and outs. This is a truly venerable mansion, as you can see, Mr. Watson. Three Presidents have set foot on these thresholds. Innumerable brides—none more beautiful than my mother—have been carried across them."

"Go find Audrey and tell her to come back," Mrs. Beneker ordered. "People will be arriving."

"In a moment, Mother," he said lazily, turning his glass around and around.

"Why can't you ever do something when I ask you to do it?" she snapped.

Alec gave her a blank, artificial smile and made a couple of hitching, straining movements as though trying to get up out of his chair and unable to. But it was too late now anyway. Giving little cries and salutations, a man and a woman in Sunday-lunch attire came pushing through the French windows, hands outstretched.

"How pretty all this is!" the woman exclaimed. She pressed her cheek to that of her hostess, who had risen.

"Vera! Dear!" Mrs. Beneker turned to the husband. "And Raymond! Have you met Dr. Beecham's new assistant at St. James's? Mr. Watson, Mr. and Mrs. Pugh."

Mr. Watson jumped at hearing his name spoken. He had been rapt in a vision—sudden, radiant—that fulfilled the earlier hint, that explained everything between Mrs. Beneker and her son. One of the miracles of reversal-into-the-opposite was going to happen to them.

His vision was of them together, as though for eternity, in a tiny, secret place, a place not a bit grand but humble rather—only the barest shelter, such as a stable was. "Silent Night, Holy Night" sang itself joyfully in Mr. Watson's head. At the bottom of everybody's life, no matter how hateful, he thought, persisted the same age-old symbol, the same right relation, that needed only time to work itself out. That time was not far off for the Benekers. No matter what base motives drew its parts, neither fire nor flood could keep love apart.

More and more people were arriving, and in no time at all the young clergyman, with his shining eyes, was being tossed about like a little boat on a sea of chatter about the stock market, jet travel, politics—subjects he knew nothing whatever about. But, with the key to everything in his heart, he smiled and smiled, listened and listened, as he practiced being all things to all men.

Mrs. Beneker, for her part, was relieved to be greeting new arrivals. It made her so uneasy when Alec kept bringing up the house in that annoying way of his. As she greeted two more newcomers, she looked over their heads and saw that Alec was making drinks, and Audrey, praise the Lord, back on the terrace where she belonged, speaking to people, fulfilling her obligations. Mrs. Beneker hoped she'd have the grace to pass canapés.

She didn't know why Alec had to keep asking her to tell about the quaint ins and outs of this old house, unless it was simply because he saw it annoyed her. Why must he be so harsh, so grim? She'd endured his unsuccessful growing up—the poor marks, the undesirable friends, the debts—always looking forward to having a tall grown-up son to lean on; but all she'd got in the end, it seemed, was an enemy.

Simply to be annoying must surely be why he did it, because she was almost positive that he couldn't have the faintest idea of the truth. She had had it put in long after he was married and gone away. She had sent to New York for the plans. Nobody but two workmen, to each of whom she had given a hundred dollars, knew that it existed right here under her feet as she stood talking.

She couldn't think it unnatural not to have told Alec. Telling him would have been the unnatural thing, what with his unpleasantness to her. As a grown-up man with a wife—furthermore, as a rich man—it was certainly his own responsibility to provide for himself and Audrey.

The fact was, she thought, even as she pressed Tom Hyde's hand and said, "How awfully good of you to come! How *is* your poor leg?"—the actual fact was it felt heavenly not to share her secret. Not with Hobart, her husband, dead for years; not with Alec; not with anybody. It made her happy just to think of it there, underfoot, cozy and snug, ready and waiting. When she walked into it, as she occasionally did to check on supplies, being enclosed made her feel as though the place itself embraced her—almost like being Aunt Lucy's baby again; back in her arms and loved. It was so nice there— the tidy shelves of canned goods, the neat bunks against the wall. She'd had two bunks put in, because she had this silly feeling that, even at her age, love might come to her. Even at her age, you never knew what strange encounter might still occur!

Her thoughts made her give Tom Hyde a sudden flirtatious smile. "Alec!" she called in her pretty, high voice. "Ask Mr. Hyde what he'll take. Quickly!"

Alec nodded. Make another round of drinks. Meet another round of people. Get through another of Mother's Sunday lunches. . . .

What Mother didn't know was that he knew. When—as it amused him to do—he called people's attention to the antiquity of this house, he could see it set up doubts in her mind about whether he possibly *could* know. Of course he knew! She was the one who was too silly to know anything.

Since he was about eight, he had been aware of the secret passage in Rosemont. He had never discussed it with her, but what had he ever discussed with her? Imagine not knowing more about a boy's nature than that! During his childhood he had not only stolen off into the secret passage but had made his own additions to it—nailed up a shelf here, scooped out a cranny there, even once constructed two steps. She'd never known it because she'd been too busy with her flirtations to know anything about the skinny, unpopular boy he had been.

On a weekend three years ago, when he and Audrey had been visiting just like this and he couldn't sleep, he had, just for the fun of it, after so many years, gone down the passage that began in the attic, wound around the drawing-room chimney, and went down two steps—*his* steps—to a shorter passage, then down the side of a stone wall that was part of the cellars. The passage used then to end up in an outlet into the terrace well. There he had encountered something strange, something new. She had built it without telling anyone. Not even him!

It wasn't locked. He had walked about in it, catching his breath after the squeeze through the passage, viewing the tidy rows of cans, the neat bunks, the water tank. She'd made it very snug, cozy. In the three years since then, there had been other weekends here, and another thing his mother didn't know was that in that time her precious secret had received a slight alteration. He had taken out a square lead-lined wooden panel backing on the passage and fitted it with nylon strips so that it could easily be removed. Then he replaced it.

If the ultimate escape ever did become necessary now, she could go down into her secret place to sit it out, to wait for the day when she would come out and start caring—caring!—for all that youth she talked about, start teaching whatever in the world she thought she had to teach. There would be time then. Plenty of time for her to reflect on all the ways she'd failed life, failed her child.

And just in case she needed reminding, why, it would be a surprise to her, wouldn't it—a real surprise—to see the end of her precious shelter begin to move. And who would come crawling in? None other than her own beloved son, if he had to come through fire and flood to get there.

JOY WILLIAMS is twenty-two years old, was born in New England, graduated Phi Beta Kappa from Marietta College, Marietta, Ohio, and received her MFA from the State University of Iowa. She has previously published a short story, "In Search of Boston," in *New Campus Writing No. 5*. She lives now in Florida where her husband is a newspaperman.

The Roomer

Tᴴᴇ house was large with a brick driveway and the curved protruding windows of doctors' old-fashioned waiting rooms. Most of the homes in that section of the city overlooking the bay belonged to doctors or lawyers or ancient ladies who spent the summer days wrapped in rugs before cold fireplaces, but the Andersons were young and from the midwest, renting the house because it was cheap and convenient and because the men in Anderson's office had recommended it when he told them that they wanted their own place —a big place, big enough for her paintings and his books. They had come in May and were still bewildered by the rotting but insistent sensibilities of the people and the archaic calm of a neighborhood so close to the city, though even that was a bit archaic, as some northern metropolises are, with its granite statue of Longfellow, supported by marble and flowers, in the square and its flatiron-shaped buildings.

After the weeks of unpacking and arranging had passed, they decided to take in a roomer, although the same men said that it was highly unlikely that they would find one, as it was not customary in the region for strangers, not even the summer students at the small college, to stay in private homes. There were many rooms however ("If you closed all the doors upstairs," Jimmie had said, "it would be like the sleeping deck of a ship.") and since they had enough spare furniture to furnish one nicely, they put an ad in the paper. It was a late afternoon in June and they were eating dinner when she came. Mr. Anderson heard the screen door being pulled back long seconds before the knocks, as if the caller were a postman fumbling with a package or a child who, after the exertion and concentration required in opening the outer door, can no longer remember what his purpose was. But then the rapping came—hollow and thin—as if the person were hitting the mahogany with a ring, not so much shy or hesitant as it was restrained.

"You advertised a room for rent," she said. The raw spring air flapped about Anderson's face like a cloth and blew the girl's long red hair across her cheeks in wisps. She stood on the steps in a chino skirt and collarless green blouse, the newspaper in her hand folded into a square. A convertible the color of hardened mustard was parked across the street, its top up. She bumped her foot against the milk-bottle box on the porch and looked vaguely at the trees or upstairs windows or sky—turning slowly about as she spoke, so that when she had finished the sentence, she almost had her back to him. She wore no lipstick and her features seemed to melt away under his gaze like soft butter, her face having the appearance of a sketch made with the wrong end of a pen. Everything was faint and fluid except the eyes which were black as buttonhooks—impenetrable and vacuous at the same time. He waved her inside.

"Yes," he said. "A nice room. Thirty dollars a month with a phone and a washing machine downstairs. You're welcome to use the kitchen too. Here, I'll show you that first and then we can go to the room. The staircase back there is shorter to the upstairs."

She walked behind him, trailing her hand over shelves and chairs, silently absorbing the room as if her fingers were porous. His wife turned from the stove where she had been boiling spaghetti when they came in. On the opposite back burner was a small crucible with chunks of lead in it and an iron ladle and scattered about the chipped drainboard of the sink were various plaster moulds and a tray of sand. A slender, pale boy, his hair combed neatly down over his forehead in bangs sat at the table clutching a jam sandwich in one hand and rubbing a mosquito bite on his chin with the other.

"This is Jimmie," Anderson said, "who wants to beat out his ma as the artist of the family." A bulletin board hung on the wall, covered with scraps of lined yellow paper of pencilled drawings. Blue and gold stars were pasted crookedly over sturdily inked printings of the name *James*.

"Child," the girl said, as if she were practicing the slur of a foreign sound on her tongue, that small pale form containing within its childishness every syllable of the word. "A child."

"He won't disturb you," his mother said quickly, eager to dispel that sense of chaos that children and dogs convey to motel owners. "He's a quiet little fellow and with the nice weather he's outside most of the time."

The girl shrugged her shoulders. "My name is Grey," she said. "You may show me the room."

She moved in the same night and in the weeks that followed she became as much a part of the house as the inanimate objects that furnished it. She was quiet and told them little about herself except that she came from a neighboring state and was attending summer school, taking credits in French and Latin. Sometimes they would not see her for days and other evenings they would come home to find that she had prepared dinner for them or cleaned the house. Her room was always spare and neat, uncluttered by pictures or a great many books, the tall bare walls hampered only by a large mirror that she had brought herself and a small copy of an early de Chirico. They grew accustomed to her—even began to be fond of her. She wooed them with silence and the fact that she was so alone, drifting in a private world like the child.

Grey's only effort seemed to be with Jimmie. Everything else she did casually, obliquely—days and people making no impression upon the empty tranquility of her face—the child's presence, like a single stone thrown in a sea pool, creating the only ripple in the dull, smooth heat of the early summer. His friendly unawareness of her was complete. She slipped as easily in and out of his mind as the games or tears of the day before, his remembrance of her being as swift and transitional as the white press print of a thumb on sunburnt skin. This indifference was most clear to her the morning she offered to take him swimming. He was playing outside, his knees stained green under the rumpled corduroy of his shorts. He looked up, interest flickering momentarily in his grey eyes and then dying away again.

"I don't want to go in your car." He squatted on the steps and examined his sneakers. "I want to go in Daddy's car."

"It's not here. He drove it to work."

"Then I don't want to go." He glanced at her quickly. "I don't like your car."

"All right," she said softly. She slipped behind the wheel, the hot

plastic of the seat covers burning her thighs, the anger towards that
small crease of paleness against stone beating at her temples like
the white splash of a dream. She stared at the sky and then at him,
the New England sun, even in summer, unable to blot him out.
His face momentarily became an orange smear but then lurched
back again, as if it would always remain there in bobbing certainty
of her initial failure.

"I'll bring you back a present."

"Ice-cream?" he asked, interested in her once more.

"Better than that," she scratched at the gear shift with her
painted nails. "Much better than that."

Jimmie wandered off to pat a collie that was trotting through the
yard, and Grey backed quickly out onto the street. Perspiration ran
down her face like tears and her loose hair hung heavy on her bare
shoulders. The clot of rage over the child's refusal pushed against
her chest and as she drove through the city and towards the sea,
she dangled her arm outside, pressing her fingers against the car's
finish—absorbing every shred of pain that the hot cruelty of the
paint could give.

Before turning off on the beach road, she stopped, drawing her
face close to a mirror clipped on the visor. Her eyes looked like
running lumps of chocolate. She had never been so hot. She wiped
her neck and face with a thick terrycloth towel and drove on down
to the ocean, using as her guide a jetty of land, on the tip of which
was a lighthouse, rising into the sky like a white cruller. When the
lighthouse was exactly opposite, she parked the car and walked
across a splintered boardwalk to the sand, deliberately stepping into
the puddle of a dropped ice-cream cone—feeling the sticky coldness
seep up through her toes.

She had counted on Jimmie to amuse her, planning her day with
him as soon as she had awakened that morning, imagining the way
he would kneel on the seat beside her, sniffing the wind and the
rushing heat like a puppy, and dressing slowly before breakfast,
rubbing tanning lotion carefully over her body, she was confident
that he would come with her. Her anger now instead of swelling
further simply throbbed as if her whole self had been sprained by
his denial of her, fearful with the thought that she had scarcely
touched that solemn little mind.

Grey had planned that he would be there, and now without paper
or books, she sat and gazed along the crowded beach. Plastic horses

reared and grinned from the water and further out, a girl on one
ski was crookedly ploughing up foam behind an inboard. A large
red ball with a clown on it bounced away from a group of children
and struck her knee. She returned it to a blond, plump boy who
swaggered over to her towel, who called her 'M'am' and wore braces
on his teeth. She watched them for a few more moments and went
to the water, scooping it up in handfulls and dabbing her neck and
arms. She walked back to the car then, slipping a shift over her
swimsuit and drove back to town.

She waited outside the photo booth in Woolworth's for over half
an hour, studying the strips of glass-enclosed pictures that covered
the outer walls. The booth was in the rear of the store by the pet
department and the air was thick with the smell of birds and saw-
dust. The teenagers finally left and she stepped behind the curtain,
plunging quarters into the slot, shifting her stance, her gaze at every
click of the light, the strips of prints, wet as birth from the devel-
oper, falling on the floor as she deposited more money. There were
thirty pictures in all, none being quite the same, but all stemming
the characteristic fluidity of her features into an awesome rigidity—
and one she considered to be perfect. She bought a sheaf of thick
paper and some india ink, and in the public library, opposite an old
man who was carefully copying the script of an Arabic newspaper
into a looseleaf notebook, she drew the picture, altering the new-
found definitions of her face as if she were carving a woodcut, and
that night she gave her strange present to Jimmie.

In the beginning she could hear his breathing—heavy and young
and careless—and she would pause by his room to stare at the motionless form sprawled on the bed as if it were boneless, watching
the moonlight sift through the screens and light up marbles in a
jar and the chrome bumper of a dumptruck. But now she no longer
had to go to the door. She merely sat on her own bed in the dark,
the blinds pulled tight to the sill, making the deepness of the night
still deeper, a pillow pressed to her lips to make even that heavy
stillness yet more quiet. Sitting there, pushing all the substance out
of her head as a child would air from a rubber toy, leaving nothing
but a tight conscious emptiness, she waited for the sound, not of
childish sleep now but of the restless amazed tossing that would
mean he had finally left the window, the white image that could
blot out the sky now lingering only under his closed lids, searing
her features, made solid for the first time by their hugeness, into

his eyes and through them, paining him, becoming as much a part
of him as the tip of his tongue burnt on hot chocolate or the warm
tickling of his bowels.

The sky, once holding stars and rockets and rain now showed
only her, night after night, not even containing her but being contained by her, giving Jimmie the tortured, delicious feeling of being
consumed, of being swallowed. He tore at the sheets and the dark,
an abyss of thought crushing his small frame, his little-boy's mind
being able only to compare it to his fear of falling from a treehouse
onto the twisted roots below.

The present being a gift of agony in the shape of a bubblegum
card but with her face there instead of a cowboy or baseball player,
and with the colors all wrong. Like a negative—the white and the
black changing places—the white milky and strong and demanding
—so demanding that he was forced to absorb it, even against his
will, and then looking at a blank wall or the sky, but especially the
sky as she had told him to, the face would slip out from somewhere
beyond the corners of his straining eyes to swim upwards, expanding
in the night until he thought that the world or his brain would
burst like a pumpkin hurled on ice, his body trembling with the joy
and terror of his yearning.

His mother, hearing the squeak of springs—the thick tumbling
of sleeplessness in that room—would come upstairs and look in, no
longer seeing her child's form, spilling light and profound as mercury
across the bed but a stranger almost whose hard body tensed and
coiled at her touch. She came up now every night, giving him some
water or a kiss and waited for him to tell her the dream, the nightmare—knowing she could dispel the night thoughts of bears or
knives or witches with lamplight, but not knowing how to break
through a boy's silence to discover a man's demons.

Distantly, Jimmie sat Indian-style, clutching the glass in both
hands, rolling its coolness against his forehead and cheeks, the picture hidden under his pillow as he once hid acorns or capguns to
frighten off dragons and waited for the alien woman-flesh of his
mother to leave him. Later, when he heard her coming up the stairs,
he would slump under the sheets, feigning sleep, and she would
only rearrange the blankets or touch his head and then go, Grey,
in the next room, being the waiting conscious witness to all of this—
the nightly, sad, spiraling ritual.

Before the images in the sky, there were never enough hours of the sun for Jimmie, and the daylight, stark and still and high, so different from the bright, rampant coloring of the midwestern summer, was a cup for him—much too small to contain all the discoveries and delights of his age. There were few children in the neighborhood—he played with others only when he went to the beach—but wrapped in the sweet cocoon of self, he did not miss them. He sailed plywood boats in the backwash of the bay and swung on a thick rope, suspended between elms in the yard, kicking the air like a jungle king and dropped to the ground, rolling on the lawn, munching on grass, burying marbles and buttons and making elaborate maps to find them again, and sometimes, after his parents came home, he would just lie on the couch in the dusky livingroom, listening to the brisk rattle of his father's typewriter, or pose stiffly and proudly for his mother as she sketched his picture in charcoal.

Now he fled from his mother, fled from the days, meaningless for him if he could not be with Grey—the night picture of her still strong but less important now in the heightened presence of her physical self. She was thinner now and brown. He noticed that her hair was piled on top of her head and no longer muffled her face, and he exulted in these discoveries that seemed to make her more for him. His parents grew concerned over his moodiness, noticing the child's deeper and deeper penetration into his own solitude, and their subsequent attentions caused Jimmie to play a more intense and conscious game than he had ever done before with top planes or trucks—controlling his anxieties and desires when with them as he would manipulate the twine of a kite, acting out what once did not have to be pretended, what never for years should have been aware of being pretended, as he would the characters in a picture book, to keep them content.

He sat at the breakfast table in the early morning with them, the eggs hardening on the plate before him into rubbery inedibility, and waited for Grey to come down the stairs. She stood in the kitchen talking to them and peeling an orange—the acrid smell of the torn fruit floating through the warm air like a tangible part of her—while Jimmie brought her books to the car.

"Your little beau," Mrs. Anderson said to Grey.

He could not speak to her. He dared not—his childish chattering cut off as if by the slam of a door whenever he was with her—his need and hers, being only that he should always be there. She took him to the beach or matinees, and sometimes at noon, instead of eating the icebox lunch that his mother had earlier prepared and wrapped in waxpaper, he would go with her to the college cafeteria and eat tomato sandwiches in huge booths. On such days, they would leave as soon as the boy had swallowed the last mouthful, talking to no one, not even to each other, and go to the library or watch students play baseball in the park. It was a solemn, silent, courtship, a bleak continuance in which the child's early bewilderment turned to acceptance and then into a necessity for proof, Jimmie learning from her, most of all, a reserve, a stoicism, a rarefying and heightening of the emotions which were honed almost to madness by his innocent precociousness.

Once, they had been in the kitchen, Jimmie playing with his mother's molding wax, heating it in a saucepan until it became liquid, poking it with the tip of a knife and making designs on a plate. Grey watched him unmoving, barely breathing, even when the pan tipped over, spilling the molten, blue wax on his hand—searing, bubbling, puckering the skin. He screamed in anguish, tearing at the hot wax and gouging the flesh, and turning to Grey, saw only her impassive, immobile face. His own face froze then. He straightened his swollen lips as if they were wire and stared back rigidly into those chunks of black that were her eyes, the useless hand trembling uncontrollably at his side. He sat beside her and she stroked his head. The whistle of an oil tanker came in from the bay while the wax hardened on the floor and she told him strange words that clutched and contained his wants and fears like a glove, knowing now that there would only be the waiting and that it too would end.

She left in the car before his parents came home. They found only the boy, standing before the stove which had been on now for most of the afternoon, the gas flames flickering up through the burner, touching only air. They found only the boy who said that he had been playing alone and who did not cry, even at the hospital where they treated his shredding flesh.

At home, they made him spend most of the week in bed. He drank gingerale and ate from a tray, never seeing Grey. He was afraid that she might have moved away, but on the third night after the accident, after he had watched television and taken a bath, the tape on his hand covered in plastic, his mother had come into his room in a black partydress, smelling sweet and powdery as she bent to kiss him, telling him that Grey would be there to watch him and that they would be home early.

For hours he seemed to wait, long after the car had rattled over the loose brick in the driveway, long after it became dark. For hours until he thought that it was so late that they would be coming back again—the moments stretching before him like interminable train tracks, time loping slowly ahead of him as it did sometimes at school or on rainy afternoons. He waited, his back leaning against the headboard of the bed, thumping his bandaged fingers against the bony protuberances of his ribs—his legs folded under the sheets, itching and thick from his very consciousness of them. His awareness of everything was acute—the furniture in the room seemingly carved out of the dark, the glass knobs on the bureau staring at him like eyes. He swallowed thickly, feeling nauseous, but it was the same exhilarating sweet nausea he had felt last Easter when he had eaten too much chocolate—chocolate ducks and rabbits and spun-sugar eggs with little scenes inside made of mint. He had discovered the candy that they were going to surprise him with hidden in a paper-bag in a kitchen drawer where they stored mittens and scarves and he had run to the cellar with it, hiding under the ping-pong table and eating slowly at first, then faster and faster, biting off ears and legs first, freshening his mouth occasionally with the candy creature's gumdrop eyes. And he had discovered that he couldn't stop—like sometimes after weeks of playing in earnest and serious calm, he would begin to giggle and then laugh—the laughter turning into a noiseless shaking that racked his body like fever. He discovered that he couldn't stop eating the sweets. Long after his stomach was round and hard as a cakepan, long after he was even conscious of eating anymore, he had gone on until the whole bag was gone, staggering, then, upstairs, white and sick and happy.

Such now was the feeling of nausea as Jimmie waited and listened to the dim sound of the radio down the hall, thinking now that Grey had forgotten him, that she had fallen asleep. Then he held his breath, stiffening, afraid that the sound was just the old house or his mind, and he watched the strip of light grow from the opening door—watched the light broaden and thicken like the flash of a sword and then shrink and disappear again. He sensed her presence now, smelled her, felt her slip quietly beside him, and he opened his mouth to scream—the shriek of it hanging in his ears so shrill and piercing that he expected the universe to crack, the house to tumble as if it were made of glass—but he didn't make a sound when she touched him—no sound at all.

CHRISTOPHER DAVIS has published four novels, the most recent *Belmarch: a Legend of the First Crusade*, as well as fiction for
children, and short stories and nonfiction in *The Saturday Evening
Post*, *Esquire*, and *Holiday*. His first novel *Lost Summer* was adapted
for Broadway as *There Was a Little Girl*. He lives in Philadelphia
with his wife and three children.

A Man of Affairs

WE MET by appointment near the church called Trinità dei Monti.
Having counted on the unexpected—his voice on the telephone told
me he was small, neat, fussy, so I expected him to be burly—I discovered him to be small and neat and to wear a fussy little moustache. He also wore the grey bowler he had told me about as
identification, and a grey topcoat with a grey-velvet collar, and black
shoes with Rome as far as St. Peter's reflected upside down in the
toe of each.

"Mr. Vicenza?"

"Good, good," he said, looking me over. His face was brown and
leathery, lined all over yet filled as tightly and neatly as a little brown
nut; the bright white eyebrows and the moustache, silver, twisted
and fixed with wax, glowed in the sunset. "Fine," he murmured.
"Yes." He waved a leaf-brown hand at Rome lying below the Spanish Steps, not himself looking where the hand pointed. "Lovely?
What do you think of that? A vista and a half."

His English was excellent. It had seemed so on the telephone,
and I wanted to ask at once why he had bothered about my advertisement, what need he had of English lessons, but I was too shy
and too scared the fish would get away, so I gazed, grinning a little,
into the twilight-filled well of the Steps, nodding. "Beautiful," I said.
"It's wonderful with those azaleas all over—"

"At Easter. No. I think it's not. Such an awful, odor-making clutter,
and such colors!" As if with reluctance, he took his quick grey eyes

from me and started down the Steps at a brisk pace, addressing me over his shoulder as I followed. "The Keats House there on your left. See the plaque."

"I know—"

"'When I have fears that I may cease to be—' Twenty-six-years old only. How old are you, Green?"

"Twenty-two."

"Good, good." "*Bene, bene,*" he would always say in Italian. I thought: a speech habit. But looking back I think he meant what he said literally. He gave the flower vendor opposite the Bernini fountain a sharp look. "All right, then." He bought a cornflower and, sticking out his lower lip with concentration, fixed it in his lapel. "Cornflowers. Forget-me-nots, but not azaleas."

He led me rapidly down the Via del Babuino, nodding right and left. "English tearoom. Not bad, but dear. Excellent tailor there. Our Roman clothes are the best. I buy my hats over there in that little shop. That man, Biondo, has good eighteenth-century prints of Rome and a few genuine Etruscan pieces and lots of—junk?"

"What?"

"I want the American word."

"Junk, I guess."

"He will cheat you in any case. I buy my shirts over there. See that restaurant? One of the most expensive in Rome and I found a spider in my spinach. That man standing in his shop door is a forger of paintings."

When we reached the Piazza del Popolo he chose his café table with care and sat down, sighing and smiling in the attitude of a man who has reached a harbor. "Good. Fine. Swell?"

I stared.

"I want the American word."

"Well—swell."

He ordered two iced camparis, then addressed me in a business-like tone.

"You guess my secret, of course. I want to learn American, as distinct from English. You observe that my English is good—good enough for all practical purposes anyhow. I am in the exporting business—cotton, which I buy up in various parts of the Mediterranean, and which, until recently, I shipped to England. Now I have American orders and I want to speak exact American. For example: the

clients when they come to Rome. I greet them personally at the
Excelsior or the Eden and I say?" He peered into my eyes.
"Well—you say—" I frowned. Now the fish would get away. "You
say, 'How do you do? I am Mr. Vicenza.' "
"That's English!"
"It's the same."
"No, no, no." He looked irritated. "I know better, Green. They
are nearly distinct languages. First cousins, perhaps, but distinct.
Another thing is that I want an American to tell me all about
America, and, inasmuch as you said in your advertisement that you
are a writer, all about American writers. Criticism is my hobby, and
I have now arrived at the criticism of American literature."
It looked good. I said, "I know something about that."
He surveyed me again in that appraising, nearly admiring way that
had come close to unnerving me earlier. "Good, good. That's what
I want. The fresh viewpoint, unspoiled by success."
"I wish I was spoiled by success."
He showed a row of white teeth under the glowing moustache.
"You're right. You imply that success spoils those who will be
spoiled in any case, and I agree. I wish you success in your work. Can
you guess something?" He had thrown his head back, disposing of
the subject of success, and was gazing straight up into the sky, the
taut, wrinkled-nut face shining. "You can't, I'll bet?" He rolled his
gaze sideways to me, proud of the phrase. "I'll bet a million you can't
guess something. I once jumped out of an airplane with a parachute
—only two years ago, and I am today sixty-three-years old—in order
to see Rome in that way. Can you believe it? No one believes that,
but it is true. I could produce the pilot of the plane tomorrow." Staring up into the sky, he suddenly trilled a complicated birdcall. "I'm
happy. I do that when I'm happy, and now I'm happy thinking of
American authors and of learning American. What a fine silence
here, despite the Roman—traffic?"
I nodded.
"Do you know the silence at twilight when the swallows go to
their nests? Like a cloister, isn't it? Once, in that silence, there was
one swallow left (I was walking in the Largo Argentina) and *pat*
like a dive bomber right on my new hat—a homburg. That to me
was a precise definition of the most humanity may hope for in
beauty—but I am cynical."
I laughed and he joined me, his grey eyes bright on my face. "Yes.

Excellent, isn't it? Wasn't that a perfect moment of its kind? I adore
irony. You'll want to discuss price, of course."

"What?"

"For the lessons. And we must decide how often they will take
place."

"Well, at your convenience."

"Of course. My work is arranged so all of my afternoons are free,
and I am free too, then, to indulge my hobby. Come now, Americans
are not generally shy in matters of business, and this is not a complicated matter." He made a picture with his hands of complicated
business by interlacing the fingers and twisting them. "However,
don't ask too much."

"I thought—" I felt myself blush "—about a thousand. *Lire.*"

"Ah. *Lire.* You thought that. Yes." He trilled a bird song. "Well,
that is too much, you know."

We talked back and forth. Vicenza changed the subject, ordered
two more camparis, mentioned price again in a delicate oblique way.
We settled at last on seven hundred, and decided that we would
meet for two hours each afternoon Monday through Friday—that he
would come at three, leave at five. It meant thirty-five hundred *lire*
a week, which was nearly all of my room rent. We beamed at each
other. I said, "Well."

He said, "And we'll begin straightaway—tomorrow?"

"Yes." I grinned. "By saying 'right away' or 'immediately,' instead
of 'straightaway,' which is English."

"*Is* it? Now, I thought that was American."

It had grown dark. Vicenza paid for the drinks and rose. "Do you
have other pupils?"

"Not yet."

"Don't take any. I will occupy your afternoons. You will use your
mornings, when you are fresh and creative, to write."

I said slowly, "All right. I'll think about it anyway. Maybe you're
right."

"Have you got a girl friend?"

"No." I was startled. "I mean I did, but—"

"It's none of my business. You are better off, I think. A serious
author avoids distractions and buys his amusements when he can
afford them. Right?"

"I don't think so necessarily—"

"I will come to your rooms for the lessons. The address in the advertisement?"

"I could come to your house."

"You miss the point. I want to go to America. I don't want America to come to me."

Returning to the Villa Torlonia area where I lived, I was at first jubilant; then I thought: "But he's coming to my room," and my joy, as I watched the headlight of a Vespa racing the bus, turned grey.

My room was large and high, with floors of composition marble, waist-high paneling stained dark brown, and sepia photographs of Roman scenes and of a smiling barefoot boy with a fish on a string that, like the boy, smiled. The room had a hot plate for cooking and, through large double windows, an excellent view of the Villa Torlonia's gardens. The landlady, Signora Nelli, a placid widow with neither curiosity nor imagination, left me to myself; the rent was low—eight and a half dollars a week—and the other tenants silent and invisible. I had come to look upon the room as something more of my own possession than the things in it that were actually mine to carry off; and when I was away from it for a time—a weekend, say—I would become uneasy, homesick I suppose; and when I returned to it, standing in its doorway and greeting each of its familiar features with affection, I, who had never lived in a place half as attractive or a quarter so much my own, would sigh with pleasure and relief. It was this that made me uncomfortable about the lessons: the prospect of sharing my room, even though it was only for ten hours a week.

At just three the next afternoon I heard Vicenza's happy bird warble below my window and, a moment later, a knock on my door.

"You heard my whistle? I deliberately whistled to warn you of my imminence." He entered the room, church-like in its saffron mid-afternoon light, sat down on one of the two chairs, and looked around appreciatively. "Very pleasant. A student's room in which the character of the student stands flatteringly revealed. I lived in a similar one when I attended the University."

I was pleased and, seeing my smile, Vicenza nodded knowingly. "Yes. There was a very small girl friend then—a blonde, I recall. Yes." He squinted into the past. "I used to smuggle her into my room because the landlady was so severe about *morality*." He laughed. "I suppose landladies the world over are like that. They are all hopelessly frustrated and secretly in love with the young men, their clients—boarders, isn't it?—and jealous of them."

I said, "Well, Signora Nelli's the exception. She doesn't care one way or the other."

"No? That's your landlady? Well." He gave the room and its contents another glance, crossed his neat legs in a swift movement, and began to speak in Italian. "How long have you lived in Rome?"

"Around three months. I lived in Florence for a year."

"I find Florence rather closed in. Don't you get the feeling there's a roof over the entire city? Well. Your Italian is reasonable, but the accent—" He smiled sadly into the grey bowler, which he held in his hands. "Then I ask myself: how does he manage to support himself all these months—this unpublished writer? But, of course, you worked and saved, and then borrowed, too. Right? But now, at a crucial moment, the great work must stand still because the bank account has so dwindled that you must choose between returning home and taking pupils. There is a great work?"

My gaze turned automatically to the desk beside the window. Then I blushed.

"Good, good." His eyes studied me, seemingly fascinated. "Good. You could write an essay on the subject of the out-at-elbows American student in Rome and perhaps sell it. No? That's not creative. Please believe I intend no irony. Irony." He sighed. "I think you are courageous to live as you do, and I, knowing I could not do so, admire you for it. The exigencies have made me one of life's moral cowards. But never mind that." The taut nut-brown face glowed happily in my room's golden light. He returned to English. "Now to work. I'm quite ready." And after a long moment during which I could only stare at him: "Nothing?"

"I don't know how to begin."

"Only begin! I want to hear an American who is a writer talk about American writers. Tell me about Steinbeck who has won that great prize, as our beloved and magnificent Quasimodo did. Do you like Steinbeck?"

"Well—"

"But Hemingway, too, has been such an influence, so much more than the others, really. And Faulkner. And what about the younger people? We read them in Italian, when there are translations. I, of course, read them in the original. The trouble is that there is such a multiplication of them. Where *does* one begin? I see your dilemma, Green. Do you know—of course you couldn't—that I once met your Gertrude Stein? And she said to me, 'Vicenza, when one really begins to write, one leaves off thinking.' Perhaps we could use the same method in our discussions in writing."

I laughed.

"I'm serious. Don't think at all. Simply begin. Arbitrarily and without thought. Say something."

I gazed at him stupidly, and then suddenly relaxed and began to talk. It was, I was sure, good talk, though I now remember very little of what we said. Vicenza was beyond a doubt brilliant. He was encyclopedic about literature—that is about all of the literature of all of Western Europe as far as I could tell; he had absorbing and original theories of his own, which he appeared to create on the spur of the moment, and which he presented with utter, almost chilly clarity. I discovered myself talking better than I ever had in my life, coming up with thoughts I never dreamed were in my mind, because, in the old-fashioned way, Vicenza had drawn me out. I felt I should have paid him and I said so.

He smiled, standing in my door. "The arrangement is exactly right. But I'm glad you mention the matter. To be frank, Green. I can pay your fee by the day or give you the lot each Friday. Only say."

I told him, hesitating, that I preferred the money on a daily basis, and at once he drew a few notes from his billfold and placed them on the desk. "Good-bye, then. So long?"

"So long."

I heard his bird whistle down the stairs and again on the street outside. When I looked at the notes I discovered there were a thousand *lire*.

Next day I mentioned it.

"Good, good. It was no mistake," he said with a pleased expression. "I had already decided that if the first lesson went well I would pay the amount you originally asked."

The lesson went well that afternoon, too, with me doing most of the talking this time and Vicenza, perched on a chair in the grey topcoat he refused to remove, holding his grey bowler, throwing in an occasional stimulating question or remark. In the meetings that followed, however, I frequently faltered and went dry (the Stein Method did not always work) and then, smoothly, Vicenza would take over and plunge us both into talk that was icily refreshing in its rationality and always excitingly in motion. Thoughts grew from thoughts, were sustained like Indian clubs between us, flashing, constantly changing and developing, so that neither of us knew or much cared where we were going or where we would end. At length, to end our sessions, he always sighed and said, "Dear Saint Benedetto Croce, hear us and be lenient," and smiled beatifically at me and at my room.

By the end of the first week, certain I had received more information and benefit than I had given and in clear possession of five thousand *lire*, I experienced a sense of pleased guilt. Obviously Vicenza was not only a scholar but a man with rare insight into the mysteries of creative literature and into the problems of the creative writer. I got into the habit, immediately on his departure, of jotting down what seemed to me the most significant ideas that had developed during the afternoon. The sessions, I realized, were becoming necessary to me, and after two weeks I learned to dread the weekends when I not only had to face my grudging typewriter but to face an empty afternoon as well. Vicenza had become my teacher and my single friend in Rome; and at last I admitted that the value of my room had increased because I had shared it.

About the man himself I learned little. I knew he was an exporter of cotton and cotton products, had gone to the University of Rome, had lived in England and in Trieste and Paris, that he disliked planes and boats for traveling, and that he had earned some kind of title. He joked about it, calling himself from time to time, casually, Commander or Cavalier or, once, with a small secret smile, Prince—so that it was impossible to know the truth. I also learned that he had a wife and two grown daughters, both of whom were married and neither of whom had children. His wife he referred to only once and then, in his odd wry way, as "that elderly lady who shares my house."

On a sunny Monday afternoon—the bougainvillaea on the Villa's walls had begun to bloom—Vicenza appeared at my door and handed me a paperbound book.

"You have heard of its author but not the work."

I took in the title—*Uomini d'affari*—then gaped at the name under it: Vittorio Vicenza. "Is it yours?"

"Don't be jealous, Green. I published it myself." He removed his hat and sat down with it in his hands. "Let the lesson begin."

"But when did you write it?"

"Years ago. When I was no older than you are. And even in those days, by way of contrast with your own situation, I could afford to indulge a sense of self-importance by having it printed." He gazed out of the window, apparently at the bougainvillaea, the little ironic smile on his lips, the moustache bright. "I recall that the applause was nearly inaudible; but do you know who liked it a little and was kind enough to say so?" He glanced at me. "Our good friend Dr. Croce. Now there was a serious moment in one's life. So long ago, however—so very many years. . . ."

"Croce! This is wonderful!" I cried. I was turning over the pages of the book. "And it's a novel!"

"Yes." The wistful tone had gone, and he was looking at me now in his fascinated way. "I bring it to you for your opinion. The copy, its pages still uncut, is a gift. Take as long as you need to read it; and if you have nothing to say about it, then please say nothing. Certainly, by now, we respect each other enough for that. Also, if you don't feel like reading it, don't read it." He waved his expensive hat, eyes glowing and contented.

"Have you written anything since?"

"No. Now the lesson," he said gently.

As soon as he had gone I read the novel. It was short—a hundred and twenty pages of large print—and I finished it in a little over an hour. Then I read it again.

The next afternoon I waited impatiently for Vicenza's sprightly whistle, but this time there was none. When I answered the knock at the door I found that my scholar-author-businessman was not alone.

"I want you to meet," Vicenza said in Italian, "Signorina Cianese. Lotti, this is my teacher of American, Mr. Green."

I was confused and I must have shown it because Vicenza raised his brows slightly. I said at last, "*Piacere*, signorina," and smiled at her. I had not fully realized how strong was the habit of the room and myself and Vicenza, with no one else; not even once Signora Nelli had interfered with our talks. The girl was young and had heavy black hair, which she wore tied in back in a horsetail that reached to her waist; she was as pretty as a movie starlet. To acknowledge the introduction, she had nodded without speaking and then moved to the nearest chair. My eyes kept resting on her face, dropping to her full figure, and jumping nervously away. Vicenza

watched her, too. She rummaged in a large straw bag, found cigarettes, and lit one.

"Miss Cianese," said Vicenza, "will join our class this afternoon."

She crossed her fine legs and looked idly about the room. I asked,
still confused, "Shall we speak in Italian?"

"No. I want her to hear English—that is, American. I am teaching
her the language." The expression in his eyes appeared to be compounded of his habitual wryness and stubborn fondness. He said,
addressing me but watching her, "She is a slow learner."

I began to talk about the novel.

"You liked it?" Vicenza asked. He sounded surprised. "I suppose
it has enthusiasm to recommend it."

"No," I said. "More than that. Much more. It's fine. I was deeply
moved by it. By the character of Carlo, with his perfect brutality—
and the schoolteacher: his, you know, inarticulateness." With the
girl there it was hard to say the things I had rehearsed. It all sounded
flat and formal. Yet, clearly, Vicenza was pleased; he sat straight on
the edge of my bed, his gaze shifting from the girl down to his gleaming little shoes, then back again. "You hear that, Lotti? Green says
my novel is fine. You didn't know I was a novelist, did you?" The
girl said, "Come?" and looked irritable. Vicenza repeated the words
in Italian.

"Oh. No, no. I didn't know." She searched for an ashtray, and I
found one, and gave it to her.

I said to Vicenza, "You should go on writing."

He replied politely, "Really? Perhaps you're right." He addressed
the girl. "Should I write another novel, Lotti?"

Miss Cianese shrugged.

"I'm serious," I said. "This one—*Uomini d'affari*—should be re-
printed by that big Milan house. It ought to be translated into English too. *Men of Affairs. The Businessmen.*"

"Well, well. Perhaps. Perhaps you will do it, Green. Now let's get
on to the lesson."

I decided to be dogged about it. "The lesson will be about your
novel. It was thirty years ahead of its time when you wrote it, and
that was why it wasn't appreciated in a popular way."

"And you feel it would be appreciated now?" Vicenza, for a moment, looked solemn, but then he made a gesture. "Really, Green,
we risk boring our guest if we discuss this. I am in earnest."

The rest of the session went badly. The girl said nothing and

Vicenza seemed abstracted. In a lifeless way he told his story about parachuting from a plane and landing just outside of Rome in a field of sharp stones and poppies; it was clear the girl had heard the story before. There were long silences, during which all three of us stared out of my windows at the traffic and at the flowering wall across the street. Twenty minutes before the meeting was due to end Vicenza rose.

"I think we'll take our leave now." Both he and the girl shook my hand. He peered at my eyes for a moment in his fascinated way and asked, "You really liked it?"

I said I did.

He sighed, tossing the rich hat in his hand. "Well, well. Good. I will inscribe your copy for you one day."

Thereafter, for a week, Miss Cianese came with Vicenza to every lesson. She always sat in the same chair, smoking English cigarettes and looking out of the window. Occasionally she would sigh to show that she was bored, and when she did both my eyes and Vicenza's darted to her fearfully. She was given to yawning, too, in a frank, loud, jaw-cracking way that halted conversation. When she was entirely silent Vicenza's gaze would wander to her, appraising her, often resting on her for minutes at a time while our discussion languished and unwound and ultimately died. Whenever she seemed too gloomy and restless Vicenza would cut the session short. I did not discuss his novel again, and Vicenza appeared to have forgotten his promise to inscribe it for me.

One afternoon he appeared alone. He announced himself with a perfunctory bird warble on the stairs, kept his hat on and his topcoat, though it was warm, buttoned up tight.

"I have a favor to ask." He did not look at me.

"Sit down. Where's the signorina?"

"Nearby." He remained standing. "It's about Miss Cianese— Lotti." He paused. "That is, we are lovers."

I said nothing.

"That is, to be explicit," Vicenza went on, "we are not yet lovers."

I said idiotically, "I'm sorry."

"These first fine spring days are, in a manner of speaking, the introduction to our affair. Of course, I have known Lotti for a long time. I knew her father, as a matter of fact, though he is now dead and naturally—" Vicenza sighed in a desperate way "—I no longer know him. Lotti and I . . . well, the difficulty is that Lotti lives with her mother, who is—can you guess? And only in the afternoons can she find some degree of freedom to . . . be herself . . . to be . . . in love." He cleared his throat. "I have several times offered to rent a flat—apartment?—but she refuses. She's ashamed and she says such circumstances would depress her. She is easily made sad. Also, looked at coldly, to rent an apartment would be a mistake for me as I am well-known in Rome, and privacy, which one values so, would be out of the question then. You see? It occurred to me recently that nothing could be safer—more discreet—than just such a place as yours." He turned. "As this. A student's room where one takes lessons or merely chats about literature. Harmless."

I stared at him. "You mean you want my room?"

"Oh, no." His tone was reassuring. "I want us to go on as we have been. Your room is yours, of course. But it occurred to me that now and then, if you feel you wish to, you would absent yourself." He shrugged. "Take a stroll. It's spring. The streets and gardens are lovely. Only for the two-hour period, which in any case is reserved time, paid for."

"I'd rather not," I said.

"Just as you say." He fixed his fascinated eyes on me.

"I'm afraid I couldn't."

"You value your privacy as I do, then? You feel it would be an invasion?"

"More or less. I'd just rather not."

"It's as you say. We'll forget I mentioned it."

He went to the door, glanced at his watch, and paused as if struck by a new idea. "See here, Green. Would it be too much if just today . . . ?" He looked very uncertain and nervous, like a small boy asking for something and knowing he will be refused. "She's waiting on the street, Green. Lotti is really extremely shy. I discover to my considerable horror that I am rather shy myself." And then, still addressing the watch: "You must find this deeply embarrassing. I know I would in your place." He laughed slightly, sadly. "It turns out that I'm imploring you, Green."

I had fully and firmly intended to say no again. I was not embarrassed; I was enraged. But instead—I think it was some memory of the novel, of the character of the schoolteacher in it—I said, "All right."

"Thank you. We will not forget."

I pushed past him. As I walked down the stairs I heard the warbling birdcall, and on the street outside I ran into Lotti. The whistle had been her signal. I nodded, feeling, against my will, righteous and put-upon; she gave me a cold glance and turned into the building.

I returned at five-thirty and found the room empty and spotless —too spotless; not as I had left it. On the bedside table was a typed note: "*Grazie, caro* Green. V." My own typewriter had been used. Under this was a ten thousand *lire* note. Vicenza's novel was propped open against the bed lamp, and he had inscribed it in English:

"Rome, April 6. To my dear good American Green, upon a happy occasion, this work is offered to show the affectionate esteem in which he is held by his friend Vittorio Vicenza"—the signature in such elaborate Italian copperplate that if I had not known whose it was I could not have read it.

I waited a week. I tried to work, but now it was nearly impossible in that room. When it was clear that Vicenza did not intend to resume his lessons I ran the advertisement again, and again I waited. There were no replies.

Once, in the currently fashionable Café Netto off Porta Pinciana, I recognized Lotti. She sat looking indolent and beautiful, the dark horsetail of hair tumbling to her waist, a frosty cocktail raised in mocking salute to the blond man (it was not Vicenza) opposite her. I nodded from the sidewalk but Lotti, remote as a nun behind her moth-wing sunglasses, did not respond.

A month later, having spent the afternoon at the American Embassy trying to borrow fare to the United States (they were willing to stake me to New York, but argued that I should make my own way to Omaha), I took the long way around to Trinità dei Monti for one of a series of final looks at my beloved Steps; and there, as if each had been waiting in the vast backstage of Rome for his cue to step under this particular spotlight, Vicenza and I confronted one another.

"Green! Well met!"

At once he took my arm and led me down toward the gorgeous fountain and the nearest café, talking non-stop as before: "Your young John Keats died there. Incredible maturity of outlook: 'My spirit is too weak; mortality/Weighs heavily on me like unwilling sleep.' And then: 'My heart aches, and a drowsy numbness pains/My sense.'" He gestured to accompany the recitation, but the gestures seemed cryptic and it was obvious that his mind was not on his words. Later, in the mahogany and cut-velvet café into which he had led me, I saw how his taut brown-nut face had fallen flaccid and how the bright darting eyes were grown dull.

"I have not been entirely well," he said when I asked. "Troubles. Business. Family. I won't bore you with details. And you? I see your advertisement now and then."

I told him.

"Ah. I'm sorry, Green. I know you wanted to make a go—is that the usage? A go of it. I too, you know. I wanted to make a go of it." He sighed. "Well, well. Well, well."

We drank sweet vermouth and soda and fell into a sighing silence, hypnotic and self-perpetuating, until Vicenza roused himself to break it, and said in a soft somehow old voice, "You remember Lotti? Well, we're finished: *kaput*. She has a German now, so I employ his sort of word." I thought of the tall pink-faced blond. "He is young," Vicenza went on, "and a partner in a firm of manufacturers of heavy farm equipment—a successful family concern." He glanced at me; in every aspect, even to the twisted ends of the white moustache, he seemed frayed. "Well, well, well. A tough break. Right? Tough. You will recall, *caro* Green, that last day? Yes. That was, apparently, too much for poor Lotti. Too—forgive me—squalid. I had hoped that would be our beautiful beginning, and so it seemed at first that day. However. . . ." He broke off and after a moment continued in an emotional tone. "I don't blame you, Green; a man's home is his castle, and I must thank you again for the gift of that brief hour. Brief. Bitter too, as all final hours are. It was—what do you say? My swan song. Yes, my swan song, Green, though I didn't know it then."

And again I heard the heavy evening silence in the café.

In parting I told him how grateful I was for the inscription in the book; I did not mention the ten thousand *lire* note.

"Not at all. Okay. You're welcome," he said with deep sadness. "Good luck, my dear Green."

"Wait." And then, at last, I asked: "You didn't want lessons at all, did you? I mean not even at first?"

He fixed me with his sad old gaze, then he murmured, "No. I wanted Lotti, Green. I still do. I tell you the truth now, and the truth is that I only meant to use you—your room. I am sorry. Lotti said I was a coward for what I did—to you, to her. She said I made you a pimp and her a whore because I was too afraid to speak my love to the world. I was not a man with her, she said. So she left me."

I watched him ascend the Steps. He made the first dozen of them briskly enough, but then he faltered, stopped, put a narrow hand to his side and breathed deeply, after which he tried a few more, paused, ascended again, until I lost sight of him in the grey-green magical haze that drops like a cloak over the Spanish Steps at twilight.

GINA BERRIAULT has published two novels, *The Descent*, 1960, and *Conference of Victims*, 1962, and a collection of short stories, *The Mistress*, 1965. She was winner of the first *Paris Review*-Aga Khan prize in 1956 and has appeared in O. Henry Prize Stories in 1958 and 1960, in Best American Stories in 1957, in *Forty Best Stories From Mademoiselle*, 1960, and, among other magazines, in *Esquire, Harper's Bazaar*, and *Contact*. She lives in California.

The Birthday Party

THE boy, wakened by the sound of his mother's heels as she went past his door, ran out into the hallway. She turned when he called to her. She had her coat on; her face was without make-up, and pale.

"Where you going?" he cried.

"Get back in bed," she called back. "You're old enough to be left alone."

"*You* get back!" he shouted.

She went on through the living room, her head down.

"It's very late," he pleaded. "I'm already in bed."

"When you wake up I'll be back already," she said. "Call Grandma if I'm not. If I'm not, then I'm never."

When the room was empty he heard, from where he stood in the hallway, the faint music from the radio. In the past few weeks, she went out often during the day or was not home when he returned from school, but she always came back before it was time for supper; she left him often in the evening, but the girl from the apartment downstairs always came in and did her homework at the desk and stayed with him. His mother wept often and brooded often, but she had never left him late at night and had never threatened not to come back. Though she had wandered the apartment all evening, saying no word to him, her jaws holding back the furor so forcibly she could not open them to eat or speak, he had not expected her to go out in the middle of the night.

He ran into her bedroom. It was untidy; a dresser drawer was out, her white negligee was on the floor, and the big, black-marble ashtray on the bed table was filled with cigarette butts. The bed's silk spread was wrinkled and there were small depressions where her fists had pounded. He crawled under the covers and lay down in the center of the bed, and the return of sleep was like her return.

The sun, and the lamp still lit, shocked him awake. Afraid that she had not returned, he leaped from the bed and ran out into the hallway, calling. She answered from his room and sat up in his bed when he went in. She was in her slip, her coat and dress on the chair.

"You said you weren't coming back!" he shouted. It sounded like an accusation that she had not kept her promise.

"That's all right," she said. "If I hadn't, you're seven years old, you're old enough to do without me. That's a sign of maturity," she said, her mouth dry—"to do without a person."

"You said you weren't coming back!" he shouted again. He stood in his pajamas in the doorway, terrorized by her troubles that had driven her out at midnight and detached her so from him that her return seemed imagined. The man she was going to marry—who was going to be a more fatherly father, she had said, than his own had ever been—had not come by to see her for many weeks, and it was to see him that she had gone out in the evening so many times, and it was probably to see him that she had gone out last night.

"I always come back," she said. "Like the cat the man was always trying to get rid of in the song. He tied her to the railroad tracks and he threw her into the ocean with a rock, but she always came back the very next day." She reached to the chair, her fingers digging into her coat pockets. "Well, no more cigarettes." She shrugged. "All I did was drink coffee at the places that stay open all night. You would have enjoyed it. Saw two motorcycle cops eating hot apple pie. They had their helmets off and they looked human. And I slept in the car a little while, but my legs got cramped. You should see the stars out there at four in the morning."

She tossed off the blankets, hung her clothes over her arm, and walked past him in her bare feet to her own bedroom. He followed her, unwilling, now that she had returned, to let her go from his sight.

"Who's going to take me to Molly's party?"

"I'll take you," she said. "Grandma's going early, and it's out of her way to pick you up, anyway. But, my God, it's not until two."

"We've got to buy a present," he said, afraid that nothing would be attended to from now on, that everything would be neglected; using the party to urge her to look after him again, to distract him again, and engage him again.

She picked up her negligee from the floor and clasped it around her and roamed the room, looking for cigarettes. She gazed into the gilded, oval mirror above her dressing table, while her fingertips felt among the jars and bottles for cigarettes. "Oh, don't you fret, don't you cry," she said to him mockingly; she gazed at herself as if she were trying to accept as herself the woman with the swollen eyelids. "We'll be there on time and we'll bring a present too. You're an anxiety hound," she said. "Oh, the champion anxiety hound."

He began to prepare himself for the party, searching for his shoe-polish kit and finding it in his closet under a stack of games. He sat down on the floor and polished his best shoes. He was not fond of Molly, who would be nine, and he saw her seldom, but he prepared himself now as if he and Molly were the best of friends. In his pajamas he went into the bathroom and combed his hair, wetting it until it was black and drops ran down his face, and combing it over and over. He slipped on a shirt, put on his suit and turned the shirt collar down over the collar of the jacket, the way his mother always did. At noon he called to her from her doorway, waking her.

In the jewelry store, where he had gone with her a few times to buy presents, they looked at a tray of bracelets. Around the walls were large, colored pictures of coats of arms; on the counter tops were silver trays and bowls and candlesticks. When she asked him if he preferred a silver chain with charms or a silver chain with one small pearl dangling from it in a silver claw, he did not balk at a choice, as he had done in the past when he had not cared and had known that even if he cared she would have made her own choice. He put his finger on the one with the pearl. Like himself in the past, she did not care, or else he had persuaded her with his decisiveness, for she nodded at the salesman, who smiled as if it were the most appropriate choice anyone would ever make and caught it up with graceful fingers.

He followed his mother down the few stone steps to the terrace above which strings of red and blue triangular flags crossed from the upper windows of the gray stucco house to the balustrade. Under the flags, a throng of children wandered in twos and threes and clustered together over games, their voices rising high on the warm, still air. His mother had a little swing to her walk that implied that parties for children were what she liked best in life, and, walking this way, went into the midst of so many children that he lost her. At the moment that he saw her again, his grandmother clapped him over the ears, lifting his face to hers and kissing him on both cheeks. Above her head, as she bent to him, the flags burned their colors into the clear sky.

With her arm around his shoulders, his grandmother led him away to the corner of the lawn, where Molly's mother was trailing her bare arm above the long table, dropping colored candy, tiny as seeds, into the red crepe-paper basket at each place. He could hear the small sound of the seeds falling because the commotion of the children was far enough away.

"We filled them all last night," she said. "Tons. But today they look half filled. Up to the brim, that's the way," she said, motioning him to cup his hands and pouring candies into them. He began to help her, awkwardly, following her to drop a few more into baskets she had already filled. "Where's your mother?" she asked.

"She just stayed a minute, to kiss Molly," his grandmother said. "She's coming back later to pick him up."

"Is that you, Elsie?" somebody called to his grandmother from the kitchen. Because his hands were empty and Molly's mother seemed to have lost all sense of his presence, he followed his grandmother. She was small and quick in her coral dress, and her large, yellow beads made a faint jangling. In the white, sunlit kitchen, Molly's grandmother, in a smock stitched with a large, red rose whose stem was as long as the smock, was sticking tiny pink candles into the high, pink cake. Her hand, small and bony, covered with brown spots like freckles melted together, was trembling. She was his grandmother's best friend; they were so close they were like sisters.

"Tell me if I ought to use the white candles, if you think I ought to use the white candles," she begged.

"You can alternate," his grandmother suggested.

"Oh, that's strange, don't you think? Who does that?" the old lady demanded crossly. One pink candle fell into the thick frosting. "Oh, pick it out!" she cried to him. "Your fingers are littler!" But while he thought about the possibility of his clumsiness, she darted her hand in among the upright candles and picked it out herself. "All the same color!" she cried decisively. "Little girls like pink." But in a moment she was undecided again. "Elsie," she wailed, "is pink all right?"

The old woman's wailing over the candles alarmed him. He wondered if his mother was gone already, and he went out the back door of the kitchen, down a narrow passage overhung with vines, and out onto the terrace again. She was not there among the children; he leaned over the balustrade, and she was not with two other mothers standing and chatting in the small garden below, and again he felt the terror of the night before. He was afraid that she would not return for him, that her threat of the night would be carried out that day, and he wished that he had not gone off with his grandmother and that he had not reminded his mother of the party, and he imagined himself fighting her, if she had remembered the party herself—clinging to the bedpost and to the railing on the front steps and to her.

A little girl passed by, ringing a bell, and he was jostled along by the other children toward the birthday table. In the throng roving around the table he looked for his name on the triangular paper flag above each crepe-paper basket. There were so many names that, after a time, he got confused and found himself going around behind the same chairs, now with children seated in them. He read only at empty chairs and found his place. Under a high, red-paper canopy affixed to her chair back, Molly sat at the head of the table. At her elbow, the many presents were piled in a red-paper cart with blue wheels. The cake was carried in by Molly's mother, followed by his grandmother bearing a great, cut-glass bowl of pink ice cream. Molly's grandmother went along behind the children, pouring pink juice from a large, white-china pitcher into paper cups; another pitcher, of glass, frosted from the cold liquid, waited on a corner of the table.

Molly braced her hands against the edge of the table and blew at the candles. Seven stayed out, two flared up again.

"You're too excited," her mother cried. "You're gasping." Although her voice was amused and loud, he heard an edge of annoyance. Molly, after a calm, deep breath, blew again, and the two little flames became rising wisps of smoke.

Molly's grandmother sat down beside her to eat a bit of cake. He was next to her, around the corner of the table, and her bony knees knocked his. "Oh, I think this is the nicest party I've ever been to!" she cried, beating the edge of the table with her fingers as if rapping time to a tune. Her voice seemed to him deliberately quavery, appealing to the children. "Isn't it, dear? Isn't it?" she begged him, patting him on the knee with rapping fingers.

Molly, under her canopy, lifted the presents one by one up from the ribbons and rustling papers. Each time she swung to the side to take a present from the cart, or clapped her hands, her long hair bounced against her back. The children nearest her, himself among them, fingered the gifts piling up before her—a long bow and a leather quiver of arrows, a small doll with a bald head and three wigs, dyed red and yellow and black, each like a puff of cocoon silk; a lifelike poodle dog of dark gray wool; a white petticoat with blue ribbons entwined in it, for which she kissed her grandmother, whose restless hands rested for that moment on the wrapping papers she was folding. The transistor radio she turned on at once, and the tiny, crackling voices of the singers went on and on under the tissue paper and other presents. She held up the bracelet, shaking it high above her head, as if it were something musical, and dropped her hands to open another present. There was a gift from each one at the table and from other people who were not there—uncles and aunts who lived in other cities. There was such a profusion of gifts that it seemed to him the reason for the party was more than that the day was her birthday. The party, he felt, was to take care of any crying to come.

On the terrace a puppet tent had been set up, a rickety frame draped with red cloth. Up high in it, like a small window, was the stage. The children sat on the ground, and behind them sat the women in bamboo chairs. From the corner of his eye he saw his grandmother in her chair; he saw the coral dress and heard the beads jangle whenever she shifted her body or clapped. Last night his mother had told him to call his grandmother in the morning, and her presence now, a few feet away, at this time when the party was tapering off and some mothers were already returning and watching the puppet show, was like proof that his mother would not return. Up in the little stage the jerky puppets with cawing voices, the Indian chief with a feather headdress, an eagle, a bluebird, and a pioneer boy with a coonskin cap, shook their arms and wings and heads at one another and sometimes collapsed over the edge of the stage. The laughter around him startled him each time, because he was watching the steps from the street and each mother coming down.

When the curtains jerkily closed, a young man with a beard, wearing a tunic of coarse cotton embroidered in red, and a woman with long hair that hung down her back like a little girl's, came out from behind the stage. The man bowed; the woman picked up the sides of her wide, flowered skirt and curtsied like a good and proper child. Some of the mothers slipped sweaters over their children's shoulders and guided them across the terrace and up the steps, and some gathered in a cluster with Molly's mother while their children gathered around the puppeteers to see the puppets put away in the tapestry satchel, each one waving as it went down. From a chair he watched the women and children climb the steps, until only one mother was left, chatting with the three other women while her two daughters wandered the terrace with Molly. He was watching the red tent carried up by the couple, swaying between them, when he saw his mother coming down, nimbly sidestepping. He saw her change the expression of her face, smiling at the couple and expecting to smile at whoever she saw next. She waved to him, the only child among the empty chairs, a wave that implied she knew the party had been wonderful, and crossed before him to the women. She had a sweater on now, as did the other women whose circle she joined. He saw his grandmother kiss her on the cheek, grasping and shaking her elbow, and his relief was expressed for him a little by his grandmother's emphatic claiming of her.

"So, Molly?" his mother called to the girl. "How does it feel to be nine?"

"What?" called Molly.

"To be nine? How does it feel?"

"Oh, I feel the same, I guess," Molly called back, a slight wonder and vexation in her voice. She went on wandering with the other girls—some purpose to their wandering that only they knew— their heads bent over something in her hands. The light wind picked up the ends of their hair and the ends of their sashes.

Molly's mother laughed. "In a few years she'll begin to feel the difference," she said.

"When she begins to feel it," her grandmother said, "you won't need to throw any more parties. She won't let you. Isn't that so, Molly?" she called, but her voice was too frail to be heard far.

"She can't know if it's so," said her mother, again with that loud voice that was both amused and annoyed.

His mother motioned to him and began to move away from the others, and his grandmother joined her. He got up from the chair and was a step ahead of them. All over the terrace the seedlike candies lay scattered, and a few ribbons, here and there, were blown along an inch at a time.

"You act like you want to get away," his mother said behind him, raising her voice a little to make sure he heard, but keeping it too low to be heard by the women they were leaving. "I came down and saw him in that chair as if he were suffering punishment," she said to her mother. "This morning he couldn't wait to go. He was ready at six."

"It wasn't that early," he said, hurt by her ridicule.

"No, he wasn't ready at six. I was out till six," she said, and the sound of the anguish remaining in her throat from the night silenced the three of them.

"Is it over? With that man? Is it all over?" his grandmother asked her as they climbed.

He turned, because he no longer heard their heels on the stone steps, and saw that his mother was covering her face with her hand and with the other hand was clutching her purse to her breasts. The way her chest bowed in and the way her fingers spread, trembling, over her face made her appear as fragile as her mother.

"Ah, not here, Lovely. Not here," his grandmother pleaded, touching his mother's fingers. So much love went out to her daughter that her old body seemed depleted suddenly. "The children, they can see you," she warned. "They can see you, and they've had such a nice day. Ah, not here." With her arm around his mother's waist, she made her continue up the steps. Before he turned away, he saw the three girls gazing up at them curiously from under the strings of red and blue flags fluttering in the wind.

GEORGE ZORN was born in Brooklyn, New York, went to Hofstra College, Columbia and Indiana Universities. He has taught for several years and has been Assistant Professor of English at Central Michigan University. His stories have appeared in small magazines; one was included in the O. Henry collection of 1964.

Mr. and Mrs. McGill

The courthouse was like all old, small town courthouses. The ceilings were high, everything narrow and dim. Five feet up, the walls were green, the rest cream—old, soured cream that caught the dust on each belly and wave of the plaster.

Rosemary McGill sat drumming her gloved fingers on the scroll arm of the bench where the secretary had asked her to wait. It was on the second floor, in the corridor, and few people passed—a fat woman in a housedress looking up with sad, cow eyes at the slack-mouthed handsome boy she had by the arm. An old man with a cane, hawking, his grizzled chin pushed forth, moving along as if he owned the place.

She found herself thinking about the men again—she couldn't imagine why she kept coming back to that. The three of them standing on the great plateau of junk, the incinerator smokestack behind them, laughing, calling to her in the way they did. Then the youngest one—skinny, handkerchief around his neck, naked to the waist—raising his arm and making that gesture.

Finally the heavy door with the pebbled-glass panel opened and Lieutenant Goist himself came out. "Mrs. McGill," he said, his voice bright, almost jovial. He shook her hand and held the door for her. The secretary left them, moved back down the hall toward the reception desk at the top of the landing.

She had difficulty for a moment once she was inside the office because he surprised her. His voice on the phone that morning had suggested a different man—much older, thin and harried, with perhaps a flaw of some sort in his dentures. The man being kind to her, telling her which was the best chair, couldn't have been more than thirty—straight pale hair, big red face, bull chest that stretched the coat of his suit at the button. Nor could she detect anything wrong with his speech except a slight affectation, a fussiness, that went with neither his appearance nor his otherwise easy and friendly manner.

"I almost gave you up," he said when he'd settled behind the desk.

"I'm afraid I got lost."

"Out by the reservation?"

"I stopped at a little store."

"Koontz's," he smiled familiarly.

She didn't know.

The office was large and neatly kept, but the air was stale and the furniture heavy and old-fashioned. A glass-fronted bookcase. A coat tree. A brown leather couch, humpy, the curve of the arm worn. The pictures were long rectangular photographs, brown with age, of groups of men—policemen, she imagined. There was a large old photograph of a boxer, arms stiffly up, a silk sash about his waist. Behind the lieutenant's desk was a bay window, the Venetian blinds drawn against the sun. But she had a feeling that the tall windows they curtained were painted shut, that even if one wanted. . . .

"I imagine you've come to pay your husband's fine." He sat up, businesslike, and leaned across the blotter.

He'd called her that morning—out of the blue—while she'd been killing flies. She'd been sitting on the sun porch looking wearily out —disappointed that among the advertisements in her lap there wasn't a letter from her daughter—when she'd become aware that there were more flies than usual. She'd thought nothing about it until one sat on her lip and in her disgust she'd gone to the kitchen and got the fly-swatter. She was almost through—she'd managed to swat four or five of them—when the phone had rung.

He'd explained that he was a lieutenant of police in Parkersville and that he had reason to believe her husband was in jail there.

She couldn't think. "Has there been an accident?"

No, he'd been arrested on a drunk and disorderly charge.

And she'd felt immediate relief at that. "I'm sure you're mistaken. . . ."

"Your husband is there then?"

No, she'd explained, Dr. McGill wasn't there. But there wasn't any question about where he was. He was in Chicago, attending a medical convention. . . .

"The woman said he was a doctor."

"Woman?"

So he'd given her the rest of the story. The man had been picked up two nights ago at a motel just outside of town. He'd given an obviously false name—Hannibal Hoo-hoo, or something of the sort —but there'd been no other means of identification. He'd pleaded guilty in court the day before and been fined, but since he couldn't pay the fine he was in jail. He was taking that all right; he didn't seem to mind it at all. But this morning the woman he'd been arrested with had volunteered the information that his name was McGull or McGill and that he was a doctor in Remus.

"Where is this?" Rosemary had asked. "Where did you say you're calling from?"

"Parkersville."

She'd never heard of the town.

"It's about sixty miles from you there in Remus. Off 26. Just past Wace. . . ." And he began to give her directions. But she hardly listened. She was sure it was just one of those peculiar—sometimes chilling—little mix-ups, accidents: like when you hear your name called by a strange voice and turn—that odd moment—only to discover the person is calling someone else. . . .

"I don't know what to say," she said. "I'm sure the man isn't my husband, Lieutenant. He'd prepared this paper . . . to read. . . ." How did one end it? "Still I want to thank you for being so concerned, doing your duty. . . ."

"It wouldn't hurt to call him, Mrs. McGill. I'd suggest you do that. Just to make sure."

"Yes."

"And you have the directions?"

She'd called Stan's hotel immediately but he wasn't in his room. Ten minutes later she'd called again. Yes, he was registered. No, he hadn't checked out. Yes, they would page him. Minutes of hollow deadness . . . she heard a coin fall into it . . . what sounded like the muffled roar of a lion far off in a cave. "I'm very sorry," the operator finally said. Once she'd got the convention headquarters and a woman told her yes, he was registered, oh just a minute, he might be right there. But that turned out to be Dr. *Frank* McGill

. . . She didn't know what to do . . . she kept trying . . . the telephone had never seemed so inadequate. Finally at one o'clock she
felt she had to decide whether to wait until evening, when she was
supposed to pick Stan up at the airport, or drive the sixty miles to
Parkersville. . . .

And here she was.

"Well, we can settle it easily enough," Lieutenant Goist said when
she'd explained her trouble.

"I'm sure it isn't my husband," she said.

He seemed hardly to hear. "I can have him back here"—he glanced
at his watch—"in . . . oh . . . say half an hour."

"Isn't he in the jail?" He'd surprised and somehow disappointed
her. She'd imagined it would be much simpler. She'd passed the jail
—a new low brick building, modern, with thick glass doors like a
bank's—on her way to the courthouse. She'd thought he'd just call
up, have the man brought to the office . . . or they'd walk down
together, across the shady courthouse square. . . .

"If I'd have known you were coming . . . ," he lifted his hands
apologetically. As he did he hunched his shoulders in a peculiar
way, as if there was a tag on his shirt that scratched his neck.
She'd noticed it before. "As it is," he said, "he'll be out with the
others. . . ."

"Out?"

"It's nothing," he shook his head. "The prisoners do odd jobs for
the county. Not much, but it gives them exercise and takes their
mind off their troubles."

"Do you mean digging?" she stared across at him.

And he laughed at that—a bright burst—as if he couldn't prevent
himself. "Sometimes," he said. "But not today. I think Charlie just
has them picking up bricks and boards . . . cleaning up. Over on
Wheeler Street. Where we tore down the old junior high."

He told her she was welcome to wait in the office—it might be
more comfortable—but she stood up when he did. She didn't want
to wait there. The office had continued to depress her. The dead
heat. The silk flag behind the desk, for all its fancy gold tassels with
a thick layer of dust on its folds. . . . The picture of the boxer—
tilted irritatingly—the slicked gray hair, the proud, sharp-jawed face
. . . standing like that. . . .

She told him that in her hurry she'd come away without lunch.

The town was so close she might just walk to a restaurant and get something.

"Good idea," he said. "Well," he looked around the office, "are we ready? Oops!" He went back to the desk, took a gun from the drawer, and put it in his shoulder holster. "That's better." He seemed to feel almost as relieved as she did that the interview was over, suddenly so gay that she thought as they neared the door he might take her arm.

The courthouse was an old red brick structure with a slatted wooden cupola, built on a square just behind the town. The lawns were patchy, with ragged continents stepped away here and there, but the trees were great pillows of leaves that shaded everything pleasantly—the railed walks, the benches, the big-bowled iron drinking fountain. . . .

Rosemary's first response, when she came through the door with Lieutenant Goist, was to the light and air. It was so good to be outside she just wanted to breathe for a moment. Her second response was to him . . . Lieutenant Goist . . . to a slight halt and sudden quickening in him when he started down the steps. . . .

The woman was sitting on a bench just below them, full in the sun, sharing something from a paper bag with a girl of about five or six who looked as if she'd been crying. Both were thin . . . the same badly curled, stringy blond hair . . . the same small mouth, tight, pinched at the corners. The woman squashed something into the girl's lap, then whispered to her, hit her playfully on the back of her head, laughing, cajoling. . . . It was hard for Rosemary to guess how old she was—twenty-five, thirty. Pretty, with a wiry, wasted prettiness. Raw white sticks of arms. Ugly shoes . . . the brace on the left leg reaching to just beneath the rolled stocking. . . .

When they passed, the woman paid no attention to them. She'd got the girl to laugh. "That's my love," she said, smacking her lightly again.

Rosemary could see her car parked across from the square. She should go home, she thought . . . walk across the street, get into it, and drive home. Had it been someone else . . . a girl . . . young . . . fresh . . . she might perhaps have imagined. . . . But not a woman like that. . . . Still, instead of making any sign to leave, she found herself, when they'd stopped at the short flight of steps that led down to the street, asking, "What is she doing there?"

"I really don't know."

"Is she from here?"

"Her name's Mrs. Kline. Mavis Kline. Her brother's Artie Hooper. Hooper's their name. There's a whole flock of them around here . . . Hoopers . . . one as bad as the other."

People were passing on the street. She saw the mechanical-eyed door of the supermarket across the way flick open as customers went in. A dumpy woman in sun glasses and soiled red slacks walking a dog. Two old men standing a distance apart, one butting the other with the rubber heel of his cane. . . .

"I wouldn't worry," Lieutenant Goist said. He had a way of holding himself, tilted back on his heels, his hands in his jacket pocket, just the pink thumbs sticking out. "You might try your husband's hotel again . . . just to check."

She told herself it was nonsense . . . that she was beginning to imagine things.

"Well, say half an hour . . . ," he smiled at her.

She watched him move along a raw gravel path toward the jail. She stood for a moment . . . working her gloves . . . resisting looking back toward the courthouse. But when she did the woman still wasn't paying any attention to her. A heavy-set man had joined them, picked up the girl and swung her high in the air while she wriggled happily and kicked him in the stomach.

The town, when she'd walked the two blocks to it, tended to buoy Rosemary's spirits. The group of stores wasn't much—a railroad crossing at one end and at the other, down the hill, a grain mill. But it looked busy, thriving. . . . The bank had been recently remodeled —slick gray and pink marble decorating the front. The Penney's looked a fair size. A movie. Grant's . . . lawn mowers on the sidewalk, sale banners across the long windows.

She telephoned from the drugstore next to the bank. She sat there caught in the spell of the droning buzz until the operator finally interrupted it.

"I'm afraid there's no one there," she said.

"It's very important," Rosemary said.

"I can have him paged."

But nothing came of that.

"Well . . . ," Rosemary said. But she remained there, wanting the operator to do more . . . there must, she thought, be something else.

"Can I take a message?"

Rosemary said she'd call back.

It was nothing . . . there could be a million and one reasons . . . , she told herself as she moved through the store out into the street again. The sun was blinding and she raised her hand, shaded her eyes to look across the street for a restaurant. And when she glanced down she saw an Indian boy imitating her, black popped eyes staring out under ridiculously raised fingers. When he caught her eyes he said something she didn't understand, burst out laughing, and ran down the street toward a heavy, lank-haired woman who held another child by the hand and was looking into a store window.

What had he said? she thought, her brow wrinkling. She'd noticed a restaurant, down farther on the other side, a faded green awning over the front. What had . . . ? She stepped down from the curb and as she did felt a sudden coil of tension which released itself in a terrible shiver down her back. He'd reminded her of the other Indian. . . .

It had hardly been anything, and if she'd been prepared for it it probably would have been nothing at all. When she'd turned off the highway she'd got lost, and before she'd had sense enough to ask at a house there hadn't been any houses . . . or at least none she cared to stop at. The countryside was flat and poor, dotted here and there with uniform gray shacks, each with a weedy patch of vegetable garden at the side. Finally though, with a sigh of relief, she'd seen from a rise in the road three or four weatherbeaten stores at a crossroads clearing. . . .

But the place, when she'd driven the mile or two to it, appeared deserted. She'd had no luck at the garage she'd pulled into. "Hello!" Honk, honk. No one. So she'd pulled down farther, beyond the crossroad, to what looked like a grocery store. And that had been open . . . she'd been able to tell by the screendoor. So she'd picked up her purse. . . . And just as she did, from the side of the wooden building, she'd heard a soft burst of child's laughter . . . then another . . . and in the next moment a tubby little girl, curls flying, her hand cupped to her mouth, had come running around the front and disappeared inside the store. She was gone before Rosemary had been able to call her . . . she'd simply flashed past . . . so Rosemary had slid over in her seat, thinking to get out . . . when the Indian had stepped around the same corner and terrified her so she'd almost shrieked.

"You loss?" he asked from the distance, smiling.

He wore khaki pants and a T-shirt that didn't quite cover his barrel stomach. Neither young nor old. Flat nose, pale brown eyes, thick brown hair. . . .

"Hey, lady."

As he moved toward her he slid one hand under his belt, inside his trousers. . . .

"You loss?" He was almost at the car window.

And she'd sat there, frozen, gripping her purse . . . actually thinking, if he opened the door, how . . . where . . . to strike him . . . when the screendoor had swung open and a neatly dressed Indian woman had come out on the steps of the store. She'd spoken inquiringly to the man and walked down to the car. And it had been then that Rosemary had learned—with a hiccough of foolish laughter she hadn't been able to control—that by some accident she had got onto the reservation.

The two of them had been kind to her—gave her directions—the woman slapping the man's arm playfully when she thought he was telling her wrong. "Don't listen to him," she laughed. "They're all the same. Men. Jokers." Both were leaning toward the car door, and Rosemary realized now that what she was smelling was the man's hair scent. The girl had come out and was standing on the top step straddling an old broom. She couldn't be theirs, Rosemary thought . . . she was white . . . that's why he'd surprised her so. "I don't go in much," the woman said, ". . . just to pick him up once in awhile. But that's the best way . . . stay on Patterson . . . then left at the old grange." In the mirror as she drove off Rosemary had seen the man give the woman a familiar pat on the buttock and turn toward the store. The girl had disappeared. But the woman had remained on the clayey slope . . . her hand up . . . smiling . . . waving after the car.

In the restaurant Rosemary ordered a tuna fish sandwich. The waitress leaned across, cleaned something from the table Rosemary hadn't even seen. . . . "We'll get it, honey," she said, bright, friendly, when Rosemary told her she was in a hurry.

The restaurant was old—metal ceiling, a pattern of decorated squares, three large overhead fans still in place. But it had been air-conditioned . . . everything freshly painted. The tables were a recent addition—gray and rose speckled vinyl or whatever it was—but she hadn't seen anything like the benches in years: scroll arms, heavy as lead, with high backs framing narrow rectangular strips of mirror. The place reminded her of—what was its name?—an ice cream parlor she used to go to as a girl.

She drew off her gloves, laid them carefully over her purse. She was happy, for some reason, to see so many people about . . . a group at the counter . . . three men in a booth . . . shirtsleeves . . . cigars . . . probably businessmen, owners of the stores. At one of the straight tables she noticed two elderly women. The one had both hands bandaged, so the other had to feed her the ice cream, but it didn't seem to bother them at all. They pecked their faces at one another, talking a mile a minute. The bigger, blowzier one, the one doing the feeding, would wait until the little one had finished a sentence, pop the ice cream in her mouth, and then dive back to her own dish.

Rosemary touched her gloves, and suddenly wished someone was with her . . . she felt so alone. She hadn't been like this . . . alone in a strange place . . . since . . . she couldn't remember. Probably since before she was married. That seemed for a minute far too long a time, but when she thought about it she realized it was true. Because before they'd grown up . . . gone off . . . like Muriel this summer . . . there'd always been the children . . . one or the other along with her. She hadn't realized until now how much she'd counted on them. . . .

She saw she was looking into the mirror of the opposite bench and was struck by her face . . . how drawn it looked. And somehow her hat had got knocked slightly crooked. She immediately raised her arms to fix it, and as she did, staring at the faded image that gazed back at her, she suddenly wondered if Stan loved her. The idea for a moment surprised her . . . so much that she hardly knew what to do with it. She hadn't thought about it . . . Stan and herself in that way . . . in she didn't know how long. After twenty-three years . . . all they'd been through . . . raising children . . . she hoped that was something she could take for granted. To start thinking about love now. . . . But as it turned out she didn't have to, for almost immediately—from nowhere—she was flooded with the unalterable certainty that he *did*. There was no question. He'd always loved her . . . through all those years. . . . He loved her now.

"Your tuna, honey."

But if he did—she was still lost in the image in the mirror—what was she doing sitting here like this, her hat crooked, alone, in a strange town she didn't like. . . .

"Honey."

She hadn't realized, until she began eating, how hungry she was . . . probably that's what was making her so lightheaded. As she ate she noticed the two women were still at their ice cream. Gab, gab, gab—plunk, the ice cream in the little one's mouth. And then suddenly, as she watched, the big one missed. The little one had ducked to blow something from her breast, her companion didn't notice, and the whole spoonful went right into her nose. The small one was prettily dressed and had looked such a dignified little lady— and there she was with a blob of ice cream on her nose. Rosemary expected her, at least for the moment, to become indignant—she herself would have; but instead, to her surprise, the woman howled with laughter, her skinny neck creaking back, her bandaged hands flapping the air at the joke. When she caught Rosemary watching, she nodded to her, as if encouraging her to join the fun, but Rose-mary, annoyed by the scene, turned her glance quickly away. Finally the waitress noticed the accident and smiling along with the two women brought a soft white cloth from behind the counter.

She'd only had time to call Stan's hotel once again, with no better luck. When she got back to the courthouse square the first thing she noticed was that the bench was empty—the woman and the girl were gone. She felt relieved at that. When she moved through the entrance, the smell inside the building seemed worse than before— like years and years, she thought, of one's painting over dirt. She didn't realize she was hurrying until, at a turn in the stairway, she stumbled and a woman coming down caught her arm: "Here we go," she helped her.

The broad second-floor landing was deserted now—not even the secretary at the desk. She saw a public telephone booth against the side wall—she hadn't noticed it before—but she immediately re-jected the idea: There wouldn't be any sense . . . she'd just called. She fixed her purse under her arm and began walking down the corridor to the right. In the dimness all the doors looked alike and she almost knocked on one before she saw the flicker of a shadow on the pebbled glass and noticed a sign in the corner—small, in chipped black paint: MEN. It was the next one . . . ! In front of Lieutenant Goist's door she took a handkerchief from her purse and touched perspiration from her nose. Her jaws ached, but she didn't realize it was because her teeth were clenched so. She raised her hand and knocked.

But there was no one . . . her fear had been needless . . . the office was empty except for Lieutenant Goist, still in his jacket and tie despite the sweltering heat. "Ah, Mrs. McGill," he raised his hand. Before he stood up to come around the desk he made the hunching movement she'd become familiar with. . . .

"Did you reach him?" he asked. He actually touched her arm this time as he ushered her to the chair. "I'm afraid he isn't here either. Our man. I thought Charlie just had him out with the others, but he sent him over to Raceville with Sergeant Eberhardt to pick up some beds. . . . But I do have something that might help . . . I brought his things."

"Things?" From somewhere about the desk she caught the smell of a half-eaten apple. He'd probably put it away in a drawer.

"We take their personal belongings . . . wallet, keys, whatever's in their pockets . . . keep them in an envelope until they get out. Here . . . wait. . . ." But when he moved to the bookcase, looked on top, his brow creased. . . . He came back and looked over the top of the desk. He smiled, snapped his fingers. "They're downstairs . . . I left them on the table. . . . I'll just be a minute." And before she knew it . . . before she hardly had a chance to understand what it was about . . . he was out the door and she was left alone in the office.

She sat quietly, almost stiffly in the chair, hoping he'd be back right away. . . . When five minutes had passed, she thought of getting up and leaving . . . just leaving—it was what, more than anything in the world, she wanted to do . . . but then she considered how peculiar that would seem. She'd begun nervously clasping and unclasping her purse, and once when she looked down she noticed her hands . . . her gloves! . . . what had she done with her gloves? She looked under the chair, then stooped to look under the desk . . . until she realized she hadn't *had* them. The waitress back at the restaurant had picked them up to hand them to her when she was about to leave . . . put them on the tray when she'd given her her change . . . and . . . and they'd both forgotten. They were still back there on the tray. . . .

Now she'd have to stop back there . . . waste more time. . . . She felt her nerves pull. . . . She sat forward and brushed something . . . nothing . . . from her skirt. . . . Then, in her distress, she closed her eyes. And with that . . . as if waiting for just such a moment . . . the image of the men immediately focused: the three of them lined in the blazing sunlight, the incinerator smokestack behind them . . . laughing, poking one another, calling to her in that crazy way across the distance. . . .

She'd only been three or four miles from town . . . on the right road . . . so she needn't have stopped at all. But the Indian couple hadn't said anything about the deserted sugar beet factory she'd passed . . . or the incinerator that loomed ahead . . . and the three men working there seemed close enough for her to just call to. So she'd pulled to the side and turned down the window. There was a chain-linked fence, then a mound of rusted metal and ashes and junk stretching as far as she could see into the glare of the white sky.

"Parkersville!" she called again, louder, when they all cupped their ears as if they had difficulty hearing. Two of them were older—one fat, with a bush of black hair. The third one was only a boy, fair, skinny—in nothing but dungarees cut off at the knees, frayed ends hanging down . . . a handkerchief tied jauntily about his neck.

The fat one yelled something, but just before he did he turned his head toward the others, so she hadn't been able to hear clearly. Then the youngest one poked the others slyly, stepped out in front of them, and shouted, "Who's winning the game?" She guessed he meant some baseball game, but it left her bewildered because she didn't know anything about such things. Perhaps it was the look on her face . . . she didn't know what . . . but the next minute they were all in hysterics. The third one, hunched forward with laughter, tickled the boy so he jumped high in the air, and while they were chasing around the fat one shouted something like, "Open your eyes, lady."

She decided they were drunk and turned away. She started the car. But as she did, something light—a clinker?—struck the roof, and when she looked up, frightened, she saw the boy had thrown it. He stood out in front of the others as before, his eyes lowered against the sun, his mouth a bright crescent of gaiety. She thought he meant to say something kind. Then, before she could escape, he raised his arm like an axe and made a quick obscene gesture. She pressed the gas pedal so hard that the car jolted her against the wheel. Only minutes later, when the mound had disappeared into a punk swamp, did she find the courage to look into the rear-view mirror.

"Here we are!" Lieutenant Goist said . . . and she almost screamed. She hadn't heard the door, his steps, anything until he was behind her.

"Oopsidaisy," he said, picking up the purse she'd let drop to the floor. He handed it to her, seeming unaware that anything was wrong. "Got it," he said, waving a large manilla envelope at her as he walked behind the desk. . . .

It took her moments to recover . . . and by the time she did he was jiggling the mouth of the envelope and letting the things tumble to the desk. . . .

And it was *over*.

"Oh," she laughed into the side of her hand.

"Well?"

She got control of herself . . . allowed her eyes to move over the things again. A comb, a marble, a gold-banded watch, two or three keys on a cheap metal loop, a wadded handkerchief. . . . They weren't his . . . they weren't even *like* him. . . .

"They aren't Stan's." She was sitting up, laughing easily now.

He ran his hand over the things . . . picked up the watch. "No wallet. There isn't really very much," he said doubtfully. "Are you sure?"

"Yes."

He hesitated . . . then dropped the watch back on the blotter. It was as if he had decided to allow her the moment. "Well, who should know better than you?" he smiled brightly. The brown eyes almost winked at her. "Well,"—he tapped the desk with his knuckles —"I guess that's it . . . I guess that ought to settle that." He kept her for a few minutes to apologize . . . explain that mistakes of the kind happened. . . .

Once outside the office she blew her nose, dusted under her eyes with her handkerchief. . . . She felt the momentary giddiness that sometimes comes with relief, but shook it away. . . . Here she'd

come all this way, she told herself . . . upset herself like this . . .
when she'd known all along. . . .

There were people in the corridor now . . . the secretary back at
her desk . . . a policeman, his shoe up, picking at a knot . . . a group
of boy scouts—their knapsacks and half their clothes in a heap on
the floor—fooling around at the water cooler. . . .

The point now of course was where *was* he? The question simply
intruded . . . was suddenly there . . . and she wanted to close her
mind to it . . . but her love of the certain . . . her distaste for the
unknown, the disorderly, and the frayed . . . forced her to listen
. . . to accept its simple truth. She *didn't* know where he was. She'd
only come here . . . gone through this whole insane rigmarole . . .
because she hadn't been able, all day. . . .

She noticed the telephone booth then across the landing . . .
glanced at her watch and calculated something. . . . It hardly
seemed likely, but it was just possible he hadn't left the hotel yet.
. . . And two minutes later, with the surprise that comes from the
totally unexpected, there he was at the other end of the line. . . .

"You're there!" She couldn't prevent the words from popping out
melodramatically . . . she had to struggle for a minute against a
catch of tears. It was the strain, she realized . . . the strain of the
whole wasteful, shattering day. . . .

"Well, where did you expect me to be?" he said. She saw the heavy
figure, head tilted, crooking the phone the way he did . . . the
serious face . . . the gentle, half-mocking eyes. . . .

"I've been trying to get you," she said.

"*You've* been trying to get *me*? *I've* been trying to get *you*. I've
been calling home ever since I got your message. What's the matter?
Where in heaven are you?"

And she was on the point of simply telling him . . . she hadn't
considered for a moment *not* telling him . . . when she suddenly
realized there was no longer any need. It was over. The whole un-
pleasant affair was over. It had had nothing to do with *them*. So
why bother, go through the whole business of. . . .

She disliked lying, but in the end she made up a story about
having had to drive—not to Parkersville, they knew no one *there*—
but to Wassau City.

"That's *it*?" he said when she was finished.

She knew it sounded a little foolish . . . so she searched . . .
found something to bolster it. "I thought this might happen. I'm

just starting back now. I wanted you to know I might be a little late picking you up at the airport."

"What?" he said. "I can't hear you."

She made a face at the mouthpiece as if the trouble was there. She could hear *him* perfectly well. "Can't you hear me?"

"Now I can."

"I said I might be a little late picking you up."

"Oh. I couldn't hear you."

She frowned. He had a habit . . . he'd always had it but it had grown increasing over the years . . . of making fun of her in a way she didn't always understand.

"Will that be all right?" she said.

"No. Who wants to be left stranded. But what can I do?"

Then, luckily, he was through with his joking. He asked how she was . . . the children . . . whether she'd heard from their daughter Muriel. . . . In the end, the mask dropping completely away, he laughed, confessed that he'd missed her . . . that he was pooped . . . anxious, as always, to get home. . . .

When she stepped out of the booth she dug for her handkerchief and touched her chin. She was dripping. The booth had been stuffier . . . more dead-smelling . . . than the office. . . . And that in turn reminded her of Lieutenant Goist. Should she? . . . there really wasn't any necessity. . . . Yet at the recollection of something . . . some vague note of condescension . . . superiority . . . which seemed now to have marked his attitude toward her from the beginning . . . she felt suddenly swell in her—even against her will—a great rose bloom of final feminine triumph. . . .

It would be simply the decent thing, she told herself, to take the extra minute to let him know what had happened . . . that she'd spoken to Stan. . . .

She was riding so high in the new glow that when she passed the secretary she smiled at her . . . only to find it was another woman. In the dimness, seeing her at the typewriter, she had simply thought . . . . And there instead was this totally unfamiliar woman bouncing up from her chair. "Oy, those kids . . . they'll be the ruin of me," she rolled her eyes at Rosemary in comic exasperation. Then she beat around the chair and began clapping her hands at the boy scouts, who had come down to the landing and were shouting and running wildly over the benches lined under the long row of dusty windows. . . .

"Tell it to the marines!" Rosemary heard one of them yell.

She moved along . . . the corridor was empty again. Lieutenant Goist's door was open now, she noticed . . . she could see a pale wash of light filtering from it into the hallway. . . . She hoped he hadn't left.

Fortunately he hadn't . . . though when she got there the fact that the door was open presented its own little difficulty . . . where were you supposed to knock on an open door? He was still inside . . . sitting at his desk. Looking more relaxed now . . . less official-looking. Somehow—the thought came to her—more *real*. He'd taken off his jacket, loosened his tie, turned back the stiff white cuffs. . . .

She knocked on the side of the door, but he didn't hear. . . . So she leaned forward, touched her purse to her breast, and said, "Lieutenant Goist."

And what happened next happened so suddenly . . . came with such shocking abruptness . . . that she actually raised her purse to her face to protect herself. The pale blond head had come up, apparently startled . . . and the left arm had flown up . . . but there hadn't been a hand . . . only the swish of a white cord cutting the air with something chrome at the end flying wildly toward his head, almost catching his cheek. But the hand remained on the desk . . . cupped and pink . . . until he'd hastily caught it up and swung out of the chair, away from her. She'd seen the broad back make a precise hunching arc, the elbow jerk toward her twice. . . .

She stood there, her eyes wide, staring out above her purse. . . .

He managed the situation better than she did. When he had snapped the hand back in place, he turned around and said, "I'm very sorry. I wasn't expecting anyone. Please come in, Mrs. McGill. Just a minute." He brushed his shirtsleeves down, walked to the coat tree and quickly slipped into his jacket.

But she remained in the doorway . . . hardly hearing . . . her mind careening after a fantastic thought that had suddenly shot up, facing her . . . eyes going, large gapped teeth . . . only to immediately turn, bright rags flying, and begin chasing toward a landscape she had never seen. . . .

He had no hand . . . he'd lost it somehow . . . there was nothing, she realized, very unusual about that. But she'd been seeing it all day . . . it had been right there, in front of her eyes, all day . . . folded on top of the other on the blotter . . . the pink thumb poking out of the jacket outside there, under the trees . . . touching her when he'd led her to the chair . . . jiggling the mouth of the envelope over the desk. . . . It even seemed now, in her bewilderment, that all day he'd been using it like a magician, purposely doing tricks with it to tease her. . . .

"Please come in," he said again. And at the new brusque tone, the flush she noticed on his cheek, she woke up . . . came to herself. What was the matter with her? What was she thinking? It was nothing . . . he'd just been thoughtless. And standing here like this she was merely embarrassing him further. . . .

When she walked into the office and explained why she'd stopped back, he said "No!" his face lighting up with surprise and pleasure. "Well can you imagine?" And that ended it . . . his bright gay burst . . . for both of them—all the awkwardness of the moment before.

She only stayed a minute.

"He's been calling me at home all afternoon," she said.

"And *you* weren't there."

They both laughed at the irony.

The things were still on the desk . . . he hadn't put them away yet . . . the marble . . . the keys . . . the wadded handkerchief. . . .

As he walked her to the door he apologized again for the trouble she'd been through.

"I knew it all along," she couldn't prevent herself from saying.

"Ho, women!" he laughed with a final easy informality.

They shook hands briefly and she heard him close the door behind her.

On the bench across from the office a girl was sitting with knees up chanting "Hoopers-ploopers!" but Rosemary hardly noticed. She did, however, recognize the blond woman talking to the secretary up ahead at the desk. There was no mistaking her—the frizzed hair . . . the greasy paper bag she'd held on the bench outside . . . the slack, wasted figure above the glinting brace. . . . But for Rosemary it was past. It was over. She was already feeling too apart from it all even to wonder what the woman was doing there . . . to care. . . . Now all she wanted was to get outside . . . back to the car . . . be on her way. . . .

And once outside, standing on the top landing of the courthouse steps, there before her—blowing away whatever cobwebs might have remained—lay the square, bright and clear in the late afternoon sun. She blinked. Jigsaws of bright sky through the leaves . . . the lawn

softly freckled . . . people about, walking, sitting on the benches
. . . pigeons fluffing themselves, pecking along the walk. A woman
passed . . . stooped over to fix a mosquito netting on a carriage.
. . . A boy doing tricks . . . no hands . . . curving away on his bicy-
cle toward the street. . . .

The light . . . the air . . . fresh air. . . . She breathed . . .
breathed. . . . She saw a handyman drawing a hose across the lawn,
yanking the end, toward a flower bed. He chased some children and
she saw them hop away, climb over the iron railing of the path. . . .
If one of the children had been with her, she thought . . . just
along to keep her company . . . there wouldn't have been any of
this . . . the whole day would have been so much easier. . . .

The main path of the square led from the courthouse to the wide
street behind the stores. As Rosemary moved down the steps she
couldn't help seeing to the end. There was little to draw her attention. A peddler's cart with an orange and black umbrella . . . an old
man attending it . . . a woman digging in her purse. Two men . . .
one young, in limp suntans, thin and gawky, but somehow official-
looking. . . . The other older, heavy set, in an undershirt, his top-
shirt hooked on a finger over his shoulder. They were eating ice
cream bars and joking, the heavier one bouncing on his heels . . .
roughhousing. . . .

She reached the bottom of the stairs and was about to turn toward the side path.

And at that moment the older one let out a sudden whallop of
laughter and swung around, facing up the path . . . and she saw it
was Stan.

She stood rooted to the pavement. . . .

His laughter echoed down the shaded path . . . the loose warm
roll of it . . . expansive . . . free. . . . He tossed the ice cream stick
in a wide baseball curve into the bushes. He pinched his nose and
said something that set the others going, even the old man at the
cart. Then he glanced up the path toward the courthouse . . .
wholly at ease in his surroundings . . . wiping his neck with his shirt
. . . enjoying the scene. When his eyes fell on Rosemary, he
squinted . . . then cocked his head in comic, affectionate surprise. . . .

She stared. . . .

He raised the finger holding the shirt several inches . . . his eyes had grown welcoming, expectant . . . he stood there smiling away more happily than ever. . . .

And for a moment . . . for a curious lightheaded moment when everything seemed to fade but the man . . . when she seemed to rise out of herself buoyed by some hope . . . some promise she had never dreamed . . . Rosemary almost responded . . . almost raised her purse in a gesture of recognition. . . .

He flapped his hand at the group at the cart, dismissing them. He touched his belt and took a step up the path. . . .

And at that instant, with a cathartic sense of relief, she remembered the telephone call. . . . It *couldn't* be Stan. . . . She'd just *spoken* to Stan. . . .

The man seemed to notice some change in her expression. He hesitated . . . his eyes straining . . . his brow furrowed in a question.

But what could she do? It wasn't Stan. She made a formal face . . . nodded her head almost imperceptibly: No.

And with that he appeared to recognize the mistake too. He blinked . . . then suddenly smiled . . . an altogether different smile . . . quick and empty and somewhat shy . . . the smile of a stranger who finds himself, to his embarrassment, staring at the wrong woman.

But it wasn't his fault, she realized . . . she'd stared first. . . . And completely relieved now, wanting to make up for her share in the little error, she was about to smile back . . . when he suddenly spat . . . clipping one of the pigeons so it fluttered its wings . . . rose under the trees. . . . He swung his shirt from his shoulder . . . hallooing . . . turning as the bird flew over the street . . . among the cars for a moment . . . then up . . . disappeared behind the stores. . . .

But she was still seeing the abrupt, ugly gesture . . . it had surprised and offended her so. She kept looking at the heavy naked shoulders as he walked back to the group at the cart. Men . . . , she thought. But she shrugged the shiver away, turned, and moved hurriedly down the side path.

And in the car she dug for her keys. . . . You try to be decent . . . kind . . . , she found herself thinking as she fished beneath the checkbook, the handkerchief, the green stamps . . . and they abuse you . . . act as if you've done . . . she didn't know *what*. She'd done *nothing* to that man. . . .

When she found the keys she snapped open the small leather case. Then she patted the cushion of the seat . . . sat back. . . .

She could see across to the square . . . the handyman watering a patch of stalky marigolds . . . the modern jail with its glass doors . . . the old courthouse . . . the dusty trees. It looked—the commonplace thought washed up as if it were of actual importance—like every courthouse square she had ever seen in her life. And if with that she felt a sudden deepening sense of loneliness, it hardly lasted long enough for her to recognize, and quickly passed in more practical matters. She had to get gas. And there were her gloves . . . should she bother? . . . but it would just take a minute to swing around into town . . . pick them up at the restaurant. . . .

She jiggled her hand at a fly on the windshield . . . turned on the ignition.

As she was pulling away from the curb a driver stopped, gave her a friendly wave, let her pull out ahead of him. She had no trouble at the restaurant . . . nor in finding her way to the highway. And when she arrived at the airport, Stan of course was there. . . .

JESSE HILL FORD lives in Humboldt, Tennessee. He is the author of two novels, *Mountains of Gilead*, for which he was awarded an *Atlantic* Grant in 1961, and *The Liberation of Lord Byron Jones*, a Book-of-the-Month Club selection in 1965. His story, "How the Mountains Are," was included in the O. Henry Prize Stories of 1961.

To the Open Water

WHEN the teal leaped from the grass it flew up so swiftly that it was already out of range by the time he fired. At the sound of the shotgun a few blackjacks put up. They rose reluctantly in the cold air and circled a moment before flying straight up channel toward the neck of the bottoms.

He quickly climbed the embankment to the road and ran to the bridge to watch the ducks. Slicing through the sky like arrows, they flew almost out of sight before they veered left, folded suddenly into a soft spiral, and went down beyond the trees.

The open water would be there, where they went down. He knew the place, a logjam island. It would be, perhaps, the only open water to be found on such a day when even the coves along the Tennessee River were frozen solid. Ice was skimming the main channel itself in places.

Even where the pale afternoon sun had shone on the windless side of the levee the air was pinching cold. Since early morning he had scouted the banks about the bottoms without venturing on the ice. Until he saw the teal he had seen only two snipe. He had killed one of them and missed the other.

He left the bridge and walked about seventy yards up the levee, then down the embankment through dead briers and dormant honeysuckle vines. The johnboat lay where he had left it, bottom upward on the bank. He stepped out on the ice.

He stamped his foot. The ice held, solid as concrete, hard as glass it seemed, too thick to break a way through it for the boat. Besides, the boat was small and of light-gauge aluminum, not meant to take the punishment of jagged, broken ice. It was made to be sculled through the bottoms on warmer days, to be ghosted along like a feather by the merest dip and twitch of the paddle, to go more quietly than man could walk or duck could fly.

He looked up. By hauling the little boat up the levee to the road he could carry it on his shoulders to the channel and put in at the bridge. He was a stout man of two hundred pounds, well used to work. Had it been morning he wouldn't have hesitated. Time, however, was against him now. Walk fast though he might, carrying the boat, and once in the channel with it, paddle swiftly though he would, there was small chance he could reach the logjam island before sundown. By that time it would be too late to shoot, and he would have labored for nothing.

His only chance was to slide the little johnboat over the ice straight out toward the logjam island, to sled along swiftly directly to his destination, pushing the little craft ahead of him and, for safety, leaning forward over the stern as he went. In that way, should he run upon rotten ice, he would fall in the boat as it cracked through.

He had gone over the ice this way many times before, but never this late in the afternoon, never with the bottoms so silent. The freeze kept other hunters close at home or sitting beside stoves in crossroads country stores. None but the most determined, not even professional guides, would try to find open water in weather such as this, even though once it was found and reached, the shooting was beyond compare. With no other place to land, the ducks would leave when jumped, only to return again and again.

The desire to be where they were this very instant made his throat ache. Once before as he slid over the ice he had cracked through in a bad place several hundred yards out and had been forced to stay where he was until after midnight, when the bottoms froze sufficiently solid for him to walk out and drag the little boat after him. Every other time, though, he had made it to the open water. There was a line of trees marking the grave of an old road buried by the winter flood. By leaping into the boat just there, it was possible to coast off the edge of the ice into the water. He had done it with never an accident, a dozen times perhaps, all before he married. Since his marriage six years ago, he had never attempted the trick.

From the time he was ten until the day of his marriage, he had hunted every day of every duck season, every day after school, even Sundays after church, though Sunday hunting was frowned upon. He had hunted them because he loved them then with the same passionate ache in his throat that he felt now for those creatures settled there on the open water by the thousands, their wild hearts calling his own, it seemed.

Marriage had pinched him down. His wife had ambitions for the farm. It wasn't enough to spend spring, summer, and fall riding a tractor, driving a cotton picker, loading and unloading his truck, working at times until long after nightfall, waiting five hours to get his cotton trailer under the suck at the gin. A wife had to have chickens and geese and cattle. Coonhounds and mules weren't creatures enough to care for, not in a wife's estimation. There must be winter duties too—even, finally, a dairy barn. God help him if he once failed to be home in time to milk.

He hadn't gone over the ice in six long years because there had been too many creatures dependent on him, nearly all of them female. First a wife, then infant daughters, and finally the wife's gentle-eyed Jerseys with their slender hips and heavy udders.

A mallard susie quacked in the distance. He turned the johnboat right side up and laid his heavy parka in it next to his gun. Besides two extra boxes of shells in the pockets of the parka, he carried twenty-three magnum loads in a shooting vest which he wore buttoned snugly about his chest for warmth. He opened his half-pint and took a drink of white moonshine whiskey. Over the bottoms the air was still.

With a practiced heave he pushed the boat out ahead of him on the ice, keeping his weight forward, ready to leap in the boat if the ice failed. As he gathered speed, his legs moving in a regular rhythm, running easily, the boat set up a screeching, thundering racket, scraping past trees and cracking through thickets. Mallards rose from the red oak thickets and flew toward the channel. Now in an open space he paused and watched them a moment. Then he pushed on, going even faster now as the open spaces between thickets got wider and wider. He began sweating a little and slowed down.

Farther out, he stopped to rest. He sat on the stern of the little boat, boots on the ice, elbows on knees, looking down at the hard, slick, olive-drab surface. He looked up at the levee, about six hundred yards away now, a long, straight elevated outline. The road was desolate in both directions. Only hunters, trappers, fishermen, or an occasional logger used it. Far down to the left, he saw the black outline of his pickup truck. He had parked it that morning before starting along the north edge of the bottoms where he had killed the snipe.

He leaned back and got the bird from the game pocket of his parka. The little body was frozen. Strangest of all were the eyes; black with life's memory, they seemed, in the instant after death, before the cold seeped into them and did its work.

He stood up and tossed the snipe into the front of the boat, turning at the same time and leaning forward. The ice cracked. The crack ran under him and on ahead of the boat through the dark-green ice. Though a crack it most surely was, it didn't seem to be a very serious one. He held the sides of the boat, leaning forward to distribute his weight, braced like an athlete preparing to do push-ups. He waited. The ice held.

Fifty yards to the right stood a duck blind. The decoys in front of it were frozen solid into the ice and glazed with white frost. Red oak saplings shaded the ice in that direction. There the ice looked pale, almost white. It would be thicker. He could turn back now in that direction and reach the levee.

Far away to his left over the long open stretches he saw the line of trees marking the lost road. Beyond the flat glare he saw the logjam island, and around it the still blue gulf of the open water, reflecting the sky. In ten minutes he could reach the trees for the final, sliding rush.

He skidded the boat left and made straight for the trees, getting up speed first and then making only so much effort with his legs as would keep the boat sliding. Now and again the ice cracked, but the boat outran the cracks, one after the other as he pushed on, keeping his weight carefully distributed forward, over the boat.

Suddenly, with no warning the ice gave under him, and he fell into the boat just in time, just before it cracked through, and not an instant too soon, for the icy water had bitten him almost to mid-thigh, wetting him well above his insulated rubber knee boots. It had happened this way before. It was like being burned, like the sting of flames licking about his legs. He lay face down and still, waiting for his trousers to freeze. It needed only a little patience. When he sat up at last, remembering to wiggle his toes and flex his calf muscles to keep the circulation going, even the splashes had frozen. They looked like drops of candle wax.

Flared by the commotion of his fall, the ducks had flown up. Now they flocked and circled low around the edge of the open water. He slipped a magnum shell into the magazine of the automatic to replace the one fired at the teal. Then he put the parka over his head and shoulders and sat very still. He quacked with his mouth. A susie answered. He quacked again. He patted his lips, making the intimate, stuttering feed call. He tried the raucous call of the wise old susie. It all proved a false hope. The entire drove splashed in beside the island with a brisk rush of sound that set his heart beating faster.

When he put the gun down and took off the parka, his toes were numb. He moved them and rubbed his legs and finally admitted it to himself. He had cracked through; maybe the ice *was* rotten. Very well, but he had broken through only one time in several hundred yards of running, after all. He *had* managed to fall very neatly into the johnboat, hadn't he?

Though it was a ticklish sort of job, there was still a chance that he could get the boat back up on the ice. He moved back cautiously and sat on the stern, balancing his weight until the bow rose high out of the water and less than four inches of freeboard remained beneath him. Then he dipped the paddle and drove the boat hard against the edge, and moving at once, fast, before it could slide off again, he went quickly forward on all fours. The ice cracked, the long, brittle sound of a marble rolling over a glass tabletop. Crouched in the bow, he waited, holding his breath, a dull pain beating in his throat just under the Adam's apple. The ice held. Cautiously, slowly, he leaned far out over the prow and caught a willow limb in his gloved hand and pulled. The boat eased forward with him. He caught another limb and then another, getting farther and farther up on firm ice, hauling the boat painfully hand over hand until at last his arms gave out and he turned carefully and lay on his back breathing the cold, clean air through his mouth, cupping his hands and breathing into them. Lying thus, looking straight up, the depth of the clear sky was blue and magnificent. When he held his breath there was not a stir of sound anywhere to be heard. He might have been the last creature left alive on earth. A feeling of independence entered him like the slow onset of sleep.

When it was time to move again he found he was tired. He moved awkwardly, stiff in his joints, his shoulders aching in the sockets, his toes numb because he had neglected to keep moving them. He took the flat, half-pint bottle from his parka and drank it empty in three long swigs and flung the bottle away. It smashed. The clear little shards of glass slid on for several yards before they finally stopped, gleaming at rest in the waning sunlight like white jewels.

The levee had never before seemed so far away. The slanting sun perhaps added to the illusion. When he stood up he could not see the truck. Willow thickets blocked the way. In the other direction, just ahead, the island loomed from the open water, a tangled mass of roots and black tree trunks. Low in the water all around it the ducks rested, very still, as though waiting for him.

Although they were out of range, he was tempted to fire at them anyway, to put them up for the joy of seeing them fly, for the satisfaction, knowing that though they might circle the whole bottoms, they would come back. The cold air would drive them down again, here, in the last of the open water, perhaps the last open water to be found anywhere about, except in the mid-river channel.

The liquor's warmth caught hold. He hadn't eaten since before daylight. It didn't matter. He had taught himself not to want food. He had taught himself not to want anything but the beautiful joy of killing. He had always hunted this way.

Now he took the bow line, and without hesitating, stepped out on the ice and put it over his shoulder and towed the boat after him. Once started, it seemed to follow him willingly, coming after him across the patch of firm, white ice like a docile beast. When the ice shaded into olive green again, he stopped and fended his way around to the stern to rest a moment before making the final dash for trees at the edge of the open water.

Once the boat slid free he would be in range. The ducks would come up and circle, dipping their dark wings to his call, and he would lovingly kill them. He would scull coaxingly after the cripples one by one, coming so slowly on them that they would hardly know the boat was moving at all. While they flirted in that final, zigzag hesitation, he would suddenly raise the gun and shoot their heads off clean. Their blood would boil below them like a cloud into the dark, clear water.

A whistling flight of teal drove in, wings already set, and pitched in beyond the island. A susie quacked. He drew a deep breath and shoved. The boat groaned against the willows and slid forward. Faster and faster, he pushed on. Exhilaration shook him like a sudden wind among dead leaves. With less than fifty yards to go, speed was in his favor. Instinctively, at the right instant, he would leap lightly forward.

As though struck suddenly blind, however, he was groping, wet to the armpits, his breath coming so fast that his chest seemed about to burst. He saw the johnboat beside him. It had cracked through. He caught its side. Water spilled in, so he pushed back, trying to swim, his hands already so numb he could hardly feel them.

"*Still, be still!*" he commanded aloud, using words he spoke to the restless cows at milking. The cold drove in from every direction like nails, driving and driving in, searching his vitals.

He must think! Of course, only keep a clear head! Make every move carefully! Sound judgment, no wasted time or motion. "*Easy, careful,*" he said, speaking to the fiery grip of the cold, which now became more powerful than anything he had ever before imagined, for it was taking him over.

In the place of the strong, obedient body he had so long been accustomed to command, he felt a strange and foolish despair at this heaving, disquieted thing that would no longer obey.

In spite of every caution to the contrary, his body suddenly fought like a cat snared on a string. Thrashing and fighting like a dying fish, he fended himself clumsily around to the prow and threw himself hard upon it. Short of seeing it, he could never have believed such an utterly foolish panic to be possible. Already, almost in the wink of an eye, he had destroyed his best hope. The incredible, the *impossible* thing happened. The boat filled almost as quickly as he had moved, and rolled down from under him.

Water covered his face. When he had fought to the surface and taken breath, he felt his hair and his eyebrows freezing.

Bottom up now and barely afloat, the boat was another creature entirely, as though it too, the docile beast of a moment before, had now lost all notion of what it was logically supposed to be, and do. When he touched it, it rolled. When he caught at it, the weird creature shook him off; it threw him a second time, and he gentled cautiously against it, the cold biting clean through his shoulders now, like teeth. His body's least twitch made the boat heave and swing. Holding the boat, huddling on it and fighting its strange movements, he realized for the first time that the shooting vest with its cargo of magnum shells was his enemy now, the perfect weight to sink a man and kill him. Propping a hand and both knees against the boat, he tried the vest's buttons. Briefly his fingers stung back to life, but they were useless against buttons.

He tried to balance himself on the boat and rip the vest apart with both hands, no trick for a strong man in his early prime, yet each time he tried it the other creature, the rebellious animal self, seized him. His arms failed. They disobeyed. His hands groped warily forward like burned stumps, to rest against the boat and balance him.

He remained thus awhile, motionless, not even shivering, such was the marvel of it, his head just above the surface of the freezing water. The thin winter sunlight and the desolate, utter silence of the bottoms, great spanning miles of it, dinned and drummed at him.

He knew he must shout soon. It would be no use, of course. No earthly man would hear. Yet soon he would begin screaming. The body would have that too; the body would have it, though he knew shouting must only exhaust him the sooner and hasten the end. Screams began gathering in his throat like a queer nausea.

If he had only thought to take off the vest before his fingers numbed, to get out of his boots, even kick off his trousers. Then he might have gotten back in the boat. He would have wrung out his clothes and put them back on and huddled under the parka until night froze the bottoms in, and then he would have walked out to the road and gotten in the truck. He would have driven it home and tottered into the house and asked his wife to draw him a hot bath. Once he was warm and rested he would have gotten a friend or two and come back after his boat and the gun.

If they ever found it, anytime within a week or two, the gun would be all right. He kept it oiled, and with the water so cold the oil would stick. The gun wouldn't rust quickly. Perhaps they would find it. He hoped they would.

Finding the gun shouldn't be hard with the boat frozen in the ice right over it. A sudden ruthless pain in his back, above the belt-line, jerked his head forward. For the first time he began shuddering. He heard himself shouting, screaming for help, the cries already hoarse though hardly even well begun. The ducks came up and be-gan wheeling and circling above him. Their curved wings were more beautiful than any he had seen before, cupping as gently as a kiss, skimming like a long caress, each pair shaped like the touch of a woman's hands in love.

He stopped yelling and slid peacefully down into the white darkness under the surface.

SALLIE BINGHAM was born in Louisville, Kentucky, and graduated from Radcliffe in 1958. Her first novel, *After Such Knowledge,* was published by Houghton Mifflin Company in 1959. She has published short stories in the *Atlantic Monthly, Transatlantic Review,* and the *Ladies Home Journal.* "On the Banks of the Ohio" appeared in the 1964 O. Henry collection.

Bare Bones

LILLY MORRISON had been divorced for almost a year. In the beginning she had wanted it, impatient of delays, as though the divorce were her reward for three years of marriage. But when the reward fell due and she was finally alone, she almost regretted it. Not him—she seldom thought of him, her gentle, dark husband. Him she did not even miss. But for a long time she felt lost without the life he had provided for her. There was suddenly so much space around her, there were such lengths of time, and her efforts to do something about it—to buy curtains or take her child to the zoo or invite friends to dinner—sank into the void without leaving a trace. She cried while she washed the dishes from her little parties, for none of it seemed substantial, none of it took up any space; and the people who had been so kind to her at dinner disappeared into their own lives as soon as the door was closed. She began to feel that she herself was disappearing, as though she had existed only as a fixed bright image in her husband's nearsighted brown eyes.

She began to be curious about him, as though he had taken away a part of herself, a secret quality on which her vitality depended. Of course she was not curious about him, but rather about what he had taken away. She could not remember ever having been curious about Jay Morrison. He had followed her too closely for that. She had never caught sight of him across that space which separated her from men who did not want her, Jay had always been so close. Besides, he was a man who suited his appearance.

Only now, alone, in the waste of her life, she began to wonder about him, and even to be angry. It seemed unfair that he had drawn off so much of her strength. How could she have known he had that power? He had never shown it before; only in leaving had he stripped her to the bone. She kept hearing from sly friends that he was going out with this woman or that, that he was giving parties. And she grew more curious about him, and more angry, as though he were living on her happiness.

It had been part of the agreement that Jay would see their little boy Willy every Saturday. Lilly felt the arrangement was for Jay's sake, rather than for Willy's. The child was mercifully vague about his father—fond of him, but lightly attached. He had scarcely known him before the break.

Jay, however, seemed to feel that his self-respect depended on his connection with the little boy. So every Saturday morning the maid dressed Willy in the clothes his mother had laid out and took him to the park, where she handed him over to his father. Lilly, of course, never went; there was a certain decorum in all their arrangements which had to be maintained. Yet for some reason she was always in the living room when the maid came back, and the scrape of the key in the lock depressed and frightened her.

"All right, Lenora?" she would call anxiously, and, "Yes, he's fine; he's with his daddy now," the maid would inevitably reply. There was nothing more to be said; the mission had been accomplished, the child had been handed over. Yet it was not the child that Lilly was missing.

Her Saturdays were so idle. She tried to believe that it was all right to be doing nothing, feeling nothing, to let time slide by. But she wasn't old enough or stale enough to be satisfied with that. She had no illusions about her life, but she did expect to be busy. During the week she had a whole range of appointments, errands, commitments; her desk calendar swarmed with tiny, precise notations. But on the weekends she had nothing. Everyone else went to the country or shrank into their families; she had only a sense of expectation. So one Saturday when she was laying out Willy's blue suit she said to the maid, quite abruptly, "I think I'll take him to the park myself, Lenora."

The maid did not answer at once. She was polishing the little boy's red shoes. "Certainly, Mrs. Morrison," she said finally.

"What do you mean, certainly? Do you think I ought not to go?"
The maid studied one of the red shoes, then spoke. "That's up to
you, Mrs. Morrison."

The cheek of her! Lilly thought. She was always hinting, and then
shrinking back into her official position. Lilly couldn't get a straight
word out of her. At that moment Willy dashed in and hurled himself against Lenora's knees. She put her arm around him. "Time to
get dressed, big boy."

While Lilly waited, a little to one side, the maid lifted the boy
onto the table and took off his overalls. She soothed him with little
chuckling endearments as she undressed him, and the child seemed
to grow limp as he listened. Lilly felt obliterated. There was something terrible about the boy's limpness; he stood there in his white
training pants as though Lenora could do anything with him. Lilly
elbowed her way in finally with the little blue suit pants. The boy
looked at her vaguely and smiled.

"I'm taking you to the park today," Lilly told him. Then she
picked up his foot and dropped it through the leg of the little blue
pants. Her shoulder brushed Lenora, and the maid stepped back.

"You want to finish him?" she asked.

"Yes." Lilly lifted the little boy's other foot into the leg of the
pants. Lenora still hovered uncertainly. "I'll manage," Lilly said
sharply, and the maid went out of the room with a tiny rustle of protest in her nylon uniform.

"See Da-Da?" the child asked, leaning against Lilly.

"Yes. I'm going to take you to meet him." She got him into his
white shirt awkwardly—he was so pliable—and then she took his
hand and led him to the elevator.

Halfway down, she realized that she did not know where she was
supposed to take him. A meeting place in the park had been decided
on, but she couldn't remember where it was—the arrangement had
been made almost a year before. She hesitated in the lobby, holding
the child by the hand. It would be too humiliating to go back up
and ask Lenora; what a triumph for the girl! So she sent the elevator
man up for the information.

He was grinning when he came back down. "She says by the
boat pond, by the statue on the far side," he told her slyly.

Lilly started off down Seventy-second Street, leading the little
boy. He dawdled, dragging his feet, his whole weight hanging from
her hand. "Carry me, carry me," he said after a while, and she picked

him up and carried him until she was tired and then put him down. "Walk, Willy—you're a big boy." But he hung from her hand, whining. They turned into the park. It was a damp, warm day, with high clouds, and hot sunlight breaking through from time to time. In that gaseous light the new leaves in the park looked poisonous. The grass too was wet, and very green. The child splashed through a puddle and Lilly shouted at him. Her voice sounded brittle and strange. She wished that she had worn her white gloves, or even a hat. She did not want to look forlorn.

From the top of the hill she looked down on the boat pond, the promenade, the wet trees. It was all deserted. On the far side the statue of the storyteller sat hunched in a small, paved square. Lilly started down the hill, pulling her son. Across the way, on the other side of the pond, she saw someone else picking his way down.

She could not tell whether or not it was Jay, and she watched intently as the dark figure came down the hillside. He did not seem to be in any particular hurry, and without thinking, she slowed her own steps; it would not do to get there before him. He dawdled along the edge of the pond, paused, kicked at something. Surely Jay would have been in more of a hurry.

Lilly stopped. Suddenly she felt uneasy. If the man was not Jay, who would he be? She was sure that whoever he was, he was coming to meet her; there could be no other reason for his appearance. But if it was not Jay, who would it be? She was not particularly timid, and it did not occur to her that the stranger might do her some harm. But he was definitely meant for her; he was practically aimed in her direction. She hesitated on the path, holding Willy, who was crying.

The man approached around the curve of the pond. She could see his overcoat and his hat. Jay never wore a hat. At that she felt a terrible sinking, as though her resistance, her physical vitality, were sinking down. She did not have the strength to move. The boy, pulling at her hand, seemed remote and powerful. Then the stranger walked slowly to the statue and stopped, looking up at it.

So Jay had taken to wearing a hat. Jauntily Lilly went on down the path. She wondered which of his lady friends had suggested that. She herself would never have dreamed of it; his thick dark hair was one of his few definite characteristics, and if it was hidden, his face would look entirely neutral. She went on, hurrying now, pulling Willy. She would hand the boy over, chat a moment and

then go off about her business. She was glad that she had worn
stockings, and for a moment she saw herself as he would see her,
striding down the hill, her skirt swinging, her legs shining. . . .
The sun broke through the clouds.

The man turned around, and she saw that it was not Jay. She
stopped and waited. He glanced at her, glanced past her and turned
away. She felt her hands grow damp and she started forward as
though to call him back. Incredulously she watched him saunter off.
It was almost as though he had not seen her; he had looked straight
through her. Looked straight through her! She knew suddenly
what that meant: She was a fragment of glass, a cellophane strip, a
drop of water. At that she picked the child up, as though to prove
her presence. The man was already on the other side of the pond.

The child clung to her, and she began to stroke him mechanically.
"Da-Da, Da-Da," he wailed. Tears ran down his cheeks. Lilly sat
down on a bench to comfort him. At the sight of his tears, she
sobbed dryly. "He'll come, Baby, he'll come." Tears ran at last down
her cheeks and dropped on the child's head. She felt utterly alone,
obliterated.

Looking up, she saw Jay hurrying toward her. He was not wearing
a hat.

"Where have you been?" she cried. "There was a man here."

He sat down beside her. The child's sobs and her tears alarmed
him. "What happened, Lilly? Did someone——"

"Oh, nothing like that!" She was outraged by the crudeness of his
supposition. She began to jounce the child on her knee to silence him.

"Well, then, what happened?" Jay asked, amazed. "I'm only four
minutes late," he added.

She thrust the child at him. "I'll expect him back at five. Be sure
to let him have his nap." She turned away, feeling naked without
the child.

Jay seemed to call after her, or to make some gesture in her direction. But she hurried off, in a fury.

For a few hours she kept herself busy, spurred on by her indigna-
tion. She took a lamp to be mended and argued with the electrician;
suddenly on the verge of tears, she stormed out of the shop. To become the kind of woman who raged at electricians! She knew he
was jeering at her behind her back. Her handsome suit, her jewelry,

her prettiness, which she had never doubted, were suddenly no protection. She felt as though she were walking the street naked, in hideous want, shamelessly holding her hand out. Every man she passed eyed her knowingly, humorously, with interest. She hurried along with her eyes down.

By four o'clock she had run through her alternatives. The living room, closed all day, was hot and stale; she did not want to be lurking there when Jay brought the boy home. In desperation she telephoned all her friends. Most of them were out—after all, it was Saturday. But even when someone answered, Lilly talked vaguely, about nothing, bored at the prospect of seeing anyone. It didn't seem worth the effort after all. She left them confused; there was a rasp in her voice that contradicted her vagueness. They could not tell what she wanted.

At last, at five o'clock, she brushed her hair and powdered her nose, and on the spur of the moment pinned a flower on her suit.

Jay smiled when he saw her. "You're looking better," he said.

"Did I look so terrible before?"

"You looked scared to death," he said, handing her the child, who was asleep.

"I wasn't scared," she said with dignity. "Why didn't you let him have his nap?" And she turned away, letting Jay go.

The child did not wake up, and she put him to bed regretfully after holding him for a few minutes in her arms. She did not think it was right to intrude on his sleep. Then she had nothing to do, and it was Saturday night. She pretended it didn't matter. Her weekend, after all, was no different from her week; she slept every day until ten or eleven o'clock and stayed out as late as she pleased. Yet it bothered her to be alone on Saturday night.

She took a bath to console herself and afterward stood naked in front of the mirror. She was still slight, almost girlish, with her pale blonde hair and her slight, limp body. Her hips and thighs were as slender as a young girl's. But there were lines around her throat, and her arms looked dry and thin. She knew suddenly that she would never have another child. Her body seemed hateful in its uselessness, and she pulled a nightgown over her head.

Then she could not sleep, and she tossed in a kind of fury. Her life had been snatched away from her. It did not seem any more that she herself had thrown it aside; it had been snatched, snatched because of her innocence. How could she have known what it would mean to be alone? Her marriage had disappointed her, and so she had decided to try something else. She had been taught to expect a great deal, and it was not her fault if she was constantly disappointed. The world was simply not equal to her expectations. In the closets and drawers of her parents' house her little dresses, her colored slippers, preserved in tissue paper, attested to her destiny. The tiny shoes were to be filled with champagne, the tiny dresses to be dismantled with kisses, and if life proved churlish, it was not the fault of her equipment. She had always asked for more and expected more, quite fearlessly. But now there was no one to give.

She got up and crept into her child's room. He was asleep, lying curled in on himself. She did not dare to kiss him, he looked so solid and self-contained. His peacefulness seemed to have nothing to do with her; he would thrive on her ruin. She went out and closed the door softly, frightened by her anger.

In the bedroom she turned on the light to look at the clock. It was not even midnight. The whole night lay in front of her, unpredictable, threatening, each of its hours strange. She lay down on the bed and looked at the round spot of light the lamp cast onto the ceiling. After a while she raised her hands and looked at them, holding them quite close to her eyes. They were slender, capable, unaffected by her age or condition. She admired them as though they belonged to someone else. She had never bothered to take off her wedding ring—it was a convenience, like her married name, to be used when she needed it—and now she looked at the thin gold band with delight. At least she still had that claim on the past. She slipped it off and looked for the initials engraved inside. They were worn almost entirely away. The karat stamp, now, was much clearer.

Superstitiously she slid the ring on again. But the thought of the lost initials, worn away already after less than three years, began to afflict her. She wondered how much else had been lost. Her memories of her marriage seemed faint, abstract, commemorative: Jay's face when the baby was born, her birthday parties. It was all disconnected, changed. She turned over on her face. Was the rest of her life—was this moment, even—to be lost, worn off by time? The intensity of her feeling seemed no proof against the evaporation of her life. She wondered if Jay had kept more of their marriage—surely he would have, since he had valued it more. Suddenly determined, she dialed his number.

The telephone rang and rang. She hung up after a while. Where would he be at midnight on a Saturday? Once she had known every detail of his life—had known, with a sense of suffocation, exactly where he was every minute of the time. Now she couldn't even guess. She remembered the gossip, the kindly hints of her friends. She had been glad then that he had found someone, condescendingly glad. Now the thought made her frantic—not with jealousy, but with the horror of her isolation. He could not cast her off as though they had never been married, as though she no longer existed. She dialed his number again.

After that she had no way of stopping. She felt as though she were keeping a vigil over her own life. She timed herself carefully; a half-hour had to pass between calls. Waiting, she lay in a trance, staring up at the spot of light on the ceiling. Around two o'clock she remembered the name that had been mentioned casually now and then: Celia Clark. She knew her—a blonde girl, exactly her own height and size. They even shared schools. That was like Jay—to fly to a second edition. She was outraged by the neatness of it. It was necessary to dial Information to get the girl's number.

The telephone rang five or six times before it was answered. There was a long pause, and then the girl said, "Yes?" She had been asleep, and her voice was hoarse. Lilly opened her mouth to say something, to question, accuse. "Yes? Yes?" the girl demanded reviving to anger. Lilly hung up without speaking.

It was two thirty. She telephoned Jay again. This time he answered.

"It's me," she said.

"Is Willy all right?"

"Of course! I've been thinking about you," she explained.

There was a pause. She heard the tinkle of ice in a glass.

"Where've you been?" she asked, almost gaily.

"Look, Lilly, it's too late for this."

"All right. I'll call you tomorrow."

"That's not what I mean."

"Then what . . . I'm lonely, Jay—I'm all alone." Her voice broke, and she poured her tears into the receiver.

"It's too late, Lilly," he repeated across her sobs. She heard the familiar tremor in his voice, but it no longer affected his words. They had become automatic. "You should have thought of this a year ago.

I knew something was up when I saw you in the park." That was to himself, with satisfaction.

"I need you," she said, blindly seizing on something.

"It's not me you need."

"I can't get on any longer by myself."

"Look," he said gently, "you'll be all right in the morning. You'll sleep late and get up and put on your pink robe and have your English muffins. Tomorrow's Sunday," he reminded her.

"I hate Sunday!" she cried. "I can't stand for tomorrow to be Sunday!" It was a cry out of the old time.

"Good night, Lilly." After a moment she heard a click. He had hung up.

She sat dazed, the dead receiver in her hand. She could hardly believe that he had turned her down. She could hardly believe, even, that she had made an offer. Yet there was the receiver in her hand, to prove that she had been turned down. He had taken something away from her and he did not intend to return it. He had stripped her to the bone. She lay on her face and sobbed and bit the pillow until the groveling sounds frightened her, and she lay still.

After a while a few words formed in the roaring void of her mind. I am twenty-six, she thought, and I am divorced, and I have a child. She had never added it up before, and the words seemed cumbersome and strange. I am twenty-six, and I am divorced, and I have a child. Is that all? she cried in anguish. And the answer came back pedantically, You are twenty-six, and you are divorced, and you have a child. It was so strange, so small and hopeless a revelation, yet small and hopeless. She turned the three facts over and over, like three pebbles in her hand. They were cool and solid and round, and she did not know what she would find to do with them. But they were—they existed; and suddenly she felt the weight of her life, of herself, laid upon her bare bones.

GEORGIA McKINLEY was born in Dallas and is a graduate of the University of Texas. She has published fiction in literary quarterlies including the *Kenyon Review, Paris Review,* and *Southwest Review,* and in *Redbook.* A collection of her short stories entitled *The Mighty Distance* was published in 1965, and she is the recipient of a Houghton Mifflin Literary Fellowship for a novel in progress. She lives in Melrose, New York, with her husband and two children.

The Mighty Distance

PART ONE

I

THE big car came into town in silken quiet and drew to the curb beside the Coca-Cola sign which flapped its kindergarten colors against the great bleak plain beyond, down at the end of the short street. Two women got out of the back seat immediately, as if to escape something which had been going on in the car, or perhaps only the confinement of each other's company, and started toward the drugstore. In the front seat, the men sat on: the Negro, having just driven 200 miles in three hours, had, while turning off the ignition, begun to let his head drop toward the steering wheel, and the white men were waiting, poking at each other, to see if he would really droop down and fall asleep against it, just like that.

The car stood at the curb, silver light running in its deep black flanks, and up and down the street the people of the town, seeing it had come from the wrong direction to be from Houston, instantly thought "Dallas" and stopped to watch. "Look, real cowboys here," one of the women said when she noticed them in their tight pants and wide-brimmed hats. The other, looking about her at the white stone buildings and roofed sidewalks, replied, "Sweet, *sweet* town," in a somewhat puzzled tone because it was quite different from the Western sets she was used to seeing on TV.

They went swiftly on across the sidewalk, their slender legs weaving and twining upward from their high-heeled shoes and ankle sox, moving them delicately and it seemed even perilously forward, for their bodies appeared more richly fruited than could be borne by such fragile flashing stems. Each of them moved in a little aura of light, in one case a silver-blue sheen, in the other a glow of yellow-gold. Ola, the older of the two, had her pouf of gray hair tinted pale blue, and her silvery eye makeup, the rhinestones in her blue plastic glasses, and the sequins on the blouse of her dress all gave back gleams of light. Bonnie Dee followed behind; her hair had been styled to spring in athletic short curves from the head and dyed a bright true yellow tipped with gold; a printed dress from Neiman Marcus' cruise collection matched both its colors. Her shoes were gold brocade, and her arms, weighted with costume jewelry, moved gently, and helplessly up and down at her sides.

Ola, who had met the younger woman only four hours before, was aware that with their rounded bodies and their air of money they looked somewhat alike. Now she reached the door of the drugstore and saw that there were several men inside who lifted their heads slowly on red necks to watch them enter; moved by their simple curiosity, she felt a sudden responsibility for Bonnie Dee, as if her presence in the drugstore might cause the men to suffer. She turned to look at her and became aware of the crucial difference between them: that the flesh of middle age had layered over and obscured the young girl she herself once had been, whereas Bonnie Dee's appeal had only been enriched and ripened by her plumpness.

It had stretched her skin to a luminous thinness, through which the pink flesh seemed vibrant with life, yet conveyed also a suggestion of the pneumatic, of the strong soft resilience of foam rubber, and Ola felt that a man, particularly an older man, would be glad to place his head upon the exquisite cushions of her body, which promised at once the excitement of the humming blood and the gift of rest. She looked, for the first time since they had left Dallas, directly into Bonnie Dee's eyes and saw that their clean, polished surfaces of blue and white were so depthless and without reflection that she appeared to be unaware that she was the custodian of her own figure. As though to signify that she herself was not accountable, Ola opened the door, stood back, and let Bonnie Dee go in alone.

They walked into a hollow of silence, only their high heels tapping across the wooden floor, and seated themselves on wire-backed chairs beside a table. The awed immobility of the men in the drugstore oppressed Ola, but Bonnie Dee leaned toward her, weighting the table with her breasts, shaking her charm bracelets into place, and said in a clear, young-girl's voice, "I just love these old-fashion' drugstores. I haven't been in one since I was little bitty." She saw the boy crouched behind the marble counter and called to him, "Bring us two *large* Cokes, will you, honey? They're gonna bring in some rum," she assured Ola, "and I just *feel* like a Cuba libre, don't you?" She showed Ola her white teeth in a gay, girls-out-together smile, which she then lifted and sent impartially about the drugstore into the gathered stillness. The men stirred and turned ungracefully away, the backs of their jug ears red beneath their Stetson hats.

Ola glanced out at the street, brilliant with the glare of the limestone buildings, and saw that the two men had got out and were standing on the sidewalk, bottles hanging from their hands, still watching the Negro's head move up and down on the long, flexible stem of his spine. Finally, they turned and started toward the drugstore, one very tall, the other short, both walking with the same gentle pace in the confidence that here, or anywhere else they chose to advance, a comfortable, well-serviced path would open directly before them. There was a meticulously cared-for look about them, as if the hairs of their heads had been straightened and accounted for and their shining skins had been lovingly bossed to the sheen of pink marble, and they projected before them an atmosphere of outdoor vigor and indoor authority. They were dressed in hunting clothes: twill shirts and trousers and laced leather boots.

"You bring the rum?" Bonnie Dee said, looking at her husband as he put down several bottles on the table. "Us girls are goin' to have Cuba libres."

"There it *is*," he said and sat down.

Ola's husband, Gus Ben Elkins, stood over the table for a time thoughtfully looking down at them all, and then finally spoke. "You sure you want to, deah? Take a drink in the middle of the day, I mean? Now, you don't usely do that."

They all looked up at him for a moment, waiting for him to go on to tell them what to do. "Yes," Ola said, "yes, I might as well . . ." She paused in incompletion; there was something she wanted to communicate to him for which she could not find the word or signal. An expression came into her eyes which had shown there only in the last few years, as if, staring out through the changed integument of her body, they would shout to him and the world, "Look for me in here; if you want to find me, I am still in here."

But he replied, "Well, if you're sure you want to. I'll just leave that up to you," and sat down.

Clayton Justice opened the rum and splashed it into the Cokes; he was so tall that even as he bent with the bottle he seemed disconnected from them all at the table, his bright skin taut as leather on his big head, his features without expression. He pushed the women's drinks forward without looking at them and turned to talk to Gus Ben.

Ola drank and felt the rum hollow out her knee joints, leaving only fragile shells for her support. After a time, Clay finished his drink and lifted his large face to Ola and his wife across the table, appearing surprised to see them still there. An undirected smile appeared, like an involuntary disturbance of his skin, and he said in an impersonal voice, "Well, girls . . . well, girls, are you all havin' fun?"

Bonnie Dee was staring around the drugstore and, since Clay himself was not looking at either of them, Ola did not know whether or not to answer. "Well, I've never been on a hunting trip before," she said doubtfully. Clay turned his opaque dark eyes toward her as if he had heard her voice and was seeking the source of the sound.

"Is that so?" he said.

She was struck by his dissociation from events around him. She had heard it said that he was rich—not in the calculable sense in which her husband was, but in a grander degree; now she felt that his mind was lost far back there within the structure of his wealth; perhaps he was thinking of the ugly oilfields which had pumped him rich, investments or speculations beyond her imagining; between him and the rest of the world there existed a barren space which he seemed to have neither the force nor desire to cross.

But Bonnie Dee was looking at her. "That's funny," she said. "You don't go on hunting trips with your husband? *He* always takes me with him. Every time he wants to get away for a while, I go too.

Some of the places I've been . . ." She raised her eyebrows in a mild amazement.

Clay turned wearily toward her; though he was in his late forties, his face was not worn, but dulled by disconnection. "Well, who would leave a wife that looks like her behind?" he said with a faint smile. He began to stare at Bonnie Dee as if he actually saw her, at first with an expression of simple appraisal; then his thick cheeks quivered to a smile, and his eyes became for the first time sharp and voraciously seeing at the centers, as if having opened at all it was upon the strong impulses of his animal nature. His mouth went slack and his right hand groped out for his wife's arm, the fingers spread like claws. "That's right," he mumbled; "now that's the living truth."

This was the response Ola had been afraid of seeing Bonnie Dee draw from some male, and it seemed more embarrassingly intimate that it had come from her husband; she could only pretend that the conversation had upheld them from what was unsayable. "Well, well," she remarked, batting her eyes to summon them to social speech. Bonnie Dee was committed to no pretense. She hit sharply at her husband's hand and looked at him with innocence hardened like a figure in china in her eyes. "Don't be *silly*," she said; "stop being silly." She brushed at the spot on her arm where his hand lay, gently touching her mounded breasts as if to comfort them; limply, his great hand dropped from the wrist and fell away and his eyes indifferently withdrew. Bonnie Dee turned to the Elkinses, silently asking them to witness how she had been affronted. Her indignant eyes spoke to them above the continuous countermessage of her body, and, as they watched her, suddenly filled with a rush of tears.

Ola looked out at the street and saw that the Negro's head had completed its fall to the steering wheel and rested there peacefully. "Look at that," she said. "Oh, aren't they *wonderful?* He's gone to sleep there. Oh," she went on to no one, and with true longing, "don't you wish . . . don't you *wish* you could just relax wherever you happened to be and go to sleep, the way he did?"

II

They had another drink and began to talk, the men to each other and the women between themselves in the way it almost always fell out. People in the drugstore started to move about again, though they still curiously watched the central island of metal table where a party seemed to be in the making in the middle of a weekday afternoon. No one around them could catch a word the four said, for they all, the two men and their women, handled language gently, their voices hardly ruffling the consonants as they passed, but melting down the vowels in a slow fall, so that the general tone of their conversation was one of soft and wondering complaint. This tone attached itself most persistently to the Negro outside; they spoke about him, veered away, returned, and, finally, the thought of him took over the conversation.

"They're *natural*," Ola said. "I wish I could just do what I feel like like that. He just felt like going to sleep so he went to sleep. They say you should be—" She looked at them, wishing she could tell them what it was she meant, her eyes tipsy and blurred behind her bright glasses. "It's not good for you if you're not," she said, after reflection, and stuck a finger through the lacquered shell of her hair to indicate that it was the brain beneath she considered.

Gus Ben looked at her judiciously, his eyes wide and solemn. "Well now, you realize, deah, that they can afford to be natural. Now all he's got to do is relax and sit still till some white man comes along and tells him what to do. I believe I could relax, too, if I knew I could get by like that. Couldn't you?" he asked Clay.

Clay looked at him; his opaque eyes seemed struggling toward life again. "They've got somebody to make all the decisions," he said.

"Now take *him*," Gus Ben said. "He just falls asleep there and it don't matter to him how it looks to have him slopping around like that all over the car. Oh, well—people probably think the car belongs to him instead of to you, anyhow," he said wanly to Clay.

"I don't care," Ola said; "I wish I could *be* like that. Don't they just *kill* you, the things they do? A girl who works for me, Olive . . ." She began a story about her maid to Bonnie Dee.

"When I first came to Dallas twenty-five years ago," Gus Ben went on, "a Buick or a Cadillac really meant something. Now, *they've* all got 'em, first- or second-hand. Sometimes I wonder what kind of car a man could get he wouldn't look up next day and see some jigaboo at the wheel of one just like it." His large pale eyes fixed them, schoolmasterish and offended. He was a small man who resembled a caricature which dwindled progressively toward the feet: his handsome, distinguished features were too large for his head, and his head was too large for his wiry body. The utter gravity of his great face, hanging, as it did, slightly below eye level for most people, made him seem to dominate every gathering of which he was a part, and gave his slightest statement an appearance of importance. "You know what I mean?" he said.

"Well, they all got rich," Clay said indifferently.

"I grew up near a little town like this," Gus Ben went on, "and every Saturday night we boys would take our baseball bats and go down through the niggertown and beat the living lights out of every one of 'em we caught out on the street. That's the nice thing about a little town—you can keep things straight. I'll bet you it really hurts those people out there to see that damned nigger slopping around all over that car with spit running out of his mouth."

Clay pushed back his chair and sat staring out the door. The women listened, Bonnie Dee staring with eyes that appeared young and eager in her late-thirties face. Ola heard her husband speak, at first with comfort and then anxiety. She was a little drunk; through the confusion of her own thoughts, his restatement of her experience steadied her; she seemed to recognize everything he said as if she were looking at an old familiar map of country where she had been born and grown up. For as long as she could remember, she had sat thus and listened to voices raised in self-righteous complaint against the Negroes. But she sensed now that something was different, for she knew that to the men these old truths no longer seemed the map of the world around them but had been compressed within their own minds to explosive tension. Their trapped convictions seemed too much for them to bear unaided and she longed to be able to comfort and help them. "Well, he ought to act better than that," she admitted, looking out at the Negro.

But Clay seemed to have come to life. He dropped his hands to his knees and pushed himself up to his great height and walked with serenity out to his car. "Raby," he called softly. "Wake up there now, Raby, I expect you had enough nap." He spoke tenderly, but the Negro did not stir. He lifted his arm and brought his open hand down on the Negro's head with such force that it cracked against the steering wheel, dropped sideways and disappeared, slowly rose again with the puffed lids of the eyes opening upon a terror so completely defined that it seemed to have been behind them all along.

252 GEORGIA MCKINLEY

"Git out," Clay said.

Raby's limpid eyes hung on the white man's face, as if his mind could find no point at which to hold and gather the force with which to act. He was normally a cheerful man; he was thirty, but at the moment he seemed much younger, his whole nature blank and unmolded, struggling simply to exist.

"You gonna take a walk," Clay said.

The Negro's eyes were afraid to leave what they had already at least seen, but turned slowly and went up the street past the idle white cowboys and off to the flat plain beyond; not daring to stop anywhere, they swung back to the white man, rolled past him, and started round again.

"Go stand out on the goddamn' prairie if you can't find any place else to go, and wait there till we call you."

The Negro began to get out, his long hands dropping slowly and tenderly across the steering wheel. After he had climbed from the car, he walked down the street toward the plain beyond. He looked back once, his face beneath its astonished vacancy beginning to tighten with anger or resentment.

III

When they came out of the drugstore after a few more drinks all around, he was still there, just off beyond the sidewalk, his hands in his pockets, standing waiting in the sun, his head turned sullenly away from them. He looked as if he had fallen asleep on his feet like an animal. "They can't sunburn because of their skin," Ola said to Bonnie Dee.

"Look at him," Gus Ben said. "That's what Ola means—they can be happy anywhere. It seems a shame to disturb his peace. We could let the girls buy the groceries so he can just rest there till we get ready to leave town."

Ola turned to him. "Oh, no—I can't buy the groceries," she said.

"Why, deah, you not too drunk to get down the street and buy a few groceries."

"It isn't that," Ola said. "It isn't that I'm drunk. But he's going to do the cooking; I don't know what to get. I don't have a list—I've never been in that store before . . ." She spoke faster and faster, and her eyes pled with him for understanding.

"My God, surely you know how to walk into a store and buy some groceries. You'll go, won't you?" he said to the other woman. "I just as soon," she answered. He turned back to Ola. "Now you go *on*," he said. "Goddamn."

Bonnie Dee had already started toward the grocery. Tilting in their high heels, the two women walked down the street. Ola began to talk. "At home, Bessie gives me a list. Sometimes if she wants to get out she even comes with me. She's shaped like a great big chest of drawers, and once she got stuck in one of those seeing-eye doors . . ."

The grocery was smaller than the supermarkets she was used to, and at first Ola thought it might not bother her. She took the basket and wheeled it into the first aisle and looked at the loaded shelves. I wonder how many things there are in this section, she thought. Her eyes began to follow the aisle to its end: the soups, the soaps, cleaning aids—maybe 2000. They are stacked deep in the shelves; I can't see them all, she cautioned herself. She began to count along a shelf. Bonnie Dee wandered about, occasionally dropping something into the basket. All the shapes were hard, dozens of little compact objects glinting in bright coverings, so densely gathered that Ola's vision was burdened and confused by their presence.

Bonnie Dee came with something to put into the basket and Ola moved it hurriedly along a few steps and stopped. How can anybody choose when there is so much? she thought. The idea of ferreting out decisions from among all those articles sapped her strength, yet they towered to the ceiling on both sides and there seemed no escape. She found herself staring into a shelf whose contents had become strange and arresting, like things never seen before. She noticed that the print on the packages was erratic, running off in odd directions: up, down, sideways. A yellow name shot obliquely across a green can; slogans such as "7-second," "special OFFER" leaped out at her in flashes. The light moving upon the jagged print made the cans appear to be a chain of silent explosions down the shelves; each, as her eyes touched it, noiselessly splintered and was reformed hard and bright as ever. As though disturbed by the repercussions, the shelves began to dance in long, sinuous ribbons beneath the cans.

"My good God," Gus Ben said, "look what you got, Ola, ripe olives and maraskeeno cherries!"

"We'd better get the nigger and let him buy the groceries," Clayton said disgustedly.

Ola hung onto the handle of the basket. What is it, she thought; is it the change?

"Git that basket and buy some groceries fast," she heard Clayton's voice say in a minute. She could already feel the soft stir of air behind her and then she saw the long black hands fall on the handle of the wheeled basket. For the first time since she had left Dallas, she had the sense of being in a situation quietly familiar and full of comfort. "Thank you, Raby," she said, and dropped back away from the basket. Her only disappointment was that he did not look at her and grin.

IV

On beyond the town, the scenery, which had not been inspiring before, was less so. The enormous blank sky grew higher as the horizon flattened and the vegetation shortened. Beneath the relentless light of the sun, the whole earth turned a uniform, endless gray: the scrub-oak thickets, the straggling mesquite, the sparse grass and the limeshale ground lying in its own floury dust. The paved road ran straight and unending across the squat world and the Negro drove the car at 80 miles an hour without bringing them to any change in their surroundings.

Ola had withdrawn into the interior happiness which had begun when she felt the Negro coming to take the basket from her. All her life she had liked the company of Negroes, and she could not remember a time when she had not lived on the most intimately friendly terms with them. Her father had been a poor corn-and-cotton farmer, but there was always a colored woman who came in from her little house nearby to do the washing and ironing. As a child Ola had sat beneath the ironing board as she worked and watched the thick chunks of the Negro's bare feet lying flat against the floor, the lovely lavender soles whispering peacefully when she moved. From those feet, the sturdy columns of her legs had moved upward into pink bloomers; her black skin emerged again at the neck of her dress in the queenly pendant of a large hanging goiter. It had seemed to the child beneath that her head supported the ceiling and her feet and legs braced and stabilized a safe place around her wherever she moved.

There were many other Negroes in Ola's country community who were friends of herself and her family. She could not recall

about whom it was that she once asked her mother the question—
one of the Negroes she knew or one who had come out of the
grownup newspaper world—for her mother's answer was so successful that it almost made her forget what had prompted it. Far back
in her childhood, some Negro had been in trouble and she had worried about it. At last, she went to her mother, who looked at her
kindly and said, "But, Ola, you mustn't *ever* worry about them, because they don't feel things the way we do. If they get cold or sick
or hurt, they just don't feel it the way you would—they can't—
they just haven't got the same feelings, that's all." She added, "I've
been meaning to tell you that for a long time." Her mother had a
long, sad, half-sick face herself, and, when Ola responded by throwing herself enthusiastically around her knees, that face warmed with
pleasure and they looked at each other for a moment, sweetly joined
in the relief of knowing that, in a world where there was so much
poverty and hardship, they at least need never worry about the
Negroes. Even in later life, when Ola had come to realize that the
Negroes, at least to some degree, could be hurt, she had felt much
the same way about them when she thought of them in their nig-
gertowns at night. She was glad in the evening when she knew they
were all together, closed away from threat of harm, carefree and
happy among themselves. She thought of their laughter and music
and love of sex and was glad they had these things.

Now her eyes rested on the black column of Raby's neck. He
never spoke or glanced away from the road when driving, erect and
quiet within himself. But the way in which he held his head looked
stubborn, and he seemed remote and cheerless; Ola hoped he
was not going to spoil the trip by pouting about what had happened in town. As she watched, she saw Clay Justice's arm loop out
around her husband in the middle. For an instant his pink hand
hung behind the Negro's head, then he thumped the back of his
neck with a fingernail, like someone testing a watermelon. "Slow the
hell down," he said. "I told you twice."

The Negro looked over at him. "I did," he said, his voice sounding
aggrieved. "I down to 60."

The flat earth and its ropes of gray, dusty grass stroked less rapidly
away from the car, and the spindly, barbed-wire fence beside the
road ran up to a three-board, dusty brown gate. They could see a
double track in the dirt which ran straight off into the plain behind
the gate, and the Negro turned the car off the road and got out to

open it. Beside the motionless car stood a shallow bank where the earth had been cut through to make the paved road. The four white people stared at the bank in fascination and concern. "Oh, look," Ola said in an anxious voice; "look at the topsoil."

"What topsoil?" Gus Ben asked between awe and annoyance. "There's *no* topsoil. What is that damn' grass growing out of?"

"Oh, yes, there's a little," Bonnie Dee said, leaning out of the window. "See—it's more gray." A film of darker dust, the color of cigarette ashes, was sifted lightly on the limeshale. Its depth could not have been measured by a ruler; it was certainly not an eighth of an inch.

"Well, now," Clay said uneasily, "these ranchers all run sheep and it don't take *too* much to keep a sheep alive." When the Negro came back to the car, Clay motioned him to wait and he sat with his hands around the wheel staring out in perfect indifference at the landscape.

"But how the hell many acres would it take even for a sheep on land like this?" Gus Ben asked. An unease had come over the four of them. The men could not for the moment remember the solid walls of their own offices or the long perspectives of plate-glass cubicles where their subordinates worked amid the crisp stir of business machines; it seemed to them unlikely they lunched in good restaurants with the presidents of corporations. Their oldest knowledge was of the packing qualities of black land, the infertility of sand, of erosion and the hard look of the sky in time of drouth ("all signs of rain fail in time of drouth," their fathers had taught them), of sandburs, bare houses, and the small proportions of the barely adequate, which might at any moment let them slip through to the not-enough. That vein of fear was present in its pure form which, even dilute in the presence of their material success, caused them periodically to go through the office wastebaskets to see if anyone was wasting paper, or led them, on their cabin cruisers, to save little balls of string. Their wives, who could not find ways to spend their allowances, thought guiltily of the food they had seen the servants throwing out and of how much money they spent on clothes, and instinct moved their muscles to gather the children closer to themselves for protection almost before their minds remembered that, in one case, there were no children and, in the other, that they were grown and gone.

The four white people sat without speaking until the Negro

pressed the accelerator and caused it to roar. Clay's head shot up as if he were coming out of sleep, and his mouth tightened. "Well, for God's sake, let's go, if you so anxious," he shouted. Then he laughed. "It's like this Texan said when he was trying to sell his ranch to this Easterner, 'There's nothing *wrong* with this grass, Mister, it just grows kinda fur apart.' If you got enough acres of it— well, we're nearly to the rancher's house now."

V

Straight and bare, offering no color or movement but a sheen of autumn heat waves, the plain stretched about them. The Negro was driving like a demon again, stirring a great screen of dust around the car, through the skeins of which they began to observe that another dustcloud was moving toward them in a straight line out of the mid-distance. They recognized it immediately, less as a result of childhood memories than of all the Westerns they had seen on TV, as a man on horseback riding fast. This small point of life moving with such felt purpose on the dead plain touched them profoundly, as if the rider were indeed coming to save them from deep trouble. "Slow down, stop, Raby," Clay said. "Let's see him come."

Within the dust veil they were aware of the high-kneed motion of a palomino quarter horse and of the rider who indifferently permitted its surging thrust to come to rest in his own rigidity. He managed the horse with his left hand and with his right held his Stetson hat over the heart in the formal gesture of gallantry. When the horse reached the car, the rider came off its back with a single motion and stood beside it, hat still in position. He had white or ash-blond hair which shone in the light, and the gleaming red skin of a cowboy, and he stood out against the dull background so intensely and suddenly that their senses were momentarily stunned. His features were short and handsome and his gray eyes were quick but rather vacant, as if from looking too long at the empty prairie. It was impossible to tell whether he was in well-preserved middle age or mature and responsible youth, but what he had, and that for which they were most grateful to him, was the look of prosperity and well-being which restored their spirits. Everything about him appeared luxurious, from the closely shaven skin of his face to the delicately woven cloth of his rancher's shirt, the soft suede of his chaps, and the fine tooling of his leather boots. He wore a heavy

Mexican silver buckle on a belt of patterned skin—it was the skin of a rattler, they saw later—and heavy silver rings on his brown hands. He looked like an outdoorsman of the old Texas type, and he also looked rich, exemplifying in his person everything they believed in. And, when he smiled, the flash of his teeth and his willingness to share with them their mutual birthright completed their happiness.

"I'm Barney Till," he said, "and I expect you're Mr. Justice and Mr. Elkins. Well, welcome, welcome," he went on, and looking out the window at the brush they felt they had come to a place for which they had always longed. "I'll ride over with you to show you the way to my house." Mounting his horse, he gestured to them to move forward again in the way they had been going.

He loped down the road as they came slowly along behind, admiring the horse's appointments. They looked at each other, pleased, for this was more than they had bargained for when they took the hunting lease; a rancher who rented hunting land in this part of the country might be anything—or nothing—at all, and this one had restored them to themselves.

"Is that man goin' to go like that down the middle of the road the whole way?" Raby asked, and they realized the car was running in low gear. He stared over at Clay Justice, expectant, more on behalf of the car than of himself, of some correction of the situation.

"He's showing us the way," Clay replied.

The Negro stared out at the endless spread of country, on which no road or path was visible except the double tire track before them, and slowly shook his head. On they went, following the rider, with nothing much for any of them to look at but the man ahead of them, his buttocks rising and falling in the ancient, monotonous rhythm of the horseman. The white people had learned to ride as children, and their muscles recalled the motion. "Beautiful horse," "the saddle," "cost a lot," they murmured to each other. Raby stared restlessly about him, here and there; then, with the look of a person gathering information, he turned and stared a moment at Bonnie Dee in the back seat. The look was too cold to be curious, but it led Ola to glance at her also: she saw that the still face had become bright, as if the woman's senses had quickened to a new atmosphere like those of a person who, after a long trip toward it, has come within reach of the smell of the sea.

VI

The rancher's house was a small, rectangular building, painted white and neat as a pin. Its yard, though it did not differ from the plain around it, containing nothing but the tough grass clumps, was outlined by a little picket fence; there was even an empty trellis over the gate—from it swung a sign which read "Till Ranch." There were no outbuildings, no fenced enclosures, nothing connected with ranching in sight. The owner dismounted with the same fluid movement and called, "I won't ask you into my bachelor's quarters. I'll just pick up the key to your place and we'll go on there."

"He could plant a *rose* there, on that thing," Bonnie Dee said excitedly to Ola; "a climbing red rose." She looked at Ola with round, solemn eyes.

"Here?" Ola said. "It wouldn't grow." She spoke somewhat bitterly. The cheerful, pert appearance of the little house in this place gave her a queer pang. She thought of the aloneness of one human unit against that large land, and the thought came to her mind: I couldn't live here by myself.

Barney Till came back and said into the window of the car to the white men, "Can he follow this road, you think? Just keep in the car tracks?" Raby's eyes flickered over toward him. "I reckon he can do that," Clay answered.

"It's about four miles by the road and only two cross-country. I'll go ahead and open up the place." The rancher mounted and took off into the scrub. Raby let the car out with a wild roar, but the road looped about so widely that Barney Till was seated on the front porch grinning welcome by the time they got there. Beside him on a little table were an icetray, a bottle of whiskey, and some glasses.

Ola stared out with an uneasiness which had grown ever since they turned off the pavement. They had come into a section where little oaks about the height of a man grew among slablike rocks; the tiny leaves were olive-green, the bark dark gray, silvered with lichen, and the stones, the grass, the earth were gray half-tones. She pressed her fingers to her eyes for a moment as if the colorlessness were lodged in them, but the dull landscape remained. The house was paintless and silvered; it was the kind of square house which stood in the empty fields of east Texas, borne down by its high heavy roof onto the squat outer walls and so to the cedar posts which held it a few feet off the ground. Ola imagined that the stunted vegetation of the place would like to sink its roots into rich moist soil and leaf and flourish; she felt the oppression of the roof of the house upon its walls as if it were some great aching forehead hanging above them. And she realized, though she had lately come to regard such places as "nigger houses," that this was very like the house in which she had lived as a child. "Oh, why do they build these roofs so high?" she asked of Barney Till, who had come out to help take in the luggage. "I've always wondered."

"Why, I believe they used to do that just to give more pitch to the roof so's the water'd run off faster; you know they didn't know how to cure the shingles right then." He opened the door and looked in at her with an expansive friendliness which seemed to flow directly from the flushed skin of his healthy body. "But the reason why I did it is I thought folks who came out to hunt would like to go back a little and live in one of the old-time houses—otherwise they might as well stay home or in a motel." He looked back shrewdly at the house. "It's coming along fine—already looks like it's been there 50 years and it hasn't been built long."

Ola walked with him up the steps and into the central room of the house. On the inside, the walls still had the faint gold of new wood. Bonnie Dee had come up behind her on her delicate heels, and, as they stared about the place, Ola saw a daddy-longlegs whose legs covered a twelve-inch span wavering up the wall. Barney walked over and struck the spider with his index finger and it fell to the floor trailing its weak spiky legs.

He looked around, saw the women, and said, smiling, "I got a fine assortment of insects here. Any kind you might want—centipedes, stinging scorpions, tarantulas—if you ladies like to make you a collection while you're here . . ." His teasing voice contained such a hearty note that Ola felt he might actually be proud of the insects.

"Ooh," Bonnie Dee burst out in a little squeal, "don't even *tell* me about them. Honestly, I'm scared of everything. I feel like I'd just *die* if I even saw a tarantula."

Her pink flesh quivered; her manner was that of an adolescent girl being teased by a big, bullying boy. She and the rancher stared at each other, perhaps in surprise to find themselves playing these roles, and such an emptiness appeared in both their expressions that they seemed in danger of losing themselves in it. Ola felt as if a central vacuum were drawing all the air out of the room; she fought against its edges, not to be sucked in too, and said the first thing that came into her head. "At home when I was little, scorpions used to get into the corn. When we'd be shucking it for feed, sometimes we'd come down on one. Our hands were tough—but the worst sting I ever had was on the . . . Well, once I got into a truckbed full of corn and sat right down on one." The men looked at each other and began to laugh.

VII

Later, they sat on the porch having drinks while the men talked hunting. Ola sat beside Bonnie Dee, not speaking, relieved that in this situation nothing was required of her, while their slow, ceaseless talk accumulated. She knew nothing of the matter and everything about the manner of such discussions: the women never interrupted or asked questions. Whether they talked to each other or not was a matter of indifference to their husbands. The men's voices very quietly reconstructed terrain, the merits of the dogs, the game and guns, the realities of past and the possibilities of future hunts. As though by unspoken rule, such conversation was always unemphatic. Ola understood that this was not because of indifference but its opposite, for, on a topic of such unquestioned importance, respectful attention was paid to each word and stress was unnecessary. Today, however, something was wrong. A note of urgency ran through the conversation, until Ola realized it was injected by the rancher; he was speaking too often of the kind and quantity of game —the wild turkey and deer—which had been taken here in the past; the insistence in his voice was that of a salesman. She saw that he was interested in hunting as a means of making money, and thought the less of him for it.

Besides, he kept watching the women, his flickering eyes considering their fragile legs in the little high-heeled shoes; Ola tried to pull her skirt down. At last he said to them, "Don't you ladies have any heavy shoes, any boots, with you?"

"No," they answered.

"You better not walk away from the house, then," he said. "There's plenty of rattlesnakes out there." That curious tendency to brag about the wilds took him. "There're more snakes around here than anywhere else in the state, and this is a bad year for them. There're probably at least a dozen of them right around the house right now."

They all looked out before them, startled. They were less fearful than slightly affronted that the prairie should thus assert itself and demand their recognition and precautions. Used to the ease of city living, it seemed to them a kind of insubordination of environment, as if the plain had stood itself up on end just to make them look at it. They did not really expect to be able to see the snakes, but, now that their attention was captured, they sat on, looking out into the distance, really aware of it for the first time, and their eyes, with nothing to stop them, sped on to the horizon. Recognition came to Ola, for it was that great space which gave the country its quality. They were all fixed, without having willed it, into the attitude of yearning which it calls forth, as if they had never left their farm-house porches. For their eyes could move so far and see so little that it seemed that what they looked for must be always forward some-where—if not here, then on, on, perhaps just out of sight beyond the horizon. The vision could not believe in emptiness, but must expect to find something—at last—out there. . . .

Ola was the first to turn away from this ancient pull, and so saw the others. The city men had stood up and were watching with sweeping, observant eyes, as if they saw an endless movement of game before them in space. Then, slowly, they looked at each other, and one of them said, "This is going to be a good place." "We're going to have good hunting," the other replied with satisfaction.

Bonnie Dee's eyes were staring out of her own vacancy, and in the emptiness beyond met those of the rancher and drew them back with her from the distance. Ola saw his eyelids flicker and draw in as if, after long vigil, they had caught the stir of a moving creature in the grass, and she was aware that the air between the two was banded with tension which was pulling them together.

Raby appeared at the door of the porch. "I got y'all a little supper fixed up now," he said. Ola gave him a brilliant smile to indicate he had done exactly the right thing, but he replied with the austere look of a person who has many things to do and went back into the house to his work.

PART TWO

I

It did not surprise her that she had found him in that bleak country, for all the men had appeared out of it just as he had, first seen as tiny marks of moving life on the wide landscape, as a cloud of dust on a lonely horizon, already appearing the negation of loneliness and those desires which fed on it.

She propped herself up on pillows and looked at her bare pink arms to see what shape she was in.

There was one tree—a cedar—in the yard of their place near Mineral Springs, its shaggy bark shined by her pants ever since she could climb it; she was up there when the first one came, looking not for him but for anything moving on the sweep of land before her. She stayed up in the tree even after it was obvious that the eruption of dust was turning in their far gate; she was only thirteen and she wanted to stay out of sight and listen to what was said, and anyhow no car had ever come for her. But this one had. "Bonnie Dee Barstow live here?" the scratchy male voice came from under the roof of the truck. "Yeah," her father said; it was a Sunday, and he had come out of the shed where he kept his bottle hidden. "I like to see her," the boy replied. "Well," her father said, starting to laugh, "you just turn your eyes up and you'll see pretty near all of her." The boy looked up into her long legs hanging out of the cedar. "You want to go to the movies?" he said impassively.

Then there was the problem of talking to him on the way to town; he was a high school senior and she was only in the seventh grade and she had no idea what there was in his world. His appearance in the Chevy pickup truck was a miracle with which her previous life had not equipped her to deal. She knew how to clean greens, shell peas, and chop cotton, where to hide to keep out of her parents' way when they were tired or drinking, how to sit all day in school without learning anything, but she didn't know what to say to a boy on the way to the movies. They chewed gum instead. "I saw you around," he said. "Baseball picture on," he said. "Ooooh," she squealed insanely. She knew, under her panic, that this was the first important thing—almost the only thing—that had ever happened to

her. As soon as they were seated in the movie their hands had
touched and locked and they had turned to each other with numbed
eyes, as if each saw the other as a great wave gathering higher and
higher until, doomed by its swell, they swung together over into the
trough of seats where no light came, tumbled in a wild embrace.
Why are we here? the part of her which was prior to this experience
dimly wondered, and the boy began to pant into her hair, "I'm crazy
about you," the husk of his voice moving hot around her ears. She
thought, Yes, that's it, and joy came to her.

They did not speak at all on the way home, but they had this
contract between them. The boy said he would come to see her the
next Sunday and she was glad it was no sooner, for she wanted to be
alone to think about the experience. She saw that she had got her
hands on something she had hardly even known existed, which she
had to explore. As she thought about it, she realized that everything
she had learned from her parents' lives and the dry earth they
farmed was a lie: all the dirty dishes and diapers and sweat and sunburn were lies, and that excitement and ecstasy existed somewhere,
up in the sky; she gave herself over to serve them only. She sat in the
tree and thought about the boy's eyes and his embraces. "It's love,"
she repeated, awed, to herself, and it was clear that they were not
the same kind of people as the others around her, she and this mi-
raculous boy.

When he came again, they drove away from the house and parked
on a hill in full sunlight. He kissed her and she prepared to enter
the new country with him. But a ghastly mistake occurred: he
seemed to have lost all knowledge of the whereabouts of his own
person, for his tongue turned up in her mouth instead of his own
—solid and cool, about the size of a large pickle, it lay and would not
retreat. Surprised, she opened her eyes and saw blurred against them
his flushed face, eyes closed, self-concerned as a feeding animal. She
noted the enlarged pores beside his nose and the sleep in one of his
eyes; his weaknesses lay open to her and she saw, shocked, that this
person was an intruder who had nothing to do with the love she had
formed, had made out of herself. The disclosure of his unworthiness
was terrible and funny to her when she had expected so much more,
and she began to laugh almost hysterically and he had to take her
home.

When, disillusioned, he left her, he did not take her love with him.
She had assumed it was a part of him, but it floated free and re-

formed somewhere just up above the events of her daily life; she got into the habit of sitting in her tree looking up at the sky or far away into the distance as if she actually could see it there. And through her researches on the subject in the popular songs of the day, in the women's magazines and by talking to the high school girls, she learned that she was right about its nature: love was altogether lovely, something of magical excitement which took place between haunted creatures who did not sweat.

From time to time there appeared on the horizon the gray dust-cloud which meant the approach of another admirer. On these young men, love always settled for a time, but they were only the boys of the country, awkward, shy, with horny, chapped hands, and in some moment this would be revealed to her. As she came to know love in all its phases, her body came to understand its practices, and it was her mind which wanted from it something more exotic than it offered. In the moments of disillusionment, the hard innocence would come into her eyes as she saw she had not achieved her goal.

When she was sixteen, she felt marriage would be the answer, and when a man of legendary importance in the area began to look in her direction this did seem to be the case, for she saw that with his money and power he could literally carry her off to another life. But this was the most surprising occurrence of all, for after they were married and she was installed in his mansion in Dallas, when it seemed to her that anyone so successful must provide her with what-ever it was her heart craved from love, she realized that he himself had never even felt it and had no interest in it. Her look of inno-cence became her public facial expression, for while she accepted her rich life as she had her poor one, and his visits to her bedroom as a part of it, in her soul she was looking again for something. Her most urgent wish was that her husband would not, as in the drug-store in town, put her in the false position of appearing to have found it with him.

But now she was glad she had gone back into the past, for she had been assured that all the possibility of loving that she had ever known was with her still. Soon now she would allow the warmth of it to rise in her brain. . . .

She lifted the skimpy shades of her room and saw by the outer light that it was near noon. She had had no breakfast and she wanted some coffee. Still she flung herself back in bed with her legs drawn up against her breasts. Now with a secret delight, she could begin to think of him. The memory of the very dust of his coming caused her heart to beat faster; then, within it, the great horse so masterfully handled, the hat at the heart touching her with his gallantry and courage, the quick grace of the slide from the horse . . . She remembered the glitter of the silver, the light of the sun on skin and hair—and then later, when their eyes had met, she had felt that he was the true strong man for whom she had been waiting, for his eyes were willing to receive and engulf her, to slide into hers, to fall together and embrace. She began to roll and tumble about the bed, her arms flung around her knees as if her body had run riot with the good news.

II

Bonnie Dee drank a cup of coffee and went out to the porch where Ola was sitting in the swing. Ola looked up and sighed. "I've been trying to write a letter to my colored woman at home," she said, "but I don't know how to. I don't know what to say to her in a *letter* —you know, she'll buy anything on time. She thinks that means you don't have to pay for it—but when I'm there I can always talk her out of it. Now, the Lord knows what crazy thing she'll do. Once they called her from a cheap jewelry store and told her she'd won the setting for a ring and all she had to do was buy the diamond. She was paying on it for *years*. But I never wrote her a letter before . . ."

Bonnie Dee looked at her with round marble eyes. "Don't ask me," she said. "I never wrote a letter to a nigger in my life." She turned toward the horizon, dreaming. "I lived in a place like this when I was a kid. From our house you could look way off down a dirt road like this." She lifted her hand and sorted the golden feathers of her hair. "Men been gone long? That—that Barney didn't go with them, did he?" She swayed against one of the posts of the porch, lifted her arms around it, and clung. "You can see a million *miles* here," she cried out huskily, "a million *miles*."

Ola got up quickly and went out to the kitchen to find Raby, thinking he might be able to tell her how to write her letter. He was just washing the breakfast dishes and she stood and watched him. "I was wondering if you might know the colored girl who works for me, Raby? Her name is Olive Taylor."

He seemed to be very busy and did not turn around. "Nome."

"She's worked for me twelve years," Ola said; "three days a week. I have a couple, too, Sam and Bessie, but they live right on the place —they have a house in back. It's a lovely little house with a bath and all. But Olive . . ."

"Umhum," he said. He was sloshing gray water across the plates and turning them upside down on a dishtowel to dry. "But of course you wouldn't know her," Ola said, startled into laughter. "Because . . . It's the funniest thing I ever heard of, but she's afraid of other colored people. She won't go near them or have anything to do with them. When she has to sit with them on the streetcar, she gets scared to death they'll rob her or do something terrible to her—and she's as dark as anybody herself. But she says there are so many *mean* niggers, it's best to stay away from them all—that's the way *she* puts it. So she and her little girl live way out in the country by themselves —but I've always thought it'd be worse for her way out there in that river bottom, if anybody mean ever did come along. What do you think, Raby?" she asked.

"Where at she live?" he asked after a moment.

"Away out—toward Mesquite. It's a mile from a bus line. She owns a little piece of land." Ola thought of the slick brown mud banks of the creek and the sad black stalks of weeds at Olive's place and sighed. "I'll tell you—I worry about her because she's kind of crazy —buys on credit, you know—but I can always stop her—she'll do anything I say. She really will. You'd think I was her mother."

Raby was wiping his hands on a paper towel. He looked round at her, bored. "Where at you say she live?"

When she had told him again, he said bluntly, "I don't know about out that way"—and went out of the kitchen and sat down on the back porch steps. She could see him through the kitchen window and she thought how dark he looked against the day, his color giving him such a power in the vision that she seemed to see him with extraordinary clarity: the young quiet head, the wide innocent neck. He did not look before him but down into his own cupped hands, making a closed circuit of himself.

Bonnie Dee had gone back to her own room. Ola sat down in the creaky swing on the front porch. There was still a hint of the freshness of early morning in the air. It seemed to her she should be starting something for the day. But there was no use thinking about her childhood on the farm—that time when there was always some-

thing that needed doing—that was all past and done. Probably nobody lived like that any more, worked that hard. Nobody.

She had felt strange all morning. She had got up and had breakfast with the men very early. After they had left in the car and she
had made her bed, there was nothing for her to do, and she had sat
on the porch. It was Friday, one of the three days a week she usually
spent buying. If she were home, she would have been dressing to
go out, with checkbook, Charga-Plates, shopping lists already as-
sembled for the assault on the stores. Looking out at the plain, she
tried to imagine upon it some of the more familiar Dallas stores:
Volk's in Highland Park Village, the Preston Hollow Neiman
Marcus, the supermarket with its air-conditioned parking lot under
a glass shell. . . . But they rose for her only in the most skeletal
form, the gray scrub showing through their plate-glass windows. It
seemed to her that Dallas must have grown by some such means,
with vast shopping centers and miles of new houses springing out of
the dry earth by a powerful act of the imagination; these swift births
had taken place everywhere in and around the city. When her husband had had their first little house built, it had stood alone in the
country; long since though, it had been enclosed by a grid of streets,
sewage pipes and sidewalks; and merchandising, formerly gathered
in the center of town, had moved out along the main arteries to
every neighborhood, where solid blocks of shops replaced desolate
acres of broomweed and Johnson grass. To Ola, it seemed these
shops were pursuing and pressing in upon her. For it meant there
were more places to which she must go, more things to pass before
her eyes and brain. In times of fatigue or confusion, the thought of
all the stocks in all the stores attacked her sanity. At other times, she
would discover that the interior of a department store had lost its
reliable outline and the counters and contents, loosed from the
floor, were heaving as to the motion of a vast sea. From these strange
signs, she went on expecting the change.

The truth was she had never enjoyed shopping. Her taste, formed
and finished at the central high school she attended, was for comfortable flat shoes, dirndl skirts, and bobbypin curls; she liked to
wear her stockings rolled and twisted below the knees, and no
girdles, garter belts, or even brassieres. She had never learned to walk
comfortably in high heels. In a home she preferred simplicity: lino-
leum floors, a few religious prints, an overstuffed sofa and some
straight chairs. But, for years, her husband's position had made it

impossible for her even to think of these things. Among their friends, standing was achieved by spending, and living lavishly was a part of her husband's business. So she went on. Having no natural instinct for fashion, there was only one criterion she could follow: to buy whatever was advertised or talked about as new and smart. This meant that life was full of fluctuation: she never wore out her clothes, and in her home only the walls seemed stable amid the rush of change which swept away the objects to which she had barely become accustomed. She sighed, thinking how far behind she would have got by making this trip, and was glad when the Negro called them to the noon meal.

After lunch, the women sat on the porch together, smoking. Bonnie Dee's eyes were fixed so straight and steadily before her that they directed Ola's thought. "I suppose the rancher's house is in behind that little grove of red oak. It wouldn't be too far to walk if it wasn't for the snakes." As if she might have suggested something to the other woman, Ola put her hand over her mouth, but Bonnie Dee apparently did not have time to look over at her. Ola watched her, fascinated by her stillness, until it seemed to her the woman's cheerless eyes were fastened upon the space, trying to suck something out of it toward her. That look is going to pull him over here, right to her. The thought came to Ola and intensified; she felt stirred and rather frightened. Oh, what's going to happen? she wondered.

She stood up. "I've got a big stack of fashion magazines I ought to read," she said. "I guess I'll go inside."

But once Ola was in the living room, an unexpected consolation came to her. She began to think about the kitchen of her home in the very early mornings when the Negroes were gathered there before starting their work. Smells of coffee, burned toast, and the people themselves would come a good way up the stairs to meet her as she started down, accompanied by their loud but never unmelodious voices quarreling or joking. But when she arrived, they always stopped whatever they were doing and looked up at her with unvarying white grins of welcome, moving back away from the table to the counters to finish their coffee while Bessie brought Ola her breakfast. Often, she would sit there with them quite a long time, either talking to them, or, her mind circled by their soft flowing voices, with her thoughts on other things entirely. Then, when she told them what she wanted done that day, each of them would grin at her with such quick, amiable intelligence that it seemed to her her orders had given pleasurable meaning to their lives.

They love me, she said to herself; they all love me—and a glow of warmth without which she felt she could not live rose in solace round her heart.

III

After Ola went in the house, Bonnie Dee sat on the porch all afternoon, her spirits resilient in the medium of hope. Just at sunset a shape emerged from the horizon and her husband's car came along the tracks, piling up rosy dust. When the two men stepped from it, the strong red light struck straight into their faces as if to penetrate to the bones, making them appear almost transparent, fragile and tired. She brought her attention to them, deferred her own hopes until tomorrow, and seeing her husband looking so worn out wished for a moment, out of her own excitement, that she might do something for him. She thought of telling him that soon everything was going to be all right for her. It seemed a shame, after all the tedium they had borne together, that they could not share this present elation of hers. "Did you all have any luck?" she called out.

They got out their guns slowly and with finality and came up onto the porch. Clayton's attention came gradually to his wife, observed the iridescence of her hair and jewels on the lonely porch. "No," he said, "we didn't." He started forward and stopped, hung on one foot reflecting over her. "Did you?" he asked. "You know, tomorrow we're goin' to a different place and try again. You not gonna mind too much if we leave you for a couple days, are you?" He stood looking down at her thoughtfully.

Bonnie Dee shrugged. "Why, no," she said, "I don't mind. You go right on, and I hope this time you get something."

In the living room, Ola, freeing her mind from the lush foliage of her magazines, looked up and saw the men standing on the porch stark and diminished, they and their guns, by the great light beyond them. She hurried toward them as if a lack had been revealed to her which might be made up out of herself. "What's the matter?" she asked, coming out to the porch. "What's wrong with everyone?"

But no one spoke to her; the three forms remained immobile in the failing light. Suddenly, Gus Ben sighed and spoke with the air of having found the surprising truth which explained everything.

"There wasn't nothing out there. Nothing. We didn't get a shot."
He took up his gun and broke it at the breach and carried it cradled
in his arms into their bedroom.

Ola ran after him. "Why, that's a shame," she said; "coming all
this way . . ." Only *she* knew how small and square his hands were,
how thin and white his feet. He sat in a chair holding his gun as if
it had been injured. She started toward him and he looked up warily;
her tenderness seemed to have reached him like an odor and his
gray eyes retracted. He would never allow her to fuss over him; there
was nothing she could do for him. When she came toward him
radiating warmth, he had the ability to withdraw life from every
surface of his body down to the changeless male center of his being,
to that unsupported self he had wielded so long against the world.

"We're goin' some place else tomorrow, deah," he said. "Just Clay
and me—can't take you girls because there's nothing but a little
shack to stay in and we may be gone two-three days. You be all right
—the nigger'll stay here with you." He watched her, his gray eyes
motionless and beautiful in their fixed purpose.

She was frightened. He still had the power to surprise her, to
pass effortlessly beyond the borders of her expectations. She thought
he must be trying her reason: that he could bring her, when she had
not wished to come at all, to this desolate spot and abandon her
for several days in the prevailing strangeness of the whole adventure
seemed at first impossible and then, without transition, as she
looked into his baby-clear, untroubled face, assured. The decision
had fallen in his mind as irrevocably as the hammer of a gun, and
she saw the event was already in motion toward her. She remembered
a time when she had accidentally come upon him while he was
hunting and seen him shoot a bird; the quail had risen before him
thrumming with its own purposes which were blanked to nothing in
the air and were quite unrelated to the bloody bag of feathers which
had fallen at his feet.

"Why, Gus Ben—don't leave me here," she said. "I can't stay here.
Why, that Nigra won't even hardly speak to me. And the woman
—well, there's something between her and the rancher, or she wants
it to be. She sits there on the porch, sort of drawing him. You know
what I *mean*, Ben? And the snakes—there's snakes everywhere. It's
so . . . lonely. I keep thinking there's something out there, away off
in the distance, and there isn't. Oh," she said in a wailing voice, as

if, fixed in the sights of his will, she must ask for the meaning and purpose of her whole life, "I don't know why I'm here at all."

"Why, we brought you along to be company to the other lady," he said. She stared at him. "Clay always takes her along and he wanted me to bring you. Well, Ola, to tell you the truth, I got a kind of deal on with him and I couldn't afford . . . But, listen, there's nothing wrong with *her*. I'll explain it to you because you never trained a hunting dog, and that kind of a woman is a little bit like some dogs. This kind of a dog I mean will be out in a field tracking birds and doing just like he's supposed to, when all of a sudden he gets the scent of a rabbit. Well, when he does, he looks so lively and happy, and if he's not well-trained he'll go off like an arrow after the rabbit and you got to beat him till he stops doing it. Now, I believe she's never been beaten out of it. But she'll be all right. Nothing's gonna come of it."

"Isn't that the main way you train a younger dog—you take it along with an older dog that knows what to do?" Ola asked thoughtfully.

"Well, that's the way you train a *dog*," he said, "but I wasn't meaning to imply you were an old hunting dog." He laughed and caught her doubled-in fingers in his hand.

"No," she said vaguely. He went on hunting and fishing trips at all times of the year without consulting her. He spent the summers in South Dakota and Colorado, he owned a fishing boat on the Gulf of Mexico which she had never seen; both her sons, from the ages of six or seven, had gone many of these places with him, and this seemed in part to account for the brevity of their childhood years and for the fact that they had been loosed so early into the world of sports cars and Eastern schools and camps which, though not yet twenty, they already understood better than she did. She had never once in all those years objected to his plans.

"Please, Gus Ben," she said, "I don't want you to go."

His eyes narrowed in surprise at her waywardness. "Well, now, please, *Ola*, I *got* to go. Why, you're asking me to give up my hunting, and I never have let anything interfere with that since I was in the fourth grade."

She stared at him without particular interest, unable to imagine why he liked it so much. "Well," she said, "you could take me to the nearest town and I could get a bus home . . ."

"Now you're talking about spoiling the trip one way or the other," he said warningly.

"Well, will you do what I ask you? Just for once, consider *me* and what I want to do. I beg you," she said.

She saw that she had gone too far; now his face frightened her. His eyes seemed enlarged and stilled in an archaic fierceness she had never seen before. His anger was so pure as to be compelling; she felt herself drawn by the centers of his furious eyes as if out of herself and into nothing; her heart swooned, her body fell away beneath her, and she felt suspended by his glance. She was surprised when he spoke and that his voice was recognizable to her.

"No, Ola," he said. "No, no, *no*. You stay here."

A relief came over her at this result. She sank down upon the bed and covered her eyes with her hands, not because she was crying but to escape from his glance which had penetrated to the quick of her self. He had overcome her upon a matter of great importance to her; her defeat had been inevitable from the beginning and had been accomplished with a careless strength she had to admire, even though it was turned against her. She was glad she had not been able to move or change him; it made him larger in her eyes. She was, in some fluttered way, glad he had won. She realized that she would not have known what to do if he had not. Suddenly, in a way she had almost forgotten, her thighs felt hard and hollow as bone; she lay back on the bed, her body vast and weak about her, netted and veined with desire. She did not know how, or even whether, this fearful longing was communicated to him. He seemed to charge upon her, still in the context of his anger, and, as she saw his face straining toward her own, she did not know until it had begun whether he intended to strike or caress her.

In the deep quiet that followed, she saw that this was the way things had always been between them; she would have preferred not to have known. He lay very still; his eyes, emptied of purpose, had in them the look of silence, as if words might never again come to his mind. Then she became conscious of the noises outside, beyond the window. They had begun some time ago, muted at the edges of the long passageway they had traveled. It was mainly the Negro's voice she remembered, though there had been another with it, harder and stronger—as hard and harsh as her own impalement.

"Git out there, go on out where they can't hear us," the voice had said.

"No, please," the other had responded, scared; "not out where they's snakes."

The tempo of the conversation had increased, words flashing faster into the pounding tunnel: "Git on," "Not beyond the light, they's snakes," "Go *on*," "No furder; I ain't goin' no furder."

The tunnel was beating its way beneath the world. The words fell into it and flashed in quicker tempo. No, no further, she thought; there isn't any further to go—because the passage had arced up and shot out into the light, and, when the silence flaked back into the exploded air, she realized the two outside must have stopped close, for she could hear their faint, strained voices.

"You gonna do like I *say*, you understand?" the white man said.

There was a pause, and then the Negro spoke, his voice scared. "Well, I been work for white people so *long* and I *know* I can't tell no white person what to do. It ain't up to me," he added sulkily.

Out of a short silence, Clay's voice spoke with a dead flatness. "I told you we're going somewhere else, Mr. Elkins and me. We got several thousand acres leased for hunting here and it's costing us money and we not gonna sit here and not use it. Now you gonna stay here to look after the women."

"*Okay*," Raby said in a sliding high voice.

"And cook for 'em."

"Yessuh."

"And just keep your eyes peeled to see that she don't leave the house. It wouldn't be safe for her to wander around here where there's snakes."

"Well," Raby said mournfully, "if you gonna take the car, how she goan wander? How we any goan wander anywhere? She ain't got only those little tiny shoes."

"Listen," Clay said, "I don't give a damn about that. *You* see she don't go out."

"Well, I don't know what I can do if she does," the Negro said very quietly.

"Jesus," Clay said. After a moment he went on, "I'll tell you what you can do if she does. I got a good hunting knife here with a ten-inch blade. I'm gonna leave that with you and now I tell you what to do with it. First, you gonna tell her not to go out of the house. If she start out, you gonna tell 'er to stop. If she don't stop, you gonna go stand in the front door and wave the knife around in her

face. Now you think *that* won't stop her? Just hold it like this pointing right *at* her."

"Jesus God," the Negro said in dismay, "I never see such a looking
knife."

"It'd take your hide off quick as a deer's if you don't do like I say."

Ola pulled aside the little shade and looked into the block of light
which came out through the kitchen windows. The two men were
standing quite close together, their heads bent toward each other
as if in intimacy, over the knife which Clay held against the Negro's
belt buckle, gently tapping it.

"Git that off my belt, please," Raby said. "Don't kid like that."

"Why, Raby, who says I'm kidding?" Clay went on tapping. Suddenly, the Negro's hand came up underneath, lifted the white hand
and the knife together, and held them rigid in the space between
them.

"What's the matter, Raby? You not getting edgy, are you?" Clay
asked.

"Gimme the knife," the Negro said.

"That's right." Clay, already starting to the house, turned and
tossed the knife backward onto the ground at the Negro's feet. Raby
stared down at the knife, leaned slowly over and picked it up, held
it at his waist level, gripped hard in his hand, turning it backward
and forward so the light from the house glinted on the long blade.
Then, to her surprise, Ola saw him bring the knife up sharply and
strike the air with it.

At dinner that evening Clay said, "You all set for tomorrow?" Gus
Ben looked at him as though surprised. "Sure," he said. "Let's go early.
The girls needn't get up with us," he added sweetly. "You all just
take it easy and have yourselves a nice time while we're gone."

PART THREE

I

It was chiefly the soundlessness from which Ola suffered. A wind
drove the dry, pale grass endlessly before it across the plain in front
of the house, out to the horizon, but when she closed her eyes no
hint of its motion came to the ear. It was so long since she had sat
unmoving in the sun that the quiet seemed to pull at her as if it

would draw her to itself, into the still hearts of trees, to the dust below the murmurless, dipping stems. On hot nights when they were children they had slept out on a little rise of ground beyond their house. They threw down a square tarpaulin, circled it casually with a rope to keep the snakes off, then lying nested in the grasses they saw them ripple like these above their heads and it seemed evident that their files were on the march, going somewhere—and so, so much the more would *they*, the two pretty sisters, when they were older. But where would they go? They talked about moving to the city, taking jobs, getting married, knotted tightly together in the night, chattering with delight about a time when they would not be there and not together. Then, one night, Ola was struck by a kind of vision: it came to her that the boy who would be her husband was already alive in the actual world, that he slept and waked and coughed and laughed just as she did. A terrible sense of disorientation came over her because she realized that, when she would be married to him, she would no longer be the self she was now, here on the tarp with her sister in the summer night, and that this self would never return to her.

Ola wished that Bonnie Dee would come out of her bedroom; she wished that anything might happen to break the quiet. Again she closed her eyes, and the silence sucked at her, pulled her down below the surface—and she remembered the seeds. In the spring they planted a vegetable garden at her home. As soon as they had tamped in the seeds and left them, they seemed to grow in Ola's mind; the black-waxy earth was heavy and packed glutinously under rain and each year Ola was afraid the seeds might not come up. She felt them lying in the dark soil, the infinitesimal quiver of the bursting skins, the stirring of the delicate runners starting up against the binding soil. She conjured the plants out of the ground, squatting between the rows, and when they cracked the surface she began to breathe again as if she herself had come to the surface from below.

To her surprise, she heard a dull "plop" in the dirt at the back of the house. She went quickly in through the kitchen and looked out. There, from the little back porch, huddled on the steps with his feet up off the ground, the Negro was bent over playing mumbletypeg, throwing the knife in a short arc, leaning sideways to pick it up and throwing it again. His hands were surprising light and graceful as he played; his face showed the intense expression of a spectator watching an important play in a game. Then he smiled. "Look at that; that's the way," he said to himself as the knife stuck in the ground.

It seemed to Ola intolerable that he should not even recognize her presence. Her voice rushed out at him. "Raby! Raby!" she called.

His eyes started dutifully around but couldn't quite leave the knife; then, though he remained crouched on the step, they rose to her face and held there, the whites very still. "Yes ma'am?" he said.

"Raby, have you worked for the Justices a long time? Have you worked for other white people in Dallas? I might know some of them —maybe some of my friends . . ."

With obvious reluctance, he got up and stood above her, the knife loose in his hands. "Well, I been work for Mr. Justice a long time, mostly to drive her car when she shop and go to beauty parlor. Before that I drove for Mr. Mandrell. Mr. B. G. Mandrell, live out on the No'thwest Highway?"

"You mean . . . Wasn't he running some gambling houses a long time ago—didn't something happen to him?" Ola was startled and concerned.

The Negro's eyes stole back to the earth where he had been playing his game, then looked at her and narrowed. "Well, yes, ma'am. He have this son, B. G., Jr., and one day they in a big argument about money and the son shot him. He shot him from down low— undah his nose—and blew all his brains up. Up the walls and ceiling."

"Oh, no! Were you actually right there when that happened?" Ola asked, distressed.

"Well, no, ma'am," he said. "I was out in the back yard hosing off the driveway. But I had to go inside and clean 'em up—both of 'em."

"Really?" Ola asked. "*Really?*"

"Yes, ma'am," Raby said dutifully, and picked up the knife again and started to throw it.

"Oh, no," Ola kept repeating; "oh, no." She went back out to the front porch and sat down.

II

For Bonnie Dee, the quiet came between her and the two others and contained her inner joy in itself. She was glad the men were gone, not because she felt any guilt or need to hide her feelings (everything would soon be out in the open anyhow) but simply because their physical presence had been noisy and had, she felt, distracted her from thinking of her new love.

She put on her robe and went to the kitchen for coffee, which she brought back into the bedroom. She drank it very slowly, looking into the mirror of a rickety dresser in her room, thinking. The house in Dallas to which her husband had brought her had a large pool in the dining room. It was edged with white marble and a bridge led across the water to a marble island in the center on which stood a very long, Spanish oak dining table. It seemed to her the clamminess of the pool penetrated even the upstairs, where she had her own apartment; she came downstairs only rarely. When she did, the household impressed her as a vast mechanism wound up and kept going from some point beyond her ken, through which in steady orbits moved the purposeful figures of servants, and in which her own duties were as routine and predictable as anyone else's.

She was glad she had been true to her own aims, that she had held herself in readiness for the change which love would bring. It had caused her to spend a great deal of time and money in shopping for clothes and in beauty parlors, where the demands of the operators grew fiercer year by year. But she had been true to her hope; she had done everything there was to be done. For she knew she had only her looks to depend on and had treated her body like the careful owner of a fine car, keeping it always in top-notch condition in case it should be needed to take her somewhere in a hurry. Now she stroked the thin pink skin of her face, as if testing it for some trial. It would happen today, she knew. Yesterday would perhaps have been too soon, but today the men were gone and she was ready; she began to make up her face. What she wanted from him lay just behind his eyes and would occur when he looked at her; when their eyes had opened fully to each other, their true union would take place across the empty air. Then it was only a question of arranging all the details. Everything else, as she knew by experience, would follow.

When she finished her make-up, she took her cup to the kitchen to refill it. Raby got up from the back steps and came into the kitchen, holding a hunting knife in his hand. He walked into the center of the room and stood there a moment. "Nobody leavin' this house today"—he shook his head vigorously—"to go outside. Or nowhere." To her surprise, he looked directly into her eyes.

She stared at him, surprised. His announcement struck her as one of those odd things which went on at the edges of her experience all the time. If she stopped to think about all the crazy things people said or did around her, it would take all her time. Still, it annoyed her that something like that, so beside the point of what she felt, should be forced upon her, and by a Negro, a person more than others of whom one should not have to think at all. What did he mean? Where would anyone go? In her own case, there was no need to go anywhere, when mere waiting was to bring her what she had always wanted. She poured the coffee quickly and went back to her room.

III

"Dear Olive," Ola wrote, "we are having a good time here but it is still hot. I hope you are all right?" After some hesitation, she signed it, "Your friend, Ola Elkins." She sat holding the card, thinking how glad Olive would be to hear from her—if, of course, there were any way to mail the card.

Around noon, as he fixed their lunch, Raby began to sing. Ola was delighted at first, then less pleased; for he sang in a low voice, so softly that one was continually conscious of a noise without hearing any melody, muttering and sawing uneasily away at something. After a while he came to the door of the front porch. "Lunch ready," he announced. Then, without turning his head in the direction of the Justices' bedroom, he shouted, "Come on out to lunch, Miz Justice." Ola wanted to warn him, for his own good, that he mustn't yell at people like that, but he resumed his singing and she did not.

When she came out, Bonnie Dee was wearing, in spite of the heat, a pale yellow angora sweater trimmed with sequins, a yellow wool skirt shot with gold thread, and her brocade shoes. She looked both exotic and sporty, as if dressed for some highly ornamental game. In her pink face, behind the mauve eyeshadow and the mascara, the expression of her eyes appeared as fresh and new as her clothes: full of unwearied innocence. "We ready to eat?" she asked.

Raby watched her sit down. "There is snakes all around this house," he said mournfully, hovering over their heads with a plate of something as they sat at the table.

"You already said that," Bonnie Dee pointed out mildly.

"Wellum," he said, and plunked the dish down.

In the afternoon, Ola and Bonnie Dee sat down together on the front porch, to look and wait. Bonnie Dee was as clearly expectant as if she had a definite appointment; she held herself very erect, figure at attention, its desirability fronting the solitude. After he had done the dishes, Raby came and sat behind them in the living room; they heard the croaking of his song, restlessly turning over the same dreary notes, and knew that he was also looking out and waiting. It seemed to Ola she could feel Bonnie Dee swelling with the intensity of her concentration, and she glanced at her, thinking, This is crazy; but Bonnie Dee responded with a strong, ecstatic smile. Her white teeth seemed to say, "Soon everything's going to be all right—just wait a little while and see." Ola felt her heart with a dry whisper absorb some new emotion and swell heavy and slow-stroking in her chest. Why should they not love? she thought. Something may still happen. *Is it too late for everything?* Tired by the heat and the tension of waiting, she went to lie down in her own room, shuddering as with a chill in the cool shadows of the bed.

Bonnie Dee felt the Negro's song picking out points of sound in the blank space behind her, pulling at the edges of her concentration. She felt she must push her attention straight out before her, or everything would be jeopardized; her contact with the rancher depended upon keeping clearly in mind the reality of him and of her feeling for him. "Raby," she said, without turning around, "go back to the kitchen."

"No," he answered. "I'm all thoo in there."

She did not want to waste energy arguing with him; everything was too precarious. The time went on and nothing happened; all was still and silent for miles around. It seemed incredible the hours should pass without occurrence when she was fully ready and waiting with an intensity which made all other waiting in her life seem like learning how to wait. Once she went into her bedroom to touch up her makeup, but she came rushing back as if nothing could happen unless she were on the porch. The Negro's song behind her had strengthened to a mournful, strong current which carried something gleaming and shining on its surface like oil on water; quick-moving, darting, the anxiety carried on his voice floated into her and it occurred to her that it might be putting a spell of some kind on all her hopes. "Raby, shut up and go out to the kitchen," she yelled at him, almost crying.

He did not reply.

But it was too late. The sun had almost reached the horizon. She had turned around furiously to look at the Negro and her thoughts were directed toward him; before she could calm herself and straighten about to wait again, the sun had set, the day was over.

That evening Ola read in her room. She had brought with her a book on needlework. She would have liked to sew, to make many useful articles; but no one needed or wanted them, so instead she read such books, going straight through them as if they were novels, reading the directions and all. Long after she thought the others were asleep she heard a strange faint sound from the living room; startled, she got up and went out into the hall to the door of the next room. "Raby?" she whispered. She could see nothing at all but the single bright bead of a cigarette; as she watched, it strengthened in the Negro's mouth and drew his skin glossily out of the darkness. He was sitting with his neck hunched between his shoulder blades, but his head was so still and prepared that he saw she had come unwarily upon him while he was keeping vigil. Unbidden, the thought came to her mind of Africa and a man crouched in inscrutable purpose beside a dark trail. "Yes, ma'am," he said finally, lowering the cigarette, "you want something?"

"What are you doing here?" she asked tremulously. "Why aren't you in bed?"

His voice came to her small and clear, the still center of his perfect isolation. "Sittin' here," he said. "That's all."

"Go on to bed—get some sleep. You need your sleep. Nothing's going to happen—you might as well go to bed." Ola fussed over him, so concerned she kept shifting about and clasping her hands.

He did not answer. "I stay here," he said at last. She saw that he had made his own decision and gone off in a direction which she could not follow. His eyes, detached, disinterested, waited for her to leave so that he might enter into the stillness in which she had found him.

When she was back in her room, in bed, she thought, He didn't even stand up while I was talking to him. But it was a long time before the thought occurred to her.

IV

Bonnie Dee appeared the next morning in time for breakfast. Though she wore the same clothes, there was a change in her appearance. The flesh around her bright eyes seemed to have fallen back from them a little, as though weary of their support, and it took a moment for her to adjust in them a look of pure expectancy; even when this was achieved, the skin of her face and neck had lost tone and sagged, creped, and sweated.

When she went to the porch, she was beginning to worry about practical things which normally would never concern her. It had occurred to her he might have gone out of town on business; she had no idea of what ranching consisted. Vague thoughts of a big cattle deal or a roundup floated in her head. Or perhaps her husband had said something—but what?—to him. She went doggedly to the porch. She smiled; she placed her eyes in readiness and waited. As soon as the hot air struck her, sweat popped out beneath the little scimitars of her hair; she wiped it away and raked the curls back into place. She would have liked to claw off the angora sweater which clung against her, but it was more becoming than anything else she had with her. She smiled and waited.

The Negro was muttering behind her. Since yesterday he had trespassed upon her attention so continually that she could not keep it focused. What was he doing? Was it all his fault? Why should he, who could have nothing against her, try to take away from her something she wanted so much? This morning his great eyelids were more puffed than ever, as if he had been awake all night; she could feel his eyes turning in silent sockets upon her back. Now, as if at the Negro's initiation, deeper doubts came to her. She knew nothing about the rancher except that he was not married. Perhaps he had a mistress; perhaps he was one of those men who liked men. No, she knew what she knew. Their eyes had met. She would wait.

Raby spoke, right behind her. "Last night I could hear the snakes hissin' out there," he said.

She turned and saw him looking beyond her, the whites of his eyes flaring out across the plain. She shuddered; things were giving way, slipping and sliding in her mind, and a thought, usually kept out of sight, rose to the center of feeling: I am getting old—how much longer can I hope? Raby began to sing again, as if of something sad and full of fear that was coming to the whole world; it was the very sound of his voice that made her feel she might be alone, connected nowhere and to no one. Then, as if he, singing behind her, had pushed her to the decision, she thought, If he doesn't come to me, I'll go to him. After that, the Negro sat undisturbed behind her as though she had accepted him, too, along with all the other conditions.

In the middle of the afternoon, the rancher arrived without anyone having seen or heard him approach. He came walking out of a mesquite thicket beside the house leading his horse and holding up by the tail the heavy body of a dead rattlesnake. He stopped in front of the porch and grinned up at them slyly. "Brought one of your neighbors to visit you," he said. "You all want to get acquainted?" He turned the thick body of the snake around so they could see the pale underbelly. "He's a nice little fellow, ain't he? I just killed him three-four hundred yards over there."

Bonnie Dee stared in surprise at the snake. "I'm so glad you've *come*," she said.

The rancher stared at her, caught by the force and sweetness of her words, and his eyes, which had been moving jerkily about, sorting the minutiae of his bare country, seemed to open upon a view of a green and hopeful land. "Why, that's nice of you to say that," he answered. Ola was again aware that the air between them was charged with a force which was pulling them together. He turned toward the porch steps, the snake dangling forgotten from his hand, and it was only then they noticed that Raby was already there, standing on the top step, the knife glittering in his shaking hand.

"Mister, you can't come up here with that snake." Raby's voice came out so huskily that there appeared to be large empty spaces among the words.

"This snake's plumb dead, boy," the rancher said, surprised. "He not gonna hurt nobody."

The Negro looked down at him. "Mr. Justice don't want no snakes in this house—dead or alive," he said. "Mr. Justice don't want nobody or nothing in this house." He paused. "Not you—*or* you snake."

"What's the matter with you?" the rancher asked, mystified.

"Git outa here, Mister," Raby said warningly, and went down the first step. "Git out of here."

The rancher stopped on the bottom step and looked up at the knife jerking around in his hand. "You gonna cut yourself," he said.

Raby plunged down the next step. "Mr. Justice tole me what to do." He thrust blindly forward with the knife. "Git *outa here*," he said on a high whine.

The rancher jerked aside, suddenly looped the body of the snake around his hand, dropped it into a saddlebag, and angrily mounted

his horse. As he rode away, he turned one long raking glance back to
the porch.

V

That night, when Ola went to bed, Raby was sitting on the front
porch, the light of his cigarette inscribing a patient pattern on the
night.

Later on, she was awakened by sounds which seemed connected
with merrymaking: the patter of a woman's shoes across a wooden
floor and a jet of clear loud laughter. Coming slowly from sleep, she
thought, The dance is about to begin—for the laughter was that of
a very young girl, pure and sweet, springing wild from unused
energies. She got up and went out to the living room. Bonnie Dee
was standing beside a lamp and another spout of laughter rose in
the room.

"I'm back," she said, "all safe and sound." Ola stared at her and
Bonnie Dee giggled. She was wearing a cocktail dress which was torn
and awry. "I tore my stockings, too. Look." She sat down on the
couch and began nimbly to take them off. "They're ruined," she
said. She held the delicate, riddled cylinders up to the light and
looked at them carefully, then with a laugh dropped them on the
floor. Her legs were torn and scratched. She stared down at them
for a moment and then in her hot face, hectic with laughter, her
round eyes rolled up to Ola in wonder. "I got all dressed up and
went over there and now my stockings are ruined," she said. "I must
have fallen into some bushes on the way back because I was
laughing."

Her cheeks began to twitch as if she had remembered the joke, and
that vigorous, pure, sweet laughter poured from her. Her face looked
tired and harassed, as if at any moment it might quiver and fly apart
in some final lack of unity; but beneath it her personality had become fixed upon the single image of a young girl.

Ola was frightened. "Well," she said, "you've got to be quiet." She
glanced continuously behind her. "What happened?"

"I went over there—over to the little house."

"Yes, yes, I know."

"No, this is funny," Bonnie Dee said. "What I found out is that
he isn't really a rancher. He just rents his land to hunters—that's all
it's good for. It used to be a ranch, but something happened, he

told me—but I don't remember; and so now he does something else. Something else." Her voice strangled for a moment; then she looked up solemnly at Ola. "He sells snakes," she said.

"Why, that's all right," Ola replied vaguely. "It doesn't matter." Then she thought of him up on a horse and the way they had all looked at him. "Sells snakes?—you mean to those snakeshows?"

Bonnie Dee was absently smoothing her hair. "Well, I think so," she said. "But, mainly, he sells the skins. No, I mean really," she added. "He puts them on green felt—he does all the work himself, he told me—and he sells them to people to hang up on the walls of their ranches like a hunting trophy. People like to say that's the big snake they killed on their ranch." She doubled over, laughed, stopped to examine a tear in her dress, and went on chattily. "He had them hanging up all over the house—like stockings on a line. He said if the men don't get any game, he'll give 'em all the skins they want to take home. He said he hopes we're all having a good time and they'll take the lease again. He was standing there with this little apron on . . . By that time I had begun to laugh and I had to run out the door. I saw his good suit hanging up on a hook and he had on a pair of old blue jeans and this little apron, and when I went in he was holding a bottle of Elmer's glue—"

Ola was frightened, but she began to laugh, too.

"As I was running out the door I could hear him saying, 'Well, goodbye, be *careful* now—remember the snakes . . .'"

Ola looked down at Bonnie Dee, slowly shaking her head and laughing. She heard a faint expiration of breath behind her.

"Now, why she do that?" Raby said. He was standing in the doorway, his eyes fixed on them still and watchful, as if he had never fallen asleep. "Why she do that; why she got to go get herself snakebit?" He spoke slowly; his voice was not loud, but the words dropped into the quiet room with flat, separate sounds which gave Ola a feeling of loneliness. She glanced at Bonnie Dee, who had looked up at him once with protuberant, unseeing eyes and then turned away.

"Do what?" Ola asked. "What's the matter, Raby? What's the matter with you?"

"Why she go out there and git herself snakebit? I try to keep her from it." He drew a clean handkerchief from his pocket and began to polish the knife he held in his hand.

Ola turned to him, arrested by his tone. "She didn't get bit," she said. "She just went out for a little walk."

"I know she went for a walk," Raby answered, turning slowly between the two of them. "A snake bit her."

"No," Ola said, "she didn't get bitten!"

Raby lifted his eyes to her deliberately, as if in a kind of trance. "I saw her," he said. "She start off the porch in those little shoes. She don't get no mo' than twenty yards out there when it happen." His eyes flickered away from Ola for a second, then returned and widened until each iris was held in a still white circle, cold as marble. "I saw the snake raise up in the bright moonlight—and it strike at her and she come running back hard as she could. Now we got to get the poison out." He bent over the knife.

Ola stared at him, dumbfounded. "Raby, none of that happened."

"It do," he said in a small voice. He nodded his head insistently, and then suddenly, quickly he licked his lips. A look of fear came from beneath the surfaces of his eyes, unmeasured, profound. She saw that he was scared, scared as he had been in the car when Clay hit him, only more so. What is it he's so afraid of? Ola wondered.

"No," she said strongly, "it didn't happen. You got a little mixed up there, Raby. Maybe you just went to sleep and dreamed it—but that's all right."

He looked at her in a second's hesitation, looked across the room at Bonnie Dee, who was studying her torn dress and taking no interest in their discussion. Then his eyes began to move around the room fast, stopping jerkily here or there, then moving again, until they seemed to lash at the air. His shoulders straightened and his face changed. "No," he said in a high, strained voice, "that's what happened and nobody gonna say it didn't. I been watchin' her all the time and I *know*." His eyes turned directly upon Ola, and she shrank back, for there was in them a light so wild and strange that fear went through her. He began to move forward with the knife, steadily and easily, and she started to back away from him, frightened less of the weapon than of his expression, for she saw that an energy of hate was leaping in his dilate eyes and bearing sharply upon her as she stood in his path. His face, set in hard, rigid lines, came toward her; she knew it to be set in opposition to her and all her kind. Stunned with surprise, she lost all strength of purpose.

"Now, get outa my way," he said, "and lemme get the poison *out*." He spoke sharply to Ola and she sank weakly down beside Bonnie

Dee. Kneeling on the floor before him, she dumbly watched his face to try to learn what was going to happen to them.

Now Bonnie Dee came out of her lethargy and she too looked up at Raby, "Did a rattlesnake bite me?" she asked. "Is that what happened?"

"He done bite you," the Negro said. Ola saw his face descending over them without expression; his knife came down unwaveringly toward the outstretched leg, touched on the pink flesh just above the ankle bone, made a shallow cut down the ankle, then lifted without hesitation and crossed its own track. As the line of blood went down the pink skin, pain rose in Ola and overflowed. Bonnie Dee gasped, her eyes glazed and dimmed as if all memory had died, and the blood ran out over her ankle and soaked into the gold shoes. Raby stared at the wound he had inflicted. "Poison blood," he said, and his shoulders shuddered. He turned around to stare at Ola and at first she did not know what he meant; when she understood, a sense of shame rose in her, for it seemed that his eyes knew her to be something that she herself had never known she was, and now had judged and sentenced her. Compelled by them, she bent over Bonnie Dee's leg and sucked and spat; she heard him leave the room, and, though she knew he was no longer there, she continued to suck at the wound and spit on the floor.

After a long time, Ola lifted herself up and made a tourniquet for the leg. Then she sat beside Bonnie Dee alternately tightening and loosening the bandage, but little blood flowed from the shallow cuts. When Bonnie Dee dropped into sleep or unconsciousness, Ola arose, washed the wound and bound it with strips of clean cloth torn from a sheet, and left her.

After that, there was nothing for her to do, and she stood absently in the hall, feeling the atmosphere of the house to have been exhausted by what had happened there; hardly knowing what she did, she made her way to the open air on the porch and sank in a chair. It was a few minutes before she realized that Raby was there too. He was sitting on the top step, not far beyond her, leaning against a pillar. There was a small, late moon, and its light modeled one side of his forehead and cheek; otherwise, his head would have been a deeper shadow on the night.

She tried to speak, and he turned his head at the sound of her weak voice. "Raby?"

Finally he responded. "I had to do it," he said gravely, his voice quiet and remote. She saw again that it was a judgment which had been on its way toward them for a very long time; but why—and for what sins? Would he not tell her that?

But already he was turning away from her, turning out toward the night. If only he would talk to her . . . She sat down behind him and waited, her heart intolerably empty as the night around her. And then she knew she was going to do something out of her deep need, something new and unexpected even to herself. She saw that her hand had lifted and started to move toward him. She did not know exactly what it meant to do; perhaps to say, There are two of us here, in the midst of emptiness. But it was the experiment of the hand—she watched it go half-reluctantly, as if it were starting off on a journey from which it might never return. Forward it went, so close to him it showed white against his neck; then she touched the wire mesh of his hair. He leaped up and stood over her, rigid, with nothing but fright showing in his eyes. "What's that?"—but then a weariness touched with anger and wonder came into them as he watched her. "Don't you know better than to *do* that," he said in a tight voice. Then he shrugged, stretched, and started back toward the kitchen where he slept.

It grew absolutely quiet.

VI

In the morning, Bonnie Dee's face was flushed bright rose with fever. The wound had pulled open and fresh blood ran out. She lay on the couch watching them with wide eyes like a sick child. Standing over her, Ola heard a car coming some distance away and knew that it must be the men returning; she dreaded to see them.

The men came in wearily and in silence, and Ola met them without speaking at the door. But, from beyond, Bonnie Dee called out in a hectic voice, "A rattlesnake bit me. I walked out a little way and a snake rose up and bit me. *He* saw it." She told the story as she had come to believe it. When she had finished, the men glanced around them uneasily. Raby did not speak, and Ola looked at him quickly, but he was not watching her; his eyes were fixed straight ahead in indifference. She saw that since he did not depend on her answer, it did not matter what she said.

"Yes, that's the way it happened." The men looked at her and at each other, puzzled and unsure of what to do next.

Clay went over and sat down beside Bonnie Dee and with strangely trembling hands looked under the bandage; his eyes were pained. "My God, we better get her to a doctor." He got up and walked across the room toward Raby and signaled him to follow; they passed out onto the front porch and down the steps. On the last one, Raby stopped.

"I not going out there," he said.

Clay turned around and grasped his arm. "What do you mean, scarring her up like that?" he asked.

"Well, Mr. Justice," the Negro said factually, "you give me the knife." When they looked out, they saw him take it from his pocket and look at it once. "Here, you take it back," he said calmly.

"Come on in our room," Gus Ben said to Ola, as if he did not think she should watch this any more. "You gotta pack. We gonna get out of this place."

As soon as he had closed the door, he said accusingly, "What's been going on here with that damn' nigger?"—but she saw that there was no force behind the question. "We ought to sue that damn' rancher for taking money on false pretenses," he went on. "There's no game on this place. Do you realize we been wandering around for two solid days out there and didn't even get a shot? Can you imagine that?" he asked furiously. "We stopped by his house this morning and gave him what-for, but there's no way to get the money back. He said there was plenty of game there." He stopped and looked at her uncertainly. She saw, puzzled, that it was no longer the Negro or even the failure of his hunting trip which engaged him. Stripped of all pretension by fatigue and disappointment, she realized for the first time, he looked old; in his cold, cautious eyes, he was gathering himself for a new contest, one more profound and secret than any she had seen before; he had pulled in to prepare to fight against time and death itself, and she knew that over the next years she could only watch the conflict.

Yet, when they were in the car and it had started roaring off down the dirt road with the Negro at the wheel, it seemed to her not only that they were traveling fast but were on their way toward something. They passed the rancher's little house without seeing him, and the dry, burned land fell behind them as if it had never existed. They came out onto the highway and on all sides about them lay the measureless distance, promising everything. For a moment, the freshness of a journey's beginning filled her heart and it seemed to her they need only travel hard to achieve some significant arrival. The faces of the others seemed to confirm this: Bonnie Dee's was fevered and in pain, but her eyes roamed the sky as if still confident her dream was before her; the men had remembered their everyday business personalities and were taut but eager to pay out their strength against familiar obstacles in order that they might know for a time how alive they were.

All of them looked forward to returning. Well, Ola thought, I'll have plenty to do—I'll go round to the stores. But the forms of those buildings to which they would in time come rose from the plain only in hollow, ghostly aspect.

She looked at the back of Raby's neck while he tutored the wheel fiercely, as though it were vital he should get away from them into speed itself. Where is he going? What does he want? she thought. She realized that since last night she had not been able to think about her Negroes in the kitchen at home. Yes, they'll go, too, she said to herself harshly; sooner or later they'll all go, wherever it is they want to be.

A great longing took her, and she began to study with feverish interest their progress through space. Soon we will come to *something*, she thought. I'll keep my eyes on this blue patch of distance and soon something will emerge from it; but when they had reached it, she saw there was nothing there. She chose another spot beyond, but nothing came of that, either. Can it be there's really nothing there in all that space? she asked herself; that I only—all my life —have rushed forward . . . into emptiness?

An intolerable vacancy grew within her, into which rushed daggers of hate and grief which turned and twisted in her heart. She began to speak in a loud wild voice: "What is it they *want*? Where do they want to *go*? Didn't we always take *care* of them like they were our children? Weren't we *good* to them? Didn't we *love* them?" The white people all turned to look at her. "The niggers," she screamed into their faces; "the niggers. Where do they think they'll go—what are they going to do? What is it they *want* that we didn't give them when we tried so *hard*? What is it they *want*?"

"Jesus, Ola," Gus Ben said, "you got to calm down."

Magazines Consulted

ANTIOCH REVIEW — 212 Xenia Avenue, Yellow Springs, Ohio

ARARAT — Armenian General Benevolent Union of America, 250 Fifth Ave., New York, N. Y. 10001

ARIZONA QUARTERLY — University of Arizona, Tucson, Ariz.

AVE MARIA — National Catholic Weekly, Congregation of Holy Cross, Notre Dame, Ind.

CARLETON MISCELLANY — Carleton College, Northfield, Minn.

CAROLINA QUARTERLY — Box 1117, Chapel Hill, N. C.

CHELSEA REVIEW — Box 242, Old Chelsea Station, New York, N. Y. 10011

CHICAGO REVIEW — University of Chicago, Chicago 37, Ill.

COLORADO QUARTERLY — Hellums 118, University of Colorado, Boulder, Colo.

COMMENTARY — 165 East 56 Street, New York, N. Y. 10022

CONTACT — Box 755, Sausalito, Calif.

COSMOPOLITAN — 57 Street & Eighth Avenue, New York, N. Y. 10019

DECEMBER — P. O. Box 274, Western Springs, Ill.

ENCOUNTER — 25 Haymarket, London, S.W. 1, England

EPOCH — 159 Goldwin Smith Hall, Cornell University, Ithaca, N. Y.

ESCAPADE — Division Street, Derby, Conn.

ESPRIT — University of Scranton, Scranton, Pa.

ESQUIRE — 488 Madison Avenue, New York, N. Y. 10022

EVERGREEN REVIEW — 64 University Place, New York, N. Y. 10003

FANTASY AND SCIENCE FICTION — 580 Fifth Avenue, New York, N. Y. 10036

FOR NOW — Box 375, Cathedral Station, New York, N. Y. 10025

FORUM — University of Houston, Houston, Tex.

FOUR QUARTERS — La Salle College, Philadelphia 41, Pa.

THE FREE LANCE — 6005 Grand Avenue, Cleveland, Ohio

GENERATION, THE INTER-ARTS MAGAZINE — University of Michigan, 420 Maynard, Ann Arbor, Mich.

GEORGIA REVIEW — University of Georgia, Athens, Ga.

GOOD HOUSEKEEPING — 57 Street and Eighth Avenue, New York, N. Y. 10019

HARPER'S BAZAAR — 572 Madison Avenue, New York, N. Y. 10022

HARPER'S MAGAZINE — 49 East 33 Street, New York, N. Y. 10016

HUDSON REVIEW — 65 East 55 Street, New York, N. Y. 10022

IN PUT — 24 Olsen Street, Valley Stream, New York, N. Y.

KENYON REVIEW — Kenyon College, Gambier, Ohio

LADIES HOME JOURNAL — 1270 Sixth Avenue, New York, N. Y. 10020

THE LAUREL REVIEW — West Virginia Wesleyan College, Buckhannon, W. Va.

THE LITERARY REVIEW — Fairleigh Dickinson University, Teaneck, N. J.

MADEMOISELLE — 575 Madison Avenue, New York, N. Y. 10022

THE MASSACHUSETTS REVIEW — University of Massachusetts, Amherst, Mass.

MC CALL'S — 230 Park Avenue, New York, N. Y. 10017

MIDSTREAM — 823 Broadway, New York, N. Y. 10003

THE MINNESOTA REVIEW — Box 4068, University Station, Minneapolis, Minn.

THE NEW MEXICO QUARTERLY — University of New Mexico Press, Marron Hall, Albuquerque, N. M.

THE NEW YORKER — 25 West 43 Street, New York, N. Y. 10036

NIOBE — 202 Columbia Heights, Brooklyn Heights, New York, N. Y. 11201

THE PARIS REVIEW — 45–39, 171 Place, Flushing 58, N. Y.

PARTISAN REVIEW — Rutgers University, New Brunswick, N. J.

PERSPECTIVE — Washington University Post Office, St. Louis 5, Mo.

PLAYBOY — 232 East Ohio Street, Chicago 11, Ill.

PRAIRIE SCHOONER — Andrews Hall, University of Nebraska, Lincoln, Nebr. 68508

PRIMIERE — P.O. Box 8008, Mobile, Ala.

QUARTERLY REVIEW OF LITERATURE — Box 287, Bard College, Annandale-on-Hudson, N. Y.

QUARTET — Lafayette, Ind.

RAMPARTS — 1182 Chestnut Street, Menlo Park, Calif.

REDBOOK — 230 Park Avenue, New York, N. Y. 10017

THE REPORTER — 660 Madison Avenue, New York, N. Y. 10021

SAN FRANCISCO REVIEW — Box 671, San Francisco, Calif.

SATURDAY EVENING POST — 666 Fifth Avenue, New York, N. Y. 10021

SECOND COMING — Box 1776, Beverly Hills, Calif. 90213

SEQUOIA — Box 2167, Stanford University, Stanford, Calif.

SEWANEE REVIEW — University of the South, Sewanee, Tenn.

SHENANDOAH — Box 722, Lexington, Va.

SOUND — P.O. Box 386, Everett, Wash.

SOUTHWEST REVIEW — Southern Methodist University Press, Dallas 22, Tex.

STUDIES ON THE LEFT — P.O. Box 33, Planetarium Station, New York, N. Y. 10024

TEXAS QUARTERLY — Box 7527, University of Texas, Austin 12, Tex.

THOTH — Department of English, Syracuse University, Syracuse, N. Y.

TRACE — P.O. Box 1068, Hollywood, Calif.

TRANSATLANTIC REVIEW — 821 Second Avenue, New York, N. Y. 10017

THE UNIVERSITY REVIEW — University of Kansas City, 51 Street & Rockhill Road, Kansas City, Mo.

VENTURE (for Junior High) — 910 Witherspoon Bldg., Philadelphia 7, Pa.

VENTURES — Yale Graduate School, New Haven, Conn.

THE VIRGINIA QUARTERLY REVIEW — University of Virginia, 1 West Range, Charlottesville, Va.

VOGUE — 420 Lexington Avenue, New York, N. Y. 10017

WASHINGTON SQUARE REVIEW — New York University, 737 East Bldg., New York, N. Y. 10003

WESTERN HUMANITIES REVIEW — Bldg. 41, University of Utah, Salt Lake City 12, Utah

WOMAN'S DAY — 67 West 44 Street, New York, N. Y. 10036

THE YALE REVIEW — 28 Hillhouse Avenue, New Haven, Conn.

June 9, 1965

H4